PRAYING FOR TIME

Carlene Thompson

To my husband Keith

This first world edition published 2020
in Great Britain and the USA by
SEVERN HOUSE PUBLISHERS LTD of
Eardley House, 4 Uxbridge Street, London W8 7SY.
Trade paperback edition first published
in Great Britain and the USA 2020 by
SEVERN HOUSE PUBLISHERS LTD.

British Library Cataloguing in Publication Data
A CIP catalogue record for this title is available from the British Library.

ISBN-13: 978-0-7278-8984-3 (cased)
ISBN-13: 978-1-78029-698-2 (trade paper)
ISBN-13: 978-1-4483-0423-3 (e-book)

All Severn House titles are printed on acid-free paper.

Severn House Publishers support the Forest Stewardship Council™ [FSC™],
the leading international forest certification organisation.
All our titles that are printed on FSC certified paper carry the FSC logo.

Typeset by Palimpsest Book Production Ltd.,
Falkirk, Stirlingshire, Scotland.
Printed and bound in Great Britain by
TJ International, Padstow, Cornwall.

PROLOGUE

Vanessa Everly squished wet sand between her toes and looked out at the ocean waves foaming beneath a nearly black sky. She sighed and her barely fifteen-year-old sister Roxanne looked at her.

'Sad that you're going back to school next week?'

'No. I've wanted to attend the American Academy of Dramatic Arts since I was twelve and I've been lucky enough to be accepted for the third-year program.'

'You like it because it's in Los Angeles.'

'I like it because its dramatics arts program is considered one of the best in the country.' Vanessa grinned. 'And because I love Los Angeles.'

Roxanne groaned, tilted back her head and shook her long, wavy honey-blonde hair that looked like her mother Ellen's. 'How can you leave me behind with Dad? He's *so* much stricter with me than he was with you. He's smothering me. I need you to stand up for me, talk him into letting me do things instead of treating me like a prisoner.'

'You get to go places.'

'Nowhere fun. He'd never let me come down to the beach for a midnight swim like this one unless I was with you.'

'It would be a bad idea to come for a midnight swim alone.'

'This is nice but he wouldn't let me come with a girlfriend.' She hesitated. 'Or a guy.'

'A *guy*? I see what this is all about. Is he a local or a tourist?'

'I didn't say there is a guy but I wouldn't want Dad to know about anyone I like. He'd ask a million questions. He let you start seeing Christian Montgomery when you were seventeen even though he's four years older than you because he thinks Christian walks on water. He believes *I* shouldn't date until I'm eighteen and then it will be some dork who doesn't even have his driver's license.'

'Don't be silly, Roxy.'

'I'm not. Since Grace came back to live with us he does what she wants,' she said, referring to Grace Everly who owned the large home known as Everly House that sat on a hill overlooking the town. 'Mommy's always on my side but even she's afraid of Dad's mother. Why couldn't she stay in France? She's been here less than a year and everything's changed for me.'

'Grace came home because she's seventy-eight. She wanted to be with her family. Maybe she doesn't believe everything you say because sometimes you fib to her.'

'Sure I do! My life is none of her business!'

'She doesn't see it that way. You're young and she's protective.' The slender, elegant woman had never wanted to be called *Grandma* or any variation. She was *Grace* to everyone in the family except her son, who called her *Mother*. 'But she – well, *no one* – would like it that I brought you here so late at night,' Vanessa went on. 'I'm not a strong swimmer. This is a secret, Roxy.'

'I'd like to have a more thrilling secret than swimming,' Roxanne groused. Then she shivered. 'Brrr.'

'Chilly in that string bikini?'

'I have a better body than most girls my age and I show it off whenever I get the chance.'

'That's one of the reasons Dad is strict with you.'

'He's *so* old fashioned. Anyway, my bikini matches my eyes. And my birthstone ring.' Roxanne wagged her finger with its sapphire and diamonds set in gold. 'My birthstone brings me good luck. You should wear your birthstone ring. The emerald matches your eyes.'

'I wouldn't wear it for swimming. I'd never forgive myself if I lost it.' Roxanne squealed as a wave washed in, submerging her feet and slender ankles in cold water, and Vanessa laughed. 'You sound like you did when you were four.'

'When I was four, you were nine and you squealed, too.'

'I didn't. I was fearless.'

Roxanne rushed forward and waited for the next wave to break and rush in. She appeared ethereal in the mist that had begun to coil sinuously across the beach. Vanessa couldn't remember ever seeing such a dense, creeping mist. It looked supernatural. To her right stood a craggy rock formation nearly nine feet high, looking as if it had suddenly erupted, solitary and sinister, from the soft sand. Such tall, jagged rocks were common on the Oregon coastline, but it had always made Vanessa think of the Dark Tower in *Lord of the Rings*. Tonight the stone did look huge and unnerving with all of its shadowy sharp edges.

And not too far down the beach lay the remains of the *Seraphim May*, a four-masted schooner that a vicious storm had driven against the shore in 1896. Like the remains of several ships on the Oregon beach, this wreck was never hauled away. The once-beautiful vessel lay forever still and lonely, its sails long gone, its oak hull slowly rotting and sinking into the sand. It was considered a harmless tourist attraction, but when she was a kid, Vanessa had thought it was haunted by the souls of the five men who had died when a merciless wind slammed the torn and gouged ship onto the beach. She used to sneak out at night and crouch near the ship's skeleton, thinking she saw floating shapes and heard thin voices of sad, lost souls calling for help. And maybe she had . . .

Oh, lord, I must be really tired, Vanessa mused. *I'm imagining an ordinary mist is eerie, making a fairy-tale tower out of a rock, and thinking I might have been right about the* Seraphim May *being haunted by desolate souls.* Still, as this time Roxanne scampered away from the incoming sea water, Vanessa called, 'It's time to go home. I'm freezing.'

'Oh, not *yet!*'

'Yes. Grace is in bed and doesn't know we're gone, but Mom and Dad will be home from the Drakes any time.'

'Oh, *them*. Simon Drake is a *pervert*,' Roxy said viciously. 'His wife's either blind or an idiot and so's their daughter.'

'Roxy, Simon is a friend of Dad's and you barely know his wife or Jane.'

'Oh, I know Simon all right! And *Janey* makes me sick the way she drools over her father like a lover. You've seen it – I know you have.'

'Well, maybe she's too physically affectionate, but—'

'No *buts!*' Roxanne ranted. 'Vanessa, sometimes talking to you is as useless as talking to Dad! You don't see what you don't want to see and you *don't* want to hear about it – you *won't* hear about it!'

'Calm down, Roxy.' Vanessa was accustomed to her sister's flashes of temper. 'Everyone knows Simon has affairs with other women. And I don't like him personally – he thinks he so cool – but he's a business partner of Dad's.'

'An *important* business partner of Dad's. That's all Dad cares about. And you, too.'

'I'm trying to be practical. Simon Drake is essential to the Everly business. His other women are his wife's problem and what do we care about how Jane acts around her father? She's not a friend of yours, and you and I aren't friends of the Drakes so what do they matter to us? We only see them three or four times a year.'

Roxanne was silent for a moment before she said with dismal foreboding, 'Mommy hates them so, when she's around them she always drinks too much and gets loud and says things that embarrass Dad, and afterward they fight and then she lies in bed for days, not speaking even to me.'

So that was Roxanne's real problem, Vanessa thought. The Drakes brought out the worst in their mother. Vanessa was usually able to ignore Ellen's dark moods but they deeply upset Roxy.

'Yes, they always have an argument, so I really don't want to walk in after they get home. An argument means if they find out about our midnight swim, they'll make an even bigger deal about it than they normally would, so let's get our robes and go home. *Fast.*'

They headed away from the ocean toward the base of a wooded hillock edging the beach, Roxanne lagging behind. Only a sliver of moon shone dully on the beach and Vanessa frowned. 'I'm not sure where we left our stuff.'

'It's right ahead of us.'

'I don't see it. It's the mist.' She looked ahead and squinted. 'Oh, there it is.'

When they reached the towels, Vanessa handed one to Roxanne. 'This one doesn't have any sand on it. Use it on your hair.'

'You didn't even get your hair wet. Trying to look glamorous?'

'Yes, I really care what I look like right now.'

'Who would around here, even in the day?' Roxanne massaged the ends of her thick hair. 'Everly Cliffs, Oregon, population eight thousand, nine hundred and forty-three, is a colossal bore.'

'Is that why we have such a big tourist trade in the summer? Because Everly Cliffs is boring?'

'I admit that the Oregon coast has a lot of pretty little towns and beautiful beaches. We have some nice restaurants and shops, and there's the golf course, and people bring their boats for the summer, but the only time this place is even halfway fun *is* in the summer when the tourists are here and they'll start leaving in a couple of weeks,' Roxanne said glumly. 'Everly Cliffs will come to a standstill in the winter and I can't bear this place when there's *nothing* to do.'

'There are things to do in winter. Plenty of them. Trust me, you'll live, Roxy.' Their robes weren't with their towels and Vanessa suddenly felt uneasy. 'Where are our robes?'

'Farther back. You're not listening to me. I won't get to go anywhere this winter.'

Roxanne's whining was beginning to grate on Vanessa's nerves but she kept her voice patient. 'I have an idea. Why don't you take the next couple of years to really concentrate on your music? You're good on the acoustic guitar but I've hardly heard you play this summer. You have a good voice that could be even better, and you write music.'

'I'm only OK at all three of those things.'

'Who told you that?'

'My music teacher.'

'That old grouch Cremeans? He's tone deaf. Why don't you switch to the music teacher at the high school? He's young, has professional experience and gives private lessons.'

'I've heard he's really demanding.'

'Which is why you've been avoiding him. He's what you need. I know him slightly. I could talk to him for you.'

'Oh, I don't know. I mean, well, I don't want to humiliate myself.'

'I don't think fear of humiliating yourself is really the problem. It's laziness.' Vanessa paused then plunged ahead firmly. 'Roxy, I don't want to criticize, but you have a gift and you're wasting your talent.'

Roxanne didn't burst into anger as Vanessa expected but instead asked in amazement, 'You really think I'm gifted?'

'Absolutely.'

'Well, I've always wanted to be the next Taylor Swift,' Roxanne said thoughtfully.

'Do you think Taylor got to where she is by not working on her craft, just sitting around complaining about how boring her life is? You have to work if you want to succeed.'

'Gee. Mommy and Dad are never too encouraging.'

'They don't encourage my acting, either. They'd like for both of us to get married, have babies, and never leave Everly Cliffs. But I want more.'

'Me, too.' Roxanne was quiet for a few seconds. 'Maybe you're right. I don't practice the guitar enough. I could write *so* many more songs than I do if I spent more time on them. And my singing definitely needs work. I could do a lot better.'

'It's not too late to change your focus. And if you really start proving yourself, maybe when you graduate from high school you'll want to come and live with me in Los Angeles. I might even have made some music industry contacts by then.'

Roxanne looked at Vanessa with a gleam in her blue eyes and excitement in her voice. 'Would you really do that for me?'

'I'd do anything for my little sister.'

They'd reached the scant evergreens lining the beach. Vanessa found her robe and gratefully shrugged into the heavy, white terry cloth. 'Now where are my sneakers?'

'They're only canvas and old – forget them.'

'I'm not walking up the hill to the house barefooted. Dammit, where are they? I wish I'd brought a flashlight.' She stepped between two trees, looked around, then saw them about four feet back where the evergreens grew more closely together. 'I know I didn't put them there.' Vanessa stepped carefully on scattered pine needles and bent over to pick up her shoes.

Something hard crashed against her head. A spear of pain shot through her and lights seemed to flash as she reached up to touch the left side of her skull. 'Wha—' she managed before another blow snapped her fingers. She wailed, jerking her injured hand toward her mouth. Then came a third bash that spun her around to face the beach and sent her to her knees.

Her vision darkened and she felt warm blood oozing down the side of her face. As her world swirled, she heard Roxanne scream and dimly saw her struggling with someone lumbering and bulky. Vanessa tried to stand but crumpled dizzily face-down in the sand. She heard Roxanne yelling, '*No!*' before she began shrieking, 'Vanessa! *Help!*'

'Roxanne,' she murmured, her mouth filling with sand. 'Roxanne . . .'

Vanessa tried to push up on her hands for balance but groaned as pain seared through broken and useless fingers. *My God, no,* she thought, still struggling to stand up, falling once, twice, her head throbbing, then losing all strength and collapsing in defeat. *Roxanne, this is all my fault, all my fault.* The words danced endlessly, agonizingly through Vanessa's mind as she lay helpless, her consciousness waning, and her sister's desperate screams fading down the lonely beach.

ONE

V anessa Everly closed her green eyes as she listened to the soaring, majestic opening song of *Kingdom of Corinna,* the hit anthology television series now nearing the end of its first season. It had already been nominated for three Golden Globes.

Vanessa had been stunned when producers had approached her to play Na'dya of Ives, the wife of Dominick Beaumond, king of Corinna, in the proposed epic fantasy show. Until then, Vanessa's professional life had consisted of guest appearances on episodic television and four supporting roles in movies that had barely broken even at the box office. She could pay her bills, but she had been deeply disappointed. She'd so hoped for a more distinguished career.

Then, two years ago, what seemed like the impossible happened when she was given the script of a new fantasy series and asked to audition for the role of Na'dya, the king's wife. She'd been dazzled by the writing, the show's energy, grandeur, and the multiple lush locations. She'd been impressed that the story was told in a ten-week arc versus a self-contained episodic format, and also that the show was not so graphic as to eliminate an adolescent audience. She'd admired the character of Na'dya, a pampered young princess who'd married a handsome, intelligent prince who became king and adored his wife – a wife who was now a strong woman and helped him rule a tumultuous empire.

When *Kingdom of Corinna* came along, Roxanne had been missing for over six years. The tempestuous, beautiful, blue-eyed girl of fifteen had disappeared like a leaf in the wind. Within hours of someone whisking the screaming girl away, a massive police search had been launched. Police looked at video of the area of the beach where Roxanne was taken, but neither of the two videos available had recorded anything except empty beach. Since her disappearance, Roxanne had not made any calls or posted on social

media. No one knew of anyone she was dating. Her few close
male friends had been interrogated, but none of them were
'boyfriends'. Posters featuring Roxanne's picture were nailed on
trees, placed in businesses, and distributed by hand all along the
Oregon coast and throughout the rest of the state. Stories ran on
the nightly local and national news along with her photo and pleas
for anyone who had seen her to come forward.

During that time, the police had one prime suspect – Brody
Montgomery, the younger brother of Vanessa's boyfriend Christian
Montgomery. When Brody was eighteen, he'd begun hallucinating,
left his freshman year at Stanford University and after going
missing for two months, returned to Everly Cliffs claiming he was
a knight searching for a lady in danger whom he must save. His
father Gerald, a surgeon at Everly Cliffs Hospital and recent
widower, had immediately sought treatment for his younger son
and was crushed when he learned Brody suffered from schizophrenia. The blow was almost too much only months after his
wife had died in a car wreck. Doctors said Brody was in the early
stages, though, and thought that rest in a convalescent center and
the proper medical protocol might control the illness and within
a year, Brody could be himself again.

At this time, eighteen-year-old Vanessa had been dating
twenty-two-year-old Christian for a year. Already in medical
school, Christian lived up to her own father Frederick's expecta-
tions. In fact, he thought of Christian as the son he'd never had.
She knew he hoped she and Chris would eventually marry and
Vanessa would give up her silly dreams about acting. She, too,
had hoped she and Christian would get married someday. She'd
loved him passionately and she knew he loved her. And unlike
her father, he didn't expect her to give up her own career desires.
She wanted to act and he'd wanted her to act. He'd wanted her
to be successful and satisfied, and not only with him. He'd
wanted her to have what would make her feel whole. He was
handsome, smart, ambitious, kind, funny, understanding, and an
ardent lover. At times, she thought their relationship was too
good to be true.

And it was.

After a year of calm, Brody had stopped taking his medication
and at twenty, began roaming throughout Everly Cliffs, once again
believing he was a knight looking for a lady he must save. He'd

had a hiding place and for nearly a month eluded the medical and police officials' searches for him.

Three days before Roxanne was taken, Brody had been captured by the local police. They had been ordered by the sheriff at the time to not divulge that Brody rambled about needing to rescue Roxanne – to take her away. He also allowed Brody to stay at home with his father until arrangements for confinement could be made. Brody was scheduled to enter a hospital schizophrenic treatment center two days after his capture, but his admission was delayed.

The afternoon after Roxanne's abduction, the police learned that Brody had not entered the medical facility until three o'clock that day. When they finally descended on the Montgomery home that evening, Gerald claimed that last night when Roxanne Everly was taken, Brody was heavily medicated with Thorazine and so sedated he could barely get out of bed. Christian had already gone back to Stanford, California, to settle into an apartment before his next year in medical school started, but a friend of Gerald's came forward and said he'd been at the Montgomery house to keep Gerald company in his vigil over Brody. He swore he'd been there all evening until after midnight and also that he'd seen Brody medicated and sleeping at the time someone took Roxanne. No case could be brought against Brody Montgomery and he'd gone free. By this time, the Everly family found out that Brody had been obsessing about fleeing with Roxanne and Vanessa and her parents were convinced that Gerald was lying about Brody being home and sedated when Roxanne was kidnapped. Over the next two months, Vanessa's relationship with Christian had exploded from the doubt and stress.

The search for Roxanne went on but after a year, even when they knew the case had gone cold, police nevertheless told the Everly family not to give up hope – miracles did happen and there was no evidence that Roxanne was dead. She could return. Vanessa's mother and father held on desperately to that hope, but Vanessa did not believe in miracles no matter how hard she tried. She pretended, for her parents' sake, to believe Roxanne would walk in the door one day, as healthy and happy as the night she'd vanished. Her grandmother Grace was without hope. She thought the same as Vanessa – Roxanne must be dead. The belief was a dark bond between them and Vanessa's pain and guilt had never abated. Her lost sister was constantly on her mind.

Roxanne had been entranced by the worlds of fantasy, royalty and spectacle in television and movies. She would have loved *Kingdom*, Vanessa thought. She would have had a million questions about the production. Vanessa could have even invited Roxy to some of the sets to watch filming. What an adventure it could have been for both of them.

Vanessa sighed in regret then forced her attention back to her flat-screen television and saw herself as Queen Na'dya. In bright sunshine, she stood on a castle balcony beside her tall, blond husband King Dominick. Her naturally black, wavy hair – doubled in thickness and length by extensions and entwined with silver ribbon – hung in a waist-length braid. She wore a pale-green brocade dress embroidered with silver thread and a delicately wrought gold crown on her head. A huge faux emerald and diamond ring sparkled on her right hand as she waved with queenly grace to the crowd below watching and cheering a parade led by knights in armor shining in the brilliant sun and carrying banners bearing the sigil of House Beaumond.

Tonight Vanessa sat in her Los Angeles apartment and smiled. The scene being shown had been filmed in Sorrento. They'd started in the morning and there had been take after take after take. By late afternoon the temperature had reached the upper eighties. In her heavy brocade dress, sweat had run down her sides and her face carefully made up with sheer products was blotted between each take and dusted lightly with translucent powder. But she'd felt most sorry for all the men wearing knight's armor. Four actors had passed out from the heat by the end of the day's filming.

The show was excellent, and she did a good job of portraying Na'dya, if Vanessa did say so herself, although she felt completely different from the composed, relentless, daunting queen. She was not as good at hiding her emotions as Na'dya. Her mind did not work as coolly and rationally as Na'dya's. She was not as brave as Na'dya. She often couldn't handle frustration and grief with Na'dya's outward equanimity.

'Unfortunately, you're not Na'dya,' she said aloud, stood up, stretched, and tucked her long hair behind her ears – a nervous habit. Vanessa always watched the show. During tonight's episode, though, she was inexplicably edgy, crossing and uncrossing her legs, fidgeting in her chair. She wanted a drink – something relaxing on a night when she felt nervous and depressed.

'Because it's almost Christmas,' she said aloud as she headed for the kitchen. Her beloved collie given to her by the cast of *Kingdom* and named Queen Na'dya, which Vanessa shortened to Queenie, rose from her bed beside Vanessa's chair and followed her dutifully into the kitchen. Vanessa handed the dog a treat and pulled a can of cola from the refrigerator, ice from the freezer, then reached for the bottle of rum. Christmas was always hard for her because it had been Roxanne's favorite time of year. Vanessa dropped ice into a glass.

Favorite? Since she was three, Roxanne had been a whirling dervish at Christmas, mad with joy as the men hung lights outside and she and Vanessa decorated the interior of the house with bows and tinsel. Roxanne wrote endless Christmas wish lists for Santa that her father had always put in his coat pocket and solemnly promised to mail, stared fixedly at the elaborate nativity scene her mother always arranged, and finally spent an evening squealing with delight as they decorated the large evergreen with glass bulbs, antique ornaments, glittering foil tinsel, and strings of lights. Even the last year Roxanne had been with the family on the holidays, she was as ecstatic as she'd been at age five.

The first Christmas after Roxanne's disappearance, Everly House had been the same as it was in the summer. No tinsel and lights decorated the large rooms, and no evergreen towered in the corner of the library, bright foil-wrapped and beribboned packages piled underneath. No Christmas music soared through the halls, Vanessa's father sat hunched over papers at his desk drinking bourbon and her mother Ellen had lain in bed half-conscious from liquor and sedatives.

The night of the attack, Vanessa's parents had come home from an evening out and gone to bed, thinking their daughters were also safe in theirs. Instead, Vanessa had regained fuzzy consciousness several times, but she didn't have the strength to crawl more than a few feet from the line of trees. Just past dawn, a young couple on their honeymoon who'd decided to watch the sunrise from the beach found her curled up on the sand, her face smeared with blood, the fingers on her left hand twisted and broken. Vanessa had barely been aware of them or of the paramedics who'd arrived minutes after the couple had called on their cellphone. They'd accompanied her to the small Everly Cliffs Hospital, the young woman murmuring encouragements all the way. At the hospital, someone had recognized Vanessa and phoned her father.

Between pain medication and shock, the following days in the hospital were a blur. Vanessa remembered her father's deeply lined face bending over her and saying she'd suffered a concussion and had surgery on her hand, which she mustn't try to move. Her mother's blue eyes, so like Roxanne's, had hovered swollen and red above Vanessa. She'd demanded over and over in an increasingly shrill voice, 'Where's Roxanne? What did you let happen to her? *Where's my baby?*' Then her grandmother Grace would appear, speaking in a calm voice, and lead Ellen from the room.

Vanessa recalled the sheriff's endless questions and the doctor requesting him to leave. 'Thank you,' Vanessa had murmured tearfully to the doctor. 'I want to go home. Please let me go home.'

But home had been worse. At least at the hospital she hadn't been forced to listen to her mother's constant weeping and lengthy alcohol- and drug-fueled rebukes for taking her 'baby' sister to the ocean at night. It was Grace who'd ordered Ellen to stay out of her daughter's bedroom. Vanessa's father Frederick was also drinking steadily although he'd mistakenly thought secretly. Occasionally he wandered in to sit on the side of her bed and stare at her with dark-green, grief-stricken eyes, which hurt her more deeply than her mother's outbursts. Vanessa felt that only Grace's gentle care and matter-of-fact conversation had kept her sane.

Vanessa returned to Los Angeles six weeks later and began school again the next term. She'd considered remaining at home until Roxanne was found, but Grace had urged her to leave. 'Staying here won't help the police. Go back to school. Do it for me.' Vanessa had worn a cast on her left hand. Over the next year she'd had two reconstructive operations and plastic surgery, which doctors hoped with physical therapy would restore the fingers to almost normal. Nevertheless, she had dived into school. When she finished, she stayed in Los Angeles, although she'd always gone back to Everly Cliffs at Christmas despite the cold, dismal atmosphere.

A few years later her father, who suffered from a bad heart and alcoholism, fell down the stairs and broke his neck. Ellen, whose drinking and use of barbiturates had spun out of control, had a nervous breakdown and retreated into an imaginary world. After a few months, she was legally declared incompetent and

sent to a professional care facility where she'd been living for
almost three years. The two calamities less than six months apart
had been a shock, especially to Grace who'd dearly loved her
grave, though damaged, son. *This year will be even worse, though,*
Vanessa thought. Alzheimer's had started its insidious work on
Grace's mind a little over two years ago and in October she had
broken a hip. Complications had delayed her recovery but she
was now recuperating at home. Still, Vanessa knew it could be
the last year that Grace would know her.

Tonight the thought sent a shiver through Vanessa and she sipped
her drink. That's why she felt uneasy, she told herself. Next week
she would be going home for Christmas earlier than usual. She
would be spending what could be her last holiday with Grace.
Even when Grace had lived in France, she'd kept in constant
contact with Vanessa, the granddaughter she said was most like
her. They'd been like girlfriends in spite of Grace's age and sophis-
tication and wisdom. Vanessa could not imagine a world without
her grandmother to confide in and ask for advice.

Vanessa gazed out the window of her fifth-floor West Hollywood
apartment at the galaxy of lights. Usually she enjoyed the sight,
and felt pleasure at so much life in a city that never seemed to
sleep, but not tonight.

She flexed her left hand. The hand surgeon had done an excellent job reconstructing the fingers and plastic surgeons had worked
miracles on the appearance. Except for a few narrow scars and
occasional pain and stiffness in the joints, her hand was almost
like it had been before the attack. Vanessa made a fist and winced.
It definitely hurt tonight. She took a deep swallow of her drink,
thinking her pain was only a symptom of what she didn't want
to admit – she did not want to go to Everly Cliffs. She hadn't
wanted to go for Christmas since Roxanne's kidnapping but she
made herself go to see Grace. And there was her friend Audrey
Willis. Their parents had shared a friendship and Vanessa and
Audrey had been close since they were children, although Audrey
was two years older than Vanessa. She had gotten pregnant when
she was an unmarried teenager and had given birth to a beautiful
daughter Cara. Now Audrey was a nurse and had been looking
after Grace since she broke her hip. She and Cara had moved into
Everly House with Grace, and Vanessa knew that Grace enjoyed
their company, especially Cara's. The girl was eleven and Vanessa

longed to see the beautiful, dark-haired sprite. Yes, going home was a must. She absolutely could not skip this visit.

She heard the concluding music of *Kingdom of Corinna* and realized she'd missed the last half of the show while standing in the kitchen sipping rum and cola and conducting a mental argument with herself. Oh well, each episode of the cable show aired at least three times a week and she could catch it later. Tonight she'd been too restless to concentrate and instead had paced around the compact kitchen of her one-bedroom apartment. *Kingdom of Corinna* had been renewed for two seasons. She could safely afford a house and she intended to buy one after the next season of *Corinna* finished filming for the year. The small apartment had suited her since she was twenty-one, but now she wanted more interior space and a lawn for Queenie. She felt as if it was finally time for her life to begin again and she wanted a real home.

Two cellphones lay on the kitchen counter: a black smartphone and a blue iPhone. The black smartphone emitted the ringtone 'Für Elise' and she quickly picked it up, glancing at the caller ID to see *Unknown.* Puzzled, she said briskly, 'Hello.'

After a moment of silence, a voice screeched, 'Is she there? Is she with you?'

Vanessa winced at the piercing shrillness in the voice although it was so ragged, she couldn't tell if it was a man's or a woman's. 'Audrey?'

'Not Audrey. I'm looking for *her.*'

'I . . . I think you have the wrong number.'

'I *don't*! *Tell* me!'

A chill washed over Vanessa at the ear-shattering voice although she knew this call could not be meant for her. 'I'm telling you I don't know who you mean—'

'You *do*! Damn you to hell if you don't tell me where your sister is!'

Vanessa felt as if her heart skipped a beat. Her *sister*? 'Who is this?' she choked out. 'What do you want?'

'Your sister!'

'My *sister*? Do you know something about her? Who are you?'

The androgynous voice suddenly sounded fatigued. 'Don't . . . don't play the fool, Vanessa. You remember that song you liked so much, don't you? "Praying for Time"? Well, you, my girl, had better be *praying for time.*'

The connection ended. Vanessa clutched the phone, shouting, 'Hello! *Hello! Please talk to me!*' But the caller was gone and Vanessa sank to the floor, her legs rubbery, her heart pounding. The kitchen whirled around her and she closed her eyes, lowering her head until the shock passed.

Because of the television show, she had a large social media presence. But Vanessa valued her privacy and used the blue iPhone, which she called her 'public' phone, for most of her calls. She called the black smartphone her 'private' phone. Not even her agent had the number – only Grace and Audrey in Everly Cliffs could call her on it. She knew that as popularity of the TV show grew, so would her loss of privacy. For now, though, she tried hard to keep her connection to Everly Cliffs unknown because she didn't want the story of Roxanne rediscovered and sensationalized. It would be painful for Grace and, if Roxanne was by some wild possibility still alive, could cause her death if her captor thought the search might be started again. If someone called Vanessa on her smartphone, it meant her Everly Cliffs number had been discovered and the results might be disastrous for Roxanne. Who could have given out that number? Grace? She probably didn't remember it. Audrey? *Never.* Then who had called her? And *why?* And who would know she liked George Michael's 'Praying for Time'? Was the caller's aim only to frighten her? After all these years? Once again, the question tolled in her head: *Why?*

Vanessa jumped when her other cellphone rang. Would the caller be playing tag with the phones? If so, she must call the police or . . .

Or do what? she wondered as she got up and staggered to the counter where the phone sounded again. Tentatively, she glanced at the caller ID. *WADE BAYLOR*, now the sheriff of Everly Cliffs, and the area code was 503. Home, Vanessa thought, suddenly trembling again.

She picked up the phone and shakily said, 'Hello?'

'Vanessa? Vanessa Everly?' came a strong, male voice she hadn't heard for years but knew well.

'Y-Yes.'

'This is Sheriff Wade Baylor in Everly Cliffs.'

Alarm rushed through Vanessa. 'Yes, I know, Wade. What's wrong? Is it Grace?'

'Your grandmother? No, as far as I know, she's fine.'

'What about Audrey?'

'Audrey Willis is OK.'

'Then what . . .'

'I know this will be a shock.'

'Tell me!'

He hesitated, then said bluntly, 'Vanessa, your sister Roxanne is home.'

TWO

'Home?' Vanessa repeated blankly. 'She's *alive*?'

'It seems so. I mean, if the woman is really Roxanne.'

'Is there some doubt?'

'Roxanne's been gone a long time. This woman is too sick to talk. She can't answer any questions.'

Vanessa's hands went cold. 'Did she come home on her own or did someone bring her?'

'Audrey Willis and her daughter are staying at your grandmother's house. Well, you know that. Anyway, earlier tonight Audrey found the woman lying unconscious on the porch. She was immediately taken to the hospital.'

'You said she's sick. What's wrong with her?'

'I don't know her condition. I only saw her briefly. She's thin and dirty. Her hands are scratched pretty badly and she has a small cut on her forehead. She's unconscious so we don't know how long she was on the porch for. There's no sign of who put her there or if she walked and then collapsed.' He took a deep breath. 'Vanessa, I'm on the way back to headquarters. The doctors won't let me question the woman right now. That's all the information I can give you. It's all I have, but Audrey is in the hospital waiting room. You should call her.'

'Yes . . . yes, of course. Thank you, Wade . . . Sheriff Baylor.'

Vanessa clicked off, her mind whirling. She'd given up on finding Roxanne years ago and now her sister had appeared, thin, scratched, dirty, and unconscious on a December night on her own front porch. This couldn't be happening, Vanessa thought. It couldn't.

But it was.

She took a deep breath, then with brittle fingers called Audrey Willis's cellphone. Audrey picked up on the second ring. 'Vanessa,' she said simply.

'Yes. Wade Baylor called. He said a woman . . .' Vanessa voice began to vibrate. 'He said Roxanne is back, that you found her lying on the front porch, that she's unconscious and thin and—'

'Slow down, Vanessa. I wanted to call you but Wade said it was his job as sheriff to notify you. Cara and I are at the hospital. We were at your house watching TV with Grace when I heard a noise at the front door. It wasn't a knock – more like scratching. I turned on the porch lights and saw a lump. I mean, it looked human, but limp and ragged. I was nervous, but I opened the door anyway and her face was turned up to me. It was Roxanne's face – dirty, a little bloody – but definitely Roxanne's face. She was unconscious and I called the emergency services. I really don't remember much after that, Vanessa. Now I'm waiting for word on Roxanne.'

'She hasn't regained consciousness?'

'Not as of ten minutes ago. Her pulse was steady, though, and her airway clear. It's around forty-eight degrees here and she was wearing jeans and a torn but warm jacket. I don't think she's suffering from exposure.'

'How did she look?'

'Very pale. Her lips were cracked but not badly. I told you she had scratches—'

'Where?'

'Well, her face and she had a cut above her left eye. Blood had run down the side of her face and dried. She didn't have gloves and her hands were bruised and scratched, too. Her hair is long but tangled and dirty. Her beautiful hair . . .' Audrey's voice caught.

'Do they think she might die?'

'Die? No, no, Vanessa. She's just worn and neglected and she probably has a concussion but she didn't appear to have any serious wounds. I'm sure—'

'You can't be sure. There could be internal injuries.' Vanessa's voice rose. 'She might have brain damage! You don't know!'

'Vanessa, calm down.' Audrey's usually gentle voice was stern. 'Now is not the time for you to get hysterical. Get a grip, girl.'

Vanessa almost smiled. How often had the cool-headed Audrey

said that to her when they were young? Audrey continued, 'What Roxanne needs now is your strength. Don't lose it like—'

'Like my mother and father did,' Vanessa finished for her. 'I know, Audrey. I need to be like Grace, not like Mom and Dad.'

'Well . . . yes.'

'Who's with Grace while you're at the hospital?'

'Jane Drake. I know you don't like her . . .'

'Roxanne didn't like her because she's Simon Drake's daughter and she hated Simon. I barely knew Jane. I know she's a good nurse. My father hired her to stay with my mother for a few weeks before he died and she stayed until Mom had to be put in the convalescent home.'

'Yes, she *is* a very good nurse. By the way, she got engaged to Wade a month ago.'

'Wade *Baylor*?'

'The very man – our sheriff. Anyway, Grace is in good hands.'

'Yes. That's OK. That's good. That's fine.' Vanessa took a deep breath. 'I should be able to think of something more articulate to say.'

'You're doing great. Oh, here's Dr Montgomery.'

'*Christian?*' Vanessa blurted in surprise.

'Yes. Just a minute.'

In a moment, a smooth male voice asked, 'Vanessa?'

How long had it been since she'd heard that voice? Eight years? It was the same only slightly more controlled, more businesslike. But it still had the deep timbre, the warm tone that touched her heart the way it had when they dated years ago. But that was ancient history, she reminded herself.

'Christian?' Her own voice squeaked slightly and she cleared her throat.

'I was on duty in the emergency room when they brought her in. She has no identification, but the woman has long wavy blonde hair and blue eyes like Roxanne's. She looks to be in her mid-twenties. I know Roxanne would only be twenty-three but this woman's been through a lot. She has an abrasion scar on her outer right thigh, like the one Roxanne got when she wrecked her bicycle against the rocks, and a birthmark on her left shoulder.'

'Like Roxanne's.'

'I don't remember exactly what Roxanne's looked like but it's a strawberry mark – roughly a circle about an inch and a half in diameter.'

'Like our mother's.' Vanessa's voice was expressionless with shock. 'What else?'

'We'll run tests and compare her dental records—'

'But you're certain it's Roxanne, aren't you?'

'Well . . . fairly certain. She's thin and weak. And . . .'

'And?'

'I hate to tell you this but she also has the scars of needle marks on the inside of her elbows.'

'Heroin?'

'I have no way of knowing. Whoever had her could have kept her drugged.'

'Is she going through withdrawal?'

'There's no heroin in her blood tests and there are no fresh needle marks.'

'I see.' Vanessa closed her eyes. 'Is Audrey close by? May I speak to her?'

'Sure. Here she is.'

'Vanessa?' Audrey's voice sounded tremulous and unsure. 'Are you all right?'

'I'm not certain. I'm so surprised . . .'

'Of course you are.'

'You said Jane Drake is with Grace.'

'Oh, yes. I wouldn't have left Grace alone. She was so drowsy when I saw a woman lying on the front porch that she didn't even get excited. I stayed until Jane arrived. I brought Cara with me. After the shock of finding Roxanne, I needed to have her close to me so I could keep an eye on her.'

'I understand. Audrey, did Roxanne say *anything*?'

'Nessa, I told you she's unconscious. But she looks . . . well, completely spent.'

Vanessa drew a deep breath. 'I'll book the first flight I can get. I'll call you when I reach Portland and then I'll rent a car and drive to Everly Cliffs.'

'Wonderful. We need you.'

'I'll be there as soon as possible, Audrey,' Vanessa said with determination. 'Tell my little sister I'm on my way.'

'When I first looked at you I thought you were a movie star, but then I thought why would a glamorous movie star be flying in coach?' The heavy-set, seventyish lady sitting to Vanessa's left let out a deep laugh, loud enough to draw the attention of several other passengers around them. She peered at Vanessa with surprisingly youthful blue eyes behind maroon-rimmed glasses. 'You really do look like someone familiar to me – someone from the movies. You're not a movie star, are you?'

'No, I'm not,' Vanessa said truthfully, wondering how anyone could mistake her for a glamorous movie star with her long black hair pulled back in a messy bun and her green eyes bloodshot from a night without sleep. 'Thank you for the compliment, though.'

'Oh, I love movies,' the woman went on. 'I see them in the theaters and my husband gets cross because he says if I'd wait, I could see them on cable, but I like going to the theater. Don't you?'

Vanessa was trying to order coffee. Originally, she hadn't been planning on leaving for Everly Cliffs until tomorrow afternoon. Instead, she'd canceled the earlier plans and been lucky enough to book a 9:40 a.m. flight for her and the dog. The three cups of caffeinated coffee she'd had at home were wearing off, though, and she felt groggy. After she'd given her order, she turned to the woman. 'I'm sorry. You asked a question that I didn't hear.'

'I asked if you liked to see movies in a theater.'

'Yes, I do.'

'Do you like to go with someone or alone?'

'Well . . . either.'

'I go with a friend. I like to talk to someone throughout the movie. People are always shushing me, but I don't care.'

Vanessa managed a polite smile.

The woman peered at her. 'Now you look like an intense one to me. You probably don't say a word and watch a movie for all you're worth. Is that what you do? Watch? Think? Analyze?'

'Maybe. Probably.' *I'd certainly like time to think and analyze now.* 'I concentrate on the movie and don't talk until afterwards.'

'Hah! Like a movie critic. Do you have family in Portland, honey?'

'No.' Vanessa's coffee arrived and she took a lukewarm gulp. 'They're in Everly Cliffs.'

'Everly Cliffs! I've been there several times. The last was two summers ago. It's a beautiful place.' Vanessa nodded and the woman continued, 'The views are magnificent! I don't go out on boats – my husband does – but I find plenty to entertain myself while he fishes. I love walking on the beach, and they have a lot of nice little shops. But of course you know that. The last time we ate dinner at a lovely new restaurant. Now what was the name? Oh, Mina's!'

'You mean Nia's?'

'Nia's! Yes, yes, that's it. I'm sure you've eaten there.'

Vanessa nodded.

'We're thinking about retiring in Everly Cliffs next year. Howard doesn't want to leave Oregon and neither do I. By the way, I'm Fay,' the woman said.

'Hello, Fay.' Vanessa smiled. 'I'm Vanessa.'

'Vanessa! Well, isn't that pretty? So you have family in Everly Cliffs and don't tell me – you're going home for Christmas!'

'Yes.'

'Oh, how sweet. I've been in Los Angeles visiting a friend but I can't wait to get home to Portland for Christmas. It's my favorite time of year. The decorations, the parties. And I hope it snows. I remember when I was a little girl and it snowed *five* inches on Christmas Eve and I got a sled and . . .'

Fay's loud voice rattled on and on while Vanessa finished her coffee, ordered another and then another. Her head hurt and she was hungry. All she could think of was Roxanne. She wondered what Fay would say if she told the woman she was going home to see her sister who'd been kidnapped over eight years ago. She'd be thrilled, enchanted, titillated. Her voice would get even louder as she asked a dozen questions. All the passengers would know within minutes.

By the time they landed at twelve fifteen, Vanessa felt jittery, stiff in every joint, and deaf in her left ear. As they waited to disembark, Fay surprised her by saying quietly, 'I know I talk a lot, but I'm not completely oblivious to other people. I can tell that you're very worried about something, dear.' She fished in her purse and pulled out a business card reading *HOWARD JENNINGS* with two phone numbers, one a cell. 'This is my husband's card but I'm Fay Jennings. I wrote my home number on the back of the card. If you should need me or Howard – he's a brilliant attorney – for *anything*, just call. I'm not being polite – I mean it.'

'Thank you.' Vanessa was genuinely touched. 'My name is Vanessa Everly.'

'Vanessa *Everly*! Are you a member of the family that founded Everly Cliffs?' Vanessa nodded. 'Well, for heaven's sake! I should have known.'

'There's no reason you would.' Vanessa was reluctant to give Fay her cellphone number. The woman would think they were best friends. Still, she didn't want to be rude. 'I'll be staying at my family's home in Everly Cliffs, so it would be easy for you to reach me if you like.'

'Well, aren't you a sweetie!' Fay beamed then cocked her head and winked. 'And it came to me about an hour ago that you're on *Kingdom of Corinna*. I didn't connect that with you being a descendent of the original Everly Cliffs Everlys, but anyway Howard and I *never* miss the show. You're wonderful in it.'

They walked to the terminal together and waited until their luggage dragged by on the baggage conveyor. Howard Jennings appeared, apologizing for being late, and helped them haul their suitcases off the conveyor and onto airport luggage carts. He was tall with a round, benign face and keen gray eyes. He was also clearly happy to see his wife. Fay introduced him to Vanessa and he greeted her enthusiastically. As the couple walked – and talked nonstop – toward the doors of the terminal, Vanessa hurried to the restroom. Looking in the mirror under harsh fluorescent lights, she was surprised Fay or anyone else had recognized her as Na'dya from *Kingdom*. She thought she looked positively blanched. She slicked on some pink lipstick, which helped a bit, tucked loose ends of hair behind her ears, then gave up improving her appearance as a lost cause and left to collect Queenie. Next, she needed to rent a car.

After looking over several options, she impulsively chose a silver three-row-seater SUV. She wanted a large car to accommodate her dog. Besides, for some reason she wanted use of this big car for a week.

As Queenie stood on the pavement, Vanessa loaded her luggage and Queenie's cage into the sizable cargo hold, marveling at how much more it could contain. She put a plaid pad on the cage bottom, left the cage door open and said, 'Get in, girl!' Queenie obediently jumped into her cage and lay down, seeming to know she wouldn't be a prisoner for long. As soon as Vanessa settled herself on the black upholstered driver's seat, she glanced over the myriad of dials on the dashboard. When she closed the driver's door and heard a satisfyingly sturdy bang, she realized that in the big SUV she felt safe, almost as if she were shut in a bank vault. She wondered if that's why she'd picked it – she wanted to be strong but hated to admit she felt vulnerable, driving into a town she'd avoided as much as possible for years, facing a situation that was both joyous and terrifying. What if Roxanne was nothing like the girl who'd gone missing eight years ago? What if she was irreparably damaged, physically or psychologically or both?

Swallowing a wave of panic, Vanessa grabbed her cellphone and called Audrey.

'Nessa!' Audrey answered as if she'd been waiting for the call. 'You're in Portland?'

'Yes. The flight was OK. I've had so much coffee I feel like I could shoot through the roof of my car.'

'You've already rented a car?'

'Yeah. An SUV. A bigger one than I'll need. I should reach Everly Cliffs within two hours. Have you heard anything about Roxy this morning?'

'Dr Montgomery called about an hour ago and said she's doing all right. He wouldn't give any details. He's waiting for you.'

'I'll go to the hospital before I come home. How's Grace?'

'I told her about Roxy this morning. She's stunned but quiet and amazingly calm. She's watching television right now and waiting for Cara to come home from school. They're very close.'

'I'm glad. I can't wait to see the three of you.'

'I'm baking brownies.'

'Oh, my favorite! You sweetheart!'

'Cara, Grace and I love them, too. You can't have *all* of them,' Audrey laughed, then paused. 'Good luck, Nessa. I hope Roxanne is . . .' Audrey's voice wavered. 'I hope she's the Roxy we all remember.'

Vanessa pulled into the Everly Cliffs Hospital parking lot, chose a spot close to the building, then sat rigid, gripping the steering wheel. Her gaze drifted up to the silky, thin white cirrus clouds stretching against the periwinkle sky. A lemon-yellow sun shone and a golden-crowned sparrow soared past her windshield. Nothing bad could happen on such a perfect day, she told herself.

She knew that in the midst of all this beauty, she could *not* walk into the hospital and find the woman who had appeared last night had no resemblance to her sister because the real Roxanne had died eight years ago when Vanessa had taken her to a beach at night . . .

Except that it could happen. It could. It might.

Vanessa pressed down the thought and walked toward the hospital. She entered the lobby and went to the desk. 'I'm Vanessa Everly,' she said to a girl who couldn't have been more than twenty-one. 'I need the room number of my sister Roxanne Everly.'

'Oh!' The girl's eyes widened. 'I'm sorry. We're not supposed to give out her room number.'

'But I'm her sister.'

'That's the rule. I was told not to give *anyone* her room number.'

'Never mind. I'll take her to Miss Everly's room.'

Vanessa hesitated a couple of seconds before looking up at Christian Montgomery. She'd never seen him in the white coat of a doctor. Other than that, he looked remarkably the same as he had almost eight years ago – the same shining, medium-brown hair, the same long-lashed hazel eyes, the same perfect, straight-bridged nose and slightly full, tender lips that had always made her want to kiss him and still did. She hadn't prepared herself to see him and was embarrassed by how vulnerable she felt and the wave of yearning for him that rushed through her. She blushed as if he could read her mind. 'Hello, Christian,' she managed crisply. 'Were you waiting for me?'

'Audrey called and told me you'd be here around two thirty. We were afraid that in spite of all our precautions, word might get out that Roxanne is here so everyone has orders not to give out her room number to anyone.'

'I understand. I appreciate it.'

His smile was slow and kind. 'I'll walk you to her room.'

Vanessa started to protest, then decided she didn't want to walk into Roxanne's room alone. She needed moral support, even if it came from Christian Montgomery. 'Is she better today?'

'As well as can be expected.' At six foot one, Christian had an imposing presence and as they walked down the hall, Vanessa noticed he still moved with the easy grace he'd had at twenty. 'It's only been a few hours. She doesn't have any broken bones, but she's malnourished and battered, Vanessa. Don't expect her to look like she did the last time you saw her.'

'I don't!' Vanessa snapped.

He merely raised his eyebrows.

'I'm sorry, Christian. I'm edgy,' Vanessa apologized.

'I understand. Here we are.'

A policeman sat on a chair outside the doorway. Vanessa turned to Christian.

'Sheriff Baylor ordered protection. It's only a precaution,' he reassured her.

'Hello, ma'am,' the officer said.

She nodded, suddenly unable to speak, and paused in the doorway of the hospital room. She felt frozen, numb. She wanted to run away and run inside at the same time.

'Vanessa?' Christian asked.

'I'm fine.' She summoned every ounce of her strength and stepped into the room. It was dim and she had to take another step inside before her eyes adjusted. She blinked twice then focused on the white sheet drawn up to a pale face and a mass of wavy blonde hair on a pillow.

Slowly the woman sat up and held out her skinny arms. 'Vanessa!' she croaked in a thin, raspy voice. 'Oh, Nessa, how much I've missed you!'

THREE

'Roxanne.' Vanessa suddenly realized that until this moment, she hadn't been certain the woman in the hospital really was her sister. 'It *is* you!'

'Yes, it's me! Please come here,' she nearly gasped, then began coughing.

'She has bronchitis,' Christian said.

'You're afraid of catching it,' Roxanne said between coughs.

'No. No, of course I'm not.' Vanessa rushed to the bed and clasped the frail woman in her arms, holding her closely. When she pulled back, she looked into blue eyes. 'Sapphire-blue eyes like Mom's.'

'At least my eyes haven't changed.'

'Roxanne.' Vanessa felt tears begin to pour down her face. 'Oh my God, Roxanne, I never thought I'd see you again.'

'You gave up hope.'

Vanessa looked into those unmistakable eyes. 'Yes, Roxy, I did. Mom and Dad didn't, but I did. I'm sorry.'

'It's all right.' Roxanne hugged her again. 'I know Dad's dead. Christian told me this morning. It's my fault, isn't it?'

'No! He was drinking too much even before you . . . disappeared.'

'No, he wasn't. At least I don't think so. He must have started drinking a lot after I was kidnapped. And Mommy . . .'

'She always depended on pills and liquor and then after Dad died, she fell apart. But she's alive and getting excellent care.'

'I feel so guilty.'

'*You* feel guilty?' Vanessa was incredulous. 'Sweetheart, there was nothing you could do. You weren't responsible for Mom's and Dad's actions. You certainly aren't responsible for being kidnapped. You've been through so much. Not that I know the exact circumstances of the last few years, but I can imagine . . . I mean, it must have been bad . . .' Vanessa ran out of delicate words and asked bluntly, 'Who took you that night on the beach?'

Roxanne shook her head. 'I don't know. I didn't know anything for a while.'

'Have you been with him all this time?'

'I've been a prisoner, Vanessa.' Her face crumpled. 'It was so *awful* – mostly sexual. I just endured it. I never saw a face.'

'Never?'

'I was blindfolded and usually drugged. When I was able to see a little bit, whoever was well, *with* me, wore a hood. It didn't always feel or smell like the same person.'

'There was more than one?'

'I'm fairly sure, but only one talked.'

'And you didn't recognize the voice?'

'No. It wasn't a natural voice – more like a growl.'

'Where were you kept?'

'I think there were three or four places but I don't know where they were except for the last place – Portland. I was there a long time. In a room . . .' She closed her eyes tightly and tossed her head. 'Oh, the *smell* and the *music*!'

'What kind of smell? What music?' Vanessa asked.

'I don't want to think about it now. I *can't!*'

'OK, honey. It's all right. But you're sure you've been in Portland for a while?'

Roxanne nodded. 'I didn't know where I was for months. Then I was alone. No one came for days.' She started coughing. 'I was starving and I felt sick. I knew I was going to die. I was tied up but I kept struggling until I got loose. I was in a basement. I crawled up the stairs and saw that I was in an old house. I found a pair of men's shoes by the front door and put them on, then I slipped out the front door as quietly as I could in case someone was upstairs. Outside I ran for what seemed like forever.

'Then I couldn't run anymore. I was dragging along beside the road and a woman stopped and offered me a ride. I would never have gotten in the car with a man. She asked a lot of questions but I kept dodging. I hardly remember what I said. Finally I saw signs saying *Portland . . .*' More coughing.

'I didn't know what to do. I thought about the police but I was afraid . . .' Roxanne started to cry. 'They'd ask a million questions and waste time and someone might come for me – one of *them*—' Coughing. Sobbing. 'I asked the woman to let me out. She didn't want to, but I got loud. After I left her car, I walked and walked and finally saw the bus terminal. I went in but I didn't have any money. I went around begging.' She held out her right hand with its ragged, broken nails. 'The fare was less than twenty dollars. A nice old man gave me more money than anyone else. I got on the bus and slept most of the way. I walked home from the Everly bus terminal. I didn't want a ride. Even a taxi. Someone might take me to the police.' She started to shake violently. 'I had to get home. Home . . . *home* . . .'

'I think that's enough for now.' Christian gently disentangled Roxanne's arms from Vanessa's. 'You need some rest, Roxanne. The nurse will give you a mild tranquilizer—'

'No! *No!*' She wrenched and screeched, 'I've had what was called a *tranquilizer!*' Her cough-roughened voice deepened to imitate someone else's making an eerie, syrupy request. '"This *tranquilizer* will make you feel better, sweetheart. So much better. Let me put the strap around your arm. Make a nice big vein for me. That's right. That's my dear girl. Now doesn't that feel good?"'

Vanessa felt as if something shriveled in horror inside her. She and Christian exchanged glances. He didn't look too steady, either, but he said soothingly, 'I'm Christian Montgomery. You've known me since you were a little girl, Roxy. Don't you trust me?'

She looked beyond him, frowning, then muttered, 'Maybe.'

'And this is your big sister Nessa. Certainly you trust *her*.'

She nodded. 'I love her.'

'Then you know that neither of us would do anything to hurt you. You're very tired, Roxanne, and you have bronchitis. You've strained your voice so much you can hardly talk. I swear that what the nurse will give you *is* just a mild tranquilizer. It might not even make you sleep. It will calm you and you can rest for a couple of hours. All right?'

Roxanne collapsed against her pillow, pressed her chapped, bitten lips together and nodded.

'Good,' Christian continued. 'You'll talk to Vanessa again later, won't she, Vanessa?'

'Oh yes.' She leaned down and kissed Roxanne's sweating, scratched forehead. 'I promise.'

'OK,' Roxanne croaked wearily. 'OK. Whatever.'

Vanessa and Christian waited until a nurse came in and began talking to Roxanne in a calm, soft voice. Roxanne didn't answer but she didn't struggle, either. The woman was chatting about her grandchildren when Vanessa and Christian slipped out of the room and closed the door. The policeman was still in place, casually looking at a vacation magazine of Tahiti.

As they walked away from the room, Vanessa had trouble catching her breath. 'Are you all right?' Christian asked.

'I don't know what I expected but not *that*.'

'It was rough. You probably thought you were only going to identify her. You didn't factor in the emotional side of it.'

'I did. A little bit. Not nearly enough.' Vanessa suddenly went ice cold and dizziness washed over her. 'Oh, Chris, I feel like I'm going to fall down.'

He wrapped his arm around her waist and pulled her close to him. She felt an unexpected urge to hug him, to hold him close like she used to do. Then she remembered. They weren't a couple any more. She stiffened and took a small step away from him.

'I'm OK now,' she said abruptly.

Christian seemed not to notice her body language. 'Let's go to the cafeteria and get some coffee,' he said.

'No more coffee for me. I've had about a gallon today.'

'You need to drink something and have a bite to eat. You're almost as pale as Roxanne. You can't drive home this way.'

Ten minutes later they scooted into a booth at the far end of the small, bland green-and-white room. 'At least we didn't hit rush hour in this gourmet restaurant,' Christian said.

Vanessa raised her glass of milk with a shaky hand and took a sip. She looked at a piece of dry banana bread. 'The few people here are staring at us, though.'

Christian shrugged. 'You're a big television star. You must be used to it.'

'I'm not a big star—'

'You are. You're famous.'

'Maybe, but I'm not used to being noticed. And now I feel like the stares are more because I'm Roxanne's sister than an actress in *Kingdom of Corinna*.'

'By the way, I like the show.'

'You watch it? I'm surprised.' Vanessa stared at him, noting the little mole beside his right eye and the small scar on the left side of his jaw he'd gotten during an adolescent brawl when a boy had called her a 'snotty bitch'.

'Is something wrong?' he asked.

Vanessa quickly lowered her gaze and sipped her milk. 'Please tell me more about Roxy's physical condition.'

'We're still doing tests.' Christian took a drink of his coffee and made a face. 'Ugh. It's even worse this time of day. She has vaginal tearing, which doesn't seem to have happened in the last few days. She has a tubal blockage from a pelvic inflammatory disease that was left untreated for too long. She suffered a broken left wrist perhaps a couple of years ago and there is some scarring around her wrists and ankles. Second, she's negative for drugs and alcohol. I told you she hasn't shot up – or *he* hasn't shot her up lately. No HIV. She has a case of bronchitis. Then there's the cut above her eye. She doesn't remember how she got it. The plastic surgeon looked at it and said it won't leave much of a scar. She's malnourished and dehydrated. She needs fluids, vitamins, and antibiotics, which she's getting intravenously . . .' He looked down at his small piece of soggy apple pie.

'And?'

'Roxanne's had an abortion.'

Vanessa closed her eyes. 'Oh, no.'

'Yes. There's quite a bit of scarring probably dating from four or five years ago.'

'How awful for her.'

'Would you rather she had that monster's child?'

'That monster?' Vanessa said flatly. 'She said she's not certain she's always been with the same man. It could have been the spawn of any one of several monsters.'

'Spawn?'

'She was kidnapped and drugged and raped. I can't think of it as a baby.'

'All right. I understand how you feel but we don't know how she felt about it.'

'You think she wanted it?' Vanessa demanded hotly.

'I don't know what she thought or how she felt. How could I?'

'Oh, stop being so dispassionate,' Vanessa snapped. 'It's not in your nature. It never was.'

'You haven't even spoken to me for nearly eight years. Maybe I've changed.'

Vanessa said nothing.

'I promised Roxanne that you'd see her later today,' Christian said. 'I was trying to calm her, but I think she's had enough for one day. She needs to rest, not to be agitated before bedtime. Can you wait until tomorrow to see her again?'

Vanessa hesitated. 'You really think it's best for her?'

'Yes.'

'All right. You seem extremely caring for her.'

Christian looked surprised. 'Why wouldn't I be?'

She leaned forward slightly and said quietly, 'Because of Brody.'

Christian drew back, his hazel eyes narrowing. She had forgotten how one minute those beautiful eyes could twinkle with humor and the next sharpen until you felt pinned to the wall. 'Are you going to start this *now*, Vanessa?'

'When it comes to my little sister who's been abused for years, you're damned right I will!'

They stared at each other and Vanessa felt them both gathering for a fight. Instead, Christian glanced around at the few people in the cafeteria, most of whom were looking at them. He paused and finally said, 'My brother is working.'

'Where? Here?'

Christian's gaze hardened as if expecting her reaction. 'Portland.'

'What a coincidence.'

'Don't be sarcastic, Vanessa. I'm not in the mood.'

Vanessa started to say something else but his steely look silenced her.

'Brody never went back to school. He was always really interested in computers and he's become a software developer. He and a friend he met here in Everly Cliffs years ago have a company named Blackbird.'

'Blackbird?'

'The name comes from the Beatles song. A lot of software companies have unusual names. Anyway, he's been very successful, both in business and in staying on his medication. I couldn't be more proud of him. Dad and Mom would be, too.'

'Who's his business partner?' Vanessa asked, taking a last gulp of her milk.

'Zane Felder. Zane's parents used to spend their summers in Everly Cliffs. Brody and Zane met then. They formed Blackbird four years ago and it's grown by leaps and bounds. They have a fine reputation.'

Vanessa could see that Christian was doing all he could to hold on to his temper. And no wonder, she thought. She'd immediately brought up a sensitive subject they'd agreed to lay to rest years ago along with their relationship. 'I'm sorry, Christian. I was out of line.'

He paused as if thinking. Then she could see him calming down. 'You've had an incredible shock.'

'That's no excuse,' she said sincerely. 'I *am* sorry.'

He smiled slightly, his hazel eyes tilting the way she'd always thought so charming. 'Apology accepted. Now, are we finished or do you want another piece of that delicious banana bread?'

'Oh, gosh darn, I'm afraid I'll have to skip another piece. Audrey has fresh brownies waiting at home.'

They left the cafeteria and walked to the lobby. 'Thanks for taking care of me, Christian. I don't think I could have faced seeing Roxanne without you.'

'I would never have sent you in her room alone.' He looked at her earnestly. 'I know she looked bad, Nessa, but she's been here less than twelve hours. Give her a couple of days. I promise she'll improve.'

'I'm sure she will. She's getting good care.'

'I'll walk you out to your car,' Christian said.

'That isn't necessary—'

'Excuse me. Christian?'

A short, stocky man with longish, curly ginger hair, a beard, and wearing jeans, a Metallica sweatshirt, and a down vest approached them. He had a deep frown and worried blue eyes.

'Zane?' Christian asked.

The man nodded.

'Vanessa, this is Zane Felder, Brody's business partner,' Christian said. 'What are you doing here, Zane?'

'I called your office but you weren't in. I'm sorry to bother you in the hospital, but have you talked to Brody?'

Christian frowned. 'Not for almost a week. Is something wrong?'

Zane fidgeted uncomfortably, then said bluntly, 'No one at the office, none of his friends have seen him or heard from him. He hasn't left any messages and I can't reach him by phone. Chris, Brody completely disappeared five days ago.'

Vanessa looked at Christian. 'Call Sheriff Baylor *now*.'

'Wait a minute, Nessa. We have no reason to call him.'

'Oh no? The man everyone suspected of kidnapping my sister going missing just when she returns is a coincidence?'

She realized what she'd said and glanced at Zane Felder. He frowned suspiciously.

'Is she back?' Zane asked.

The lobby suddenly seemed full of people, everyone staring at the three of them. 'Let's go to my office,' Christian said. 'And no one say anything until we get there.'

Christian led them down a hall to a small, sunny office with framed degrees hung on the walls and a tall, full lacy-leaf philodendron in a woven basket beside a bookshelf. He motioned toward two leather chairs across from his desk. 'Please, sit.'

They obeyed and Vanessa felt like a child called to see the principal as Christian sat behind a vast desk whose chair was at least four inches higher than hers. She sat up straighter. 'I still say we should call Wade Baylor.'

'And I say we should wait.' Christian's voice was firm. He looked at Zane. 'When did you last see Brody?'

'Friday around six o'clock when I left our office. I usually get at least one phone call from him over the weekend, but not this time. I called him twice but my calls went to voicemail. Monday he wasn't anywhere on the first or second floors at the business or up in his loft apartment. He hadn't left any word about being gone on Monday so by that afternoon, I started making calls. No one I know had seen or heard from him. The same yesterday.'

'Does he have a girlfriend he could be with?' Vanessa asked.

Zane looked at her, obviously slightly surprised. 'No. At least not one I know of. Besides, he wouldn't let even a girlfriend distract him from the business, especially when there's something important we needed to discuss. Our company's going public soon.'

'Has he been acting differently?'

'Well . . . he's been really wound up. Kind of hyper and short-tempered. But that's understandable considering what's going on with Blackbird. I haven't been a model of patience myself. I'm nervous, can't sleep—'

'Was Brody not sleeping?' Christian asked.

'He never said but his eyes were red and he looked tired.'

Christian raised his eyebrows. 'Why didn't you call me when he didn't show up?'

Zane shifted in his chair, looking guilty. 'I didn't want to alarm you. I also know how suspicious people around here are about him. I had my fiancé Libby call you and use a fake voice to ask if Brody was home for Christmas yet.'

Christian looked annoyed. 'That spacey woman was your *fiancé*?'

'You've met Libby. She is *not* spacey,' Zane returned indignantly.

'She sounded spacey on the phone when she called twice – Monday morning and yesterday afternoon. Why did she use a fake voice?'

'We didn't want to scare you. We thought we were being thorough but discreet.'

'Thorough but discreet? Is that what you call it?'

Zane's hands clenched on the chair arms and raised his voice. 'Look, I'm here now, aren't I? I didn't want to jump to conclusions, start an uproar over nothing, but now I know this has gone beyond a lapse on Brody's part. This is something serious.'

'All right. Arguing won't get us anywhere. Was there anything unusual in his loft?'

'No. Well, it was messy. Brody's usually meticulous when it comes to his living space.'

'Did you check the bathroom? That's where he keeps his medications. Were they there?'

Zane hesitated. 'I don't know everything he takes for the schizophrenia. Nothing was in the medicine cabinet except aspirin, bismuth, antihistamine, a couple of other over-the-counter things.'

'His prescription medicines were gone?'

'Yeah. At least they weren't in the bathroom or kitchen.'

'When did you discover this?'

'A couple of days ago.'

'And it didn't occur to you to call me, Zane? You didn't think that might be something serious?'

Zane's eyes narrowed. 'Look, Chris, he's not only my business partner, he's my best friend! You think I'm not concerned about him?'

Christian took a deep breath and closed his eyes for a few seconds. 'Please lower your voice, Zane,' he finally said calmly. 'I know you're concerned. So am I. That's why I wish I'd known sooner, but I suppose you did what you thought was best for Brody.'

Vanessa tried not to sound sharp. 'And now what do *you* think is best for Brody, Christian?'

'If you can't find his meds, it sounds like he has his medicine with him. That's good as long as he's taking it. But he's not answering his phone. That's bad.' He sighed. 'I know nearly every place Brody could be in Everly Cliffs. I'll make calls to people who might have seen him. I'll go to the places he could be that are deserted.' He paused. 'He might even be at our house. Dad left it to Brody *and* me. I still live there but he has keys to every door.'

'How could he be in your house and you not know it?'

'There's a guest house. It's small but he always loved it. He used to hide in it when he was a kid.'

'And if he isn't in any of the places you think he might be?' Vanessa asked.

'Well . . . then I'll call Wade Baylor.'

'Isn't he the sheriff?' Zane burst out. 'Oh no. No way, man. Not after what Brody's been through in this town!'

Vanessa looked at Zane. 'You don't understand—'

'I understand fine, thank you. I know you're upset about what happened to your sister but you've got it in for Brody. You always have. I know all about you.'

'You don't know one damned thing about me!'

'Hold it, you two,' Christian said sharply. 'Brody is my brother. He's the only family I have left. I care about him more than anyone in the world, Zane, but I have to think about his mental condition.'

'You're going to let all hell loose because *she* wants it!'

'Listen to me, Zane,' Vanessa said. 'If Brody *isn't* taking his meds, he could act erratically, get himself blamed for something he hasn't done. Don't you understand that Christian has to notify the sheriff for Brody's own good?'

'She's right, Zane.'

Zane glared at Christian and Vanessa. Finally he muttered, 'I still don't think it's the best idea.'

'I'm sorry you don't see it that way.' Christian shifted an intense gaze at Vanessa. 'I *will* call Wade Baylor.'

'When? You can't wait until tomorrow—'

'Just give me until . . . say eight o'clock tonight.'

'That's a long time.'

'No, it isn't, considering that I'm actually going to a few places, not only making calls.'

'I don't like it.'

'Come on, Vanessa, be reasonable. Like Zane, I don't want to start an uproar over what could be nothing.'

'Oh, all right,' Vanessa huffed, then stood and reached for a pen and piece of paper on Christian's desk. She wrote down the number of her public phone. 'This is my cellphone number. If you find out anything, call me immediately. And call me before you call Sheriff Baylor. *Don't* call my grandmother's house.'

Christian glanced at the number. 'Yes ma'am! Any further orders, Your Majesty?'

'I don't mean to interrupt whatever the hell is going on between you two,' Zane said with weary sarcasm, 'but is it *really* true that Roxanne Everly is back?'

Vanessa and Christian exchanged looks before Christian said, 'Yes, Zane, it's true. She turned up last night. She's in bad shape and in this hospital. The sheriff put a guard on her room – she's safe – but you can understand that we want to keep her return on a need-to-know basis for her sake and for the family's.'

'Sure, I see why you want to keep it on the down low and not only for her sake or the family's – for Brody's, too. He went through hell when that girl was kidnapped! He's never gotten over it.' Zane took a couple of deep breaths, clearly fighting for control. 'Libby and I are staying in town tonight at the Everly Cliffs Motel. I'll give you my cellphone number and I'd appreciate it if you'd let me know anything you find out about Brody.'

'I will, Zane. What about your girlfriend? Will she . . . well . . . be talking to people?'

Zane bristled. 'She's my fiancé and despite you thinking Libby's spacey, she isn't. She's intelligent and loyal and kind, and she loves Brody – like a friend, of course. She hasn't told anyone he's missing and I won't tell her the Everly girl is home. Satisfied?'

'Yes. And I'm sorry I said she was spacey.'

'Thank you.' Zane looked around aggressively. 'She's probably smarter than all three of us put together.'

Vanessa almost smiled at Zane's obvious love for his fiancé, thinking it would be nice to be so admired and cherished. It would be better than nice.

'I'd better get to work,' Christian said. 'I have to see three patients and then my day here is done. I'll make all my calls on my cellphone – none on the hospital phone.'

Vanessa nodded. 'Good idea.'

Christian's gaze met hers. 'I really will do my best, Vanessa.'

'I know you will. You love your brother.' She paused. 'But if I don't hear from you by eight o'clock, then *I'll* call Sheriff Baylor.'

FOUR

Vanessa tried to calm herself down as her car climbed the hill toward Everly House. The news that Brody Montgomery had gone missing just when Roxanne had returned was beyond upsetting. Hadn't Roxy said her captor had disappeared and that's why she'd been able to get away? Could Brody have left Portland, left Roxy, giving her the chance to escape? It seemed probable if he was her captor, but she'd promised to give Christian a few hours to search for his brother and a policeman sat right outside of Roxanne's room. Certainly she was safe enough for now?

As Everly House came into view, Vanessa smiled. Grace's grandfather, Abraham Everly, had inherited a fortune built decades earlier through the Oregon fur trade with the Native Americans and increased tenfold by maritime business with England. In 1905, he'd commissioned the house, abandoning the tall, elaborate Victorian mode in favor of the newer Edwardian style. The house was longer and wider than most Victorian houses but only two stories high except for a four-story red-domed tower in the shape of a lighthouse Abraham had added so he could look at the Pacific Ocean. Vanessa's grandfather Leonard, Grace, and Vanessa had loved the lighthouse and spent hours in it, but her father didn't like it and her mother Ellen said it made her nervous. Roxanne simply wasn't interested in looking through a telescope at the ocean.

Built of brick, the house featured balconies, porches, and verandahs, all decorated with elaborately carved white wooden railings. The windows were large, flooding the house with light during the day. Vanessa had lived at Everly House all of her life and the grounds had always been kept immaculate and the house in first-rate condition by Pete McGuire, who seemed like part of the family and lived in a small cottage near the home. She pulled up in front of the house, got out of the car, and looked out over Everly Cliffs. Somehow the little town looked bigger from up here.

A stiff breeze blew loose strands of hair around Vanessa's face. She took a deep breath, appreciating how clean and bracing everything smelled.

'Miss Vanessa, you're here! And driving a silver Ford Tahoe of all things. Is it big enough for you?'

Vanessa looked to her right and saw Pete walking toward her. He seemed thinner than the last time she'd seen him, his face a bit gnarled, his thick hair gone entirely white, but his smile was as warm and affectionate as ever.

'Pete!' As he neared her, she rushed into his arms, taking him by surprise. 'I'm so happy to see you!'

'And I to see you!' He drew back and looked at her. 'Still the prettiest girl alive.'

'Oh, you always were the charmer.' His gray eyes were slightly faded and the lines in his forehead were deeper than she remembered. 'Got a new girlfriend?'

'A girlfriend! Who'd have me?'

'Any woman with an ounce of sense.'

'Am I interrupting a romantic moment?'

Audrey Willis stood in the open doorway of the house, her arms spread wide, her blue eyes alight. Vanessa hurried up the porch steps and Audrey swept Vanessa into a hug. Vanessa pressed her face into Audrey's long, auburn hair that always smelled of lavender. 'I feel like I haven't seen you for a year,' Vanessa said. 'Where did the time go?'

Audrey smiled. 'Faster for you than for me with your busy shooting schedule and continent hopping. It obviously agrees with you. You look beautiful!'

'I look worn out. I feel at least fifty.'

'You don't even know what fifty feels like, silly girl.' Audrey glanced past her at the SUV. 'Why the big car?'

'What is it with you and Pete and the size of the car? I brought Queenie along. I needed room for her cage. Besides, I just *wanted* it!' They both laughed. 'It's a three-seater. Think Cara will like taking a ride in it?'

'She'll love it. She hates our tiny compact.' The women watched as Pete opened the back of the vehicle and let out the dog. 'Now come in while Pete gets Queenie out of prison. Grace can't wait to see you.'

Vanessa hurried through the living room to the opened, wide sliding doors that led to the library, which had been converted to a first-floor bedroom since Grace's fall. Her hospital bed and the metal tables for food and medicine looked out of place in the elegant mahogany-paneled room with its beamed, cream-colored ceiling, chandelier hanging from a gold ceiling medallion, and the ivory, rose, and light-blue Aubusson carpet on the gleaming mahogany floor. At the sight of Vanessa, Grace held out her arms. 'My darling! How wonderful to see you!'

Vanessa embraced her, noticing how frail she felt beneath her cashmere robe. Her shining, silver hair reached her shoulders where it was turned into a slight pageboy style and she wore pearl stud earrings as well as sheer rose-colored lipstick, and blush. Behind her beige-framed glasses, she'd put a bit of mascara around her green eyes that were so much like Vanessa's.

'Surprised to see me down here in the library?' Grace asked and before Vanessa could answer, she rushed on. 'I couldn't stay tucked away in my bedroom upstairs. When the doors are open,

I can see all of the living room and the entranceway. I have to be here where the action is.'

'I don't blame you, Grace.'

'It also makes things easier for Audrey than running up and down the stairs.' Grace smiled. 'Well, my girl, you're looking fine.'

'That's what Audrey said, but I think you're both just being nice. I hardly slept last night, and all I did this morning was wash my face and brush my teeth and pin back my hair. I was in such a hurry to get here.'

'Yes, of course you were. Who in the world would have thought Roxanne would come back?'

'I didn't think she *could* come back until now.'

'Well, if I were religious, I would thank God.'

'Oh, Grace, you only say you're not religious to be shocking,' Vanessa teased. 'I see right through you.'

'You always did. We're kindred spirits, you and I.' Grace winked at her. 'Audrey baked brownies and she wouldn't let me have even *one* until you got here. Please may I have one now, Audrey? I'm starving.'

'Grace, I would *too* have given you a brownie earlier!' Audrey protested.

'You'd better hurry up and start serving. The children will be here soon and there won't be *any* food left.' Grace grinned.

'Children?' Vanessa repeated. 'Is Cara bringing friends?'

Audrey was already heading out of the library. 'One very special friend,' she tossed over her shoulder.

'Oh, a boyfriend.'

'Don't call him that. She's too young to have a boyfriend.'

As soon as Audrey disappeared, Grace smiled at Vanessa. 'He *is* Cara's boyfriend. Sammy Sherwin. He's very nice. You'll like him.'

'And so do you.'

'He's well-mannered and polite. He's also bright and quite charming. I do like having children around, Vanessa. They make me feel less decrepit.'

'You will never be decrepit.'

'Tell my hip that. Of all the silly things to do! Break my hip right before the holidays.'

'What happened?'

'I got up in the night and tumbled down the staircase.'

'Just like Dad.'

'Well, not *just* like him. I hadn't been drinking. That's not kind but it's true.' She leaned closer to Vanessa. 'I had a dream that you were calling for me downstairs. Maybe I was still half-asleep, but I got up and started downstairs without turning on a light. I've never done something so silly. Thank heavens I had my pager tucked in the pocket of my robe. I called Pete. I don't know how long I would have lain at the foot of the stairs if he hadn't come immediately.'

'You really shouldn't live alone in this big house, Grace.'

'A cleaning lady comes in three days a week.'

'I'm not talking about someone who comes to clean a few days a week. I'm talking about a companion or—'

'Ah, the brownies at last!' Grace cried and looked up with relief and Vanessa knew she didn't want to discuss the subject of living alone. 'Audrey, I've never had brownies served on a silver tray.'

'With doilies, silver flatware, and freshly brewed tea in the Wedgewood china service.'

Grace cut a piece of brownie with a silver fork, popped it in her mouth, and muttered, 'Hmmm. Delicious. Vanessa, she makes them from scratch with lots of dark chocolate.'

'Glad you like them, Grace. Vanessa?'

'They look scrumptious and I want at least two. I don't need a plate and fork.'

'Yes, you do,' Grace said. 'Otherwise you'll drop crumbs.'

After Vanessa had taken her first bite of brownie and sip of tea, Grace asked abruptly, 'How is Roxanne?'

Vanessa knew the woman could tell if she was trying to soft sell Roxanne's condition, but she didn't want to be brutally honest, either. 'She's dehydrated and undernourished. She has quite a few bruises and scrapes – nothing that won't heal. Mentally, she's in and out. One minute she was talking lucidly to Christian and me and the next she was confused. I'm sure once she's rested and medicated, she'll improve.'

'Did she say where she'd been?'

'Different places but she's not sure where. The last place and maybe the longest was Portland, although she didn't know it until she escaped. She took a bus home although I don't know how she managed it considering her condition.'

'And she doesn't know who took her, who kept her captive all of these years?'

'No. She has no idea, Grace. She was kept blindfolded . . . and—'

Grace suddenly held up her hand. 'I don't want to hear details. Not now.' Her voice shook. 'I'm still processing that she's home. I hope I don't sound unfeeling. It's just . . .' Her eyes filled with tears.

'There's plenty of time to talk about it later.' Vanessa put her arm around Grace's shoulders and patted her back. 'Don't think about it now.'

The doorbell rang twice and Vanessa jumped. Audrey smiled. 'It's the kids home from school. They always ring twice to let us know it's them.'

Vanessa leaned over and watched through the open library doors as Audrey opened the wide front door, mahogany halfway up, glass stained with red and pink roses above and matching sidelights. A girl's voice immediately piped, 'Is that Aunt Vanessa's car outside?'

Then a boy's announced, 'It's really cool. Will she take us for a ride?'

'Yes, it's Vanessa's rental car and yes, it's cool.'

Queenie ran toward Cara and barked.

'Oh, wow!' Cara exclaimed and dropped to her knees, hugging the dog's neck. 'It's Queen Na'dya. See, Sammy? I told you about her!'

'She's great! Can I pet her?'

'Sure. She's the friendliest dog in the world, aren't you, Queenie? Where's Vanessa?'

'Right in there with Grace,' Audrey said.

The girl finally noticed Vanessa, who stood as Cara raced toward her, throwing her arms around her waist and hugging tightly. 'Oh, Aunt Vanessa, I've missed you so much!'

'And I've missed you, Cara. Take a step back and let me look at you.'

Cara did so, beaming with her golden-brown eyes. She had medium-toned skin and long, wavy black hair. She didn't look at all like Audrey. She resembled her handsome father, who'd left Everly Cliffs as soon as he learned Audrey was pregnant.

'You have grown at least two inches since I saw you last and gotten even more beautiful!' Vanessa said.

Cara blushed then prodded a boy forward. 'This is Sammy Sherwin my . . . best friend.'

Sammy looked slightly abashed, smiling shyly at Vanessa. His thick blond hair shone in the sunlight coming through the window and his eyes were the color of blue hyacinths. Sammy Sherwin was going to be devastatingly handsome when he grew up, Vanessa thought. 'Hello, Miss Everly,' he said softly. 'I love your show. Cara talks about you all the time. I'm glad I finally get to meet you.'

'It's lovely to meet you, too, Sammy, and please call me Vanessa. I see you've made friends with Queenie.'

Sammy grinned down at the collie, who sat obediently by his side. She had long white, tan, and black hair and weighed around sixty pounds. She was friendly and especially loved children. She looked at Vanessa with her intelligent melting brown eyes.

Sammy stroked the dog's head. 'She's gorgeous.' He beamed as the dog dropped her small look-alike stuffed collie toy and nuzzled into his hand. 'What's her toy doggie's name?'

'King Dominick.'

Sammy grinned. 'Like your husband on the TV show?'

Vanessa nodded. 'We call him *Dom*, don't we, Queenie?'

The dog barked again and the children fell into fits of laughter. 'Queen Na'dya and King Dominick together on TV and off,' Cara giggled as the dog shifted back and forth on her front paws as if enjoying the fun. 'Oh, I love you, Queenie! And you love Sammy, too, don't you?' She looked at everyone and pronounced, 'Sammy loves dogs. I knew he and Queenie would hit it off.'

Grace smiled. 'I'm quite in love with Queenie myself.'

Finally Sammy tore his attention away from the dog. 'Hello, Mrs Everly.'

'It's *Grace*.'

'Yes ma'am. Hello, Grace. How are you feeling today?'

'Hello, Sammy. I'm feeling tip-top.' Grace looked at the group. 'I always tell Leonard I want a dog, but he says it must stay outside. I want a dog that can stay in the house and keep me company. I'm going to keep arguing. I can always wear him down.'

All the laughter died. Leonard had been Grace's husband who'd died over twenty years earlier yet she was speaking about him in the present tense.

'Why don't you kids take off your jackets and have some brownies?' Audrey asked quickly. 'I made a fresh batch.'

'That sounds great but Queenie can't have any. Chocolate can kill dogs,' Sammy told her solemnly.

Audrey nodded. 'I know. That's why I picked up a new bag of treats for her this morning. Let's go to the kitchen.'

The kids trailed after Audrey, shedding their navy-blue puffy quilted jackets. They looked almost fashion coordinated. Vanessa nodded an *OK* at Queenie, who picked up Dom the stuffed dog and walked sedately behind the children, as if trying especially hard to behave herself in the house.

'Does Sammy always come home with Cara?' Vanessa asked.

'He doesn't *always* come. His father is Derek Sherwin. Do you remember him?'

'I don't think so.'

'He's older than you. He's become a developer. He owns the Everly Cliffs Café and the restaurant Nia's. He named it after his wife.'

'He owns *Nia's*? I've never met Nia Sherwin but I'm impressed with the restaurant.'

'He also owns something downtown that he's going to demolish and build . . . I've forgotten what . . . and some little houses near the beach. I think.'

'He sounds like quite a go-getter.'

'He is. He and his wife are divorced. She left Everly Cliffs a few months after the restaurant opened. I've heard that she met a Hollywood producer a lot older than she is and left Derek for him. No one knows much about the divorce but he got full custody of Sammy, which says something about his wife.'

'How could I have missed this scandal?'

'Derek worked hard to keep things quiet for a couple of years for Sammy's sake. By the time the details leaked out, I guess I forgot to tell you about it. Anyway, someone stayed with Sammy after school until his father got home from the restaurant. Then a couple of weeks ago, she quit. Cara asked if he could come here with her until his father finds a replacement after the holidays. I'd already met Sammy and liked him – he's a dear little thing and Cara has *such* a crush on him. Derek picks up Sammy here after he leaves work each evening. He's a conscientious father. *And . . .*' She lowered her voice to a whisper, '. . . I think he and Audrey like each other.'

'Really?' Vanessa was determined to keep the conversation light and cheerful for Grace's sake. 'She hasn't said a word about him.'

'Well, she wouldn't. Audrey isn't a gossip.'

'Telling me she likes an unmarried man wouldn't be gossip.'

'Perhaps she doesn't want people to think she's pursuing him now that he's divorced. He's quite good looking and successful, and I believe every single woman under fifty is interested in him. I think he would be perfect for Audrey, though. She has class. She's a lady. And their children get along beautifully.'

'Maybe you can do some matchmaking.'

Grace tilted her head. 'Maybe I already am. After all, he comes here almost every day!'

Vanessa smiled. 'You're too smart for your own good, Grace. I need you to go to work for me. I haven't had a date for months.'

'Darling, I'm so sorry. You should move back here from Las Vegas so you won't be alone.'

Vanessa waited a beat. 'I live in Los Angeles, Grace.'

'That's right. You moved. Have you been able to get any acting jobs lately?'

Vanessa swallowed. 'Well . . . yes. I'm on a television show.'

'How nice! I love television. There's one show in particular I never miss. It's about old times when there were kings and queens. The girl who plays the queen looks a lot like you. I've told Audrey and Cara I think so. They agree.'

'I think I know the show you mean.' Vanessa looked away so Grace wouldn't see the tears in her eyes. 'Do you mind if I go to the kitchen and talk to the kids for a few minutes? I haven't seen Cara for ages and I'd like to get to know Sammy.'

'You run along, dear. And don't fill up on all the gingerbread and sauce Audrey made before it's dinner time.'

'Dinner smells extra good,' Sammy said almost two hours later as he sat at the kitchen table with Queenie lying beside him.

'You and your dad are welcome to eat with us,' Audrey told him. 'There's plenty of food.'

'He told me this morning we're eating at Nia's tonight. He likes for us to eat there at least once a week. I believe he thinks it's his duty or something because it's his restaurant.' Sammy sounded slightly downcast.

'Nia's is the nicest restaurant in town.'

'I like the food. But when we're there, Dad spends most of his time talking to customers. He doesn't mean to ignore me, but I don't have a very good time.'

'Maybe you should tell him,' Audrey suggested gently.

'Oh no, I wouldn't want to do that. He'd feel bad because he always wants to make me happy. It's OK. I don't mind going.'

The doorbell rang. 'That's him!' Cara piped. 'Are you sure you don't want to ask him to eat with us?'

Sammy looked resigned. 'Maybe tomorrow evening or the next. He likes to make plans and stick to them.'

'I'll get the door,' Vanessa said, wanting to make certain she got a look at Derek Sherwin.

In a minute she was gazing at a strikingly handsome man of medium height and build and a penetrating gray gaze. He looked about Christian's age although his brown hair was lightly silver-laced. He greeted Vanessa with a pleasant, relaxed smile. 'Hello. I'm Derek Sherwin. I'm here to collect my son.'

'Please come in. Sammy's getting into his coat and gathering his books. I'm Vanessa Everly.'

Derek Sherwin stepped inside and shook her hand. 'It's a pleasure to meet you. An honor, really. My son is crazy about your TV show.'

'That's nice to hear. A lot of people don't let twelve-year-olds watch *Corinna*, but I don't think it's so graphic.'

'I agree with you. There are a dozen other shows I don't let Sam watch, but I've seen *Kingdom of Corinna*. I think it's tame compared to the other costume dramas. It's also captivating. I'm not surprised he's a fan. So am I.'

Vanessa smiled. 'Thank you. I'm glad you approve.'

Sammy came into the entranceway and grinned at his father. 'Hi, Dad.'

'Good day at school?'

'Awesome.'

'Oh.' Derek pulled a face. 'That means you were bored silly. Oh well, you only have one more day before Christmas break.'

'Sammy said you're having dinner at Nia's tonight but we wondered if you might like to have dinner here another night.'

'That sounds very nice,' Derek said carefully, 'but I know things are a bit hectic here.' Vanessa stiffened, thinking he knew about Roxanne's return, but he went on easily. 'Mrs Everly doesn't always feel like having company for dinner, I'm sure. We wouldn't want to intrude. Can we play it by ear?'

'Sure,' Vanessa said, relieved. 'You two enjoy your dinner tonight. Nia's is a lovely restaurant.'

'You've been there?'

'Twice.'

'Then maybe you'll be able to come again on this visit. In fact, we're having a Christmas party tomorrow night. Everyone in town is invited.'

'Sounds like fun. Maybe I'll make it.'

Derek looked beyond her. 'Hello, Audrey.'

'Hi.' Vanessa noticed that Audrey's color had heightened slightly. 'How are you, Derek?'

'Fine. It's been a busy day. People are arriving for the holidays.' He grinned. 'Town's booming!'

'The kids will enjoy our few Christmas festivities with more people here to make them seem like a real celebration,' Audrey said. 'I always did when I was young.'

'I liked it, too.'

Cara appeared by Audrey's side. 'Mr Sherwin, since you'll be busy with your Christmas party tomorrow night, can Sammy stay here for the whole night?'

Derek looked startled. 'That's very nice of you, Cara, but I'm afraid we've already imposed on your hospitality too much all ready.'

'No, you haven't. Honest and truly.'

'Honest and truly,' called Grace. 'We love having Sammy.'

Derek glanced at his son who nearly moaned, 'Oh, *please*!'

Derek looked back at Audrey. 'Well, I won't be finished at the restaurant until well after midnight. I'd thought he could sleep in my office, but if you're sure he won't be a bother . . .'

'Sammy is never a bother,' Audrey said, and Cara beamed.

'All right then.' Derek's voice lightened as he spoke to Sammy. 'I'll guess we'll put pajamas in your backpack tomorrow morning. Don't let anyone at school see them or they'll laugh at you.'

'Oh, I won't, Dad,' Sammy said excitedly. 'This will be super-secret.'

'Great. Ready to go, son?'

'Sure.' He looked happily at Vanessa. 'It was great to meet you.' Then Audrey. 'Thanks for the brownies.' Then Cara. 'See you tomorrow.' And finally he called, 'Goodbye, Grace!'

'Son, it's Mrs Everly,' Derek corrected.

'No, it isn't,' Grace returned loudly. 'I'm Grace to everyone I like. Goodbye, Sammy.'

Derek raised his eyebrows. 'Well, I suppose that settles it. Have a nice evening, ladies.'

Audrey and Vanessa watched the two walk to their car. Night was falling and from the hill they could see the myriad of Christmas lights that decorated Everly Cliffs. The number of brilliant lights was surprising for such a small town.

'I like Derek,' Vanessa said.

'Yes, he's quite nice.'

'Quite nice? I think you find him more than *quite nice*.'

'I never could hide anything from you. Let's hope Derek doesn't see it. That would be so embarrassing.'

'Not if he feels the same way about you!' Vanessa laughed.

Two hours later Vanessa excused herself from the library where she'd been watching television with Grace, Audrey, and Cara, and went to what had been her father's study, looking at the grandfather clock to be certain it was eight o'clock and carrying her cellphone. She waited five minutes, impatient, thinking if Christian didn't call her, she would call him. If he didn't answer—

Her phone buzzed and she nearly barked, 'Hello!'

'It's me.' Christian's voice was tired and lifeless. 'I've looked every place I can imagine Brody might be, called everyone he knows, and I haven't found him. You asked me to tell you before I notify the sheriff, so that's what I'm doing.'

'You're really going to call Wade Baylor?'

'I said I would. We've been apart a long time, but you might remember that I keep my word.'

'Yes, you do. It's one of the things I always lov— admired about you.' Even though she was alone, Vanessa blushed for almost letting her tongue get carried away. 'Are you sure you can do this?'

'It won't be easy, but I have to. It's only right. And there's one other thing. Have you looked at the internet tonight?'

'No.'

'The news about Roxanne's return hit a couple of hours ago.'

'Oh, no! So soon? How?'

'Maybe someone from the emergency services leaked it. Maybe someone from the hospital. I knew it wouldn't be long.'

'Damn. This means we'll have news people all over the place by tomorrow.' She paused and asked carefully, 'Did you see anything about Brody being missing?'

'No, but that won't take long, either. God, what a night.'

'Chris, I'm . . . I'm sorry about Brody. I really am.'

'So am I, but Vanessa . . .' Christian's voice sharpened. 'I'm still certain my brother had nothing to do with either Roxanne's disappearance or reappearance and I will stake my life on it.'

By ten thirty, Grace and Cara were sound asleep. Audrey followed Vanessa into the large kitchen at the back of the house. 'How about a drink before bed?'

'If you mean warm milk, fine. I never drink liquor when I have a patient.'

'You're the best nurse in the world.'

'Yes, I am,' Audrey deadpanned.

'Fix your milk. I'm having a rum and cola. If there's rum around, that is.'

'Spiced rum. Grace still wants a spiced rum and cola every night before she goes to sleep since she broke her hip. She was really mad at me when I told her she couldn't mix alcohol with her medications.'

'She's used to getting her own way.' Vanessa asked seriously, 'How do you think she's doing with the Alzheimer's? She could hardly follow what was on TV tonight and kept telling us what a character had said ten minutes ago.'

'It's always worse at night, Nessa. "Sun downing", they call it. But she's declining.' Audrey hesitated then plunged on. 'She can't live alone anymore. When her hip gets better, she'll have to get a companion or go to a convalescent home.'

'She's that bad?'

'I don't think she can navigate this big house anymore. I'm not a doctor, though. When her hip is better, she should have an MRI to see how far the Alzheimer's has progressed. But don't worry about it tonight, Nessa.'

They fixed their drinks and sat down at one end of the long, wooden kitchen table, Queenie settling down beside Vanessa. 'Tell me about Derek.'

'I met him at the school's fall festival. He attends all of Sammy's school events he can. We talked quite a bit that day. He asked me out to dinner. I hadn't had a date for over a year but he made me so comfortable. He was charming yet sincere. Then we went out to lunch. Then we took the kids for a long walk on the beach.'

'And then?'

'Then your grandmother broke her hip.'

'Oh, what bad timing! Couldn't another nurse have taken the job?'

'Probably, but Grace wanted me. She also had no problem with Cara staying here with me.' Audrey smiled. 'And I have to earn a living.'

'Grace told me Derek is divorced.'

'Yes. His wife Nia left Everly Cliffs over two years before Derek started divorce proceedings, which took another six months to be finalized. He's been legally divorced for four months but Nia has never tried to see him or Sammy since she left town.'

'She didn't want custody of Sammy?'

'No, but oh Lord, Derek doesn't want Sammy to know that! It would break his heart to know his mother didn't want him. You see, Nia had another man who didn't want Sammy.'

'And Nia chose the man. How could a woman give up her child so easily?'

'Don't ask me. Cara is the center of my life. But Nia was a different kind of woman. She's beautiful and Derek said she was always drawn to other men, to put it politely. She never settled in to being a wife and mother, especially a mother. Sammy sensed it. He wasn't close to Nia like he was Derek. Still, knowing you were rejected by your mother—'

'Would be a bitter pill to swallow. My mother didn't love me like she did Roxanne, but at least she made an effort to appear that she cared. Sometimes.' Vanessa shook her head. 'Children always realize the truth, though.'

Audrey patted her hand. 'I'm so sorry you didn't have a mother like mine. If I can be half the parent she is, I'll be happy.'

'You are, Audrey. Cara knows how much you love her. I can see it in her eyes when she looks at you. Are you missing your mother this Christmas?'

'Yes, but she's visiting her sister in San Francisco. I know they're having fun together.'

Vanessa took a sip of her drink and said thoughtfully, 'I was having a rum and cola when Wade called me about Roxy. If I hadn't had rum to bolster me, I think I would have fainted.' She took a deep breath. 'But I had another call that sent me to my knees.'

Audrey raised her eyebrows. 'Why? Who called?'

Vanessa closed her eyes. 'I don't know.'

'What do you mean you don't know?'

'I mean it was an anonymous call. And it came on the smart-phone – *our* phone, Audrey.'

'But how did someone get the number?' Audrey stiffened. 'You don't think *I* gave it out, do you?'

'I know you didn't give it to anyone.'

'I don't have it written down, Vanessa. Not *anywhere*. I didn't open my purse and drop a piece of paper out with your private phone number on it. Is that what you think happened? That I was careless?'

Audrey's cheeks were red. Her blue eyes were large and her hands clenched with indignation.

'Audrey, I trust you with my life – with my grandmother's life. I certainly trust you with a phone number. I don't know how someone got it. Maybe there are a dozen ways someone could – I'm not a tech wizard. I'm only trying to tell you what happened last night. Please don't make it about you because it isn't.'

Audrey's breath came fast for another minute before the color in her face began to fade and she slowly relaxed. She took a sip of her milk then said softly, 'I'm sorry, Vanessa. You're going through so much and I'm throwing a fit. I know you didn't mean to hurt my feelings. You'd never try to do that.'

'You're going through a lot, too. As for my never meaning to hurt someone's feelings, I don't think Christian Montgomery would agree after the things I said to him this afternoon. I was awful.'

Audrey took a drink of her milk then said carefully, 'I have my opinion about you and Christian, especially seeing your face when you talk about him, but I'm not going to venture into that subject tonight. Now tell me about the phone call. When did it come?'

'Right before Wade's call telling me Roxy was home. I looked at the caller ID and it said 'unknown'. A couple of seconds after I picked it up, this godawful voice asked, "Is she there? Is she with you?"'

'What does a "*godawful*" voice mean?'

'Grinding. Screeching. It was mechanically altered. I couldn't tell if it was a man or a woman.'

'And then?'

'I said something about the person having a wrong number and they answered, "I don't. Tell me!" Finally they told me not to play the fool and to remember a George Michael song. I'd better be "praying for time".'

'Praying for time?'

'Don't you remember George Michael's "Praying for Time"? It's not my favorite song but it would be in my top ten. Audrey, who would know I liked a song that came out in 1990 and that I didn't even hear until I was a teenager?'

Audrey's lips had parted. She looked thoughtful, surprised, and frightened at the same time. 'I don't know,' she murmured. 'I don't even know the song.'

'That's what I mean. It isn't as if I went around singing it all the time. Or ever. I can't remember mentioning to someone that I liked it, even when George Michael died.'

'Somebody you told casually without even realizing it.' Audrey's blue eyes grew anxious. 'That call came from someone you know, Vanessa.'

Around eleven o'clock, Audrey checked on Grace, who slept peacefully, and Cara curled up in a bed in the big combination sitting room-bedroom off the kitchen that had once been used by the succession of cooks the Everlys had kept until about fifteen years ago. 'It's large enough for two – a full bed, a dresser and chairs, and keeps me fairly close to Grace,' Audrey told Vanessa. 'I have a baby monitor hidden beside Grace's bed in case she calls out or tries to get up. She'd be outraged if she knew I was keeping track of her with a baby monitor!' Audrey laughed. 'She's so independent.'

'She always was. Does Cara mind sleeping in the downstairs bedroom?'

'She loves it. There's a big window with a nice view. We have a television and a desk for her schoolwork and plenty of closet space. And frankly, she didn't want to sleep upstairs. She thinks it's creepy because of the lighthouse, which she's sure is haunted.'

Vanessa grinned. 'Maybe it is, although I slept upstairs for eighteen years and made it to adulthood.' She yawned. 'It's been a long, stressful day to say the least. I think I'll go to bed, too. Upstairs. But don't worry – I have Queenie to protect me.'

'Sleep well, Vanessa. Everything will look better tomorrow.'

'I'm holding you to that, Audrey.'

Vanessa climbed the curving staircase to the second-floor landing. Long ago Grace had told her that Victorian houses had several stories, but Edwardians like Everly House usually only had two floors and fewer, smaller fireplaces because the use of electricity had become more common. Vanessa had always loved the house and thought her ancestor Abraham had done a wonderful job with its design.

Queenie walked behind her, all the while clutching her beloved Dom in her jaws. 'Which bedroom shall we sleep in tonight?' Vanessa asked the dog. 'There are five up here. *Five!* Can you imagine? We're not used to more than one!'

Vanessa peeked into the bedrooms: the guest bedroom done in shades of blue; Roxanne's old bedroom, a pink confection that hadn't been changed one bit since she was seven; Vanessa's lavender and pale-yellow bedroom; a room Ellen had occupied in her later years drearily furnished in gray and white, and finally the master bedroom that Grace had redecorated after her son died and Ellen had departed the house.

The walls were painted a muted, light gold. A large Persian rug in brown, beige, olive-green and peach lay on the mahogany flooring beside a four-poster bed covered with an olive-green and gold bedspread and cream-colored embroidered pillows. Gleaming Sheraton furniture sat around the room holding various colorful porcelain and glass collectibles. An oval mirror sat above a beautiful dressing table.

But it was the fireplace that grabbed her attention. It was black cast iron with a golden oak frame and canopy. There were sliders at either side of the fireplace opening that were lined with tile sets showing beautiful climbing green vines and yellow roses, Grace's favorite flower.

'Wow, quite a difference for us!' Vanessa exclaimed to Queenie, who was inspecting herself in a tall, framed cheval mirror, Dom still clutched firmly in her mouth. 'Grace outdid herself!' As she looked around the room, Vanessa noticed a twenty-four-inch flat-screen television sitting on a modern stand. 'Thank goodness. I can't go to sleep without watching at least fifteen minutes of TV.'

She knew Grace must have been sad to leave her beautiful room and move downstairs. She'd only gotten to enjoy it for a short time. But maybe, when she recovered from the broken hip, she'd be able to return for a while. *Maybe*, Vanessa thought wistfully, although the reason for her fall made that possibility unlikely.

Pete had carried her luggage to this room. He'd known her mind even before she'd decided to stay here. But then Pete had always known her mind, just like Grace did.

'This is it, Queenie,' she said. 'I'm sorry you don't have a doggie bed. I'll get one for you. I'm afraid it's the floor for you and Dom tonight.'

Vanessa had remembered to bring flannel pajamas for the cooler temperatures in Everly Cliffs. She buttoned up the top and gazed at herself disconsolately in the mirror. 'Hardly a sex symbol. Queen Na'dya wouldn't be caught dead in these.' She laid her velour robe and house slippers near the bed, then went into the adjoining bathroom to wash her face and put on a layer of expensive night cream, an indulgence she'd allowed herself when she signed on for *Kingdom of Corinna*. She needed to keep her complexion looking its best for the cameras.

Back in the bedroom, she slid under the elegant sheets and blankets of Grace's bed and flipped on the television. Leaning back against the thick down pillows, she realized how desperately tired she was, yet her thoughts raced. She could see poor, thin, scratched and bruised Roxanne. She replayed the scene where Roxanne held out her arm and in a horrific voice imitated someone cajoling her into making 'a nice big vein' for an injection. An injection of what? Heroin? And a demoralized Roxanne who had simply turned her head, waiting for what would come. Then there had been news of the abortion. When had it been performed? When she was a teenager? Had she gotten proper care afterward? Had it been the only one? And finally, she'd learned that Brody Montgomery had disappeared from his home and business in Portland. Schizophrenic Brody Montgomery, who had been the number one suspect in Roxanne's kidnapping. Now she was home and suddenly he was missing. Where was he? Had he followed Roxanne to Everly Cliffs?

Throughout the evening Vanessa had tried to seem calm for the sakes of Audrey, Cara, and Grace, but really she'd never been as shaken in her life except for when Roxy had been kidnapped. Tonight, in front of Grace, she had performed the greatest acting job of her life by acting cheerful and casual and now she was exhausted. But not sleepy. Anything except sleepy.

'Oh, this is useless.' Vanessa reached for the remote control and turned off the television. She needed the oblivion of sleep, but the scenes from the day kept flashing behind her closed eyes. She thought of going downstairs and asking Audrey if she had any mild sleeping pills, but she didn't want to disturb her and Cara. *If I lie here long enough*, she thought, *I'm likely to fall asleep out of sheer fatigue. After all, I didn't sleep last night, either. My body is worn out.*

Vanessa burrowed determinedly under the covers and forced her eyes closed. Maybe a sleep mask would help, but she didn't own one. She tossed twice, frustrated. Then, in less than ten minutes, she heard a muted thudding noise. Queenie's head shot up as she gazed at the wall.

She sat up in bed and looked at the left side of the bedroom, where the wall separated the room from the four-story lighthouse-inspired tower Abraham Everly had built so he could look out at the ocean. The tower was narrower than a real lighthouse, with a spiral staircase that led to a top room furnished with a few pieces of furniture and a telescope placed in front of the circle of storm windows. A small door opened to a railed gallery outside of the windows so they could be cleaned and maintained regularly. Although there was no rotating beacon light that spun in the night, the tower was wired for electricity. The lighting had been updated over the years and now flush florescent sconces lined the walls leading to the top, which was called the Lantern Room. Abraham, the father of five young children when he built the house, had been adamant that there be no entrances from the house to the tower for fear that a child would find its way into the tower and fall on the steep stairway. The only entrance was an outside ground-floor door that was always locked.

Vanessa sat looking at the wall. Nothing. *I must have imagined it*, she thought. Then she heard what sounded like a footstep on the stairs. The step was stealthy but the foot that made it definitely wore a shoe. And then she heard another.

She climbed out of bed and crouched by the wall. Queenie got up and came to stand beside her, her head tilted slightly. For five minutes Vanessa held absolutely still against the wall. 'Pete?' she finally called, although she couldn't think of a reason why Pete would be in the tower. Only silence answered.

At last she said loudly, 'I must be having nightmares, Queenie,' hoping her voice carried through the wall. 'Let's watch TV then go back to bed.'

She turned on the television then padded loudly back to the bed. She watched the minute hand of the clock move. One, two, three – she slid quietly out of bed, tiptoed back to the wall and pressed her ear against it. She heard a faint scratching noise, about five feet to her right. She went cold all over.

Someone was in the tower.

Who?

Brody Montgomery?

Nearly blind with panic, Vanessa looked around for her cellphone and called Pete. He answered with a sleepy, ''Lo?'

'Pete, someone's in the lighthouse!' she hissed. 'I can hear him on the stairs!'

Pete's voice was husky with sleep. 'What? Oh! Be right there soon as I find my key. Don't go outside, Miss Vanessa.'

Vanessa dropped her phone, slid her feet into her house slippers and shrugged into her velour robe. Queenie was turning in circles, alarmed, but followed Vanessa as she opened the bedroom door, rushed from the room and down the stairway to the front door. Vanessa found the key to the tower in the drawer in a small white antique bureau desk beside the door, thinking that Pete might not be able to find his key and the door locked from the outside. Maybe the intruder had gotten locked in – *I should call the police*, Vanessa thought in a distant, reasonable place in her brain. Instead, she grabbed her grandfather's large oak walking cane that had rested in the umbrella stand ever since his death. *I should stay inside like Pete said*, she told herself as she opened the front door and braced herself against the cold air. But her body wasn't listening to her mind.

She stepped out on the porch and looked around her. Two carriage-style lamps softly illuminated the walkway up to the porch. Much farther down the bank near the road, halogen lights shone brightly. A gentle wind blew the limbs of the three evergreen trees near the house and the full moon cast a surreal, metallic glow over the grounds.

Something hit the inside of the tower door with a loud thud and Vanessa jumped. She turned on her flashlight then began creeping down the porch stairs. A voice inside her screamed for her to stop. This was dangerous – beyond dangerous. But the thought of an intruder being so close to her grandmother, to Audrey and Cara, terrified her to the point of overcoming caution. She hardly realized she was edging toward the tower, holding the cane like a baseball bat, Queenie barking uproariously behind her.

Then Pete McGuire ran past her, nearly reached the tower door, let out a wail and fell hard.

Vanessa rushed to him. 'Are you all right?'

'Damn! Wrenched my knee. Get back on the porch!'

But she didn't. She took four steps closer to the tower door. With a crash it flew open, slamming into her body, hitting her forehead, and knocking her flat on her back. She was vaguely aware of someone dashing out and heading away from her. 'Get him!' she yelled at Queenie, but the dog stood firm, licking Vanessa's face. Her head swam as she struggled to push Queenie aside and managed to sit up in time to see someone disappear into the nearby woods.

'Could you see him?' she called to Pete.

'Not really but he was strong enough to break that door.'

Strong like six-foot-two athletic Brody Montgomery would be. Vanessa rubbed her forehead as Queenie barked viciously at the spot where the man had vanished. 'Clearly you're not meant to be a guard dog who protects her mistress,' Vanessa said, reaching out and rubbing the dog's side reassuringly. 'Pete, I think we should call the police now.'

FIVE

'Brody? Brody are you here? If so, come and talk to me. That's all I want to do – talk.'

Christian stood in the living room of the small, two-bedroom guest house he'd already searched twice. He wished desperately that Brody would appear, having hidden himself away in some cubbyhole Christian didn't know about, but he knew that was silly. Brody wasn't in the guest house. God knew where he was.

Christian went outside, locking the door behind him then unlocking it in the dim hope that Brody would find sanctuary in the guest house in the middle of the night. Yeah, sure, he thought sarcastically as he strode toward the main house. After all of this time, Brody would hide in the first place he knew his brother would look.

He'd tried to be calm in his office in front of Zane. He'd tried to be calm on the phone with Vanessa earlier in the evening, but underneath the act, he was seething. Vanessa had backed him into a corner. She'd *threatened* him – if he didn't call Wade Baylor, *she* would. How dare she?

Because she's terrified for her sister, a tiny voice inside him said. Because Roxanne has reappeared after eight years just as Brody has disappeared. It looked suspicious.

But it is *a coincidence*, he told himself. It's a horrible coincidence with possibly dangerous repercussions for Brody. Christian was sure Brody had absolutely nothing to do with Roxanne's kidnapping. He'd been heavily sedated with Thorazine and under the watch of his father the night when Roxane was taken. Gerald would not have eased up on Brody's medication or lost track of his son for several hours. Besides, Ben Johnson from next door had been at the house. He'd known Brody was upstairs.

But he had not seen Brody. He'd sworn to the police he'd been at the Montgomery house an hour longer than he had and looked into Brody's room to see him dead to the world. Ben had been Gerald's best friend for twenty years. He hadn't given a thought to stretching the truth for the sake of his best friend's son. He'd died three months later of cancer. Gerald had told Christian the lie was Ben's parting gift. And after all, Brody was innocent, Gerald had reasoned. But is that why Gerald hadn't told Christian about Ben's lie until the night he died? Christian remembered that after telling him, his father had looked at him doubtfully and reassured him that Ben's 'exaggeration' hadn't hurt anyone. *Except for me,* Christian thought. *That lie has haunted me for years.* Why was it necessary?

If only I'd been here, Christian mused as he entered the main house. *If Dad had called me as soon as Brody was caught and returned home, I could have done something to help, if only to keep another pair of eyes on Brody. And I would have watched him like a hawk. Is that why Dad didn't let me know Brody was home, why he didn't tell me exactly what was going on? Because he didn't want Brody to feel like a prisoner? Instead, Dad didn't call me until the afternoon of the day Roxanne was kidnapped. Brody was already a suspect. I was too late to do anything to help him.*

Christian paced around the softly lit living room decorated in calm blues, grays, and ivory with occasional touches of burgundy for contrast. His mother had refurnished the room six months before her death in a car wreck and been so proud of it. After she died, his father hadn't changed a thing and later neither had Christian.

Accent lights glowed from the built-in shelving on either side of the fireplace. The top shelf on the right drew Christian like a magnet. He stared at the fourteen-inch-high gold trophy gleaming beside a framed color photo of Brody dressed in white shorts and shirt with a red, white and blue headband crossing his tanned forehead and holding down his longish, sun-lightened hair as he grinned rakishly while holding a trophy. As a child, Brody had been dreamy and removed, preferring to read and write fantasy stories. A natural athlete, when he was thirteen, he'd become fanatical about tennis. He'd always devoted himself to what caught his imagination and his idol had been Björn Borg, the sex symbol tennis champion famous in the Seventies. Brody's expression in the photo said he felt as successful as Borg winning Wimbledon, even if he'd only won a state tennis championship. In the background, people were standing and cheering and when Christian looked closely, he could see Vanessa and Roxanne Everly, Jane Drake, Zane Felder and Derek Sherwin in the stands. The picture had appeared in newspapers throughout the state and on the internet and Brody had been ecstatic. A year later, the first symptoms of his illness manifested themselves and the golden boy had begun a tragic tumble into murky depression and heartbreaking confusion.

Christian's chest tightened and he felt as if he couldn't breathe. He rarely drank, but he decided tonight of all nights called for something that might ease his tightening muscles, his growing apprehension.

He retrieved an excellent brand of cognac from a kitchen shelf and poured it into one of the tulip glasses his father declared was *the* best glass for fine cognac, making his wife roll her eyes. 'You act like you were raised on the stuff, Gerald,' she'd tease. 'When we were teenagers, we drank the cheapest wine right out of the bottle.' Christian smiled at the memory and carefully holding his glass, he stretched out on the long, wide blue couch and took a sip, absently swirling the warm, smooth liquid in his mouth before swallowing and forcing himself to breathe slowly.

He closed his eyes, wondering if Brody had gone off his meds and why. He'd done it years ago, thinking he didn't need them, but afterward he'd told Christian he'd learned his lesson. Maybe now a girl was involved – a girl Brody had never mentioned to Zane. He was extremely sensitive, particularly about his illness. He might have confided in her and she rejected him. He would have been crushed. Christian took another sip of cognac. Or it could have been something about the business. They were taking Blackbird public. That's huge, Christian thought. Maybe Brody had gotten extremely agitated, stopped his meds and run from the source of his stress.

Except that agitation would have made Brody even more conscientious than usual about taking his medications. He would have wanted to be in top form. He wouldn't have wanted to let Zane down.

'Brody, where *are* you?' he asked aloud. 'Don't you know the longer you're missing, the worse suspicion of you gets?'

Which is why he'd given in so easily to Vanessa and called Wade, he admitted to himself. He'd known Vanessa too long to let her intimidate him. He'd decided it was better for Brody that he be found and prove he had nothing to do with Roxanne's reappearance than let people build a case against him, maybe even hurt him if they found him.

Christian readily admitted he knew a lot about Brody's illness but not everything – not the way his mind worked. He'd tried, but he didn't have Brody's illness. He didn't understand all the twists and turns Brody's thoughts could take. He didn't understand Brody's various delusions. When his father had died, Christian had promised he would take care of Brody. He'd said he'd never let anything happen to him. He felt tears rise in his eyes. And now look . . .

His cellphone rang. Christian jerked, nearly spilling his cognac, then wiped away the tears. He leaned forward anxiously and picked it up from the coffee table, nearly barking, ''Lo?'

A familiar voice chirped, 'Chris? I mean Dr Montgomery? This is Jane Drake in the emergency room. You asked that we call if anything came up concerning Roxanne or Vanessa Everly.'

Christian tensed. 'Who is it?'

'Vanessa.'

* * *

Christian drove quickly to the hospital, praying that whatever had happened to Vanessa had nothing to do with Brody. Before he got out of his car, he popped a breath mint into his mouth. He wasn't on call and he'd only had two sips of cognac, but some of the staff had noses like bloodhounds. Tomorrow the rumor that Dr Montgomery arrived at the hospital drunk could have spread like wildfire. He hurried past the emergency room desk, called, 'Dr Montgomery,' to the on-duty nurse and rushed back along the hall. Only one room was occupied.

Wade Baylor stood outside the room. He was slightly less than six feet tall, sturdy, brown-haired, and looked older than his thirty-three years because of a perpetually hang-dog expression and sad, dark eyes. Smiles didn't come easily to Wade but his perpetual calm and air of authority gave people confidence in him.

'What's going on?' Christian asked.

'A break-in at the Everly House.'

Christian tensed. 'A break-in?'

'Vanessa was sleeping in the room next to the tower. She heard someone in there. I don't know what possessed her but she went tearing outside. She had her dog with her – it's a collie – and was getting near the door at the same time the guy gave it his all and broke the doorframe. Pete McGuire had shown up by that time but he fell and twisted his knee. He's getting treatment now. The intruder made it into the woods.'

'Is Vanessa all right?'

'Not sure. The door flew back and hit her. I think she's in X-ray, but she's conscious.'

'Can I go in and talk to Pete?'

'Be my guest.'

A doctor working on Pete looked up at Christian. 'He's wrenched his knee.'

'Of all the stupid things to do!' Pete ranted, his white hair rumpled above his rage-red face. 'No snow on the ground, nothing in my way, and I fell down like an old man!'

'Didn't the dog chase him?'

'That big lump of love didn't care for anything except her mistress. Vanessa was lying flat and Queenie was licking her and nosing her and whining to the sky.'

'Pete, did you get a look at the guy's face?' Christian asked, feeling as if there was a band around his heart.

'Nope. He had on a bulky quilted coat with the hood pulled up. I never got a glimpse of his face or a look at his hair as he ran away.'

'Was it a kid? A teenager?'

'Doc Montgomery, I told you I didn't see his face. It could've been a teenager.'

'How tall was he?'

'I'm not sure. Six feet?'

'Are you sure?'

'No, I'm not sure! He was running!' Pete glared, then his look softened. 'Sorry. My knee hurts like the devil. I'm only guessing. Maybe he was a little taller than me. I told the sheriff all this.'

'I apologize, Pete. I shouldn't be grilling you. Six feet, you say.' Christian hoped no one heard the relief in his voice. Brody was six two. 'I'm glad you're all right.'

'Except for the pain. I'll get some pain killers for that but I'll be limping around for days.'

'More like a couple of weeks with a brace and a crutch,' the doctor said, and Pete groaned.

Christian stepped out of the room at the moment a nurse rolled Vanessa down the hallway in a wheelchair. Chris was surprised to feel his heart give a little leap of joy and he strode toward her.

'How are you, Nessa?'

'They say some bruises and a mild concussion. This means I have to spend a *second* night awake.'

Christian could tell she was trying to joke but her voice was thin and her hands trembled. He knew she was thoroughly shaken. 'Why in God's name did you go after an intruder by yourself?'

'Oh, Chris, I don't know. PTSD, a hero complex, no common sense.' She looked deeply into his eyes. 'We didn't get the guy.'

If it was Brody, her gaze seemed to say, and he had a sudden impulse to kiss her for not saying the name aloud.

'I know but Pete thinks it was someone around six feet. Maybe it was a teenager up to a prank. That's happened before, hasn't it?'

'Well, yes, over twenty years ago. But it was summer – not cold. Tonight it was cold in the tower.'

'Kids don't think.'

'*If* it was a kid – a teenager. We don't know *who* it was—'

'It wasn't someone trying to break into the house. There aren't any openings between the house and the tower.'

'No, but maybe the person didn't know that. I don't think it was a kid—'

'Wade will find out, I'm sure. At least you're not badly hurt.'

'Tell that to my head. I have a helluva headache.'

Another nurse appeared, beaming. 'Oh, hi, Christian, Vanessa!'

'Hello, Jane,' Christian said, seeming to know from Vanessa's blank expression she didn't recognize her. Jane Drake's thin mouse-brown hair was now lush and blonde, and her long, needle-thin nose was shorter and slightly turned up. Her small teeth wore perfect brilliant white veneers. 'Vanessa, you remember Jane Drake.'

'Hello, Jane,' Vanessa said after a beat of surprise. 'It's been a long time.'

'I'll say!' Jane grabbed Wade Baylor's arm. 'Have you heard we're engaged?'

'Yes, Audrey told me. I'm glad for you both.'

Wade looked embarrassed but gave them a small, tight smile. He gently removed Jane's hand from his arm.

Christian said, 'I think Vanessa's all finished here. I'll take her home.'

'It isn't necessary,' Vanessa said.

'Why?' Christian smiled. 'Did you drive yourself here?'

'Very funny, Dr Montgomery, but maybe Sheriff Baylor—'

'Should stay here with Pete,' Christian interrupted. 'Besides, I'm sure all of this gave your grandmother quite a shock. I can check her over and reassure her that her granddaughter is in fairly good shape. Now get dressed and we'll fill out your release papers.'

While he waited, Christian approached Wade again and said quietly, 'Wade, Pete says the guy was about six feet tall.'

'I know. But he's approximating.'

'Yeah, but Brody's—'

'Taller. I know.'

'Have you released the news about him being missing?'

Wade nodded. 'I was going to give it another day and release it tomorrow on the six-o'clock news, but after tonight, I can't take any chances. I'm sorry, Chris.'

'I understand.'

'Brody wouldn't have gotten into so much trouble when Roxanne was kidnapped if our former sheriff had done his duty and kept police supervision on Brody instead of turning him over to your dad. It's not that I didn't respect your father, but most people thought he'd do anything to protect his son. There should have been an officer at the house until Brody left for his stay at the rehab hospital.'

'I know that, too. I'm sure we'll find out something about Brody tomorrow. His partner Zane Felder is here in town searching. He probably knows Brody better than anyone except me.'

Wade nodded slowly. 'That's good. I wish we could have had another day without publicity.' He looked solemnly at Christian. 'When we were teenagers, Brody and I were friends. I don't want to hurt him and I want you to know that I get no pleasure from hunting him down like a criminal. Sometimes I hate having to follow my duty instead of my feelings.'

SIX

After a night propped on firm pillows while watching television in Grace's bed, Vanessa finally toppled sideways during the morning news. She knew that everyone dreams every night, but her sleep seemed blessedly peaceful and dreamless. At one point she was vaguely aware of the room becoming brighter and a dull pounding noise somewhere in the house, and she pulled a pillow over her head and went back to sleep. Finally, slowly, consciousness returned. With her eyes still closed, she fumbled on the bedside table until she found a clock, then opened one eye: 12:45 p.m. People argued loudly on the television and she grappled for the remote control, shut off the TV set, and groaned. How could she have slept until afternoon? And why did her head still hurt?

Vanessa slowly descended the stairs and saw Audrey carrying Grace's lunch tray to the kitchen. 'Well, you're finally up!' She frowned at Vanessa's forehead. 'With only a bump on the forehead and a shadow around one eye. Not much in the way of battle wounds.'

'They feel worse than they look. I need some aspirin.'

'Come in the kitchen. Aspirin and coffee coming right up.'

Vanessa sat down at the long kitchen table and swallowed the aspirin Audrey brought her along with some water. Then came a steaming mug of coffee and a spiced muffin. 'I'm not sure aspirin and coffee are going to help,' she complained. 'Shouldn't I feel better by now?'

'You will. I didn't get banged on the head but I was up all night, too. I had to make certain you didn't go to sleep.'

'Oh, Audrey, I'm sorry!'

'I wasn't sleepy anyway. Too much excitement for me.'

'How about Cara? I hope she wasn't frightened.'

'She was at first. Then she was glad that you weren't hurt and finally elated that Queenie had gone out with you and stayed to protect you. She hugged that dog half to death last night while you were at the hospital. This morning she couldn't wait to tell Sammy all about it when she got to school.'

Vanessa sipped more coffee. 'Sammy's staying here tonight, isn't he?'

'Yes. It's the Christmas party at Nia's.'

'You don't think Sammy will be afraid to stay here after the break-in?'

Audrey looked at her incredulously. 'Sammy? He'll love it. And if you're thinking about Derek objecting, Sammy will probably have the foresight not to tell his father about the incident.'

'Ah, a wily child. Audrey, did the police search the woods?'

'Yes, but they didn't find anyone.'

Vanessa remembered Christian insisting last night it must have been a teenager playing a prank and his harping on about Pete's approximation of the intruder's height. She hadn't had the heart to tell him that Pete had been half-asleep – that's why he'd fallen – and he couldn't have accurately gauged the man's height. Christian wanted desperately to believe it wasn't Brody – so desperately he'd grab at any straw.

'The lock on the tower had been picked,' Audrey went on. 'The police think someone got in, left the door open slightly but the wind slammed the door behind him and locked, and he was trapped. He must have heard you coming and was ready to burst out with a bang.'

'A bang on my head.'

'It could have been worse. They didn't find anything in the tower. Not a sign of an intruder.' Audrey shook her head. 'This morning the door frame was fixed and a steel door with a deadbolt installed.'

'Good. That should have been done at least twenty years ago. The frame and wooden door were old and weak. Gosh, I must have really been out of it not to hear all that noise.'

'You sure were after two nights without sleep.'

'You're certain they didn't find anything in the tower?'

'That's what Sheriff Baylor told me.'

'I wonder why someone was in there.'

'Maybe he thought there was an entrance from the tower into the house. Or maybe he thought he could hear something.'

'Only my TV.'

Audrey shrugged as she rinsed dishes and put them in the dishwasher.

'You seem very calm about the whole incident,' Vanessa said.

'I agree that it was probably some prankster. Who else would pull such a dumb trick? It couldn't have been someone pursuing Roxanne. She's in the hospital. Still, I took Cara to school this morning instead of letting her walk and Derek will be bringing her and Sammy back this afternoon.'

Vanessa suddenly remembered that Wade Baylor hadn't put out the alert about Brody until after midnight. No doubt Audrey hadn't heard that he might be in the area, that he might have been the person in the tower. All she knew was that a thick wall had protected the family from whomever decided to hide in the lighthouse. She could tell Audrey now about Brody, but she decided to wait until Cara was home from school and safe under the watchful eyes of her mother.

Audrey looked at Vanessa and smiled. 'We're having company today at three.'

'Company? And I look like I've been in a bar fight.'

'I knew you'd love it.'

'Who's coming?'

'Max Newman.' Vanessa frowned in thought. 'You might not remember him. He's around your age or a year younger. He went to art school in San Francisco and a few years later came back here. He opened a store called the Artisan and does a fairly good business with the tourists in the summer – the ones who want real photos, not selfies – and he still does watercolors and oil paintings. Grace commissioned him to do three paintings of lighthouses in memory of her husband and he's bringing the first one.'

'I remember Grandfather's fascination with lighthouses. He must have inherited it from Abraham because Dad wasn't interested. And I remember Max. He had high cheekbones and the most incredible dark brown eyes. Did he ever marry?'

'No. I heard there was an engagement before he came home but his mother made quick work of that. She was the most over-bearing woman I've ever met and determined to keep her only child at her beck and call. She died three months ago and now Max is free.'

'I'm going to visit Roxanne today.' Vanessa rubbed her temples although she could feel her headache fading. 'Visiting hours start at one o'clock. I should be back in time to see Max and the painting. I don't want to tire Roxy. I have to try not to ask questions. They upset her.'

'You could tell her about your TV show.'

'When she was a child, she was crazy about fairy tales. She loved dressing up and playing a queen.'

'There you go! Now *you* are getting to play a queen. That should please her.'

'I'm not so sure. I think she wanted to be the queen, not me.'

'Oh well, she won't mind. Maybe if she fully recovers, she could be on the show.'

Vanessa laughed. 'Slow down, Audrey. I'm not a producer and they don't listen to me about whom to cast. I wouldn't want to get her hopes up.'

'No, but it would be fun to work with her, wouldn't it?'

Fun? Not if she was the competitive, diva girl she was at fifteen, Vanessa thought, then immediately felt guilty. Roxanne had been a spoiled adolescent. The past years would surely have changed her, even more than Vanessa could fathom. 'I don't know whether or not to mention it to her. After all, she's never even seen the show.'

'As far as you know.'

'True. I know very little about what her life has been like the last eight years. Part of me doesn't want to know.'

'Then find something else to talk about. Something cheerful like your life in Los Angeles.'

'That's not as exciting as you might think, Audrey. I'm not out at clubs every night.'

'Then pretend, Vanessa. Roxy's traumatized. Keep things light for now.'

Vanessa smiled. 'You're right, as usual. You should have been a psychiatrist.'

'I like what I do, but it would be nice to have a psychiatrist's salary. There's so much I want for Cara. Oh well, these things have a way of working out.' She glanced at her watch. 'It's time for Grace's massage. She always enjoys it.'

Vanessa gazed at Audrey with admiration. Almost always she looked on the bright side. Even when she had discovered she was pregnant and that her boyfriend of six months wanted nothing to do with the child and moved south, Audrey didn't despair. She simply told her mother, saying that if she wanted Audrey to leave, she would find a room to rent and a part-time job. Luckily, her mother had sympathized and then looked forward to having a grandchild. She'd taken care of Cara while Audrey went to nursing school and was loving and supportive while Audrey cherished her baby.

Roxanne's eyes widened. 'What happened to your head?'

Vanessa thought she done a fairly good job of covering the bump on her head by combing her hair differently, and her black eye by applying extra concealer. But the curtains were opened wide in Roxanne's room and the day was bright. 'I fell down.'

'Fell down? On your face?'

'Yeah. I tripped on a rug.' Roxy was looking at her dubiously so Vanessa rushed on. 'It's so beautiful today I wish you could get out of here and we could walk around town. But the doctors tell me you need another day to build up your strength.'

Roxanne smiled. 'Walk around town? Years ago that would have sounded *so* boring. Now it sounds wonderful.' She sighed. 'Freedom. You don't appreciate it until you lose it.' Her voice sounded so lost, so mournful, that Vanessa's throat closed with unshed tears. 'Has town changed much in the last few years?'

'Oh, a little bit. There's a beautiful new restaurant called Nia's. It's owned by Derek Sherwin, whose son Sammy is Cara's boyfriend, only he doesn't know it.'

'Cara?'

'Audrey's daughter.'

'Oh, my, I forgot her name! She was so young when I . . . left. Is Audrey still single?'

Vanessa nodded in response.

'How are she and Cara doing?' Roxanne asked.

'Great. Audrey's father died a while back, and they live with Audrey's mother now. Audrey is a nurse. She does a lot of private duty work. Right now she's at Everly House taking care of Grace after she broke her hip. I think Grace loves having Audrey and Cara there. And Sammy. He visits quite often.'

'It's hard to think of someone taking care of Grace. She was so . . . indestructible.'

'She's not indestructible now with her Alzheimer's and broken hip.'

'She never liked me.'

Vanessa looked at her, surprised. 'Of course she did! You're her granddaughter.'

'Just because you're related to someone doesn't mean you like them. I was too much like Mommy. Grace didn't like either of us.'

'You're wrong, Roxy. She was impatient with Mom but she cared about her.'

'And what about me?'

'She thought you were saucy!' Vanessa laughed. 'She wished you'd been more mild-mannered. But she loved you. She really grieved for you when you were taken from us.'

'They blamed you, didn't they?'

'Well, yes, and I was to blame. I should never have taken you out on the beach so late.'

'Nessa, I was fifteen, not five, and it wasn't even midnight. I begged and pestered you until you gave in one night.'

Vanessa looked out the window, seeing the dark, eerie beach in her mind. 'But the wrong night. The worst night possible. The night when someone was watching.'

Roxanne took her hand and squeezed it. 'I don't know who, but I think someone had been watching for a while. He didn't just happen to be watching the one night we went out. After all, I used to make quite a show of myself, particularly that summer. I attracted as much attention as possible.' She shook her head ruefully. 'God, I was a brat.'

'Oh, Roxy, you weren't.'

Roxanne smiled. 'I was and you know it. You can be honest with me – you don't have to treat me like I'm made out of spun sugar. The last few years have made me tough. Miserable but tough.'

Vanessa had never felt closer to her sister than at that moment. They laughed and hugged and suddenly Vanessa felt as if everything was going to be all right. After eight long years, everything was going to be all right.

She told Roxanne about a few changes in the town, including that Max Newman, whom Roxy barely remembered, had a new store and was doing some paintings for Grace. But it was Vanessa's show that Roxanne wanted to hear everything about. 'You're the star of an international hit show! The nurses have told me all about it. I can't wait to see you playing a queen. Queen . . . what's your name?'

'Na'dya.'

'Oh, I love that! And your husband is Dominick. Is he a good kisser?'

'Well . . . yeah, he is!'

'Great. It would be awful if you had to keep kissing a guy who slobbered on you or had bad breath and act like you're enjoying it!'

'Part of the auditions were a couple of "chemistry" scenes between us,' Vanessa confided, grinning. 'They wanted to make sure we had convincing sexual chemistry. They told us it would be two scenes but it turned into five. In one we were actually naked although there's no nudity on the show. We were both so uncomfortable and awkward that we ended up laughing hysterically. After that, we were comfortable together in more intimate scenes.'

'Is he married?'

'No.'

'Do you date in real life?'

'He has a beautiful girlfriend with sense enough to rarely let him out of her sight!'

An hour later, Roxy's voice was beginning to get hoarse and Vanessa glanced at her watch. 'It's ten minutes past visiting time. I've worn you out. I need to go.'

'Please stay a little longer.'

A nurse looked in and before she could say a word, Vanessa said, 'I'm on my way out,' and kissed Roxy on the forehead. As she left the room, she noticed that the security guard hadn't moved. She wondered if Roxanne was even aware of the guard. Before seeing her sister, Vanessa had decided she wasn't going to mention Brody Montgomery being missing and as she left, she knew she'd made the right decision. Roxanne was happier and looked better than she'd expected. Some color had come back to her face. Vanessa wouldn't have wanted to spoil the afternoon for her sister.

She only hoped that no one else would tell Roxy the man who'd been suspected of kidnapping her could have come back to town.

SEVEN

'Hello, Grace. You're looking well.'

'Aren't you going to say I look beautiful? Honesty is so disappointing, Frederick.'

Max Newman's smile froze on his high-cheekboned face and his dark eyes lost their confidence. Almost immediately Audrey stepped in. 'Grace, *Max* doesn't know you're teasing him!'

Grace looked at him closely, blinked twice, then smiled. 'Of course I'm teasing. Honesty is one of the greatest qualities a man can possess. How nice of you to come and visit me today. You didn't bring your mother?'

'No, not today. I wanted you all to myself.'

Vanessa breathed easier as Max decided not to explain his mother was dead.

'Charmer. I remember now. You painted a picture for me and you were going to bring it today.'

'That's right!' Max looked like he knew he'd sounded too enthusiastic about Grace getting an answer correct and softened his tone. 'It's the first of three. I hope you like it.'

'Well, don't keep me in suspense. Show me! I can't wait.'

Max went into the entranceway and carried back a package covered in brown paper. Slowly he unwrapped it to show a painting measuring approximately thirty by forty-five inches.

Grace clapped her hands together, beaming. 'Max, you said you were going to surprise me! Yaquina Head! Leonard's very favorite lighthouse. Oh, I *am* pleased!'

Relief as well as pleasure shone in Max's smile. 'I thought Oregon's tallest lighthouse might be a good start.'

Everyone stared at the image of the towering white lighthouse sitting on the bluff above the Yaquina River. Max had painted the wooden lighthouse against the background of a sunset. Gold, crimson, maroon, turquoise, and royal-blue streaks melded and led up to a slate-colored sky against which the light shone.

'I seem to remember that the lighthouse is ninety feet tall,' Vanessa said.

'Ninety-three,' Max corrected with a smile. 'And the light can be seen for six miles.'

'Magnificent,' Grace whispered. 'Leonard and I saw it a number of times – day and night – and you've certainly done it justice, Max.'

'I'm glad you're pleased, Mrs Everly.'

'Max Newman, I've known you most of your life. It's *Grace*.' Max nodded.

'I'm going to hang it here in the library so Leonard can see it every day.' She glanced around. 'In spirit. I know Leonard is gone.'

Everyone breathed more normally. Grace was having a good day. She realized her husband was dead. She also knew that some days she didn't know he was dead.

'Two more to go, Max,' she said. 'Have you decided which lighthouses you'll paint?'

'I thought I'd surprise you unless you have specific requests.'

'Not at all. You surprised me with this one and I couldn't be happier.'

'I'm so glad.'

'Max, are you going to the party at Nia's tonight?' Grace asked.

'Yes. I'm looking forward to it, even if my girlfriend and I broke up two weeks ago.'

'Oh!' Grace tried to look sympathetic and failed. 'I think it would be wonderful if Vanessa could go. Perhaps you would escort her.'

Vanessa flushed in embarrassment. 'Oh, no. I'm sure Max has other friends he's taking to the party. Besides, I'd enjoy staying here with you and the children.'

'Oh, pshaw! You couldn't possibly have any fun with an old lady and two noisy children. Max, you don't have another date, do you?'

'Well, no. I was going alone.'

'That's no fun, either. Poor Audrey has to stay and look after me, but wouldn't you be happy to take our beautiful Vanessa?'

Vanessa felt like a thirteen-year-old writhing in her chair, humiliated and angry that her grandmother was nearly shaming Max into taking her.

'I would love to take Vanessa,' Max said gallantly.

'No, Max, really, it's not necessary.'

'I know it isn't necessary but it would be a blast. C'mon, Vanessa, we're both dateless. Let's have a good time.'

'Yes, Vanessa, it would be a blast,' Grace repeated gleefully. 'Oh, don't turn Max down. He just broke up with his girlfriend – right at Christmas. He needs cheering up. And Roxanne will be coming home tomorrow. I know you'll want to be with her every evening. It's your last chance to go out and kick up your heels. Please, as a favor to an old woman. I'll imagine you having the time of your life like I used to do fifty years ago! *Please,* for me?'

'Yeah, Vanessa, *please* for Grace?' Max begged, grinning.

'Oh, OK, I'm outnumbered,' Vanessa said, then quickly turned to Max. 'I'm sorry. That sounded like a put-down. I'd be pleased to have you as an escort.'

'And I'm thrilled.' Max stood up. 'I believe the party starts at eight. I have to go home and start primping. Shall I pick you up about eight thirty? We want to make a grand entrance.'

Vanessa couldn't help giggling. 'Eight thirty it is. And thank you, Max.'

'Audrey!' Smiling broadly, Derek Sherwin strode toward her wearing jeans and a red sweater. 'I was afraid you wouldn't be able to come.'

'I needed to do some grocery shopping. I had the perfect excuse to leave.'

'Do you need an excuse?'

'No, certainly not. I didn't mean to make it sound that way.' She looked around the entrance of Nia's where tiny white Christmas lights glowed from thick strands of holly and red ribbons. 'The restaurant looks beautiful.'

'Come into the main room.' Derek took her arm and led her into a large dining room. Chandeliers sparkled in the afternoon light and in the corner stood a giant evergreen tree decorated with white and gold ornaments and tinsel.

'Oh, it's magnificent, Derek!'

'I think it looks pretty good.' He gazed into her eyes. 'I wish you could be here tonight.'

'So do I, but I have responsibilities.'

'Including my son. I feel guilty for pushing him off on to you this evening.'

'Don't! Sammy's such a good kid he's no trouble at all. And Cara adores him. She'll be so much happier with him at home with us tonight. So will Grace.'

'I know *he* will be happier at Everly House than he would be here. He tries to make me think he enjoys coming here, but he doesn't.'

'He does!'

Derek shook his head. 'He pretends to enjoy it for my sake, but he only tolerates it. Sam tries so hard to please me that I sometimes think he's afraid I'll take off and leave him like his mother did.'

'I don't believe he worries about you leaving him. But he is a child who tries hard to be perfect.'

'Kids shouldn't have to be perfect to win their parents' love. Anyway, I bring him here once a week because I don't want him to think I'm ignoring him in favor of the restaurant.'

'You never ignore Sammy and he knows why you bring him. He loves you dearly.'

Derek grinned. 'And you're a dear for saying so.' He tilted his head and kissed her on the cheek in spite of the staff hurrying around them with tablecloths and centerpieces. 'As soon as Grace is well, I'd love to have dinner with you again.'

'Sounds wonderful.'

'And I'd love to have lunches and take long walks – sometimes *without* the children – and watch movies and . . . well, about a hundred things.'

'A *hundred*?' Audrey laughed. 'Are you sure you can think up a hundred things for us to do around here?'

'They don't all have to be around here. There's a whole world beyond Everly Cliffs, Audrey.'

'So I've heard. I never thought I'd see it.'

'I didn't either. And I didn't have any desire to.' Derek looked at her, his slate gray gaze tender. 'Not until the last few months. I do think you've brought me back to life, Audrey Willis.'

A mixture of happiness and apprehension rippled through her. She'd loved once and been deserted. Since that time, she'd had occasional dates and three casual relationships, but her heart had never really been involved. Her love was reserved for Cara and she'd come to believe it would always be that way. Then she met Derek Sherwin. He was handsome and intelligent, kind and gentlemanly, but there was something else about him that had immediately drawn her to him. Maybe it was his sensitivity, his gentleness, his empathy for other people. His qualities seemed to develop an almost instant affinity to her own and after a couple of months of intense introspection, Audrey had finally decided to let Derek into her life and her deepest emotions. She had decided to try love again.

She hoped she wasn't making a mistake.

'I don't have anything to wear,' Vanessa said.

Audrey smiled. 'In the closet in your room I saw a beautiful cocktail dress you left a couple of years ago. Did you forget about it?'

Audrey went with Vanessa, opened the closet door and pushed a few items of clothing around on the rack and removed a dress from the closet. It was a bateau-necked forest-green crepe with ruching around the waist and long sleeves that ended with a delicate spray of sparkles above the wrists.

'It's perfect,' Vanessa agreed. 'I'd completely forgotten I'd left it here.'

'Along with dark green high-heeled pumps.'

'I wore the outfit to a party I attended with Grace two Christmases ago. I think it was her last party.'

'Well, it's a lovely dress and I don't think you should associate it with anything sad. I'll bet Grace had a good time that night.'

Vanessa laughed. 'She did. She drank too much champagne and sang 'I Want to Hold Your Hand' by the Beatles. Loudly. She was the hit of the evening!'

'You'll have fun tonight.'

'I should stay here with Grace.'

'The best thing you can do for Grace is to make her happy and you going to the party will make her happy.'

'I wish you could go, Audrey. I feel guilty.'

'Don't. There will be other parties for me. Tonight I'll enjoy Grace and the kids.'

At eight thirty sharp Max rang the bell and when Vanessa answered, his eyes widened. 'Well, I know who'll get all the attention this evening. You look beautiful.'

'And you look quite handsome in your white dinner jacket.'

When they were in the car, Vanessa added, 'I feel like I was forced on you. I'm sorry.'

'If I didn't want to go with you, I wouldn't have said my girlfriend and I broke up two weeks ago. It was months ago. I was trying to get sympathy to persuade you to go with me. If you're embarrassed, you shouldn't be. You're giving Grace a great vicarious experience and me a night I'll never forget.'

'Gosh you're nice!' Vanessa exclaimed, laughing. 'You know what to say to make a person feel good.'

'I'm a natural charmer, no matter what my mother thought. I couldn't say or do anything to please that woman.'

'That's a shame, but I understand. I had the same relationship with my mother.'

'Well, here we are.' Max turned into the crowded parking lot of Nia's, the largest and most elegant restaurant in town. Lights shone at every window and had been strung in the evergreens – large and small – surrounding the restaurant and lining the entrance, with its red carpet and awning.

Vanessa wore her diamond and emerald birthstone ring and Grace had loaned her a narrow diamond necklace, small diamond earrings, and a black faux-sable coat. Even when she was young, Grace had refused to wear real fur. Vanessa pulled the coat around her and stepped from the car when Max opened the door.

'I feel like trumpets should be sounding,' he said. 'Queen Na'dya has arrived.'

'I'm undercover tonight, acting like one of the common people,' Vanessa returned, already enjoying herself. Max was an entertaining companion.

Inside, the restaurant's three chandeliers glowed over the dark-gold and ivory furnishings. Candelabras held white candles flickering with flame, exquisite pots brimmed with crimson poinsettias, and a Christmas tree decorated in white and gold towered in a corner.

'It's gorgeous!' Vanessa exclaimed as she slid out of her coat.

'I'm so glad you think so.' Derek Sherwin stood behind her dressed in a tuxedo. She thought he looked even more handsome than when he'd stood at the door of Everly House. 'I didn't know you were coming tonight.'

'I didn't either. My grandmother shamed poor Max into bringing me.'

'As if any man would have to be shamed into bringing Vanessa Everly to a Christmas party,' Max intervened. 'I'll be telling my grandchildren about this.'

'Speaking of children, is Sam behaving himself?' Derek asked.

'Perfectly. He picked out the blue guestroom upstairs. Cara sleeps on the first floor with her mother. When I left, he and Cara were playing with my dog Queenie.'

'I've heard about her.' Derek looked at Max. 'The two of you need a drink. Champagne?'

'Sounds great. We're headed for the bar, aren't we, Vanessa?'

'Yes. The party looks wonderful, Derek.'

'Thank you. I hope you have a nice evening.'

Derek moved on to other guests while Vanessa and Max walked slowly to the long, mirrored bar. 'Champagne isn't usually my drink, but it seems appropriate for Christmas.'

'It isn't mine either, Max, but if I have several rich eggnogs I'll pop right out of this dress.'

'Every man here would consider that the highlight of the evening,' Max laughed.

No sooner had they each taken their first sip of champagne than Vanessa heard, 'Nessa! Nessa! Over here!'

Vanessa looked blankly at a woman with thick blonde hair, her dress a blaze of glaring fuschia pink sequins and cut to reveal impressive cleavage. After a beat, she realized it was Jane Drake. She and Max slowly made their way over to Jane, who was waving and squealing.

'Nessa! Oh, how nice of Max to bring you since you're all alone. You remember Daddy, don't you?'

Vanessa's gaze moved to the man sitting with studied sophisti-cated ease. She knew Simon was in his mid-sixties, but his hair was jet black without a trace of gray, even at the temples, and slicked down with absolute perfection. His teeth were extremely white and his forehead was so tight the skin shone. He was tanned even though it was December and he wore a navy-blue jacket with a blue and gold silk ascot. Vanessa had only seen a man wearing an ascot in old movies.

'How very nice to see you, Vanessa,' he said smoothly. 'You're more beautiful than ever. It's been far too long. Your father's funeral, wasn't it?'

Vanessa managed a smile. 'Yes. And I was sorry to hear about your wife's death.'

'We received your flowers. She died quickly like your father. I think she, too, had been drinking.'

Jane chirped, 'Isn't this great? Daddy's my date.' She rubbed a hand affectionately back and forth over her father's shoulders. 'Wade couldn't come. He has important official business.'

Looking for Brody Montgomery, Vanessa thought, and hoped Jane didn't know about Brody. 'I'm sure Wade would like to be here, Jane.'

'He's certainly not a social butterfly but I can change him after we're married.' She smiled pertly. 'Oh, sit down, Nessa. You too, Max.' Jane wore heavy blue eyeshadow over deep blue eyes that used to be pale gray. Colored contacts obviously. She kept flipping her long, thick blonde hair over her shoulders. 'So, how is Grace? I've heard she's not doing too well.'

'It takes a long time for a broken hip to heal,' Vanessa said. 'She'll be fine.'

'At her age? I don't know. And you, you poor thing. To get banged on the head like you did last night! How awful! Did they catch the man?'

'No.'

'Well, you look fine. You can hardly see the bruises on your face.'

Vanessa's legs were crossed beneath the table and her foot was beginning to jitter with annoyance. Still, she managed a calm, 'Thank you. The wonders of make-up.'

'I don't see any bruises,' Simon announced, 'but Janey knows all about the magic of make-up. Make-up and a few surgical tweaks and some fake hair have done wonders for her.' He flipped a lock of Jane's golden hair and flashed Vanessa a smarmy smile.

Jane's face fell and Vanessa said quickly, 'On the show, I wear extensions, too. My hair isn't nearly as long and thick as the queen's.'

'I wouldn't know. I don't watch your show,' Jane snapped.

'I've seen it. Some people think it's quite entertaining,' Simon offered in a bored voice. 'Tell me, how is Roxanne faring?'

Vanessa stiffened. 'She needs rest and fluids. She's doing well.'

'Where has she been all of this time?'

'She doesn't remember.'

'Doesn't *remember*?' Simon exclaimed. 'How can you forget eight years?'

'I don't know. I'm not a doctor.'

'Will her memory return? Oh, you wouldn't know that, either. Well, I'm sure she hasn't forgotten a thing, but she won't tell the truth until she feels like it.' Indignation rushed through Vanessa but before she could verbally slap back, he raised his glass and announced, 'I need another drink.'

'No, you don't, Daddy.' Jane looked earnestly at Vanessa and Max. 'Daddy has type one diabetes. That's serious. He must be very careful. His diet is strict and his alcohol intake is minimal. Or, it's *supposed* to be minimal. Daddy doesn't always follow the doctor's orders. I'm his watchdog tonight.'

Simon's entire face went red and feral. He looked as if he'd like to bite Jane. Vanessa knew he wanted to seem young and virile but Jane had made him sound old and ill. She wasn't certain if Jane had done it deliberately.

'I'm sorry, Simon,' Max said. 'My mother was diabetic. What a bummer. I didn't know you're sick, too.'

'I am not sick. It's a condition that I manage quite well on my own.'

'When you're careful about your insulin dosage,' Jane said. 'You're not always careful.' She leaned toward Vanessa and Max. '*And* he has heart problems. His daily schedule is atrocious. He goes to bed at one or two in the morning and he doesn't get up until after *ten*, usually too late for me to come by his house and check on him before I go to work. If he'd let me live with him—'

'Isn't that Nia Sherwin, Derek's wife?' Simon asked, cutting off Jane.

She peered. 'She's Derek's *ex*-wife.'

It took all of Vanessa's control not to whip around to see her. She'd thought Nia had left Everly Cliffs after the divorce and never cared to return. Why was she here now?

'Well, that's surprising,' Jane said, looking unhappy. 'She's got some nerve after treating poor Derek the way she did. They aren't getting back together, are they?'

'Oh, I don't think so. Why would she come back here?' Simon asked everyone. 'She's living the high life with a producer in Los Angeles. Perhaps you know him, Vanessa?'

'I don't think so.'

'Probably not. He's a very successful and famous *movie* producer.'

Max quickly turned his head. 'I see a friend over there I want to say hello to. Vanessa, can I introduce you to him?'

'Certainly.'

'So nice seeing the two of you,' Max muttered to Simon and Jane as he and Vanessa escaped. On their way across the room, he whispered, 'That was excruciating.'

'For you, too? I can't imagine Wade engaged to Jane. He's so nice.'

Max laughed. 'I think he's trying to please his mother who's sick and harassed him into proposing. She wants grandchildren and Jane doesn't have a lot of offers. But Wade is a sensible man. I'll have to see a marriage happen before I believe it.'

'Oh. Maybe that explains a few things. Where is this friend of yours?'

'Nowhere. I couldn't stand sitting with them anymore.'

'Neither could I. I never liked Simon and Jane is . . . well . . . weird.'

Max smiled and touched a passing man on his forearm. 'Mr Hardwicke, nice seeing you. Do you know Vanessa Everly?'

For the next hour, Vanessa and Max mingled. Once she looked up and saw Derek Sherwin talking to Nia, who strongly resembled Sammy. The woman was frowning and Derek looked strained. Finally he strode away from her and she hurried after him.

'Something wrong?' Max asked.

'I was watching Derek Sherwin and his ex-wife.'

Max smiled ruefully. 'She took off with a wealthy man twenty-five years older than she is and, as far as I know, she hasn't been back in Everly Cliffs since the divorce, even to visit her son. Maybe she's here to get Sammy back, even if the guy in California hasn't married her.'

'You certainly are a fountain of knowledge about the local folks,

Max,' Vanessa teased. 'I thought you only came home a couple of years ago.'

'My mother's mission in life was collecting Everly Cliffs gossip. Before she died, she passed her vast collection of data on to me. I try to forget it – I really do – but it's been burned into my brain.'

'Well, you're handy to have around at a party where I know next to no one.'

'I think everyone here knows you. At least they know *of* you. How many times have you been asked for an autograph? I lost count.'

'Eleven times.'

'And now it looks like Nia Sherwin is being asked for *her* autograph by none other than Simon Drake.'

'What?' Vanessa's gaze shot around the room until she saw Simon, his super-white teeth gleaming against his overly tanned skin as Nia wrote something on a card and handed it back to him, smiling. 'Well, well. Is Simon picking up young women here at the party?'

'It's what playboys do, Vanessa,' Max said with mock solemnity. 'But I think Jane is going to break up their little tête-à-tête.'

Jane had appeared beside her father, her fuschia pink-sequined dress looking garish compared to Nia's elegant ivory gown. Jane clung to her father's arm possessively.

'Oh dear. If Simon had plans on following up with Nia tonight, I'm afraid he's out of luck. His sparkling watchdog has appeared.' Vanessa laughed.

Another woman approached Vanessa, praising *Kingdom of Corinna* and asking for an autograph. After she'd left, Vanessa told Max, 'That makes twelve.'

'If you're annoyed, you don't show it. You're very gracious to everyone.'

'I'm very pleased people like the show.'

'Nevertheless, I know it's draining. I don't mean this as an insult, Vanessa, but you're looking a little tired. Would you like to leave?'

'It's not an insult at all, Max. I'm *very* tired and in spite of my charming companion, I would like to go home. My head is starting to hurt from that crack on the forehead I got last night.'

As they stepped out of the brightly lit restaurant into the night, Vanessa shivered and pulled her coat closer around her. 'You stay here under the awning and I'll bring the car around,' Max said.

As soon as he'd left, a curly-haired man in a down jacket rushed up to her. 'Vanessa?' he asked as if in disbelief.

'Yes.' She looked at him closely. 'Zane?'

'Sure. And this is Libby.' He pulled a slender young woman with long, straight brown hair closer. 'What are you doing here?'

'Well, it's a party—'

'A *party*!' Zane sounded as if she'd said *orgy*. 'Why are you at a party?'

'I was invited. My grandmother wanted me to come . . .' Annoyance washed over her. 'Why shouldn't I be at a party?'

'Because Christian is out looking everywhere for Brody. Libby and I are looking everywhere we can think of since we don't know the town. I thought, well, *we* thought that you—'

'Would be helping to search for Brody?'

'You think he's come here after your sister. I'd think you'd want to find him.'

'Zane, the sheriff, the police, and apparently you and Christian are looking for Brody. Why would I be running all over town in the middle of the night looking for him, too?'

Zane opened his mouth but Libby took his hand. 'Zane, please calm down.' Her voice was soft and young. 'You can't expect Vanessa to be out on a manhunt.'

'Why not? You are.'

'I'm with you. And I'm Brody's friend.'

'She *used* to be Brody's friend,' Zane fumed. 'She used to be in love with Christian.'

'What's going on?' Vanessa had not seen Max pull up and get out of the car. 'Zane, is that you?'

'You know Zane Felder?' Vanessa asked.

'I sure do. I met Zane here in Everly Cliffs one summer years ago. Much later I moved into an apartment in Portland close to Zane's. We ran into each other by accident and renewed our friendship. Zane was at Brody Montgomery's every day. Libby got to know Brody and Zane, too. How are you, Zane?'

'Not good,' Zane snapped. 'Brody's missing. We think he might have come back here because it's his home.' *Not because of Roxanne Everly,* Vanessa could imagine him thinking.

Vanessa's gaze flew to Max's face but she saw no surprise. 'I know the sheriff issued a search for him,' he said. 'I suppose people think he'd be most likely to come home. That makes sense.'

'So what if he wanted to come home? He hasn't done one damn wrong thing, but Vanessa here nearly lost her mind when she found out we can't contact him! You should have heard her – making demands, issuing a high-handed ultimatum to Christian about telling the sheriff.' Zane was seething. 'Maybe Brody went off his meds. He's done it before but even then, no one's proved he's done anything destructive, much less *hurt* someone, yet people act like he's a serial killer on a rampage!'

'I think they're trying to locate him so he doesn't injure himself or put himself in harm's way,' Max said calmly. 'I wouldn't get so worked up over it.'

'Oh, you wouldn't, would you? Well, you're his friend, too, Max. Isn't he, Libby?'

'Yes.' Libby looked about twenty with wide, brown eyes and a kind face. 'We're all friends. Brody's real smart but he never shows off. He's an awful nice person.'

'He sure is,' Zane blustered, 'but it seems like not that many people care about him. Not Max. Not Miss TV Star.'

'Zane—'

'What, *Vanessa*? Are you going to deny you planned to marry his brother? That you were in love with Christian before people got it in their heads that his little brother kidnapped your sister? Some ignorant people *thought* he did. That's all it took for you to drop Chris cold. That's *some* love, if you ask me. And Christian is still torn up over losing you. He *still* loves you, don't ask me why.'

Vanessa was astonished. 'He d-doesn't.'

'He *does*. Brody knows he does and he's wounded because he thinks he's the cause of you leaving Christian. It seems to me you've done more damage than Brody ever did and now he's some-where, being hunted down like a rabid animal and *you're* at a party!'

'Trouble here?' Derek Sherwin had appeared behind them.

Zane cast Derek a murderous look. 'You. Still Mr Big Shot.'

'I don't know what you mean, Zane.'

'You were an arrogant jerk when you were young and you still are. Mind your own business, Derek.'

'I will if you leave right now, Zane. Otherwise, I'll have to call the police.'

'To hell with you, Sherwin!'

Vanessa was left open-mouthed as Zane stalked away, pulling Libby behind him.

Max looked at Vanessa. '*Damn.*'

'Yeah. Double damn,' she murmured. But she wasn't sure she didn't deserve everything Zane had dished out.

Derek went back to the party after he made certain Zane had left and Vanessa and Max were all right. When they got into Max's car, Vanessa asked, 'So Zane knows Derek Sherwin?'

'From way back. He always hated Derek.'

'Why?'

'I don't know. A lot of reasons. Derek's handsome, he comes from an upper-class family, he used to act sort of high and mighty, he married a beautiful woman that Zane had a crazy crush on when he was a teenager. He always gave Derek a hard time. He even told Derek when Nia was having her first affair after she married Derek.'

'What a mess and Nia was in the middle of it.'

'Yeah, even though she was a little older than Zane, she flirted with him, made him think she was really attracted to him, even went out with him a few times then dropped him for Derek. Nia's like that – she can't get enough male attention. She had affairs all through their marriage – none with Zane. Anyway, Zane hates Derek. He even blocked him investing in Blackbird.'

'And now it's going to be a big success.'

'Hopefully for Brody and Zane. Zane did the same thing to Simon Drake – prevented him from buying shares. Simon knows a good thing when he sees it.'

'But this time he's not going to see a dollar from Blackbird.' Vanessa smiled. 'I repeat, you are a fountain of knowledge, Max.'

EIGHT

Christian unlocked his front door, walked into the lit living room, and flung himself on the long couch. He felt as if every bone and muscle in his body ached after hours of walking all around Everly Cliffs and down to the beach, where he'd sat for a while on a rock looking at the wreck of the *Seraphim May*. He and Brody used to play around the beached schooner, making up different stories about how the boat had crashed and which one of them had been a secret sixth sailor that had lived but never told the true story of what had caused the disaster.

He's probably not even in Everly Cliffs, you fool, Christian thought. He probably went off his meds for God knew what reason and went somewhere exciting like San Francisco. He loved San Francisco. Besides, he never pored over the internet for gossip. He most likely didn't even know Roxanne Everly had come home, even if it had mattered to him.

Christian's head pounded, and he got up and found some coated aspirin, poured water from the sink into a plastic cup sitting on the counter and gulped down three pills. Then he looked at the cognac he'd left sitting on the counter. Without thinking he dumped the water out of the plastic cup and poured in a healthy dash of cognac. As he drank, he wondered if this ordeal was going to turn him into an alcoholic. Not considering whether or not he even wanted a drink and then dumping it into the nearest cup possible weren't good signs. But he was in an unusual situation, he told himself. He was in an alarming situation. His brother was lost.

He poured more cognac and began pacing around the living room the way his father had when he was worried. *Gerald, sit down. You're going to wear out the carpet*, Christian's mother used to tell him. 'And now I'm doing the same thing, Dad,' Christian said aloud.

He was circuiting the room a second time when he glanced at the built-in shelves beside the fireplace. His eyes fastened on the top shelf. It was empty. The picture of Brody winning the tennis tournament and the trophy were gone. Shocked, he went to the shelf, as if looking at it more closely would make the memorabilia appear. He gazed around the room, but neither the photo nor the trophy appeared.

Someone must have been in the house to steal the objects, but he always kept the place locked, even the windows. But Brody still had all of his house keys. With dread, Christian set down his drink and started toward Brody's room. Every Christmas, his mother had placed a big green candle in Brody's window and a red one in Christian's, even when they'd complained that the candles looked babyish. Still, neither of them had ever removed the candles set in thick glass holders on the windowsills and flickering through parted curtains. Neither had lighted the candles after she died.

Christian slowly opened the door to his brother's bedroom, which he'd kept shut since Brody moved to Portland. He hadn't removed anything from the room, even the posters of rock and tennis stars Brody had hung on the walls when he was a teenager, or the books of his childhood and notebooks full of Brody's own creative writing piled on shelves. Immediately the smell of evergreen washed over him. He looked at the window where a dark-green, scented candle burned brightly, like a beacon in the soft, dark night.

Christian walked slowly down the stairs, sat down, and put his head between his hands. So it was true – Brody had come home to Everly Cliffs.

'I'd ask you in but Grace is sleeping downstairs and I don't want to wake her,' Vanessa said as they stood outside the front door of Everly House.

'I understand. I had a great time tonight.'

'So did I, Max. For the most part.'

Max shrugged. 'Running into Zane was a real downer. He can be a hothead but he's a good guy. Anyway, don't worry about him or anything he said.' He leaned forward and lightly kissed Vanessa on the cheek. 'Sleep well.'

'You, too. And thank you for a lovely evening.'

Vanessa stood on the porch, waving as Max drove away, but she didn't go inside. Instead she stared down on the town, thoughts of Christian roiling in her head. For the last eight years, not a day had gone by when he hadn't flashed to her mind, but actually seeing him had been different. When he'd approached her in the hospital, drawing close and looking at her with his beautiful hazel eyes, the rush of loneliness and longing had almost floored her. After the things Zane had said to her at Nia's, she'd realized the truth. She could no longer ignore her feelings for Christian Montgomery. She loved him now and she always would.

When she was certain Max was well out of sight, she dug her keys out of her clutch purse and walked to her SUV, quietly opening the door and closing it behind her. She was certain no one would expect her home this early and there was somewhere she must go.

Vanessa pulled into the driveway of the pale limestone and stucco French-Country-style house Gerald Montgomery had built for his family in 1995. She'd always thought the house beautiful inside and out. Even though it was almost eleven o'clock, all the downstairs lights were on and glowed over the shrubbery and brick walkway leading to the front door. When she reached it, she raised the knocker and tapped gently, fighting an urge to run away. She wouldn't have had time, however. Christian opened the door almost immediately, his hair mussed, his shirt untucked.

'Were you asleep?' Vanessa asked. 'It's late. I shouldn't have bothered you.'

He blinked at her in surprise, then said, 'I wasn't asleep. I'm a mess because I'm tired. It's been a long day but please come in.' He shut the door behind her. 'Can I take your coat?'

Vanessa slipped out of the faux fur sable and handed it to him. His gaze swept over her quickly. 'You look beautiful.'

'I went to the party at Nia's tonight. I hadn't planned on going but Max Newman came over to bring a painting to Grace and when she heard he didn't have a date, she nearly begged me to go with him. I was embarrassed, but she said it would be a vicarious experience for her and . . . well, you know how Grace can be.'

Vanessa realized she was talking too much and too fast, but Christian merely gave her a tired smile as he hung up the coat. 'Yes, I know how Grace can be. I think she should be in charge of foreign policy – she could talk down any country on the verge of invasion.'

Vanessa laughed. 'I'd never thought of that, but she certainly is a force of nature.'

'Come in and sit down.'

'The living room looks the same as the last time I was here.'

'Neither Dad nor I wanted anything changed after Mom died.'

'She would have liked that. I cared very much for your mother.' Vanessa smiled. 'Anyway, the room is still lovely, but you look worn out.'

'I am. I've been looking for Brody for hours.'

'I know. I ran into Zane and Libby when I came out of Nia's. He was furious that I'd gone to a party when the three of you were scouring the town for Brody. He made quite a scene.'

Surprisingly, Christian laughed. 'Zane is a great guy, a brilliant guy, but he's also volatile. I don't think anyone who's not as mellow as Libby could put up with him as a boyfriend.'

'She's very young.'

'Twenty-three although she looks eighteen. But she truly loves Zane, and he's crazy about her.' He frowned. 'Brody didn't have a girlfriend and I think sometimes looking at Zane's and Libby's devotion made him sad.'

'He could have had that with the right woman, Christian. As long as he stayed on his medication, he was fine – the Brody we'd always known.'

Christian shook his head slowly. 'No, he wasn't. When he learned his diagnosis, his self-confidence nose-dived. He buried himself in work. He never dated. He rarely even laughed or had a good time.'

'Max didn't tell me that.'

'Max must have told you that by coincidence he lived near Brody. He was always nice to Brody and Zane, interested in their work although technology isn't his thing. But the guys didn't hang out together. Brody was a loner.'

'He used to be so social, so extroverted.'

'That all changed after he learned he was schizophrenic. It didn't have to, but it did for him.'

'I'm sorry, Christian. I really am – sorry for Brody, sorry for all the drama when Roxanne was kidnapped.'

He gave her a piercing look. 'Does that mean you no longer think he took your sister?'

Vanessa paused. 'The more I learn about her abduction, the harder it is for me to believe he did it. But I'm not absolutely sure he didn't. I know that isn't what you want to hear—'

'But you were always honest.'

'To a fault. I never learned to be tactful.'

'Your honesty is one of the things I loved about you, Vanessa. I'm glad to see you haven't changed.'

Vanessa's heart beat harder, and she felt flustered and awkward. She was thankful Christian's manner became brisk. 'I didn't even offer you anything to drink. I don't think I have much except beer and rum and cognac.'

'I had three glasses of champagne at the party. I shouldn't have anything but I can't resist a weak rum and cola. If you have some cola, that is.'

'I bought a twelve pack of Coke yesterday. I think I'll have one, too.' Christian walked into the kitchen and opened the refrigerator door. She heard glasses clinking and the tabs on cans popping. In moments he handed her a glass and sat near her on the couch.

Vanessa took a sip. 'I said a *weak* drink.'

'You only live once and you visiting me is an occasion.' He looked at her and cocked an eyebrow. 'Why have you come to see me?'

She bought time by sipping more of her drink. 'Tonight Zane reminded me of how close we used to be. Brody was my friend and not because he was your brother. You and I were . . . more than friends.'

'Much more. We planned to get engaged at Christmas.'

'Yes. And then Roxy was taken at the end of summer. It was so shocking, so unbelievable, so devastating.' Her throat felt dry and she took another drink, noticing that her hand was trembling slightly. She saw Christian notice, too. 'Brody was sick. He'd been wandering around, thinking he was a knight looking for his lady. Everyone was talking about him, afraid of him.' Christian winced and Vanessa had to look away from his face. 'No one could catch him.'

'The police caught him *before* Roxanne was kidnapped, Vanessa. You knew that.'

'I did. I also knew he'd been turned over to your father and he'd made arrangements for Brody to enter a mental health facility the day before someone took Roxanne. Frankly, I wouldn't have taken her out on the beach late at night unless I thought Brody was safely locked up. I know that sounds brutal, but it's true. After she was kidnapped, I found out there had been a delay and Brody was still in town that night.'

'He was in my father's house. Dad was looking after him.'

'I know he was supposed to be in this house but he could have sneaked out.'

'He was heavily medicated. My father swore—'

'Your father could have been lying. Brody was his son, for God's sake.'

'Ben Johnson also swore Brody was here.'

'He was your father's best friend.'

Christian sighed. 'Vanessa, we've already had this conversation more times than I can remember a long time ago. Why are you bringing it all up again now?'

'Because I've had a lot of time to think. When Roxy was kidnapped, I was so frightened, mystified, incredulous and . . . and paranoid. Everyone kept saying that Brody wasn't mentally stable, that he'd seemed fixated on Roxanne when he was in Everly Cliffs and she was taken. They said it over and over until I couldn't think of anything else.'

'And what's different now? She's back and Brody is missing. You seemed sure enough yesterday that there was a connection.'

'I know. And I was. But it was an automatic response. I've believed for so long that Brody had something to do with Roxanne's kidnapping I didn't take the time to think. But as hotheaded as Zane was, he said some things that hit home with me. He said that Brody has never hurt anyone. Until this week, I thought Roxanne was dead but even though I was convinced Brody kidnapped Roxanne, I never thought he murdered her – I thought he took her and something happened, something he didn't plan, something that ended in her death. But it didn't.'

'No, she's alive and well and there's no proof that Brody's ever done anything bad, even when he's off his meds.'

'What about the beating I took on the beach? It took months for my hand to heal.'

'I'll repeat that there is *no proof* about Brody's guilt. If he didn't take Roxanne, he didn't beat you.'

'I realize that now. It took years, but it did sink in, Christian. And our relationship aside, I'd been Brody's friend too. Yet I turned on him within days. And I decided your father, whom I'd always admired, was lying to cover for him. I think I did those things in a kind of hysteria. Roxy was missing, it was my fault, my parents were distraught, I'd been beaten and concussed, and thought my hand would never be the same—'

'And you thought Brody would do that to you?' Without waiting for an answer, Christian picked up her left hand and looked at it closely. 'They did a wonderful job of reconstructing it.'

'Yes. I have some scars, an enlarged knuckle, a couple of stiff fingers . . . Some days it hurts and I can't make a fist. But I'm so lucky that it's as near normal as it is.'

'You were on a lot of drugs after the beating you took. Do you think the things people were saying to you about Brody were distorted by the drugs? Did they alter your perception of what was being said?'

'I have no idea. My father didn't say much of anything. My mother was a screaming shrew and she hated Brody before Roxanne's kidnapping. She started hating him after she learned his diagnosis. I think she was aware of how fragile her own mental stability was and she thought she was headed down the same road as Brody. She hated what she was afraid of becoming and in her mind schizophrenics were raging violent maniacs. The medical people were kind to me, but the doctor in charge constantly made insinuations about Brody being a possible suspect.'

Christian smiled ruefully. 'Shapiro. He couldn't stand my father.'

'I didn't know.'

'Vanessa, you took a helluva beating, and I'm not talking about just your hand. Do you think Brody would have beaten you?'

'He could have. He's tall and strong.' She hesitated. 'But he was always gentle.'

'And what do you think about the possibility of him going off his medication and being in Everly Cliffs at the same time your sister returned?'

'I don't know, Christian. I wish I could say it must be a coincidence, but my God, what a coincidence. Of course, we don't know that he's here.'

Christian still held her left hand. He raised it and kissed it gently. 'He's made no attempt to get to Roxanne.'

'She's in the hospital.'

'Would that make a difference if he's irrational?'

'How would I know? I'm not a psychiatrist. I don't know how he would or wouldn't behave without his medication.'

'At least you're not acting like he's a monster coming after your sister like you did at the hospital when Zane told us he's missing.'

'But I did, didn't I? Zane gave me hell for that tonight, too. And rightly so. To say I overreacted is an understatement. Which is really why I'm here. Or partly.' She took a deep breath. 'Christian, I'm sorry for the way I've behaved to you for the last eight years. I was close to your family, to you, to Brody. I saw how all of you suffered when you found out Brody was schizophrenic and I saw how your father made certain he got the very best of care. I suffered for him, too, and it made no difference in my feelings for you. Yet when Roxy was kidnapped, I simply went off the rails, making accusations—'

'You never directly accused Brody.'

'I didn't defend him, either.'

'How could you have? You didn't see who took Roxanne.'

'That's true. How could I say "It definitely wasn't Brody Montgomery although I didn't see who it was"? But I hammered you with questions. You and your father. I all but accused your father of being a liar when he said Brody was under his supervision when Roxy was taken. I was as bad as my parents—'

'No, you weren't.'

'Well, almost. That was unforgiveable because I loved you. And you loved me.' Christian remained silent, still holding her hand. 'And that's the other part of why I had to see you tonight.' She took a deep breath. 'Zane said that you were still in pain over losing me. That you're still in love with me. When I heard that, I felt as if someone had punched me in the stomach. Worse. Chris, is it true?'

He stared at her with his beautiful eyes, the planes of his face soft and filled with tenderness. 'Would it make a difference?'

'Yes,' Vanessa said shakily. 'Yes, it would, because I've realized I'm still in love with you.'

'You're going to get your dress wrinkled,' Christian murmured in her ear as they lay side-by-side on the wide couch.

'Is that a hint for me to take it off?'

'Not if you don't want to.'

'I don't want to turn this into one of those scenes when people say they love each other and three minutes later start ripping off their clothes and violently make love.'

'It's been twenty minutes but all I want is to savor this time to just hold you and hear that you still love me.'

'Good. You feel so warm and familiar – just like I remember. And I don't care about the dress.'

'By the way, it was great to hear that realizing you still love me was like being punched in the stomach.'

Vanessa giggled. 'No one has ever accused me of being a poet.'

'It may not have been lovely, but it was effective. I don't think I've ever been as surprised in my life. I thought you hated me.'

Vanessa lifted her face to his. 'Never, Chris. *Never*. Not even in the worst of times. I think I was furious that things weren't working out for us. I'd led a privileged life. I wasn't used to hard times. I certainly didn't take them gracefully or even sensibly.'

'So if we have hard times again, I don't have to look forward to eight more years of silence from you?'

She nudged him gently and laughed. 'No, you dope. I've grown up a lot.' She paused. 'But we're talking as if everything's the way it was, like we're a couple again. After all these years . . .'

'After all these years you have someone else in your life?'

'No. I've dated of course but I've never been serious about anyone. You?'

'The same. Well, I have to confess I went out with Jane Drake a couple of times and she decided we were getting married.'

'*Jane Drake!* Christian, how could you? Was this after she had her nose and boob jobs?'

He burst into laughter. 'I did not check out her boobs.'

'How could you miss them?'

'I meant I didn't check them physically. And yes, she had them. And the new nose. And the ton of blonde hair. She'd had all the work done over the course of a year yet I heard no one asked her to the hospital Christmas party, so I did.'

'You saint.'

'Yes. I didn't have a good time but somehow I was roped into having lunch the next Saturday afternoon. Within two days I think she'd told everyone at Everly Cliffs Hospital we were a "thing". I backed away – I hope I wasn't cruel because I've always felt kind of sorry for her – but she's tenacious. She pursued me for weeks but finally she left me alone. I was shocked when six months later, I found out she was engaged to Wade Baylor. He's a smart all-round great guy. She's a good nurse and I get the feeling she's basically a hurt little girl, but her demand for constant attention drives people away.'

'Jane adores her father although he's never been particularly nice to her. Maybe all she needs is a strong, kind, supportive man like Wade.' Vanessa paused then exclaimed, 'Oh my God! When you mentioned Jane being a nurse, I thought about Audrey. She'll be wondering where I am.'

'Is she your warden now?'

'She worries.'

Vanessa grabbed her cellphone and called Audrey. 'I'll be a little later getting home than I expected but I'm fine.'

'Where are you?'

'With . . . Christian.'

'*Christian!*'

'Yes. Everything is OK. I'll talk to you tomorrow. Bye.'

'Nessa—'

'You didn't even wait for her to say goodbye before you clicked off.' Christian grinned.

'I didn't want any more questions. You should have heard her when I said I was with you.'

'I did.'

'You can't blame her for being shocked. We've only seen each other twice before tonight since I got back.'

'It feels like more than twice.'

She relaxed again and Christian hugged her.

'And before that, in one way it feels like it's only been weeks.'

'And in another?'

'Eight years. Every single day of eight years.' His beautiful, soft lips brushed hers. 'Dear God, don't let it be another eight years.' He paused. 'Vanessa, you've been totally honest with me tonight but I haven't been with you about Brody. At least I don't think I have. Something's happened tonight. Well, I can't be sure but I think someone was in here in the house.'

'Brody?'

A mechanical *ping* interrupted him. 'Damn, a text,' Christian muttered as he reached for his cellphone. He looked at the small screen and frowned.

'What is it?' Vanessa took his phone. 'It's from Zane.' She read the message: *Chris, come to Diamond Rose now*. 'Diamond Rose?'

'The Diamond Rose – the nightclub downtown.'

'I don't remember a nightclub.'

'It's on the outskirts of town. It was built in the early Seventies and caught fire twenty years later. The owner of the property refused to have the remains torn down and the town council turned a blind eye.'

Vanessa frowned. 'I *do* remember that place. I forgot the name was the Diamond Rose. We called it "the ruin".'

'My grandparents told me it was elegant and a great draw for tourists. They went there a lot. They loved to dance.'

'Why would Zane want you to come to the wreckage of an old nightclub at one in the morning?'

'It has to be something to do with Brody.'

'Why doesn't he say what it is?'

'It's a text. He's being as brief as possible. I have to go.'

'Oh, no, Chris. Not now. It's late – or early – and dark and Zane is so cryptic. You don't know what's going on.'

'You think he's luring me into a trap?' Christian gently pushed her aside and got off the couch, stretching as he stood. 'You know how determined Zane is to find Brody. This has to be serious.'

'You're not even certain the text is from Zane.'

'Who else knows I'm waiting to hear from him?'

'Then call Wade before you go.'

'I don't have time for Wade to pull himself together and drive to the Diamond Rose. The text says *now* and I'm only ten minutes away.'

'Then I'm going with you.'

Christian was already shrugging into his jacket and gave her a stern look. 'No, you aren't. You'll stay right here and wait for me. I promise to call as soon as I know something.'

'I'm going.' Vanessa slipped into her shoes, put on her coat and picked up her purse. 'I'll wait in the car.'

'Vanessa—'

'I'm *going*, dammit.'

Christian closed his eyes and sighed. 'You were always the most stubborn woman I've ever known.'

Five minutes later they pulled out of the Montgomery driveway in his red Buick Regal GS. 'I never thought you'd drive a red sporty car,' Vanessa said, trying to take the edge off her nerves.

'Dad thought doctors should drive oatmeal-colored sedans. Don't ask me why. After he died, I bought what I wanted. Do you like it?'

'Very much.' Vanessa still wished they were in her sturdy SUV. 'Aren't you driving too fast?'

'Yes, but there's no snow or rain or much traffic, and I'm in a hurry.'

The main street of Everly Cliffs looked completely different during the Christmas season with red, green, white, and navy-blue lights blending into a bright, magical glow that transformed even drab buildings like the dry cleaners into seemingly beautiful, fairy-tale structures. She had the bizarre feeling of being in the middle of a deserted amusement park and she clasped her hands together so Christian wouldn't notice they weren't quite steady.

They drove past Nia's. The party was over and only tiny Christmas lights glowed on the shrubbery and around the windows. All the merriment had died at the stroke of midnight, Vanessa thought.

'There's the Rose and Zane's car in the lot.' Chris turned into the large parking lot of the only dark building in town. What once had been a glittering, opulent nightclub was now a blackened, charred skeleton hulking in the night. He reached across her, opened the glove box and withdrew a large flashlight.

'That's all you have? A flashlight?'

'What were you expecting? A Glock 21? It's a twelve-hundred lumen tactical flashlight – very bright. Don't worry.'

'I don't see any other lights in the building.'

'There's no electricity.'

'I *know* that. I meant a flashlight, Chris. Zane isn't sitting in there in the dark.'

'Maybe he is. I'll be careful. Stay here.'

Christian closed the door quietly and began walking slowly toward the west end of the building, which was the most badly burned. Vanessa thought of the first time she'd seen the Diamond Rose. She'd been eight, and it was a rainy autumn night. They'd been driving home from a wedding in Portland and all the way home, Vanessa's father had been pouring liquid from a thermos and sipping it, drawing angry looks from his wife. Suddenly he slowed the car down to a crawl. 'Look at that place, Nessa, Roxy.' He'd nodded to the burned building. 'It used to be like a magnificent palace full of light and happiness and good times. My mother and father came here dressed like a queen and king to drink champagne and dance. Then an evil spirit from the blazing depths of the Earth crawled up and set the whole place on fire – the biggest fire this town has ever seen – a fire that lasted for hours and hours. A hundred people burned to death, screaming in agony, while the evil spirit huddled nearby and laughed and laughed.'

'Frederick!' Ellen's voice lashed at him. 'What a terrible story to tell the girls! They'll have nightmares for weeks!'

Roxanne giggled, '*I* won't!'

Vanessa had asked, 'What kind of evil spirit was it?'

'An ugly, creeping, twisted, horrendous mosgrum that was a thousand years old.'

'Stop it right now, Fred!' Ellen was furious. She turned toward the back seat. 'Girls, there is no such thing as a mosgrum. Your father drank too much at the wedding reception and he's been drinking ever since we left. You're a drunk, Frederick! A low-down drunk!'

'It takes one to know one!'

'Did a hundred people really die in the fire, Dad?'

'Certainly not, Vanessa,' Ellen stated. 'Your father is making up stories. He's ridiculous!'

Frederick had speeded up, snickering in a way that made Vanessa deeply uneasy, while Ellen glared at him. Roxy sat in a corner of the backseat, laughing, but the story had frightened Vanessa. If Grace had been home, she might have asked her about the mosgrum. Grace had just left for France after Grandfather's death, though. Vanessa hadn't wanted to ask anyone else about the fire and the mosgrum – she was too afraid it was true – so she tucked it away in the corner of her mind where she hid the things that scared her.

As she watched Christian enter the Diamond Rose, all she could think of was the mosgrum. She'd never known what caused her father to uncharacteristically invent a ghastly story with an imaginary monster to tell two little girls, even if he'd had too much to drink – but the mosgrum had lurked in her subconscious for twenty years and now she knew it was inside the building. Not an actual twisted and ugly thousand-year-old creature, but something creeping and horrendous embodied in the idea of the mosgrum. Vanessa shuddered. It was waiting for Christian.

Vanessa reached in her clutch purse and pulled out the small flashlight she always carried at night since her attack on the beach.

She climbed out of the car and started toward the burned building, wishing she wasn't wearing high heels as she hurried carefully over the scattered trash, twigs, and moldering leaves that littered the parking lot. The concrete walkway to the wide front entrance was riddled with cracks full of moss and dead weeds. Once she caught sight of a flash of light inside but it disappeared quickly as if someone had turned it off.

She reached the concrete steps leading up to the entrance and stood for a moment, telling herself not to be afraid. She slowly climbed the steps and passed through what had once been the doorway to a beautiful, glittering club full of elegantly dressed people, a live band, and a dozen waiters serving drinks and delicious gourmet appetizers. She stopped and gazed around, noticing that the fire had destroyed most of the west side and a huge chunk of the back where she knew there had been a terrace used in the summer. When it was whole, it had been twice the size of Nia's. What a shame it had burned, she thought.

Vanessa pulled herself from her thoughts, knowing she was stalling and that was the last thing she wanted to do, although she was frightened to her bones. She'd come to help Christian.

'Chris?' she called. 'Christian, where are you?'

'I'm over here but I told you to stay in the car. Go back!'

She turned her flashlight in his direction. 'Turn on your flashlight. I can't locate you.'

'Go back—'

'*No!* Now where are you?'

He turned on his flashlight and they walked toward each other, the lights drawing closer until they met. Christian immediately put his left arm around her shoulder. 'You shouldn't be in here.'

'Neither should you. Where's Zane?'

'I called for him but he didn't answer.'

'Maybe he left.'

'Without his car? He's here, Vanessa. I can feel it.'

'But if he's here, why doesn't he answer?' *Because something's happened to him,* she answered herself silently.

They each swept their flashlight beams around what had been the central room of the Diamond Rose. All that remained were singed walls, crumbling railings around the stage where bands used to play, the tall windows – most of them broken – and bedraggled cobweb-festooned chandeliers, and at least sixteen cracked and broken floor-to-ceiling arched mirrors. Vanessa had a brief flash of images she'd seen of the Hall of Mirrors in Versailles. The floor – partly covered with ragged carpet, partly with scratched and scorched hardwood – was littered with debris, some cracking beneath their feet although they tried to turn a flashlight beam on their path before they took each step. Vanessa shivered. Someone was watching them – she could feel the gaze as if it were touching her.

'Christian?' He didn't answer. 'Christian, let's leave.'

Finally, he stopped. 'I don't see him. Maybe something scared him off.'

'What scared him off? Another person? He asked you to come. He wouldn't run if he heard footsteps. I don't think he's here. *We* shouldn't be here.'

'I can't leave until I'm absolutely sure—'

'Wait!' Vanessa's flashlight was focused on the dais where a band had once infused life into the room. The beam danced over some sagging music stands and a ramshackle piano. Suddenly the breath went out of her as her stomach clenched. 'The piano bench,' she said in a tiny voice.

They inched closer. Beneath her coat, chills ran up and down Vanessa's arms as she and Christian both turned the beams from their flashlights on to a form sitting at the piano. Or rather, bent over the piano. Vanessa suddenly wanted to run out of the building and hide from whatever was slumped there, but she forced herself forward, keeping up with Christian. They stepped up on the dais then moved slowly to the piano.

'Zane?' Christian asked in a shaky voice. 'Zane are you . . . all right?'

You know he's not all right, Vanessa thought. *You're only hoping, beseeching.*

'Zane? C'mon, guy. You're scaring me. Answer me.'

Oh God, oh God, please, no. The phrase tolled over and over in Vanessa's mind as Christian touched Zane, gently took hold of his curly hair and tilted back his limp head to reveal a cascade of blood spilling from a thin, vicious slit in his throat. His legs jerked, his body convulsed, and then he was still, his dying blue eyes fastened on a shattered chandelier above him.

NINE

Vanessa pulled her coat tighter as she huddled in Christian's car. The heater was running at full blast but she still shivered, her clenched hands icy, her feet numb. Christian had called Wade Baylor, and they sat in the Diamond Rose parking lot waiting for him to arrive.

'Maybe we shouldn't be here,' she said. 'Wade told us to leave the scene.'

'We might see the killer.'

'He was in the building when we found Zane. I could feel him.'

'I didn't hear anything.'

'Neither did I, but I *know*. If he's still here, he might come after us.'

'We're in a locked car,' Christian argued. 'What's he going to do?'

Vanessa sighed and trembled. She knew she would never get the image of Zane Felder's blank, dying face out of her mind. Or the blood spilling down the front of him. So much blood . . .

Headlights swung into the parking lot and a patrol car pulled up beside Christian's. 'Thank God. Wade's here,' he said.

'Make sure it's Wade before you get out of the car.'

Christian sat still until Wade emerged, walked to Christian's car and rapped on the window. Chris got out, apologizing. 'I know you told me to leave, but—'

'Too late now. Tell me what the hell is going on.'

Christian shut the door. Vanessa could hear his voice but not make out any words as he explained to Wade why they were here and what they had found. Or *who* they had found. Just two hours ago Zane had been alive – vibrantly alive – and furious with Vanessa as he held tightly to his girlfriend's hand.

Libby! Her young, innocent face flashed in Vanessa's mind. Did Libby know Zane had come to the Diamond Rose? Good lord, had she come with him? Was she in the building, too?

Vanessa jumped out of the car. 'Libby!' Wade and Christian

looked at her. 'Zane's fiancé! She was with him less than two hours ago. Where is she? Inside?'

'Oh, no,' Christian groaned.

Wade's face remained impassive. 'Take it easy. We don't know anything yet.'

'We should call her to make sure,' Vanessa said.

'Do you have her cellphone number?' Wade asked.

'No.'

He looked at Christian. 'She might be hiding inside. I'll go in.'

'I'll go with you.'

'No, you won't, Christian.' Wade looked at another squad car pulling into the parking lot. 'I have backup. You and Vanessa get back in your car.'

Two officers accompanied Wade into the derelict nightclub, all three carrying high-intensity flashlights. Vanessa and Christian watched as beams of light moved inside the building, flashing through the broken windows and the burned-out west end.

'Did you tell Wade that Zane is at the piano?' Vanessa asked.

'Of course.'

'They're going all over the place.'

'They're looking for anyone else who might be inside.'

'Maybe we should have called the ambulance before we called Wade.'

'Zane would have been dead within a couple of minutes, if that long. There was nothing anyone could do.'

'Was Zane's throat slashed with a knife?'

'I think it was a sharp wire. Maybe a piano wire.'

'A *wire*! Why a wire?'

'Maybe I'm wrong. But I saw a wire—'

After a moment, Vanessa said darkly, 'Someone would have to be very strong to hold Zane still and strangle him with a wire.'

'Strong like Brody? Is that what you're saying?'

'Well, I couldn't do it.'

'And *I* could. So could a lot of other men. You wouldn't have to be extremely strong so don't say any more. Don't even mention Brody's name.'

'I wasn't going to.' Vanessa sank even lower in her seat and drew the collar of the black coat up around her face. She shouldn't have brought up Brody, even obliquely. He wouldn't hurt his best friend. But lord, she thought, Christian had to be thinking the same thing. She knew Wade would.

It seemed like an hour before Wade returned to them but the clock in the car told her it had only been fifteen minutes. Christian lowered his window.

'We found only Zane Felder, no one else. I have the county crime-scene people on the way. In the meantime, I have to get in touch with his girl . . . what's her name?'

Vanessa leaned across Christian. 'It's Libby. I don't know her last name but they were staying in the Everly Cliffs Motel. I'm sure their room is listed under his name.'

Wade nodded as he took in the information.

'I saw her this evening. She's his fiancé. Could I come with you when you tell her? She might feel better with another woman around. She doesn't know anybody in Everly Cliffs, much less any other females,' Vanessa asked.

Wade looked as if he were automatically going to say no, then he slowly nodded. 'All right. This isn't how we usually do things but – well, we don't have many murders here. Certainly not like this one. I'll call and make certain she's at the motel and if she is, we'll tell her there, not on the phone. Chris, will you follow and bring Vanessa?'

'Sure, Wade. Anything. Damn it, poor Zane. Poor Libby.'

Wade found out Zane's room number and he knocked softly on the motel door, Vanessa and Christian standing behind him.

'Zane, is that you?' a young voice called through the door.

'No, ma'am, it's Sheriff Wade Baylor. I need to speak to you.'

Libby jerked open the door, her face pale, her brown eyes wide and scared. 'Is this about Zane? He's been gone for over an hour. He's not answering his phone. Have you found him? Is he hurt?'

'Ma'am, I'm afraid I have some bad news for you,' Wade said gently. 'May I come in? I have Vanessa Everly and Christian Montgomery here. You don't have to worry about being alone with me.'

'Vanessa Everly?' Libby looked doubtfully past Wade. Vanessa tried to smile reassuringly. 'Oh, Vanessa. And Brody's brother. Come in.' They filed past her and stood awkwardly in the small motel room. 'Where's Zane? In the hospital? Tell me he's in the hospital.'

Her voice was pleading. She even held out her hands as if begging for news that if the man she loved wasn't here, he was safe.

'Ma'am, I'm so sorry to tell you that Zane is dead.'

Libby blinked at him. 'That's not possible. No, you're mistaken. I've been with him all evening.'

'I know you were with him most of the evening. You were with him when he saw Miss Everly at Nia's. Where did the two of you go after that?'

'We were tired. We've been walking around this town all day. I was cold. Zane was upset. We came back here. I took a shower to warm up. Zane said after my shower he'd give me a foot rub.' She thumped down on the double bed. Her face crumpled and she began to cry. Vanessa quickly sat down beside her and wrapped an arm around her shoulders. Christian pulled a tissue from the box on the nightstand and handed it to Libby, who sobbed into it.

'Um, ma'am—'

'Please call me *Libby*, Sheriff. I can't stand *ma'am*,' Libby snuffled.

'Libby. Is that short for Elizabeth?'

'No. I'm just Libby.'

'Libby what?'

'Libby Hughes. What does that have to do with anything?'

'I need your full name for reports, ma'am. Libby.'

She nodded.

'What happened after your shower?' the sheriff continued.

'I was still in the shower when Zane stepped into the bathroom and said something. I couldn't hear him over the water running. I yelled, "What?" and he said something else and then I turned off the water and got out of the tub, toweled off and walked into the bedroom. He was gone. I opened the room door and he was taking off in the car. I thought he'd gone to get us something to eat or some wine. But he never came back. I called him at least five times but it went to voicemail.' Her pale lips quivered as she looked up at Wade. 'Where did he go?'

'To a place called the Diamond Rose. It used to be a nightclub but there was a bad fire. The remains are still standing.'

'Why would he go there?'

'We don't know.'

Christian said, 'He sent me a text telling me to meet him there. Otherwise we wouldn't have known where to look for him.'

'Why didn't he tell me?'

'Maybe he did, but you didn't hear him when you were in the shower. Or maybe he didn't want you to go with him.' Libby frowned. 'He might have thought it was dangerous.'

Wade took over again. 'Christian went to meet Zane. When he got inside, he found him . . . dead. I'm sorry, Miss Hughes.'

'Not Zane.' She drew back and announced loudly, 'Zane wouldn't leave me. He's not dead. He *cannot* be . . .'

Her head dropped to her chest, her long, light brown hair falling around her face. When she began sliding forward, Vanessa grabbed her, afraid she would faint and fall off the bed. Finally, her head still bent, she asked, 'How did he die? Did he fall or have a heart attack or . . .?'

'He was murdered, Miss Hughes.'

Libby's head snapped up. '*Murdered!*'

'Yes.'

'How?'

'He was . . . strangled.'

'Strangled? Who strangled him?'

'We don't know. Christian and Vanessa found him and Vanessa felt as if someone were still in the building—'

'Vanessa? I thought he only texted Christian.'

'I was with Christian when he got the text,' Vanessa said. 'I insisted on going with him.'

'And you saw Zane strangled, too?' Libby seemed to want confirmation from a woman. 'You're sure he was strangled?'

'Yes, I'm afraid so. I'm so sorry, Libby.'

Libby held up her left hand and looked at her gold engagement ring set with what looked like a full carat diamond. Then she made a long, gut-wrenching sound like a wounded animal and collapsed against Vanessa.

Vanessa sat at a table in the Diamond Rose. Above her chandeliers glowed and their light shone over and over in the beautiful, tall mirrors encircling the main room. She wore a long, strapless, black satin gown, opera-length black gloves, and an ivy-patterned diamond bracelet. A perfect red rose stood in a crystal bud vase on a white damask tablecloth. Vanessa raised her martini and held it toward Christian, dressed in a tuxedo and beaming at her across the table, his beautiful hazel eyes full of love. Music began to play from the dais only a few feet away from them. It was a piano solo – 'Love is Blue'.

'I love this song,' Vanessa murmured.

'So do I,' Christian answered. 'Especially when it's played with such feeling. He's a real virtuoso.'

As if hearing him, the pianist turned his head and looked at them. Vanessa smiled at him until she saw the slash across his neck, the blood spilling down the front of his white shirt, his dead-blind blue eyes. Zane Felder.

Vanessa woke up with a scream stuck in her throat. Her gaze darted madly around her and a nightlight showed her Grace's bedroom at Everly House. Still breathing heavily, she looked at the bedside clock: 5:05 a.m. She'd wearily dragged herself into the bed at three thirty to curl into a fetal position and shiver until a dream-torn exhausted sleep had overwhelmed her. She covered her face with her hands. How could she face this day? How could she ever forget the horrible sight she'd witnessed last night? She couldn't. It would haunt her until the last of her days.

Finally her black private smartphone rang. She reached for it nervously and said, 'Yes?' The grating mechanical voice she heard the night Roxanne returned home screeched in her ear.

'You can stop praying for time, Vanessa. You've used all your time and now the end has begun.'

TEN

In shock, Vanessa clutched the phone after the caller had hung up, listening to the dead air. At last she realized her hand was shaking and tossed the phone to the foot of the bed as if it were poisonous. So someone knew, she thought. Someone knew of all the horrible events of the evening. It could be anyone – maybe even another policeman – but she knew it wasn't. It was the person who had called her the night Roxanne reappeared after eight years. It was a threatening, all-knowing being.

She wanted to call Christian to tell him about the call, but she didn't want to wake him. Instead, she tried to sleep again but could only doze before awakening with a terrified jerk. She lay in bed until the day's light showed through the parted drapes then put on her robe and slippers and went downstairs. Not even Audrey was awake yet so Vanessa put on coffee and took a couple of aspirins as she sat at the table waiting for the coffee to brew.

Last night dealing with Libby had almost been worse than finding Zane. She'd cried hysterically, unable to stop, until Christian brought in a medical bag from his locked car trunk and gave her a mild tranquilizer. Even that had only calmed her slightly but not made her drowsy. Finally Vanessa tucked her into bed and offered to stay with her, but Libby had turned her down. 'I need to be alone now. I want to be alone. Please.' On their way out of the motel room, Christian told Vanessa to call Libby around seven to make certain she was all right. They agreed that, at nine o'clock, she would pick Libby up and take her to the police headquarters where Wade Baylor wanted to get a statement from the three of them.

At six, Audrey walked into the kitchen, looking with surprise at Vanessa. 'I expected you to sleep late after your big night at Nia's!'

Vanessa groaned. 'If only it had *just* been a big night at Nia's. Will Cara be getting up soon?'

'It's Christmas vacation. She and Sammy will probably sleep until seven thirty or eight.'

'I forgot about Sammy sleeping over. I'm glad he did and was surrounded by people.' Audrey looked at her quizzically. 'Please pour some coffee and I'll tell you what happened last night.'

Vanessa spoke in a low voice, starting with her and Max's arrival at Nia's, and didn't stop until she and Christian had found Zane's body and Libby was recounting to Wade that Zane had left but she didn't know where he'd gone. When she finished, Audrey's face had paled and her mouth was slightly open.

Vanessa looked deeply into Audrey's eyes. 'Are you going to say something?'

Audrey picked up both of their mugs, refilled them with coffee, and sat down again. She reached out and took Vanessa's hand. 'You're all right. Oh, thank God, you're all right. If something happened to you . . .' A tear ran down her face. 'And Christian is all right. I didn't know Zane, but . . .' She lowered her head. 'Oh, that poor, poor man.'

'His fiancé is shattered. She's so young – only twenty-three but she seems younger – and it's obvious she adored him.'

Audrey nodded. 'Do you have any idea who would do this to Zane?' Vanessa shook her head. 'What about you and Christian? Why were you even there? Why on Earth did you two go to the Diamond Rose?'

'I was at Christian's – I'll tell you why later – and he got a text telling him to come to the old nightclub. It was signed *Z* – Zane. Zane had been looking everywhere for Brody.'

'Ah – Brody,' Audrey said warily. 'I know he could be in this vicinity.'

'I think it's more than *could be*. Chris is certain Brody was in their house.'

'That would mean Brody is definitely roaming around Everly Cliffs. He's here because Roxanne is back.'

'Maybe. It could be merely a coincidence if Brody has gone off his meds.'

'Well, perhaps.' Audrey paused. 'Do you think Brody killed Zane?'

'Why on Earth would Brody kill Zane?'

'Lower your voice, Vanessa. You said Brody was off his medication.'

'If he is, that doesn't make him a killer.'

'For years you thought Brody kidnapped Roxanne.'

'Yes, but I didn't think he'd murdered her.'

Audrey frowned. 'Yes, you did.'

'I thought something had happened to her but not that Brody had killed her. Not intentionally, that is. There was less than twelve hours between the time she was taken and the time Gerald Montgomery delivered Brody to the hospital—'

'A lot can happen in twelve hours, Vanessa.'

'I know. I'm not saying I'm convinced Brody didn't take Roxy, there was an accident and she died. But Zane was Brody's best friend and the murder was so deliberate, so brutal—' Vanessa put her head in her hands. 'That wire slicing into his throat!'

'Stop picturing it,' Audrey said sharply. 'Tell me about you and Christian. Why were you with Christian last night? Because Zane made you feel guilty about not looking for Brody?'

'At first. And then . . . well, I realized I still love Christian. After all these years, Audrey! How could I not have known?'

Audrey smiled slowly, warmly. 'I knew, honey.'

'What? You did?'

Audrey nodded.

'Why didn't you say so?'

'It wouldn't have done any good. You'd made up your mind you didn't love him. You wouldn't talk about him. You avoided him. But I thought – I hoped – that when you saw him, you'd know. And you do.'

Vanessa swallowed hard to prevent tears. No one in the world knew her better than Audrey, except maybe Grace. She wondered what her grandmother would say about this news.

As if reading her mind, Audrey said, 'It's time for me to check on Grace. I won't say a word about the murder. Oh Lord, it gives me chills to say the word *murder*.'

'And don't tell the children, either,' Vanessa said.

Audrey tilted her head at her, and her eyebrows raised and mouth quirked.

'Oh, here I am giving orders about children when I'm not a parent and you and Derek are. Is Derek coming by this morning to pick up Sammy?'

'He said he would but I know he'll have a lot to do at Nia's, cleaning up after the party and getting things back in order. I told him Sammy could stay here today. Derek won't be here until evening.'

'Good.' Vanessa didn't think this was the time to tell Audrey she'd seen Nia at the restaurant and that Max had said perhaps Nia was trying to get back custody of Sam. After all, it was gossip. Besides, if it were true, Derek should be the one to tell Audrey. 'Wade wants Christian, Libby, and me to be at police headquarters at nine o'clock to give our statements. I'll call Libby now to make sure she's awake. Then I'll pick her up. At one o'clock, Roxy is being released from the hospital and I'll bring her home. I don't know how much of what's happened she'll already know. I'll deal with that later.' Vanessa stood up. 'I'd better get to work.'

Audrey rose and hugged Vanessa tightly. 'Sometimes life can be unbearably hard, Nessa, but if anyone can handle it, you can. Don't forget that.'

Vanessa knocked lightly on the door of room six of the Everly Cliffs Motel. She shifted from foot to foot, then knocked again. Had Libby gone back to sleep after Vanessa had called her? She raised her hand to knock a third time when Libby opened the door.

Her hair hung lankly around her alarmingly pale face and her lovely brown eyes looked almost sunken, lost in dark circles.

'Did I wake you?' Vanessa asked.

'No. I just can't seem to get it together. Could you help me get dressed?'

'Sure.' Vanessa stepped into the room, flipped on the overhead light and closed the door. 'I know what happened is awful, Libby. Devastating. Did you get any sleep?'

'A little.' Libby stood in front of her dressed in underpants and a bra, barefooted, her arms hanging limply. 'I feel like I've been beaten up.'

'That's understandable. I stopped on the way here and got you some coffee and a warm pastry. I know you think you don't want anything right now, but I guarantee caffeine and sugar will help.' She took the coffee and pastry out of the bag and handed them to Libby. 'What do you want to wear today?'

'I only brought jeans and sweaters.'

'That's fine. I'm wearing jeans and a sweater, too.' Vanessa sorted through Libby's clothes still folded in the suitcase. 'Any particular sweater?'

'The lavender one. Zane gave it to me.'

'It's beautiful.' Vanessa waited until Libby had finished her coffee, took the empty cup from her hand, pulled the sweater over her head, then found a brush and ran it through the girl's brown, silky straight hair. 'Put on your jeans and socks and boots and we're ready to go.'

The day was gray and rain had started about ten minutes earlier. Vanessa turned on the windshield wipers and Libby murmured, 'The sky is crying for Zane.'

Vanessa didn't know what to say. She kept quiet, occasionally glancing at Libby who remained expressionless. The trip seemed longer than it was and Vanessa was relieved when they turned into the parking lot of the city building where the police headquarters were housed.

'Here we are.' She turned off the SUV. 'Ready?'

'No, but that doesn't matter.'

They walked into the lobby of the square, shingled building and found Christian waiting for them. He stood and smiled at Vanessa. Libby stared at the floor.

'Wade wants to take our statements separately,' he told Vanessa.

'He wants me first since I was the one who found Zane.' He glanced nervously at Libby. 'Sorry. I didn't mean to sound insensitive.'

Libby shrugged. 'What does it matter who found him first? He's still dead.'

'You're right. But it's police procedure and Wade Baylor is an excellent sheriff. He's totally professional and dedicated to his job.'

'That's good. Zane deserves the very best.' Libby clenched her hands and stared out a window. Finally she said, 'Zane's parents are dead and he didn't have any brothers or sisters. There's no one to notify. His parents died in a fire but before that, they spent their summers at Everly Cliffs. That's where Zane met Brody and they were friends right off the bat. From the time Zane was sixteen, he lived with a grandfather who couldn't stand him. He thought Zane was a nut because of all the computer and tech stuff. When he died, he left his house and all his money to charity.'

Libby shut up like a toy that had wound down. Vanessa said, 'I'm glad he had you, Libby.'

'Oh, I'm nowhere near as smart as Zane. I know some of his friends wondered what he saw in me, not that he had many friends. Except Brody. And Max. Max was nice. Brody had a kind heart like Zane.'

'Libby, I'm sure you're a lot smarter than you think you are. And more importantly, *you* have a kind heart. I could tell the first time I looked into your eyes.' Vanessa smiled.

Libby's eyelids batted away tears. 'Oh gosh, I sure did love Zane.'

'And I know he loved you.'

Half an hour later, Vanessa saw Wade after he'd interviewed Christian. She told him about the evening as concisely and exactly as she could remember it, although she omitted her overwhelming fear of the mosgrum. It made her sound crazy. 'Now tell me what happened, Wade. Please.'

Wade looked at her with his sad, downturned brown eyes. 'The assailant attacked Felder with a Taser. It incapacitates the neuro-muscular system of the victim at a fifteen-foot range. Felder had been hit twice. I'd say he was limp and that's how the assailant dragged him to the piano and got him on the bench. That would have been fairly impossible if Felder was struggling.

Then the attacker used piano wire as a garrote and strangled Felder, cutting the carotid arteries, and finally slashed the jugular veins with a razor-sharp knife with a serrated edge to make sure he bled out.'

For a moment the room swam around Vanessa and she was afraid she'd pass out. But then Grace's face flashed in front of her. Grace wouldn't faint. For now, she would pretend she was Grace. 'I suppose Christian and I are in the clear.'

'For now. From what Libby said last night, she was in the shower and Zane called in to her that he had to go somewhere. Do you know if he got a text asking him to come to the Diamond Rose?'

'No, I'm not sure, but he sent a text to Chris to meet him there. Can't you check Zane's texts?'

'We could if we had his phone, but it's missing. We've searched every inch of the Diamond Rose, hard as that was to do. That place should have been torn down over twenty years ago.'

'Why wasn't it?'

Wade leaned across his desk. 'It was owned by Zachary Barnes. He *loved* that place and refused to have it torn down after a kitchen fire got out of control. He wouldn't even let the wreck of a piano be hauled away. The city council let him get away with it, which is a disgrace. Anyway, Barnes died eight months ago, his widow sold the land, and the Rose will be torn down this spring.'

'Who bought it?'

'Derek Sherwin.'

'Derek Sherwin?' Vanessa swallowed, thinking of Audrey. 'The man who owns Nia's?'

'Yes. He's a developer. He owns Nia's, the Everly Cliffs Café, some shacks down by the shore, and the Diamond Rose.'

'Do you know what he's going to build in place of the Diamond Rose?'

'An office building. I give him kudos for making plans to tear down that old eyesore.' Wade paused. 'And now the scene of a vicious murder.'

After seeing Wade, Libby had decided she was too shaken to drive back to Portland, so a friend was coming to pick her up. Zane's car would be retrieved when the police released it. Christian went back to the hospital and Vanessa dropped Libby off at the motel, exchanging phone numbers with her. Although neither one said it, they both knew the first call would probably be about Zane's funeral.

Glancing at her watch, Vanessa saw that she couldn't pick up Roxanne for nearly two hours still, so she decided to shop for clothes for her. Roxanne was two inches shorter than she and at present, at least twenty pounds lighter than Vanessa. She had nothing to wear, even home to Everly House.

Town wasn't crowded this morning and Vanessa wasn't surprised. No doubt news of the murder had circulated and a lot of the population had decided to stay in their homes on this dreary, rainy morning, which made the situation seem even more forbidding. She parked and darted into Jeans 'N' Things and bought two pairs of jeans a size smaller than she wore, a red and a sky-blue crew-necked cable-knit sweater and a pink turtleneck sweater. Pink had always been Roxanne's favorite color.

'Excuse me,' she said to a young female clerk, 'do you have shoes, socks and underwear?'

'Nope. You have to go down the street to Tanya's for underwear and Fordman's for shoes and socks.'

'I haven't shopped downtown for a long time. I've forgotten where everything is.'

'Well, there's not much of anything to choose from if you ask me,' the girl said glumly, reminding Vanessa of Roxanne eight years ago.

Vanessa walked down the street in the drizzle and bought underwear in Tanya's. Roxanne had been busty since she was thirteen and Vanessa chose two lace-trimmed bras along with five pairs of matching panties. Next she hurried to Fordman's for athletic shoes and socks. Finally she dashed into a discount store and bought a big, cushioned doggie bed for Queenie.

As Vanessa left the discount store, the vision of Zane Felder's body hunched over the piano flashed in front of her out of nowhere. She suddenly felt weak and disoriented, and stopped in the middle of the sidewalk, drawing in a deep breath. A flashback. An after-shock so strong it left her trembling. She knew if she didn't sit down, and have something to eat and drink, she'd be lying flat on the sidewalk.

She was afraid she wouldn't make it back to her car with her purchases. A few feet ahead of her hung the blue-and-white awning of the Everly Cliffs Café. Vanessa forced herself to walk steadily into its cheery interior of pale oak floors, blue-and-white striped booths against the walls, dark tables with cane-back chairs lining the middle of the restaurant, and glowing globe lights dangling from the ceiling. Vanessa sank down at one of the tables, piling her bags and Queenie's bed as close to her as possible so no one would fall over them. In a moment, a smiling dark-haired woman appeared beside her with water and a menu. 'Do you still have apple strudel?' Vanessa asked.

'Yes, ma'am. We have a fresh batch, as a matter of fact.'

'Oh, bless you. I'll have a double order and a large coffee with milk.'

'Coming right up, ma'am.'

Vanessa searched in her purse for her public cellphone. Earlier she'd given her private phone to Wade Baylor. She'd told him about the two anonymous phone calls she'd received – the first the night Roxanne was found and the second last night. She'd explained about the two phones – one for everyday use and the other strictly for communication with Audrey and Grace. She'd assured Wade that Audrey had protected Vanessa's phone number with her life and Grace probably couldn't even remember it. Wade had taken the phone, assuring Vanessa he would trace the number of the anonymous caller. 'He talks in a mechanically altered voice,' Vanessa had told Wade, 'but he remembers that I used to really like the George Michael song "Praying for Time". I don't know who could possibly recall that after all this time.'

'Do you ever listen to it when you're on set?' Wade asked. 'I mean in your trailer or wherever it is that you dress and wait for your takes.'

'Maybe. I listen to a lot of music, but I don't remember that one in particular. People give me playlists with more recent songs. I have to admit I'm fonder of the older stuff than rap or hip-hop though. Anyway, I should have told you after I got the first call, but I was so shocked about Roxanne's return that I forgot.'

'I understand,' Wade had said kindly. 'I'll get to work on it immediately.'

Now Vanessa called Roxanne to reassure her she would come to the hospital at one o'clock to collect her and that she was bringing clothes for Roxy to wear home. She was putting away the phone when a striking woman with long blonde hair stopped by her table and asked in a slightly cooing voice, 'Are you Vanessa Everly of *Kingdom of Corinna*?'

'Yes, I'm on the show.'

'I don't mean to intrude' – the woman said, pulling out a chair and sitting down, showing she had every intention of intruding – 'but I'd love to have your autograph, if it's not too much trouble.'

She slid a notepad and pen toward Vanessa and looked at her with eyes like Sammy's. 'My name is Nia. Please make it out to Nia.' Vanessa wrote, *Best wishes to Nia, Vanessa Everly*. The woman took back the notebook and frowned. 'I'd hoped it would be a bit more personal, but this is all right.' Vanessa stared at her, not offering to rewrite the note. 'I'm Nia Sherwin. I saw you last night at the Christmas party at the restaurant. My husband Derek owns it and he named it after me.' She smiled brightly. 'You looked lovely.'

'Thank you.' Vanessa studied her pretty face that didn't look as young as it had last night under the flattering lighting. 'I saw you, too. I thought you were Derek's *ex*-wife.'

'Oh, yes. I always forget to say *ex*. You were with Max Newman?'

'Yes, I was.'

'Max is so handsome. It's a shame he doesn't have a wife or at least a steady girlfriend.' Her perfect eyebrows rose slightly. 'Unless you two are dating now?'

'No. We were only out for one evening.'

Vanessa's order of coffee and double apple strudel arrived. 'My goodness!' Nia exclaimed. 'Are you going to eat *all* of that?'

'Every single crumb.'

'I've always thought it would be so nice to not worry about one's weight.'

'It is. I couldn't care less when I'm not filming.'

'Well! Aren't you a wonder! Of course, you look like you're naturally slender. Tall and naturally slender. Elegant. No wonder they chose you to play Queen Na'dya.' Vanessa wondered where this compliment fest was leading. Then she knew. 'I know you've met my husband, Derek Sherwin.'

'Yes, I've met your *ex*-husband. And Sammy.'

'Oh, Sammy, my little darling! Isn't he the sweetest?'

'He's a fine boy. Derek is doing such a good job raising him.'

'He's doing the job *I* started. Sammy and I weren't separated until he was nine,' Nia returned with an edge in her voice and color rising along her high cheekbones.

Vanessa took a sip of her coffee. 'Everything is really good here. Aren't you going to have anything?'

'I had a blueberry muffin. Well, half of a muffin. That's all I allow myself.' There was criticism in her tone as she watched Vanessa start on her second piece of strudel. 'I wanted to spend the day with Sammy, but Derek told me he's at Everly House with his little friend . . .'

'Cara Willis.'

'Cara . . . Cara Willis. I don't believe I remember a Cara Willis from Sammy's elementary school.'

'Maybe they weren't friends back then. She's Audrey Willis's daughter.'

'Audrey Willis. I think I remember her. Auburn hair?'

Vanessa nodded.

'Who is Cara's father?' Nia inquired.

'He's out of the picture. Audrey is a single mother. Do you have a problem with Sammy being friends with Cara instead of a little boy?'

'Heavens, no! I want Sammy to have lots of friends. It's only that I didn't know until Derek told me that Sammy is a frequent visitor at Everly House. I hope he hasn't been a bother.'

'Just the opposite. We all think he's delightful.'

'Do you suppose anyone would mind if I pop in to see Sammy?'

'My grandmother has a broken hip. We try to keep visitors limited, so today probably wouldn't be a good time.'

'Oh.' Nia's lids dropped down and Vanessa expected to see tears. Either Nia couldn't work up any or she knew that would be a step too far. 'I think I know what's going on. Derek has enlisted you to keep Sammy away from me.'

'I don't know of any such plan.'

'You wouldn't admit it, of course. You're doing it for Derek. You think he's a saint and I'm a whore.'

'I don't know much about either one of you.'

'Then you don't know that I had good reasons for leaving. Derek Sherwin isn't what he seems.'

Vanessa looked at her. 'What *is* he?'

'I prefer not to malign my son's father.'

'How very discreet of you.' Vanessa dabbed at her mouth with her napkin. 'Well, I'm full and I have somewhere to be, so I must hurry.' She stood up. 'I hope you enjoy your visit to Everly Cliffs, Nia.'

'I thought you'd forgotten all about me!'

Roxanne sat on the side of her hospital bed, her legs dangling over the side, her feet bare, her blonde hair hanging messily. But she was smiling.

'It's only twelve thirty-five! Your release time isn't until one o'clock.'

'I know, but I can't wait to get out of here and go home.' She glanced at the bags Vanessa was carrying. 'Are those clothes for me?'

'No, I thought we'd save money and just wrap you up in a blanket.' Roxy made a face at her. 'Of course they're clothes for you. Not a lot – I'm not sure about sizes. If they don't fit or you don't like them, I can exchange them.'

Vanessa laid the bags on the bed and Roxy began pulling out jeans and sweaters. 'They're perfect!' She held up a lacy bra. 'And these are beautiful! It sounds dumb, but I used to think I'd never wear a lace bra again and that made me cry.'

Roxanne slipped out of her hospital gown and began sorting through the clothes. Vanessa didn't stare but she couldn't help seeing Roxy's thin legs and arms marked with healing scratches and fading bruises. In record time Roxanne was dressed in jeans and the sky-blue sweater. Everything was a bit loose on her but the shoes fit perfectly. 'A few good meals and the clothes will be just right. Thanks, Nessa. I don't suppose you brought any make-up.'

'I forgot. But I have some pink lipstick.'

'I can rub some lipstick on my cheeks. I'm white as a ghost. And they have this piece of white gauze and white tape on my forehead to cover the stitches. I don't want Grace to see it. Do you happen to have a flesh-colored bandage?'

'No. But she probably won't notice. Don't worry about it. You look great.'

Roxanne grinned. 'You really *are* a convincing actress. Let's say I look better than I did when I got home.'

Vanessa opened the last bag. 'I also got you a wool jacket with a scarf and hood. I have to warn you there are news people out front. I let the hospital administrator know and he agreed to let us go out the emergency entrance. The car is close by.'

'Oh thanks, Nessa. I haven't looked at newspapers or the internet since I've been here. I haven't watched any news shows on TV.'

Thank goodness, Vanessa thought, although Roxanne's mood obviously expressed that she didn't know anything about the murder last night.

'That's good. You can catch up on the news when you get home.'

'I know. But when it comes to people seeing me leave the hospital, I feel . . .' Roxy frowned, 'embarrassed by what happened to me. Humiliated. I know everyone can imagine what I went through. But all I want now is privacy. Privacy and my family.' She looked at Vanessa and gave her a beautiful smile. 'Please take me home.'

ELEVEN

In spite of having left via the hospital emergency exit, they'd picked up a couple of paparazzi – one group in a van and another in a car. As Vanessa sped up the hill to Everly House, she used the remote control to open the double garage doors. She made a quick turn into the shelter and closed the doors behind her.

'That was slick!' Roxanne laughed. 'How long do you think they'll sit outside waiting for us?'

'I'd say in twenty minutes they'll realize we've entered the house through the garage. Of course they could always wait to catch sight of you at a front window.'

'Can't Pete chase them away?'

'Pete wrenched his knee the night we had the intruder in the lighthouse tower. He's still not very mobile.'

'No one told me he was hurt!'

'We didn't want to upset you. Anyway, I called earlier and asked Audrey to close the drapes so no one can spy on us.'

'Vanessa, you amaze me. But after all, you've become a big television star nearly overnight. You've had to learn press-dodging tricks in a hurry.'

'I'm not as famous as you seem to think. The show hasn't even finished its first season.' She smiled. 'Ready to go inside?'

'More ready than you can imagine.'

They opened the door leading from the garage into what they called the mudroom, with the washer, dryer, ironing board, racks for freshly washed clothes, pegs for coats and shelves for outside shoes. Vanessa and Roxanne took off their coats and hung them up, then hurried into the kitchen where Cara and Sammy sat at the table playing a game. They both looked up blankly, then Cara cried, 'Aunt Roxy!'

'That's right! How did you know? You've never met me!'

'Mommy told me you were coming home today and that you're blonde and beautiful! Isn't she blonde and beautiful, Sammy? This is Sammy Sherwin. Sammy, this is my Aunt Roxanne Everly.'

Roxanne went to Cara and hugged her tightly. 'Oh, you're a beautiful one!' She pulled away and looked at her face. 'I've not known you almost all of your life.' Her gaze turned to Sammy. 'And what a handsome friend you have! Sammy, I've heard you're a wonderful boy!'

Sammy's face turned bright red. 'Thank you, Miss Everly.'

'It's *Roxy*. I'm so pleased to meet you.'

'Me too. You, I mean.' Sammy turned even redder. 'Welcome home.'

'Roxanne?' A scratchy voice called from beyond the kitchen. 'Roxanne, is that you?'

Roxanne ran from the kitchen to the living room and then into the library. She stood at the door a moment, looking at Grace lying in her hospital bed wearing a blue bed jacket. 'Grace! Oh, Grandmother!' Roxy rushed to Grace, sat down gently on the edge of the bed, and embraced the frail woman. 'I never thought I'd see you again.'

Roxy's tone surprised Vanessa. She sounded almost desperate for her grandmother's joy and tenderness, a major change from her attitude when she was fifteen.

'Did you miss me?' Grace asked coolly.

Roxy pulled back, her blue eyes searching Grace's solemn face. 'Did I miss you? Of course! Every day. Every single day.'

'And you were missed, child. This house turned into a dark place without you. But you know that, don't you?'

Vanessa was taken aback by her grandmother's detached voice and lack of facial expression. Roxanne's smile faded. She looked bewildered and definitely disappointed.

'Certainly your grandmother is overjoyed to see you,' Audrey intervened. 'How could she not be? It's a miracle, Roxy.' She smiled regretfully. 'It's also past Grace's nap time. She's almost too tired to talk.'

'I'm not,' Grace returned querulously. 'If I could have a rum and Coke, I'd be fine!'

Audrey nodded. 'In honor of the occasion, you'll get exactly what you want, Grace. A rum and Coke coming right up!'

Vanessa followed her to the kitchen. 'What's wrong with Grace?'

'She's been cantankerous all day. I don't think she feels well but she won't admit it.'

'Are you really going to give her rum and Coke?'

'What difference does it make? She absolutely refused her noon medicine and I'll only put a dab of rum in her drink. Maybe she needs to think she's in charge for a while.'

'Does she know about the murder last night?'

Audrey put a bit of rum in a glass, poured in Coke and dropped in three ice cubes, then stirred. 'I don't think so. She's dozed through most of the television news shows. The children don't know either, but I have to tell Derek when he comes to pick up Sammy. He may not want his son to stay here after he knows that you . . .'

'That I what? Murdered Zane Felder?'

'*Found* him. And lower your voice. The kids will hear. Let's get back to Grace and Roxanne.'

'Wait. Audrey, I have to tell you something.' Audrey paused. 'Nia Sherwin is back in town. She was at the party last night. Today I stopped for a snack at the café and she sat down with me. She wanted to come here to visit Sammy.'

Audrey's expression froze. 'She was at the party with Derek?'

'Not *with* Derek. Sort of following him around.'

'Oh. Well, she *is* Sammy's mother. She must want to see him.' Her voice sounded robotic. 'It's really none of my business.'

'Audrey, it's me you're talking to. You're interested in Derek. And he's interested in you. It certainly is your business.'

'Audrey!' Grace nearly screeched. 'My drink!'

'Geez. She *is* in a mood,' Vanessa said. 'I thought she'd be so happy that Roxy's home.'

'So did I. I'm concerned about her,' Audrey muttered as they hurried into the library to find Grace scowling and Roxy still sat beside her. She looked hurt. 'Here we go!' Audrey handed Grace the glass. 'This will make you feel like a new woman, Grace!'

'Thank heavens.' Grace took a slurp and spilled some down her chin. 'Goddammit!'

Grace never cursed. They all gaped at her for a moment before Roxy grabbed a tissue and dabbed her grandmother's chin. 'There. All better.'

'How embarrassing,' Grace said angrily. 'I can't even drink properly!' She turned to Roxanne. 'Did you expect to see your grandmother in this condition?'

Vanessa could tell Roxy was groping for a tactful answer. 'Anyone can spill their drink when they're drinking lying down. I spilled plenty when I was in the hospital. It's not a big deal.'

'I didn't offer anyone else anything to drink,' Audrey declared. 'Roxanne?'

'Oh, a Coke.'

'OK. Vanessa?'

'I think I could use a rum and Coke, too,' Vanessa said. She followed Audrey to the kitchen again. As they passed the dining-room table where the kids were working a puzzle, she asked the kids, 'In the mood for Cokes?'

'Sure,' Cara said. 'Unless Sammy wants milk.'

'I do *not* want milk.' Sammy sounded offended as if Cara had insulted his manhood. 'I'll have a Coke, too. Please.'

'I know you won't be having a rum and Coke, being on duty and all,' Vanessa said to Audrey when they reached the kitchen, 'although don't be insulted if I say you look like you could use one.'

'I would like to have a very strong margarita. What a day! You found a dead body less than twenty-four hours ago, Brody Montgomery is probably roaming around town off his meds, Roxy is home after eight years, Grace is acting strange, *Nia* is back.' She looked upward. 'God, *why*?' Vanessa couldn't help laughing. 'I'm glad you think it's all funny, Nessa,' Audrey snapped.

'Oh, I don't. Believe me, I *don't*. I think I'm hysterical. Honestly.' Suddenly tears rose in Vanessa's eyes. 'I've been on auto-pilot since we found Zane – running around, shopping in the rain, putting on a happy face for Roxy, having an unwanted conversation with nosy Nia Sherwin – but inside' – she let out a tiny sob –'I'm s-shaking . . .'

Audrey pulled her into a hug. 'Calm down, honey. I'm going to call Christian tonight and ask him to come over. I'm worried about Grace. I'm worried about you. For now I'm fixing *you* a very strong rum and Coke.' She made Vanessa's drink and gave her the glass. 'Drink this. And then maybe you'll need another, but right now let's get back to Grace and Roxy.'

To Vanessa's relief, Grace was smiling at Roxanne, who looked more sure of herself. 'Your hair is still long and that lovely shade of blonde although you look at bit pale, dear,' Grace commented. 'Vanessa, don't you think Roxanne looks pale?'

'She just needs a good dinner and a night's sleep in her old bedroom.' She looked at Roxy. 'You do want to stay in your old room, don't you?'

'Sure I do. Could we go up now? I'd like to see it.'

'Certainly. Let's take our drinks and leave the clothes until later.'

In a minute they stood in the pink creation that had been Roxanne's bedroom since she was five. She gazed around, then burst into laughter. 'Exactly how many shades of pink are in this room?'

'Six. I've counted. Mom let you have as much pink as you wanted.'

'Even the carpet is pink. *Hot* pink! And the magenta-colored tassels on the valances are too much!'

'Do you hate it now?'

'I love it! I wouldn't change a thing.' Roxanne walked over to her white dresser and opened the jewelry box. Inside a ballerina began turning and the sounds of 'Waltz of the Flowers' tinkled through the room. 'You don't know how many times I danced to that until I got a CD player.'

'I was so glad when you got that player. I was sick of "Waltz of the Flowers".'

Queenie stood at the doorway, looking at Roxanne. She bent and held out her hand. 'Come here, beautiful girl!'

The dog cast a look at Vanessa as if asking permission. Vanessa nodded her head and gestured toward Roxy.

In a moment Roxanne was rubbing the collie's face. 'She's a lovely dog, Nessa. You said she was a gift from the cast of your show?'

'Yes. They knew I loved dogs and a few of them thought I'd done a good job this year and deserved an award. Frankly, I'd rather have her than an Emmy.'

'Sure about that?'

'Well, I'd like to have both, but I'm certainly not counting on an Emmy, especially considering the staggering talent of some of my castmates.'

Queenie walked over and gently touched Roxanne's guitar with her nose. 'Have you missed playing?' Vanessa asked.

'Yes. I should have taken my practicing more seriously.'

'You were good.'

Roxanne picked up the guitar, tuned it, and stumbled halfway through the introduction to 'Tears in Heaven'. She stopped and laughed. 'Oh yeah, I was one of the greats, Nessa!'

'Don't be so hard on yourself. I doubt if you've had much time to practice the last few years.' Roxanne's smile disappeared. Her expression went stony. 'Oh, Roxy, I'm sorry! What an insensitive thing to say. Please forgive me.'

Roxanne gave her a tight smile. 'It's OK. You're right. I haven't held a guitar since I left here.' She set the guitar aside. 'Tell me about Grace. Is her health worse than you let me know or did she not want to see me?'

'Roxanne, of course she wanted to see you. When she found out you were back, she said it was a miracle, and Grace doesn't believe in miracles, if you remember. She's having a bad day with the Alzheimer's and the broken hip that isn't healing as quickly as we'd hoped. I think she's in pain but she won't admit to weakness. And she's mad at herself for being sick and having to depend on other people. You know how independent she's always been.'

'I used to resent her. Mommy would let me have and do anything I wanted, but not Grace. I was glad she went to Paris after Grandfather died. I hated it when she came home. I've told you before, I was a spoiled brat and I know it.' Roxanne smiled slightly. 'She cramped my style. But now I appreciate the woman she was – is. I don't want to see her weak and sick.'

'She'll bounce back. All it took was a little bit of rum to improve her mood this afternoon!'

'Yes, it did, but she can't drink rum all the time.'

'If Christian comes tonight, he'll know what to do about her.'

Roxanne grinned. 'What do you mean *if* he comes? I'll bet nothing could keep him away if you're here.'

'We didn't expect to see you so early,' Audrey said when she opened the front door to Derek. 'It's only four o'clock.'

His smile was weak. 'May I come in and talk to you privately? It's about Sam.'

He knows about Vanessa finding Zane Felder and he also knows about Brody Montgomery being in the area. He doesn't want Sammy to come here anymore, Audrey thought. She couldn't blame him.

'Certainly. I was getting ready to start dinner. Would you mind joining me in the kitchen?'

Grace was dozing, the children were playing a video game, and Vanessa was upstairs with Roxanne. Audrey led Derek into the kitchen without having to say a word to anyone. The many white cabinets brightened the dreary day. The caramel-colored oak floor gleamed and a yellow table runner decorated the rectangular antique pine island.

'This is very nice,' Derek said appreciatively as he sat down on one of the stools at the island.

'Grace remodeled it three years ago. The appliances were ancient. Ellen Everly didn't do much cooking and they haven't had a full-time cook for a long time.'

'Maybe full-time cooks are a thing of the past.'

Audrey pulled a covered platter of chicken breasts from the refrigerator. 'We're having chicken with bacon and cheese. The kids love it.' Audrey turned on the oven and began rinsing the chicken breasts. 'You wanted to talk to me about Sammy?'

'Yes.' Audrey heard the reluctance in his voice. 'Something totally unexpected has happened. Nia has come home.'

'Oh. She wants to get back together?'

'With me? Absolutely not. She's still with the movie producer she left me for, but according to her, she misses Sam desperately and wants him back in her life.'

Audrey stopped rinsing, turned and looked at him. 'You mean she's just now missing him desperately?'

'Funny how that happens, isn't it?' Derek asked bitterly. 'One day you pack your bags and leave, for three years you never even try to see your son, you send him a Christmas and a birthday card. One year the birthday card was six weeks late.'

'Maybe you'll have to give her visitation rights.'

'I wouldn't want to do that much but even if I did, it wouldn't satisfy her. She wants full custody.'

Audrey gaped at Derek. 'That's ridiculous!'

'That's what I told her but she didn't seem to take me seriously.'

'Vanessa told me she saw Nia at the party last night and again today in the café. Apparently she was talking about how she missed Sammy and how much she wanted to see him. She knew he was here, and all but invited herself for a visit.'

'That's my problem. She's determined to see him and I don't want her to – not even for an hour. Her leaving without so much as a goodbye to Sam nearly broke his heart. He cried every night for months. His schoolwork suffered for two years. The school counselor asked to see me because Sam's behavior had changed so much – he was withdrawn, silent, barely looking at the other students. He'd been a popular kid. He gradually got better, but he didn't act like his old self until he made friends with Cara this year.' Audrey saw the misery and fear in Derek's eyes. 'I can't let her do that to him again. I *won't*!'

The fine lines in his forehead looked deeper and his face was taut.

'You've seen her this afternoon, haven't you?'

'She came into the restaurant announcing herself to the staff as my *wife*. She started out by trying to charm me. When that didn't work, she tried playing on my pity. She said she'd made a mistake in not even trying to get custody of Sam. She realized that now. When that failed, she got nasty. She's the boy's mother and courts favor the mother, she told me. Even if she didn't get custody of him, did I want to drag him through a nasty court battle? Because she was more than ready to fight me.' He sighed. 'I don't want her to see him, Audrey. When I asked if he wanted to see her, he got really agitated.'

'He has been a bit different today. He got touchy when Cara suggested he might want milk.'

Derek smiled tiredly. 'Milk? Well, it's beginning. She upsets him.' Derek looked at her sheepishly. 'I won't leave Sam at home with a stranger. If I take him to the restaurant with me, Nia will barge in demanding to see him. I wonder if . . . well, I hate to ask, but he's so happy here and I wonder if he could stay full time for a few days. If it's any trouble at all, I want you to say no. You won't hurt my feelings or offend me or—'

'Derek, I know Sammy would be welcome here, but this might not be the safest place in the world.' Derek frowned at her. 'I'm sure you've heard that Brody Montgomery is missing. Years ago the police thought he kidnapped Roxanne.'

'But he was cleared.'

'Well, yes, but he *is* schizophrenic and Roxanne has moved back into this house as of this afternoon. If he's come after her—'

'That's a big *if*, Audrey. As far as I know, no one has seen him in Everly Cliffs.'

'Not that I know of. But there was the murder of Zane Felder. Vanessa *found* him.'

Derek's frown deepened. 'How awful for her! Was she alone?'

'No, she was with Christian Montgomery.'

'God, that's terrible. I'm so sorry for her.' He paused. 'So I'm sure with everything going on, you'd rather Sam didn't stay here. I understand. It was too much to ask.'

'No, you don't. I'm only trying to be completely honest. This isn't like an FBI safe house. We're having a few problems. To tell you the truth, I won't feel completely safe until Brody Montgomery is found.' Audrey hesitated. 'But given the alternative, I think Sammy *should* stay here. It's safer than your home with a stranger or the restaurant where Nia could walk in and take him. Here he'd be surrounded by people who care for him and I guarantee Nia will not make it past the front door. Of course, I'd have to ask Nessa—'

'Ask Nessa what?' Vanessa strolled into the kitchen. 'Are you two hatching nefarious plans?'

'Only to have Sammy stay here for a few days,' Audrey said. 'You see, Derek is in a spot—'

'In a *spot*?' Vanessa looked at him compassionately. 'Nia has come home after three years and she wants to insert herself into Sammy's life. Of course you're in a spot! Derek, we won't let Nia tear up Sammy's life again if we can help it. Sammy is welcome to stay for as long as you and he want. All he needs is some more clothes from home.' She smiled warmly at Derek. 'He's already like one of our family. And if Nia causes any trouble, Grace will give her a send-off she'll never forget!'

Derek's face relaxed and the look in his eyes softened. 'Thank you so much, Vanessa.'

'It's our pleasure,' she said casually as she left the kitchen.

Derek looked at Audrey. 'You don't know what this means to me. And . . .' his voice thickened, '. . . and you, with your warmth and your honesty, don't know what *you* mean to me.'

Grace coughed and Vanessa sat down beside her on the bed. 'Do you feel all right, Grace?'

'I've felt better.' She reached for Vanessa's hand. 'Darling, I may not be long for this world—'

'Don't say that!'

'Not saying it doesn't make it true.' She looked into Vanessa's eyes. 'You know I'm leaving almost my entire estate to you. You will be the guardian of your mother and see to all of her expenses, of course. She can't cope with them herself.'

'I know that. I'll always see that Mom gets the best of care.'

'And I've left a bequest to Pete.' She smiled. 'For meritorious service for all these years.'

'Yes, certainly.' Vanessa paused. 'But now that Roxy is home . . .' Grace cocked her head. 'Well, I thought you would want to make changes to your will. I believe that after Dad died, you left everything to me because Roxy had been gone for years. We didn't think we'd ever see her again.'

'I didn't think she'd be back.'

'But now that she is, you'll want to amend your will, won't you?'

Grace looked down, then back up at Vanessa with faded green eyes. 'Where has she been?'

Vanessa was startled. 'A lot of places. She was a prisoner. Her kidnapper dragged her around—'

'Never mind.' Grace patted her hand. 'There's time enough for changing my will.' She started coughing. 'When I'm feeling better.'

Three hours later, Grace was still coughing as Roxanne sat beside her. 'Are you sure you're OK?' Roxanne asked.

'I have a tickle in my throat.' Grace looked at Sammy and smiled. 'Frederick, why don't you come and read Mother a story? You read so beautifully.'

Sammy's gaze skimmed uncertainly around the room. Audrey came to the rescue, as was becoming increasingly common. 'Yes, *Sammy*, if you don't mind, why don't you read a little bit to Grace? She'd enjoy that.'

'OK.' He sat down by Grace's bed and picked up one of the several books that lay on her bedside table. '*War and Peace* by—'

'Oh, that's far too long, Frederick,' Grace said. 'How about a short story by Poe?'

All the child needs is to be scared silly by a Poe story, Vanessa thought. 'Maybe the beginning of Halprin's *Winter's Tale* would be better. Is that all right with you, Sammy?'

'Sure. Whatever Grace likes, but I like Edgar Allan Poe, too. My favorite story is "The Tell-Tale Heart".'

'Oh, I love that one!' Grace exclaimed.

Vanessa looked at Audrey and shrugged. 'Whatever you two want, but don't wake Audrey and me up at two in the morning when you're having nightmares.'

'Don't worry about *us*,' Grace announced cockily. 'We're fright-proof!'

Grace and Sammy thought this was hilarious. Grace actually cackled and Vanessa hadn't heard Sammy laugh so joyfully for days. His entire expression had lightened after his father had told him he'd be staying with the Everlys over Christmas and Derek would be visiting every day.

Sammy had only read the title when Cara pulled a chair near Grace's bed, sat down and began listening intently, tilting her head until her gleaming black hair was almost touching Sammy's bright blond. Vanessa noticed that in an attempt to impress her, Sammy pitched his voice deeper. They were joined by Queenie, who carried her beloved toy Dom and lay down beside them.

'"I think it was his eye! Yes, it was this!"' Sammy read with husky drama. '"One of his eyes resembled that of a vulture – a pale, blue eye with a film over it. Whenever it fell on me, my blood ran cold; and so by degrees – very gradually – I made up my mind to take the life of the old man"' – Sammy's voice took on a shiver – '"*and thus rid myself of the eye for-e-verrr . . .*"'

The doorbell rang. Cara shrieked, Sammy flung the book in the air, and Queenie jumped up, barking furiously.

'I knew Poe was a bad choice,' Vanessa said drolly as she went to the front door. She opened it and faced a smiling Christian.

'Anyone here need a doctor?'

'Several more of us than five minutes ago.'

Christian stepped inside and winked at Vanessa like he used to do when they didn't want to make a public display of kissing. 'How's everything going tonight?'

'Fine. We've found out that Sammy will be spending Christmas with us and we're overjoyed, especially Grace. It turns out they have the same taste in literature. He's been reading "The Tell-Tale Heart" to us at Grace's request.'

'Oh, shoot. And there I thought Cara was squealing with joy because I'm here!' Christian teased as Cara giggled and lightly elbowed Sammy in his side as if to let him know he had a rival. 'I suppose Queenie is barking with ecstasy at my arrival, as well.'

'Of course. Everyone is over the moon.'

Roxanne sat curled into a chair. 'Hi, Christian. Hard day at the hospital?'

'They're all grueling, beautiful. I know you're glad to be home.'

She smiled. 'I can't begin to tell you, Poe and all.'

'You feeling all right?'

'Fine. Better than fine.' She held up a cup. 'Chamomile tea. It's supposed to be calming so I'll sleep well.'

'I had *rum*,' Grace announced. 'What do you think of that, Dr Montgomery?'

'I think rum isn't prescribed.'

Audrey hurried to Christian's side and murmured, 'She's been extremely difficult today. She wouldn't take her meds at noon. Later, I let her have a tablespoon of rum in a Coke. She settled down then.'

'If she hadn't had any medication, a tablespoon of rum certainly wouldn't have hurt her. If it made her happy, you did the right thing,' he reassured her.

Audrey looked relieved.

'Did she eat much dinner?'

'No. She only nibbled,' Audrey said. 'And she's been dozing and coughing more than usual today.'

'All right.' Christian raised his voice as he walked into the library. 'So what's up today, Grace? Are you on a diet? Going on strike against your medication?'

The children and Queenie scattered as Christian sat down by the bed. 'I'm just not hungry today,' she said. 'I don't see what all the fuss is about. As for my medication, I don't think it's doing me one bit of good. I still can't walk.'

'It's too soon for you to be walking. You're not Superwoman.'

'I used to be. Funny that when you're young, you never think about how lucky you are to feel well and when you're old, all you think about is how well you once felt.' It wasn't like Grace to indulge in self-pity or refer to herself as old. 'I'm so sick of lying on this bed,' she went on, 'but I feel tired all the time, especially today. And I'm peevish. I *hate* being peevish!'

Christian laughed. 'You're allowed to be peevish now and then.'

'I'm afraid it will become a habit.' Grace sighed then brightened. 'Did I tell you that I had rum today?'

'Did you really? Three or four glasses on the rocks?' Christian smiled and Grace laughed. 'Let's get your temperature and take your blood pressure. You'll have to take off that pretty bed jacket.'

'Leonard bought the jacket for me,' she explained, although Vanessa had given it to her for her birthday. 'He has wonderful taste.'

'Aunt Vanessa, your cellphone is on the dining-room table and it's ringing,' Cara told her.

Vanessa went in the other room and picked up her phone. 'Hello?'

'It's Wade Baylor. I'm sorry it took so long for me to get back to you. The anonymous calls you received were made from a prepaid cellphone. TracFone. It's possible to trace calls from them but extremely difficult.'

'Oh, darn,' Vanessa said. 'Well, at least you have the phone to which the calls were made. Maybe another one will come. Or the caller might start ringing me up on my other cellphone.'

'That still wouldn't help us track the origin of the calls. And we have no idea how the caller got your private number. I hope you don't get any more.'

'Me, too, although *you* might get one on my phone. The caller doesn't know I turned my private phone over to you.'

'I'm sure he has your public number. You still might get another call. If so, let me know immediately.'

'OK.'

'How's everything else going, Vanessa?'

'Oh, so-so after the horror of last night. I brought Roxanne home from the hospital today. She doesn't seem to feel bad physically but Grace hasn't been her most welcoming. I don't know what's wrong with her. Christian is here now giving her a quick check-up. And Derek Sherwin asked if Sammy could stay with us because his mother has come back to town determined to take him away with her.'

'I barely know Derek but I thought Nia didn't want Sammy.'

'That was three years ago. I don't know what's up with her. Anyway, Derek doesn't want to keep Sammy at the restaurant with him – her access to the boy would be too easy – so he's staying here. He seems happy and we're delighted. We all love Sammy.'

'At least something is going right. We still don't have any leads on Zane Felder's murder, by the way. The killer was very careful not to leave any physical evidence. Did his girlfriend leave for Portland today?'

'Yes. The poor thing was a wreck.'

'No wonder. It will be a couple of days before we can release the body. We're looking for relatives. All Libby knew was that his parents are dead and he has no siblings. I've tried reaching Zane's lawyer today but he wasn't in. I'll try again tomorrow.'

'Libby mentioned a grandfather to me. Zane's parents died when he was sixteen and Zane lived with the grandfather who died a few years ago.' She paused. 'I just remembered Max Newman knew Zane! Maybe he can help you.'

'Max knew Zane? How?'

'He lived near Brody and Zane in Portland. I don't think he was close to Zane – not like he was to Brody – but he still might know something about Zane's background that Libby is too shaken up to remember.'

'I'll get in touch in with him. Are you OK, Vanessa? You had a terrible shock last night.'

'It hasn't been a great day but I'll recover once I stop flashing back to visions of Zane at that piano. Lord, what kind of ghoul would think up that horrid scenario? Why not kill him and leave him lying down?'

After a pause, Wade said, 'Zane was posed at the piano because we *are* dealing with a ghoul – someone who doesn't only want to murder but to create a horrible image no one would ever forget.'

And he had.

TWELVE

Vanessa lay in bed listening to Queenie breathe in her own bed on the floor where she slept with Dom safely tucked under her chin. The dog's presence was calming and Vanessa was once again thankful that the crew of *Kingdom of Corinna* had given her the gift. On her own, Vanessa might not have gotten a dog because of the time she spent away from home, but she'd always wanted one not for protection, but for love.

She'd stayed up later than anyone else. Grace had fallen asleep early and Audrey had taken advantage of Grace's drowsiness to go to bed before her usual eleven o'clock. Christian had pronounced Grace well, although he told Audrey and Vanessa he'd heard a bit of rattling when she coughed, which would be caused by phlegm in her lungs. He wanted Audrey to keep track of her coughing in case she was developing pneumonia. Audrey had been concerned, but Vanessa was certain her mind was on more than Grace. Probably it had something to do with her long talk with Derek before dinner.

On her way to her bedroom, Vanessa had peeked in Sammy's door. He lay sprawled in the middle of the double bed, his mouth open. Further down the hall, she'd quietly opened the door to Roxanne's room. Roxy had rolled into a ball, her hands clenched into fists, the sheet and blanket thrown off her thin body. Vanessa tiptoed to the bed and pulled the blanket up to Roxy's chin. She'd murmured incomprehensibly then snuggled deeper under the blanket. She'd slept the same way when she was a little girl.

Now in her own bed, Vanessa looked at the Jane Austen novel that lay open on her lap. She couldn't concentrate. She sank even deeper into the down pillows piled behind her and worried about Libby. She was a delicate girl full of emotion and tenderness. Vanessa also realized how much Libby had loved Zane. *Poor, shattered girl*, Vanessa thought. She'd gotten Libby's home landline phone number and her address before she'd left the young woman in the motel room to wait for her friend to take her back to Portland. *I'll call her in a couple of days*, Vanessa told herself. *I'll go to Zane's funeral and I'm sure Christian will want to go, too. We'll offer all the support we can.*

Then there was Roxanne. Was Roxanne all right? She knew Roxy was doing well physically – better than expected – but Grace's cool reception seemed to have hurt her. True, telling Roxy that Grace had changed during the last eight years was one thing. Confronting the reality was something different, especially when Grace hadn't really seemed at all glad to see Roxy. Vanessa had received a warmer greeting when she'd arrived for Christmas.

But Grace wasn't doing well. Vanessa could tell when Christian was trying to downplay a worrisome situation. She didn't know if Grace's condition was bad, but clearly she wasn't doing as well as they'd hoped. The Alzheimer's seemed worse, she was losing her appetite and she had a rattling cough. Maybe she was having a bad day or perhaps this was the beginning of many bad days.

Vanessa finally felt her eyelids grow heavy and then shut. Images began floating through her mind: the party at Nia's with good-looking, happy Max; Nia trying to wheedle her way into Sammy's life as she talked to Vanessa at the café; Roxanne's disappointed expression as she joyously greeted her blasé grandmother; Sammy reading 'The Tell-Tale Heart' with Cara's head leaning toward him—

Out of nowhere, she heard a shrill scream. She would have thought she was dreaming of Cara's scary-story inspired shriek when Christian knocked on the door earlier, but Queenie jumped up from her bed, barking loudly. The dog shot to the open bedroom door and out of the room.

'Wait! Queenie!' Vanessa floundered in the sheets and blanket then her feet found the floor and she ran after the dog, not bothering with slippers or a robe. As she emerged from her bedroom, she saw Queenie heading down the hallway at the same time as another scream tore through the house. Vanessa passed Roxanne's closed door and Sammy's open one. She glanced in. He wasn't in bed. He was in trouble, she thought frantically.

She held the banister as she ran down the staircase, afraid she'd trip on her pajama legs that were a tad too long. When she reached the bottom, Queenie had already disappeared but her barking came from the direction of the kitchen. Vanessa stubbed her toe on a chair leg, yelled 'Ouch!' then limped into the kitchen where Sammy stood rigid and white-faced while Audrey and Cara milled around him.

'What's wrong?' Audrey nearly shouted. 'Are you hurt? Did you cut yourself with that knife?'

'*Knife!*' Vanessa cried. 'Sammy, why do you have a knife?'

Cara stroked his arm. 'You don't have to tell the grown-ups what happened. Just tell me. I won't let you get in trouble.'

Sammy finally focused on Cara, who took the knife from his grip. 'It's only a dull dinner knife,' she told Audrey and Vanessa. 'Show them your hands, Sammy, so they can see you aren't dripping in blood.'

Sammy turned mechanically and held up his uncut hands. The women both let out deep breaths. Queenie had stopped barking but went to the boy's side, as if to protect him. 'What's wrong, Sammy?' Vanessa asked gently. 'Why did you scream?'

'I woke up and I was hungry. I came downstairs to have a peanut butter sandwich. I put the bread on a plate and spread the peanut butter – I didn't use a ton of peanut butter, I promise – and I was cutting it because Dad told me that was the polite way to eat a sandwich. I was standing right here beside the sink and I looked up and—'

All gazed anxiously at his pale face and big blue eyes.

'And?' Cara prompted.

'And a man was standing outside staring in at me. That's what was so scary. He kept staring at me. Peeping Toms run away. He didn't. Even when I screamed he didn't move.'

'What did he look like?' Vanessa asked.

'He had light brown hair that was longer than most guys' hair around here. His eyes were blue. He seemed younger than my dad. I believe girls would think he was handsome. He looked sort of like Dr Montgomery.'

Vanessa willed herself not to glance in alarm at Audrey. Could the man have been Brody Montgomery? Or had the Poe story Sammy read earlier frightened him into thinking he saw someone staring at him – staring at him with a blue eye like the man in the story? Only Sammy didn't say this man had only *one* blue eye. And he said he was young and handsome.

'Are you sure it wasn't Pete McGuire who works here?'

'Mr McGuire? He's *ancient*!' Sammy exclaimed.

'When did the man run away?' Cara asked.

'When I screamed the second time.' Sammy's face had turned red. 'I screamed like a scared little girl. I'm sorry I woke up everyone.'

Cara smiled at him. 'Anyone would have screamed. Even a grown-up man. It doesn't mean you're not brave.'

'All right. We had a *staring* peeping Tom,' Vanessa said. 'We're not going to let it ruin our night. The doors and windows are all locked and we have Queenie to protect us so we're as safe as safe can be.'

'Are you sure?' Cara asked.

'Yeah, she's sure. We're safe.' Sammy's voice suddenly sounded more mature and Vanessa knew he was trying to recover from his embarrassing screaming fit. 'I'm not a bit sleepy.' He looked at Audrey. 'Can Cara have a snack and stay up to watch TV with me? Just for fifteen minutes.'

'Fine,' Audrey said. 'Do you want a peanut butter sandwich, Cara?'

'I sure do,' Cara announced. 'What do you want to watch, Sammy?'

Audrey nodded at Vanessa and they walked out of the kitchen. They saw that Grace was sleeping and looked more peaceful than she had all day. 'Good.' Audrey paused. 'Nessa, who do you think it was?'

'You know I think it was Brody,' Vanessa said reluctantly.

'Are you going to call Wade Baylor?'

'No. I'm going to call Christian.'

Max Newman buried his hands in the pockets of his wool pea coat and stared out over the ocean. He'd never liked walking on the beach at night. He didn't think it was romantic – only lonely and sad, especially on dreary days and after sunset. But his business was photographing and painting the beach. Occasionally someone like Grace Everly wanted something different like paintings of lighthouses, but they were still associated with the sea. He supposed it was his destiny to be dependent on a part of nature he didn't like. His dreams of creating avant-garde art for gallery showings in New York City galleries had died years ago.

He sighed and reached into his pocket for his cigarettes, cupping his hand against the wind to light one. He didn't smoke a lot, but he also didn't drink a lot because he didn't handle alcohol well, but tonight he'd done both and he'd probably drink even more when he got home. Home – the two-story house decorated in 1970 and not touched since then. His mother had made him promise before she left him the house in her will that it would remain exactly the same. Even some of his grandmother's things lay stored in the attic. Sometimes he could still smell the potpourri his mother had sprinkled all over the place. Of course he could redecorate and she'd never know now, but he didn't have the money or the enthusiasm. He didn't care how the damned house looked or smelled as long as everything worked.

Tonight he was in a funk. He'd sold a painting and a large, framed photograph at the store. That should have made him feel somewhat happy since it was winter when sales were always down, but it didn't – not after Jane Drake dropped in and announced that not only Christian Montgomery but also Vanessa Everly had found the body of Zane Felder. Wade had told Jane that they'd been together when Christian got a message to come to the Diamond Rose. Vanessa and Christian *together*! Jane had smirked when she told him, knowing he'd been with Vanessa just hours earlier at the party. *She dumped you and ran straight to Christian*, her eyes said. *What do you think of that, you loser?*

It wasn't as if Max had a 'thing' for Vanessa. He hadn't even seen her for years. But they'd had such a good time at Nia's. She'd looked beautiful and she'd seemed pleased to be with him. He'd been thrilled to be with her – the television star. He knew they'd made a striking couple. He knew she'd had a good time, even though she acted strained when they'd sat with Jane and Simon Drake. Then there was that unfortunate confrontation with Zane as they were leaving. Damn Zane! Why did he have to attack her and try to make her feel guilty for not pounding the pavement looking for Brody? Zane was an oddball and unpredictable, but he'd never made Max really angry until then. Apparently something he'd said had gotten to Vanessa, though. She'd run straight to Christian, which Max felt was a slap in the face to him.

He finished his cigarette and dropped it in the sand. Then he realized he was nearing the *Seraphim May*. The shipwreck was a big tourist attraction and when he was young, the local kids had been fascinated by it. He'd taken photos of it but he'd always hated it. He would never have admitted it, but the wreck gave him the creeps. And there it was, an ugly rotting hulk stuck in the moist sand and looming against the nightscape. Max wished it would turn to dust and blow away.

He was pulling another cigarette out of the pack when his gaze turned from the ship and saw a man walking toward him. He was tall and moved with long, energetic strides, his arms swinging as if he were bursting with energy. 'Max!'

Max felt alarm spike through him. 'Brody?'

'Yes. What are you doing out here? You hate the beach at night.'

They were only a few feet apart now and Max's stomach fluttered. Everyone was searching for Brody Montgomery, the dangerous schizophrenic off his medication. Max knew the alcohol he'd consumed had befuddled his thinking, made him so careless he was taking a risk by walking the beach alone at night. He hadn't given Brody a thought. But now Brody was smiling. Max decided the safest behavior was to keep things light and casual.

'I was bored and restless at home. Nothing good on TV. The house suddenly felt like it was closing in on me. What are you doing on the beach?'

They were face to face now, Brody a couple of inches taller than Max. His longish hair blew in the slight breeze and his face was thinner than the last time Max had seen him. His jacket hung open over a dark sweatshirt, his hands were empty, not holding a weapon as Max had feared. 'I'm looking for someone.'

'Oh, who?' Max went cold, mentally kicking himself. 'Not that it's any of my business. Maybe I should just let you look.'

'You can help me.'

'Well, I might go home.'

Brody's smile faded and he stared at Max who felt like Brody wasn't going to *let* him go home.

'Or we could go to Hoppy's Bar for a beer.'

'Hoppy's Bar?' Brody repeated slowly. 'Is it still open?'

'I think it was the first business in Everly Cliffs and it'll be the last!'

'I don't want a beer.'

'They have other drinks, guy. What was it you used to like? Bourbon?'

Brody said flatly, 'I don't drink anymore. I don't play tennis anymore. I don't have friends anymore.'

'You don't have friends? What am I? C'mon, let's go to Hoppy's.'

Brody's expression suddenly changed from blank to suspicious. 'Why are you determined to get me to Hoppy's?'

Max was so tense he couldn't move. 'I don't want to go home. I'd like to have a few drinks with a friend. I don't have any alcohol at home . . . I just . . .'

'You just *what*?' Brody's voice deepened and took on an edge. 'You just want to get me in a public place so someone will call the police? They're looking for me.'

'They are?' Brody stared. 'Brody, settle down. I didn't give it a thought.'

'Are you the one who's been watching me, spying on me?'

'Spying on you? I don't even know where you're staying.'

'You're trying to trap me.' Brody's blue eyes narrowed and his body twitched. 'You're against me. You've *always* been against me, even in the tournaments—'

'The tournaments? What tournaments? Oh, the tennis tournaments? We were competitors! Sure I wanted to win. That's only natural. It was only a game and we were kids, Brode-man.'

'*Do not* call me *Brode-man*. I am Sir Brody, you,' Brody's voice rose, 'you, traitor, lurking around the beach at night trying to catch me! Do you hope to get a reward? Is that it? Don't you have any honor? You are supposed to offer protection and aid to a fellow knight!'

'I'm not a—'

Before Max had a chance to move, Brody's right fist punched him in the abdomen, knocking what felt like every ounce of air from Max's body. He groaned and bent double before a fist struck his jaw. He heard a sickening grinding sound in his jaw and tasted blood. The world spun before it went black and he fell to the damp beach sand.

THIRTEEN

As Christian drove up the hill to Everly Cliffs, he saw that every porch light shone. He stopped the car at the front porch steps and hurried to Vanessa, who sat huddled in a robe, house slippers, and a blanket. She jumped to her feet when she saw him and in a moment he was hugging her tightly.

'Chris?'

'Yes?'

'I can't get my breath.'

'Oh, God, I'm sorry,' he said, loosening his grip but not letting go. 'What are you doing out here?'

'Waiting for you.'

'But if someone's wandering around . . .'

'He's not going to snatch me off this blindingly bright porch. You can probably see me from downtown.' She buried her head against his chest. 'I'm so glad you're here.'

'So am I. I wish I'd stayed when I was here earlier. Is Grace all right?'

'She slept through everything. I checked on Roxanne and she was asleep, too, which surprises me.'

'You never get much sleep in a hospital. There's noise all night. She's probably just catching up. And Grace wore herself out today. Anyway, tell me again what happened.'

On the phone she'd explained to him about Sammy getting up to fix a sandwich and a man looking in at him. 'Sammy said he had light brown hair, sort of long, with blue eyes, and he looked like you.'

Christian sighed and closed his eyes. 'Well, that pretty much nails it. Brody was here looking in your kitchen window.'

'And he wasn't scared off easily.'

He sank down in the rocking chair Vanessa had abandoned as Pete McGuire limped up the walk leaning on his crutch. 'Don't even bother telling me nothing's wrong,' he said. 'The place is lit up like a carnival. What's happened?'

'Nothing you can help with, Pete,' Christian said.

'I've got a sore knee. Big deal. I'm still strong as an ox.'

Vanessa and Christian exchanged looks. Even when he was young, Pete never had above-average strength – only a talent with tools and machinery.

'Pete, we've had what's probably just a peeping Tom, but we're not sure,' Christian told him. 'We're not going to call Wade because you know the cops are looking for Brody so we don't want to distract them. I'd like to have a chance to find this guy myself, but I'm not comfortable leaving the women and kids alone. Would you stay with them while I scout around and see what – or who – I can turn up? I'd feel better and I know they would.'

'Well . . . well, sure. A house full of young women need a man to watch over them.' Vanessa swallowed a groan, forgiving his sexism. 'I'd be glad to stay. I'm not one bit sleepy and I can still put up a fight, bum knee or not.'

Vanessa knew Wade should be here – Wade with backup. But she had to give Christian one last chance to catch his brother and safely take him home, even if she knew it wasn't the safest course of action.

She stood on her tiptoes and kissed Christian hard on the mouth. 'Be careful. I love you.'

'Love you, too.' Christian looked at Pete. 'You take good care of those women.'

Vanessa almost made a face at him, knowing he was teasing her. 'Yes, Pete, we'll all feel safer with you guarding us. The kids are watching TV but they'll go back to bed in a few minutes.'

Pete hobbled into the house. He'd never mastered the crutch and Vanessa was glad he'd only need it for two or three more days. Meanwhile, Christian turned on the flashlight and gave her a bracing smile. 'Everything will be all right. Don't worry about a thing.'

But Vanessa knew the words were hollow. Christian knew there was a lot to worry about, especially if he found Brody.

Christian circled the house although he knew no one would be lurking beside a home with lights glowing from almost every window as well as a number of outdoor lights illuminating the lawn. After one circuit, he started down the steep hill toward the beach. He didn't take the path. If someone were hiding, they wouldn't place themselves in plain view on the path. He poked through knee-high brush, angled past scrub pines and slid on mossy spots growing under foliage. He aimed the flashlight at the ground, not wanting to shine it all around him and announce his presence. A breeze blew in the smell of ocean water and a full moon shone with cold, silvery light, making the beach look unreal and eerie.

The peeping Tom could have run down the hill in front of Everly House, but Christian felt he wouldn't have gone in that direction because of the lights illuminating most of the hill. *I'd run for the beach*, Christian thought. *No one would be likely to navigate the cliff to chase me.* He paused. What was really driving him toward the beach? Brody's love of it, especially at night. He was certain, after all, that he was searching for his brother.

When they were young, they'd spent hours walking on the beach, trying to get tans without looking like they were tanning, exploring the *Seraphim May*. Their bond wasn't linked only to the ocean, though. Their father used to charter boats to take the boys fishing on the Columbia River and although neither

Christian nor Brody excelled at the sport, they always had a good time.

Christian wondered as he trudged along, discreetly flashing around his mechanical beam, how long had it been since he and Brody had walked on the beach together? Three years? No, longer. Five years. It had been a warm, crystalline afternoon and Brody was happy until he'd seen some people he'd graduated from high school with. Most had turned their heads, refusing to acknowledge him, and the word *lunatic* floated from the group. Brody had nearly run from the beach and didn't leave their house for two days until he returned to Portland.

A mist was rolling in and Christian stopped. This walk on the beach was accomplishing nothing except stirring up memories. He wanted to bellow 'Brody!' but it would only alert the few people he had seen on the beach that Brody Montgomery was near the ocean. He looked at the luminous dial on his watch: *12:45*. Vanessa had called him at 11:20. Sammy saw the peeping Tom around 11:10. If Brody had been around then, he was long gone, tucked away in a hiding place Wade and the other cops hadn't found.

Reluctantly, Christian turned around and began walking back toward the path up the hill. The wreck of the *Seraphim May* lay ahead of him, but he knew without looking that Brody wouldn't hide inside it. Although he would never admit it, Christian knew something about the wreck had always made Brody uneasy. When he was off his meds, Brody tended to be paranoid. He wouldn't take refuge in a crumbling wreck that had caused him anxiety even before he got sick. Christian dismissed the shipwreck and looked at the towering rock formation jutting out of the sand not far from the *Seraphim May*. He remembered that Vanessa used to say it should have been in *Lord of the Rings* with its ominous jagged edges pointing to the sky. He smiled, thinking of what a vivid imagination she'd always possessed.

Then he heard it: a soft groan. He slowed his pace. There it was again. He squinted through the mist but saw nothing. Still, he knew he had heard *something*. Something that sounded like a man. It could have been Brody.

He walked to the rock and looked around it at the side that faced the ocean. There huddled a man, his knees drawn to his abdomen, his face turned to the sand. Christian kneeled and peered

at him, then gently turned his face just enough so he could identify
him. His jaw jutted unnaturally to the right, blood ran from his
mouth, and his eyes were closed, but Christian knew without a
doubt he was looking at Max Newman.

Christian called Vanessa on his cellphone and told her he'd found
an injured Max and to call an ambulance. He was afraid to move
Max without a cervical collar for c-spine stabilization. He couldn't
examine Max here on the beach at night so he didn't know how
badly Max was injured. All he could do was sit beside him,
frequently taking his pulse and checking his breathing as he waited
for help. The emergency team couldn't get Max to the hospital
for at least twenty minutes, having to descend the cliff and then
ascend it wielding an ambulance stretcher and he didn't know how
long Max had been lying here. He took off his jacket and spread
it over Max, wondering why he had been wandering on the beach
at this hour. He didn't remember Max having any particular fondness for the beach but then to be fair, he barely knew him. It was
Brody who'd been friends with him. And his number one rival on
the tennis court. But that was ten years ago.

  Christian had told Vanessa he and Max were at her Dark Tower
rock, but after twenty minutes, he turned on the bright flashlight
so the emergency workers could find them more easily. As soon
as the light beamed, Max groaned again, but he still didn't wake.
Christian knew he had a concussion but he wasn't sure if Max's
jaw was broken or dislocated. He'd run a finger around the inside
of Max's mouth and found a loose second bicuspid on the left
side. Max could have swallowed it and choked. The rest of his
teeth seemed all right, even if a couple were slightly loose. His
lip was split and would probably require a stitch or two. Without
X-rays, though, Christian couldn't assess the true extent of the
damage.

  He looked up and saw lights coming slowly down the path. He
felt as if he'd been sitting here an hour although the emergency
services had actually arrived with amazing speed. Christian stood
up and waved the powerful flashlight Vanessa had given him to
help the squad find him.

  Twenty minutes later they arrived at the emergency-room
entrance of the hospital, where the staff were busy with an elderly
man who'd gotten a bad shock when plugging in an old string of

Christmas lights he'd placed on his roof. Max was taken to a second room and transferred to the examination table. To Christian's dismay, Jane Drake was on duty and dashed to the side of the new patient. She frowned at his face then asked Christian, 'Isn't that Max Newman?'

'Yes.'

'What happened to him?'

'I'm not sure.'

A doctor named Parker stepped in to begin the examination. 'Has he regained consciousness?' he asked Christian.

'He's groaned a couple of times but that's all.'

'How long ago was he injured?'

'I don't know, but I found him around half an hour ago.'

'We need to get him to X-ray,' Dr Parker said. 'I don't think his jaw is broken but—'

At that moment, Max's brown eyes opened slowly then shot from left to right in panic. Dr Parker leaned close, within Max's range of vision. 'You're in the hospital. You're safe. Blink twice if you understand me.' Max blinked twice. 'That's good. You're going to be fine.'

Jane leaned over him and smiled. 'It's me – Janey Drake. Don't worry about a thing, Max. You're in the best of care.'

Max seemed to relax slightly and so did Christian until Max's injured jaw moved slowly, obviously painfully, and he ground out, 'Brody.'

'Brody Montgomery did this to you?' Jane shrilled.

'Brody,' Max repeated. 'Brody . . .'

FOURTEEN

Vanessa stood at the top of the house's tower, looking out at the lights dancing like fireflies on the beach. At least eight policemen were searching for Brody Montgomery and she had a view of the entire area surrounding Everly Cliffs as they hunted him.

Audrey had tried to keep her out of the lighthouse. 'It's freezing in there!'

'No, it isn't, but I'll wear a coat.'

'You'll be all alone!'

'Audrey, calm down. I'll take Queenie with me and lock us in with our new deadbolt. No one else has a key. Believe me, Brody is not going to storm the lighthouse tonight.'

'And how do you know that?'

'Because Brody is running for his life,' she said bleakly. 'He's not going to come here, even for Roxanne.'

Audrey glared. 'I don't know what the hell makes you think you can read his mind, Vanessa.'

'I don't either. Please don't be so mad. Pete is staying in the house tonight but we all need you.'

'Apparently *you* don't need me, but I know there's no changing your mind when it's made up, even if you're being foolish.'

'That's right. Even when I'm being foolish.'

Which is exactly what Wade Baylor told her when she called him after she heard from Christian, who said Max had regained consciousness in the emergency room and said Brody had attacked him. Wade already knew – Jane had immediately been on the hotline to him.

'Why didn't you call me after Sammy saw Brody at the kitchen window?' he'd demanded.

'Sammy didn't know who was at the window. He gave a vague description.'

'How vague?'

'He said the man was young and had light brown hair and blue eyes and . . . and looked a little like Dr Montgomery.'

'Oh. And that was so vague it didn't occur to you he'd seen Brody? Don't bother answering. That's why you called Christian instead of me. Vanessa, you astound me! Brody Montgomery probably murdered Zane Felder. *Murdered* him! He also probably kidnapped your sister eight years ago. I know you used to be friends with him. I know you were in love with his brother. Maybe you still are, but you can't expect me to believe you thought calling Christian instead of me was the sensible thing to do.'

Vanessa had sighed. 'No, Wade, I knew the *proper* thing to do was to call you. However, I believed you'd arrive with a search party and if Brody was around, he'd run. I thought that maybe if he saw his brother—'

'He'd throw himself into Christian's arms?'

'No, but he might not . . . I don't know . . . flee the area. I don't know how else to put it. I believed if he saw only Christian, Brody might hide but not vanish.' She drew a deep breath. 'I still believe that.'

'What you're saying sounds good but it doesn't make sense in light of what Brody's done and I'm sure that no matter what you're telling yourself, you know it.'

'I'm sorry, Wade. I'm sorry I didn't do what you think was the right thing and I'm sorry you don't understand it.'

Wade had taken a couple of deep breaths then said more calmly, 'Do you think Brody's close by?'

'I don't know. Honestly, Wade. I'm not hiding anything from you.'

'You hid something when it really mattered. I'm ordering an immediate search for him, Vanessa, and we won't give up until morning.'

Wade had hung up on her and she understood his anger and frustration. Perhaps Brody was a violent threat to Roxanne, although he hadn't tried to break into the house. He might have been in the lighthouse a few nights ago, though. And he'd beaten Max, although she didn't yet know the extent of Max's injuries. She couldn't bear to think about Zane Felder. Surely to God, Brody couldn't be capable of slitting his best friend's throat.

But who else would have done it?

Vanessa pulled her coat tighter then bent and stroked Queenie, who seemed uneasy in this unusual space reached by a four-story wooden spiral staircase, surrounded by glass and topped by a metal dome. The dog had left Dom in Sammy's room as if for safekeeping. She'd explored her surroundings, sniffing the black leather loveseat, the table with maps and tide charts stored beneath a glass lid, some low shelves holding books and candles, and the small serving table on which Vanessa had placed a thermos of coffee, a few chocolate chip cookies, and some dog treats. Finally Queenie lay down on the thick, gray shag area rug Vanessa had bought and placed in the room two years ago.

'Do you like it up here?' Vanessa asked. The dog looked at her with mournful eyes. Vanessa smiled. 'I'm being selfish.

You'd rather be with Cara or Sammy but I need you tonight, sweetie.' Queenie let out a long, beleaguered sigh that made Vanessa laugh.

Vanessa sat down on a padded leather chair on rollers and pulled it up to the telescope, aiming it at the beach directly ahead. Squinting through the lens, she watched waves roll in, crest, and break. If she'd been looking through the telescope earlier, she would have seen Brody on the beach, she thought with regret. Maybe she could have prevented the attack on Max, wondering how badly he was hurt and knowing the assault had only made things worse for Brody. That's what she should have done as soon as Sammy saw Brody at the window, she thought. She could have been searching for Brody through the telescope while calling Christian, a call that had enraged Wade but for which she still didn't feel entirely guilty.

Her cellphone rang.

'Hi, Chris. How's Max?'

'He has a concussion, a dislocated jaw, a missing tooth, and a cracked rib. He's in quite a bit of pain but he'll be OK.'

'And he definitely identified his attacker as Brody?'

'Yeah. He hasn't described how they met on the beach, though. What are you doing?'

'Sitting in the lighthouse looking at the cops searching for Brody. They seem to be everywhere. Do you have any idea where he went?'

'Absolutely none.' He paused. 'You always liked the lighthouse but I didn't expect you to be there tonight.'

'You thought I'd be huddled in terror with my family?'

'I don't know. I suppose we should have called Derek and given him the option of picking up Sammy.'

'Derek's getting a good night's sleep and Sammy is safe. You didn't want them both up half the night.'

'Wade is trying to be the best sheriff he can, especially considering the poor job his predecessor did.'

'I understand. And technically, I did do the wrong thing by calling you.'

'I'm glad you gave *me* a chance to find Brody, even if I didn't have any luck.'

'You found Max.'

'The police would have, too, if you'd called them.'

A short silence spun out before Vanessa said, 'I plan on spending most of the night in here. It's cold but would you like to join me? I know you must be tired but—'

'I'll be there in fifteen minutes.'

Vanessa led Queenie down the spiral staircase to the first floor of the lighthouse so the dog wouldn't charge ahead and perhaps fall. She glanced at her watch and after exactly sixteen minutes, Christian tapped on the door. Queenie barked once. Vanessa flipped the deadbolt and opened the door.

Christian smiled, the fine lines around his eyes deeper than usual. 'Hiding out?'

'How did you know?'

'Because you used to retreat to your tower to brood when you were upset.'

'What a memory you have! I was a kid when I did that.' She leaned forward and kissed him. 'I'm glad you're here.'

'I parked halfway up the hill. I didn't want to disturb anyone in the house.' He held up a bottle of wine, a corkscrew, and a plastic bag containing two glasses. 'For our nerves.'

'I need it. Please come in, sir.'

First Christian kneeled and rubbed Queenie's ears, then he followed the two of them upstairs. He opened the wine, poured two glasses, and handed one to Vanessa before they sat down on the love seat. He took a gulp of the white wine, leaned back his head and closed his eyes. 'God, I'm tired.'

'No wonder. You can't be getting much sleep considering how you're stressing about Brody. Then last night you found Zane and tonight Max. I'm surprised you can stand up.'

'I can't. Not for a while at least.'

Vanessa pulled the blue wool afghan on the arm of the love seat over their laps. Then she grasped his right hand and put her head on his shoulder. 'I always loved this tower. The only other person who did was Grace. She and I spent a lot of time here talking and looking out at the ocean.'

'I didn't know that.'

'I never told you. Anyway, I think it's cozy. That's why I always came here. I felt safe, locked away from the world, high above it all.'

'The tower isn't really very tall.'

'You have to use your imagination.'

'You've always had more imagination than I have. That's one of the things that makes you such a good actress. You can lose yourself in a scene, act as if it's all real.'

'Thank you. My parents never understood why I wanted to spend my life "pretending", but you did.'

'I didn't think talent like yours should be wasted, even if it took you away from me.'

'Even if I were as talented as you seem to think I am, it wouldn't have taken me away from you.' Vanessa hesitated. 'It was something else.'

'You mean *someone*. Brody and what you believed he did.' He tilted her head up so their gazes met. 'Vanessa, even when he was in the midst of his worst episodes, I never knew him to be violent. Whoever took Roxanne beat you. I knew Brody couldn't do that to anyone. And then tonight . . .'

'Max was beaten and you know Brody did it. You can't run from that realization.'

Christian seemed to deflate, to somehow shrink into himself. 'Something has changed with him. I have to accept it now. But murder? No. My brother is not a murderer. Someone else killed Zane Felder. I don't know who, I don't know why. I only know that my brother didn't slash his best friend's throat.' His voice rose. 'He didn't, Vanessa. He *didn't*—'

'Stop, Chris.' Her voice was firm. 'I don't want to talk about this anymore. I don't want you to think about it anymore. Not tonight. You might not know it, but you're at your breaking point.' His eyes shifted away from hers and he stared almost sullenly at the opposite wall. 'I want you to try to forget everything bad that's happened and relax.'

He laughed sharply. 'Forget everything bad that's happened? Yeah, that's easy.'

'Don't be sarcastic. I'm trying to help. I'm worried about you, Christian.'

'A week ago I wouldn't have believed you could be worried about *me*.'

'I never stopped caring about you or thinking about you. Not for one day. But now you need more wine.'

She refilled his glass. He took a gulp, then rested his head against hers. 'Your hair smells good.'

'These days I use ridiculously expensive shampoo and conditioner.'

'It always smelled good. I remember. We used to lie beside each other and you'd spread your hair over my chest. I loved that. It felt so intimate, so protective.'

'Then let's trade Queenie the love seat for the rug. It's thick and soft.' In a minute, Queenie lay on the leather seat and Vanessa and Christian arranged themselves on the shag rug. Vanessa covered them with the blue throw, then put her head on his shoulder and spread her hair across his chest. 'There. Does that feel the same?'

'Not quite. You used to spread it on my bare chest.'

'Then take off your shirt.'

Vanessa unbuttoned his shirt and opened it, then lay down and arranged her hair once again. 'How's that?'

'Wonderful.'

'Are you cold?'

'Not at all. I feel like I'm floating on a warm breeze while I'm holding you in my arms.' He raised his head and took another drink of wine. Then he lay back and was quiet for a while. Vanessa thought he'd drifted to sleep until he asked, 'What made you follow me into the Diamond Rose?'

'I was worried about you, naturally.'

'There was something else. When I first saw your face, you looked terrified. I know a lot of people might be terrified in that situation, but not you. You looked panic-stricken but also kind of *knowing*. What did you think you knew?'

Here it was, Vanessa thought dismally. She was in love with Christian. There could be no more evasions with Christian. She would have to tell him the truth, even if he thought she was crazy.

'When I was a child, my father told Roxanne and me a story.' She went on to recount the tale of the night the family had driven past the Diamond Rose at night and her father had told them about the mosgrum. 'He said it was a thousand-year-old evil spirit that crawled from the burning depths of the Earth and set the Diamond Rose on fire then laughed as the people burned. The story scared me so badly that for years I was haunted with fear of that terrible creature. The night you went in the building, all

of my fear of the mosgrum came flooding back. I thought . . .
well, that it was waiting inside for you.'

'A mosgrum? What a horrible story to tell two little girls!'

'It was a couple of months after his father died and his first
bout of heavy drinking.'

'Nevertheless . . .' Christian was quiet for a moment before
he asked, 'And even though you're still afraid of the mosgrum,
you came rushing in to protect me.' His arms tightened around
her. 'You dear girl.'

'I don't believe in the mosgrum anymore but last night the fear
of it washed over me as if I were eight again and had just heard
about it. I didn't think twice about coming after you.'

'You love me.'

'Yes, Christian, I love you. You know I do.'

'It seems too good to be true. I've missed your love for so long.
Right now your love is the only bright spot in my life.'

'I know how much Brody means to you. He always has. There
was never any sibling rivalry.'

'No. That may have been because we were so different. I was
always the scientist, even when I was a little boy. Brody was the
kid who read fantasy novels, who was intrigued by medieval tales
of King Arthur and the Round Table, who wrote magical stories.
He wasn't interested in chemistry sets like me.' Christian was
silent. 'He was the charmer.'

'He was charming, Christian, but so were you. My God, do
you think I would have been attracted to a guy who couldn't talk
about anything except science? You knew everything about current
affairs and history. You had an overwhelming desire to help other
people through practicing medicine or participating in charities.
And you were . . . you seemed . . . devoted to me as a person,
not just a girl you thought was pretty.'

'That's exactly how I felt about you. You're four years younger
than I am. When we started dating, you were seventeen. So many
people thought I was taking advantage of a young girl, but you
never seemed young to me. You had a sensibility and wisdom
that far surpassed mine. That didn't threaten me. I thought you
were the most intriguing person I'd ever met.'

'Wow,' Vanessa said weakly. 'I didn't know that's what
you thought of me.'

'But you knew I loved you.'

'Yes, I did. I thought we'd always be together, that nothing could drive us apart.'

'But something did.' Vanessa didn't know what to say. She lay quietly as Christian stroked her hair. 'Do you know that I never got a hint that my brother was interested in Roxanne? Never. She was just your little sister.'

'She was very beautiful and looked older than fifteen. She managed to be around him every chance she got. I always thought she had a crush on him.'

'He's almost six years older than she is.'

'That wouldn't matter to a young girl who's infatuated with a man.'

'But Brody wasn't infatuated with her. I would have known if he was. He never flirted with her. He never stared at her, no matter how skimpy her outfit was. I don't think he paid much attention to her at all. He was interested in Beverly Cowan. They even went out a few times.'

'Beverly Cowan! I'd forgotten all about her.'

'She was what we called a "computer nerd". She wasn't especially pretty and certainly not popular, but Brody thought she was fascinating. When he got sick the first time, she disappeared from his life. Three or four years later she married a guy from Texas and moved to Dallas. But my point is that Brody liked girls his own age – not adolescents like your sister.'

'Then why did he fixate on her when he got sick?'

'I have no idea.' Christian turned on his side to face her. 'Let's not talk about Brody anymore.'

'You brought him up.'

'I know. It's hard for me to get my mind off him.' He smiled. 'There's only one person who can completely wipe him from my thoughts.'

'And who is that?'

'Don't be coy,' Christian teased. 'It's you, of course.'

'And you tend to wipe everyone and everything from my thoughts, too. What a strange coincidence.'

'Astonishing.'

Christian leaned down and kissed her forehead, then each cheek, then her chin, and finally her lips. He drew away but she put her hand behind his head and pulled him down again. She kissed him long and deeply, wondering how she could have lived eight years without kissing those warm, soft lips she loved so much. How many times had she kissed them in the past? A hundred? Five hundred? Not enough.

'Are you warm enough?' Vanessa asked.

'I've never felt warmer in my life.' He kissed her again. 'How about you?'

'The same as you.'

'Do you think we should shed some of our clothes or would Queenie be too shocked?'

Vanessa glanced at the dog lying on her side across the full length of the love seat, her eyes closed and snoring softly. 'I don't think Queenie even knows we're alive.'

Vanessa stood up, took off her coat and pulled her sweater over her head and slipped off her jeans, glad that she'd worn her prettiest bra and panties. Then she slid back under the blue afghan.

'You still have the most beautiful body I've ever seen,' Christian murmured.

'I'm glad the years haven't taken too much of a toll.' She grinned. 'Now you.'

Christian stripped, got under the cover, and pulled her close to him. Vanessa ran her hand down his side to his thigh. 'And you still look like someone from Greek mythology.'

'Who?'

'Achilles. He was extremely strong and beautiful.'

'A force to be reckoned with except for the tendon in his heel.' He was silent for a moment. 'Brody is my Achilles heel.'

'No, he isn't. He won't be the cause of your downfall, Christian. I know it.'

'You have great faith in me. Honestly, I don't know if my father was lying and even if he was, I wasn't supporting his lie.' He looked deeply into her eyes. 'I have *never* lied to you, Vanessa, and I never will.'

'*Will*. That sounds as if you think we have a future.'

'Don't you?'

She closed her eyes and pulled his body closer to hers. 'Yes, Christian. I want to have a future with you. You are my one and only, my other half, and you always have been.'

They kissed and caressed and murmured endearments, joining their bodies long into the cold and lonely night.

FIFTEEN

'Are we going to get a Christmas tree today?' Cara asked. Vanessa smiled. 'We certainly are! Your mom wants to stay with Grace, but Roxanne is coming with Sammy and you and me to pick out the perfect tree. Does that sound like fun?'

'Lots of fun. Is Aunt Roxy really coming with us?'

'I was surprised, too, but she says she wouldn't miss it. She hasn't gotten to help select a tree for years.'

'Oh.' Cara's beautiful face turned solemn. 'Is that because the people who captured her wouldn't let her?'

'Uh, yes.' *The people who captured her.* Had Audrey said that? It didn't sound like her. Cara had heard it somewhere else, maybe in school before the holidays. 'Anyway, she's really looking forward to coming with us. When she was a kid, she loved Christmas more than anyone.'

Cara smiled. 'Then I'm glad Sammy and I get to be with her for this one. It's gonna be awesome.'

Two hours later Vanessa, Roxanne, Cara and Sammy stood in the middle of a big lot filled with evergreen trees. 'Wow, these are the prettiest Christmas trees I've ever seen!' Cara exclaimed. 'How about you, Sammy?'

'They're lots bigger than the trees Dad and I've had for a few years.'

Cara took his hand. 'Let's go look at all of them. Is that OK, Aunt Vanessa?'

'As long as you don't leave the lot.' Cara took Sammy's hand and pulled him along, chattering and smiling. Vanessa turned to Roxanne. 'Does this bring back good memories?'

Roxanne had been quiet and didn't look especially happy although she'd asked to come with them. 'I'm not sure.'

Vanessa was surprised. 'Roxy, you loved Christmas. Even Mom stayed on her best behavior.'

'Because we had a lot of visitors at Christmas.'

'I don't think she cared about the visitors. She was really trying, especially for you.'

'But it was always as if she was never really there.' For a moment Roxanne seemed forlorn. Then abruptly she shrugged and smiled brightly. 'Oh well, that's water under the bridge. I want to forget the bad times and only remember the good.'

'Great. And this is going to be a wonderful Christmas, Roxy. I'm sure of it.'

A middle-aged man in jeans and a heavy red-and-navy-blue plaid jacket walked up to them, beaming. 'Looking for a Christmas tree, ladies?'

'Yes. A nice big one. This is a special Christmas for us,' Vanessa said.

'We've got some beauties this year. My name is Jackson. I'll take you on a tour.'

Vanessa called for the children who joined them as Mr Jackson led them around the lot, telling them about the various trees. 'This is a Douglas fir.' He gestured at a beautiful evergreen almost seven feet tall. 'It has a full body and you'll notice the tapered appearance – perfect for a Christmas tree. It also gives off a strong pine scent.'

They moved on to another one. 'This is a Nordmann fir. It has very strong branches that will hold heavy Christmas ornaments.' He grinned at the kids, who grinned back. 'It lasts longer than a lot of evergreens because the needles have waxy cuticles, but you don't want to hear about cuticles. As you can see it's very full. Beautiful.

'And here is a Noble fir. It has strong branches, and it's a lovely blue-green color. It also holds the needles for quite a while.'

'It was always my wife's favorite.' All five of them turned to see Simon Drake standing behind them. He wore an elegant black cashmere coat with a burgundy scarf rakishly draped behind his neck and left to dangle on either side. His jet-black hair was plastered into perfection. 'What a delight to see all of you.' His small, dark eyes shot to Roxanne. 'Particularly you, my dear. How are you?'

Vanessa was shocked to see that her sister had turned completely white. Her blue eyes looked huge and her lips trembled slightly. 'Fine,' she managed. 'I'm fine.'

'So glad to hear it. What an ordeal you must have been through.' Simon shook his head and clicked his tongue. Then he looked at Sammy. 'Are you Samuel Sherwin?'

'Yes, sir,' Sammy answered in a small voice.

'I know your father. Fine man. I can tell that you'll be a fine man, too, some day.'

'He already is,' Cara piped up.

'Oh, is he?' Simon turned his oily smile on her. 'I think *you* have a crush on him, young lady. You're a lovely girl. Don't waste all of your beauty on one boy.'

Cara turned bright red and Vanessa felt like kicking Simon. What an embarrassing, inappropriate remark to aim at the young girl. But then Simon had always enjoyed embarrassing females.

'Daddy! Daddy!'

Vanessa heard Jane's voice. She ran up to them, waving a small white bag at her father. 'I've been to the drugstore and picked up your sleeping pills.' She looked at everyone. 'You know how it is with the elderly – they have trouble sleeping.'

It was a perfect moment, and Vanessa almost burst into laughter as dark blood rushed to Simon's face and his lips tightened before he pried them apart and said, 'I am not elderly, as my daughter seems to think. I simply have a lot on my mind. Business affairs. I think about them so intensely I sometimes have insomnia.'

'Yes, well, whatever,' Jane said dismissively, then turned her attention to Roxy. 'Is this your first day out in the world?'

Roxanne nodded yes.

'Not a great start, I'd say. But then some people like the whole Christmas experience including picking out a tree to mess up the house,' Jane continued.

'Sweeping up a few needles is a small price to pay for having a beautiful Christmas tree,' Vanessa said as Simon tucked the white bag in his coat pocket and began wandering away, using his cellphone. 'We always went all out at Christmas.'

'Oh, I remember!' Jane's voice was loud. 'Lights everywhere! Music booming through the halls of Everly House! Quite grand. Quite a show.'

'Yes, it was. We won't be quite as grand this year, but we still intend to have a gorgeous tree.' Vanessa turned back to Mr Jackson. 'Excuse us for keeping you waiting. I'm going to let the kids decide which tree they want.'

Cara clapped while Sammy beamed. 'Let's look at them all again before we make up our minds,' Cara said to Sammy. 'This is *really* important.'

'I'll leave them to make the big decision. Call me when you need me,' Mr Jackson said, and turned to other customers.

'How's Grace?' Jane asked.

'All right. Getting tired of not being able to walk.'

'Oh, yeah, what a drag considering how active she always was.' Jane looked at Roxy. 'I think it's brave of you to come out today considering they didn't catch Brody last night. Wow, did he do a number on Max! Dislocated jaw, cracked rib, tooth knocked out. Wade should be the *first* to know if anyone's seen Brody.'

So Jane knows I called Christian instead of Wade when Brody was at the window, Vanessa thought. If we still had a town crier, Jane would win the job by a landslide vote.

'Have you come to pick out a tree?' Roxanne asked suddenly.

'Yes. I don't really care about it, but Wade wants a tree.'

'Then shouldn't he be helping you pick out one?'

Jane laughed. 'Oh, Vanessa, you know Daddy has better taste than Wade!'

Suddenly the children appeared, running to Vanessa. 'Sammy's mom's here!' Cara blurted. 'She's here!'

Sammy turned to stone as Nia Sherwin strode toward them, her blonde hair loose, her slender face intense.

'Sammy? Sammy, don't run away from Mommy!'

'Oh, do something, Aunt Vanessa,' Cara begged.

'Let's be calm, kids. Nothing is going to happen.'

Sammy didn't appear to believe that for an instant. He drew closer to Vanessa and looked almost fearfully at his approaching mother.

'Thank heavens I found you!' she exclaimed to the boy. 'I've been trying to see you for days.'

'He's been with us,' Vanessa said. 'Hello, again. This is my sister Roxanne Everly.'

Roxanne held out a hand and Nia gave it a quick, limp shake. 'I knew he'd been staying with you but I didn't think he was still there. It's Christmas. He should be at home.'

'Alone?'

'I know Derek only thinks about business, but Sammy wouldn't be alone. He'd be with me.'

Jane was taking in this exchange almost breathlessly, but Vanessa ignored her. 'I believe Derek thinks about his son a lot. Sammy wants to stay with us.'

Nia gave Vanessa a quick, wary glance as if knowing her approach and tone of voice were all wrong to accomplish what she wanted. She relaxed her face, gave Vanessa a smile, and lowered her voice. 'No wonder he likes staying at Everly House. It's a beautiful place. And he has his little friend . . .'

'Cara Willis,' Cara announced. 'I'm Sammy's *best* friend.'

'How sweet.' Nia gave Cara a pinched smile then looked back at Vanessa. 'Since I haven't seen my son for ages and he's right here, I'd like to take him for a short walk.'

'I'm sorry, Nia, but I believe Derek wants him to stay close to us.'

'*Derek wants—*' She caught herself. 'I'm his mother, Vanessa.'

'And Derek has custody.'

Anger flickered in Nia's large blue eyes but she said in a cajoling voice, 'I understand that he wants Sammy to be with you so maybe I could go home with you and spend some time with him there. You are going home after you buy a tree, aren't you?'

By now Sammy was pressing against Vanessa. She could feel his slight tremble. 'Yes, we're taking our tree home, but I'm afraid I can't invite a guest. My grandmother is very ill.'

'I won't bother her.'

'Having a stranger in the house will bother her.'

Nia finally glared. 'Why are you making this so hard? Because of Audrey?'

'What about Audrey?'

'I've heard rumors about Audrey and my husband. He wanted Sammy to stay with you because it gives him an excuse to be near Audrey. I know her type.'

'Oh? What is her type?'

'Really, Vanessa? Are you going to make me say it in front of the children?'

'Look, Nia, I'm sorry but you can't visit with Sammy now. You'll have to get permission from Derek—'

'*Permission!* I'm his *mother*!'

Vanessa simply stared at the woman steadily.

Finally, Nia said, 'I won't forget this, Vanessa. And I *will* see my son, eventually. I'll probably even take him away from Everly Cliffs.'

'Derek will have something to say about that. And so will the courts. They gave Derek full custody for a reason.'

Nia looked as if Vanessa had slapped her.

'Now if you'll excuse us, Nia, we need to buy a Christmas tree.'

They drove home in silence with a seven-foot Noble fir tied to the top of Vanessa's SUV. The children had chosen it because Mr Jackson said it was strong enough to hold heavy ornaments and even small wreaths.

Sammy sat rigid in the backseat with Cara close to him, almost touching. Finally he asked, 'Do you think we're strong enough to carry the tree inside?'

'Christian and your dad are coming this evening to have an early Christmas dinner with us, then bring in the tree and help us decorate,' Vanessa said.

'Dad's coming?' Sammy's voice had risen joyfully. 'Do you know what time?'

'He said he'd trust the dinner service to his manager. He'll be there at six.'

'Oh, boy! I didn't think he'd leave the restaurant for *anything*!'

'He would for you, especially on such a special occasion.'

'And Christian's coming, too?' Cara asked. 'He doesn't have to do any operations or anything?'

'Well, he's not a surgeon, so he never does operations, but he's leaving the hospital promptly at five o'clock. He promised.'

Vanessa glanced in the rear mirror to see the kids high-five each other. All the fear had left Sammy's face and Cara looked radiant.

When they got home, the children entered quietly, thinking Grace might be asleep. Instead, she called from the library, 'Did you get a tree?' Vanessa nodded at them and they ran in to tell Grace all about the different kinds of trees they'd seen and why they picked the Noble fir. Vanessa watched from the doorway for a moment as Grace listened to them with what looked like fascination.

Roxanne went straight up to her room and Vanessa went to the kitchen, which smelled of roasting turkey. Audrey was making pie dough. She looked up and smiled. 'Mission accomplished?'

'Yes. We got a beautiful tree, but it's stuck outside until the men help us move it.'

'Don't let Pete hear that. He'll try to wrestle the tree into the house by himself to prove he's a man.'

'He *is* a man – an injured man. I'll tell the guys to ask him to supervise, though.' She peered at the two dough shells Audrey was carefully placing in pie pans. 'Something happened while we were looking for trees that I think you should know.'

She told Audrey about Nia Sherwin as Audrey gently shaped the dough. 'When I said Derek wanted Sammy to stay with us through Christmas, she said it was because of you. She claimed to have heard rumors about you and Derek.'

Audrey looked at her, clearly troubled. 'What kind of rumors?'

'She didn't say. I'm sure some people noticed that you've been seeing Derek for a while, which is no big deal, but she has it in for you. I thought you should know.'

'I'm glad you told me.' Audrey began pouring cherry filling into one of the pie shells. 'Do you think everyone in town is talking about Derek and me?'

'No. I think a couple of people mentioned it to her and she's decided to run with it. She must believe it will help her get back Sammy.'

Audrey raised her head and looked at Vanessa with resentment in her eyes. 'Why? Is it because I was a teenage, unwed mother? Does that make me an inappropriate companion for Derek, a bad influence on Sammy?'

'It certainly doesn't, but I can't speak to what Nia might say. I think she has a nasty streak and I'm fairly sure she's determined to get what she wants. She's not thinking about what's good for Sammy – only for herself.'

'Well, there's nothing I can do about her. It was bad luck that she came to the evergreen lot, though.'

Vanessa frowned. 'Bad luck? I'm not sure. Simon Drake was there, too. At the Christmas party, he seemed quite taken with her and I think he got her phone number. Today he walked away from us and I saw him on his cellphone. Not long afterwards, Nia appeared.'

'So you think he told Nia where Sammy was?'

'It's a possibility.' Vanessa watched Audrey press her thumb round the rims of the pies. 'Do you need any help with those?'

Audrey looked up slowly, grinning. 'Great timing, Nessa. They're ready to go into the oven.'

'Oh, sorry. The people who eat the pies won't be – my cooking is still terrible – but the least I can do is open the oven door.'

Audrey put the pies on a cookie sheet and carefully slid them into one of the kitchen's two ovens.

'Since you have dinner under control, I need to talk to Roxanne,' Vanessa said.

'Is something wrong?' Audrey asked.

'I don't know.'

Vanessa found Roxanne in her room, lightly strumming her guitar as she sat in a wooden rocker near a big window swathed in pink voile ruffles. She stared at the floor, her blonde hair falling forward over her face.

'Am I interrupting?' Vanessa asked.

Roxanne looked up, her face grave, then gave her sister a half-hearted smile. 'No. I was only making noise on this thing.' She lifted the guitar. 'That's what I always did.'

'No, you didn't.' Vanessa entered the room and sat on the edge of the bed. 'You were good. You would have been *really* good if you'd practiced more.'

'I don't know if I would have ever been really good, but I didn't practice enough.' She set the guitar aside. 'You look like you want to talk to me.'

'I do. Rather, I want to ask a question. When we were shopping for Christmas trees today, you seemed fairly happy. When Simon Drake walked up, though, you stopped talking and every bit of color left your face except for your eyes, which looked frightened. What was the matter, Roxy?'

Roxanne turned her head for a moment and sighed. Then she looked at Vanessa solemnly. 'I've always hated Simon Drake.'

'I remember.'

'But I didn't just hate him, I feared him. Dad taught me to fear him. He knew Simon was a slippery character, Nessa, not that it stopped him from doing business with Simon.'

'That's why you hated him?'

'Well, I thought he was a creepy guy.'

'Let me be blunt. Did he ever molest you?'

'What? No.' Roxanne looked at her steadily, her voice normal. 'I mean he made excuses to touch me, but that's all. I felt like if he did more, I couldn't say anything. Maybe that's why he scared me.'

'Why couldn't you have said anything?'

'Because he was important to the family business and I thought he and Dad were friends. But nothing happened. I don't know, Nessa. I haven't been back very long and after what I've been through, seeing someone I used to fear and hate shook me. Badly. And what's worse, I think he knew it.'

'He didn't seem to be singling you out for his attentions, slimy as they are.'

'He's too smart for that.' Roxanne fluttered a hand in front of her face as if she were shooing away a fly. 'Oh well, it doesn't matter. He's an old man who doesn't have nearly as much power as he did or a lackey like Dad was. I think he's past his heyday in this town.'

'I don't know if Dad was his lackey—'

'He was. After Grandfather died, the business would have gone down the drain without Simon, but he took more than his share.'

'How do you know that?'

'I heard Grace talking to Dad about it. I used to eavesdrop, you know.'

'Was Dad's relationship with Simon the reason you didn't like Dad?'

Roxanne was quiet for a moment. 'Partly, but Dad and I didn't get along before Simon. We just clashed, probably because of Mommy. He didn't treat her right.'

'I think he treated her very well considering her unstable mental condition.'

'He tolerated her. Then he began emulating her. Then he got rid of her.'

'He got the best medical care for her, Roxy. He even had a private nurse staying with her near the end.'

'The *end*. She isn't dead, Vanessa. Do you go see her in that home where she is?'

'It's a very nice facility for people with problems like hers, and no, I don't go to see her. I tried after she first went in, but she doesn't want to see me.' Vanessa paused. 'You were so close to her. Do you want to visit her?'

Roxanne twisted her hands together. 'No, nooo. Not now. Maybe after a month or two. At this point, I can't bear seeing her put away.'

'She's very comfortable, Roxy. She has a nice private room and a few friends. She's as calm and as happy as Mom is capable of being. You don't have to worry about her. But you don't have to go running to see her before you're ready. In fact, we didn't even let her know you're home.'

'I'm glad. I need to focus on myself now, not a mother I can't help.'

'You're absolutely right.' Vanessa stood up and smiled. 'Coming downstairs soon?'

'In a few minutes.' She picked up her guitar again. 'I'll just fool around with this until I can stop thinking about Simon Drake.'

'Who gets to carve the turkey?' Vanessa asked as she, Audrey, Roxanne, Cara, Sammy, Christian, Derek and Pete sat around the dining-room table.

'Dr Montgomery should 'cause he's a surgeon,' Cara said.

'I'm not a surgeon, Cara.'

'She knows that but she's determined to make you into one,' Vanessa laughed. 'Derek, you're the restaurateur. I think you should do the carving.'

Derek smiled. 'I own a restaurant, I'm not a chef. However, I'll be proud to carve this beautiful turkey that Audrey has roasted for us all.' As he began to slice, he said, 'I can tell it's succulent. Cooked to perfection. Cheers to the chef.'

'Cheers!' everyone repeated as Audrey blushed.

The table looked lovely covered in an ivory damask cloth, the best Wedgewood china bordered with pale sage vines and tiny red flowers, a silver candelabra holding six ivory taper candles, and crystal wineglasses. The children drank cola out of theirs while the adults had white wine.

They all laughed and talked while eating turkey, baked sweet potatoes with marshmallows, glazed carrots, and French-cut green beans with almonds. For dessert, Audrey served slices of her pies with whipped cream. Afterward, Roxanne rose from the table and began fixing a plate for Grace. Audrey offered to serve her, but Roxy said she wanted to do it herself.

While Audrey and Vanessa cleared the table and began cleaning up, the men went out to rescue the Christmas tree from the roof of Vanessa's SUV. Pete insisted on helping although he still had his crutch. Vanessa knew he would merely be supervising, offering suggestions where none were needed, feeling important. When they got the tree into the house, they carried it into the living room where Pete began giving orders about how it should fit securely into the tree stand.

When Vanessa and Audrey finished with the dishes, Grace imperiously called to Audrey. 'I don't want to lie in bed eating my Christmas dinner like a baby,' she announced. 'I want to sit in my wheelchair.'

Christian sauntered in and Grace repeated herself. He tilted his head as if thinking, then smiled. 'Of course you can sit in your chair, Grace. We should have thought of that earlier and you could have joined us at the table.'

Clearly put out, Grace muttered, 'Hmmmph.' But she let Christian lift her into her chair. Then Roxanne neared her with a tray. 'Is it OK if I sit with you while you eat, Grace?'

'Yes, but I can feed myself. I don't need to be spoon fed.'

'I know,' Roxanne said tentatively. 'I just want to join you.'

Vanessa wondered why Grace was being so cold to Roxy. She never said anything rude, but she didn't say anything warm and welcoming, either. Vanessa could see disappointment and confusion on Roxy's face every time Grace all but rebuffed her. For once, Vanessa was annoyed with her grandmother.

Earlier the kids and Roxanne had carried Christmas tree decorations down from the attic. Now they carefully unpacked them, squealing in delight after they unearthed one carefully wrapped treasure after another. Derek said lights should be put on first so Pete found a four-foot stepladder in the mudroom and Derek climbed it, holding the end of a string of miniature multi-colored lights. It took four strings to completely cover the tree.

At this point, Roxanne wheeled Grace into the living room. 'I never miss the decoration of a Christmas tree,' Grace said with her usual vivacity. 'Christian, if you order me back to bed, I'll mutiny.'

Christian grinned. 'I don't see anything wrong with you just watching. If you get up and try to decorate it yourself, I'll have to put my foot down.'

'I swear I won't,' Grace said. 'Carry on, troops!'

Next came the ropes of fluffy gold tinsel that they draped in loops around the tree. Then the children began handing Derek and Christian ornaments to hang on the top two feet of the tree. Cara and Sammy placed the special decorations at a lower level: a six-inch angel with long blonde hair and silver sparkles on her satin dress and cloak; a bamboo reindeer wearing a white fur-trimmed red velvet horse cape; a small wreath covered with green silk vines and pink silk roses that had belonged to Grace when she was a girl; red- and green-dressed pixies wearing pointed hats with pom-poms on top; golden bells that actually chimed. Then came a multitude of satin-covered Styrofoam bulbs and glass bulbs in all colors and some with names written on them in glitter. There was a green one reading *Grace*; a red one reading *Roxanne*; a blue one reading *Vanessa*; a gold one reading *Leonard*; a purple one reading *Audrey*; a yellow one reading *Pete*; a silver one reading *Cara*; and a white one reading *Sammy*.

'My name!' Sammy exclaimed when he saw it. 'You just made this one, didn't you?'

Cara smiled impishly. 'Yesterday. I did it all by myself. White with gold glitter. Do you like it, Sammy?'

'It's great! Dad, did you see this?'

'I certainly did. It's the prettiest Christmas ornament I've ever seen. Thank you, Cara.'

Her face turned pink and she looked at Christian. 'I think it's time to plug in the lights.'

'As you wish, my lady,' Christian said. Suddenly the big tree bloomed with tiny lights of every color that made it look both bright and ethereal. Everyone gasped and clapped, even Grace.

'I think this is the most beautiful tree we've ever had,' Vanessa said. She looked at Roxanne and then at Christian. 'And it's truly the most wonderful Christmas of my life.'

Brody stood slightly beyond the driveway in front of Everly House, past the glow of the porch lights and slightly inside the narrow rim of woods above the cliff. His hands were buried in the pockets of his jacket and his brownish-blond hair hung long and tousled on his forehead.

They hadn't drawn the draperies in what he knew was the large living room of the house. Instead, he had a clear view of a tall evergreen and several men hoisting it into position, then draping the lights over it. A man he didn't know stood on a short stepladder, but occasionally Christian came into view – well-groomed, laughing Christian who'd been welcomed into the beautiful house and no doubt the company of Grace and children and the lovely Vanessa. He'd won back Vanessa. *In spite of me, she's his again. Thank God,* Brody thought. *Thank God I didn't ruin his life.*

The glittering, joyful scene in the house literally made his chest ache. Such scenes weren't for the likes of him. He couldn't watch anymore.

Brody walked down the hill, staying to the side of the road and close to the trees in case he saw headlights. Maybe more people would be coming to Everly House. Certainly not Max Newman. His meeting with Max was hazy. He remembered walking along the beach, then running into Max and feeling threatened, trapped, and striking out to protect himself. Afterward he'd run and run – he didn't recall in what direction – but when he had no breath left, he stopped, crawled into a small, dark space, and slept. When he wakened the next morning, he knew he'd done something bad to Max although he didn't remember exactly what it was.

Now he wasn't just wandering. He had a specific destination in mind and he didn't want to run into anyone who would delay him. So often he felt confused, not sure where he was or what he was doing, but tonight his mind felt oddly clear. He couldn't count on that clarity to last, though. He remembered feeling sharp, calm, in charge of his emotions and his life, but for some reason those feelings had vanished. He didn't know why and at times the world felt like too much for him. Often he sat and cried like a lost child. He wished someone could save him, but he didn't trust *anyone*, not even his own brother. Christian wanted to capture him like everyone else did – capture and put him away in a cage. Forever. He knew if he entered the cage, he would never emerge.

Brody walked at a normal pace but kept close to tree lines, avoiding lighted areas and hugging the shadows. At last he made it to his home – the house where he'd grown up and where Christian still lived. He had a set of keys to the locks that had never been changed. Slipping a key into a backdoor knob, he heard a satisfying click. The door swung open into the kitchen. He'd brought a small flashlight and turned it on, keeping it aimed near the floor. As usual, Christian had left a living-room lamp on as if that would fool anyone into thinking someone was home. Brody avoided the light from the lamp and headed for his old bedroom.

He danced the flashlight beam around the room. His candle still sat on the windowsill although it wasn't lighted. He already knew that every poster he'd put on the wall when he was a teenager was still in place. He went to the low, built-in bookshelves that lined one wall. Sitting on the floor, he smiled when he saw his favorite old books about conquerors such as Cortez, Attila the Hun, Julius Caesar and Alexander the Great. Especially worn were copies of books about King Arthur and the Round Table: *Knights of the Round Table*; *A Boy's King Arthur*; *Le Morte de Arthur* Volumes I and II; *The Mists of Avalon*. He'd read them over and over. He moved on to the notebooks full of stories he'd written about kings and knights, lords and ladies.

Finally he came to his last and favorite – *The Rescue of Roxanne*. Only a couple of months after he'd written it, he'd met Zane Felder. They'd liked each other immediately. Zane talked a lot about computers. Before, Brody had been bored by the intricacies of computers, but Zane made them sound interesting – even fascinating. That's when he'd started learning all he could about computers – particularly software – and let his obsession with kings and queens take a back burner. Still, he now wanted to reread *The Rescue of Roxanne*. He folded it and tucked it inside his jacket.

Slowly he made his way back to the kitchen, listening for the sound of Christian's car in the driveway. He'd looked like he would be spending the whole evening at Everly House, but that had been a while ago. Brody went to the widest drawer atop the cabinets. He opened it and looked carefully at the cutlery inside.

At last he picked up a carving knife with a razor-sharp ten-inch stainless steel blade, wrapped it in a dishtowel he found on the counter, and put it inside his coat along with the notebook. Then he quietly let himself out the backdoor just as headlights from Christian's car shone through the picture window and swept through the living room.

SIXTEEN

Grace had already begun nodding in her wheelchair when Vanessa said, 'I think all of you have created the most beautiful Christmas tree ever, but we're all tired, particularly Audrey who did all the cooking. Shall we call it a night?'

She'd expected objections from the children, but Cara was

looking at Grace. She was the most considerate child Vanessa had ever known. 'I sure am tired.' She yawned hugely and nudged Sammy. 'How about you, Sammy?'

He followed her lead and yawned unconvincingly. 'I'm worn to a frazzle. I could sleep for days.'

Derek looked at his son with a mixture of perplexity and relief. Clearly Sammy was acting differently from how he had for the last few years and Derek was glad to see the change. Vanessa had told him about their encounter with Nia in the Christmas tree lot. He'd been angry with Nia but expressed his gratitude to Vanessa for standing up to her and the entire family for 'babysitting' Sammy during this difficult time.

Roxanne wanted to help Grace back into bed but Grace insisted that Audrey do it. Christian checked Grace's vitals and told her she was doing great. She fell asleep within minutes. Later, in private, he confided to Vanessa and Audrey that he was still concerned about her breathing. He hoped she wasn't developing pneumonia.

Afterward, Christian and Derek left and Pete went back to his small cottage. The children sat quietly staring at the Christmas tree for about fifteen minutes before Audrey declared it was bedtime for both of them, too.

Vanessa had already changed into her pajamas and was watching television in Grace's upstairs room when her cellphone rang. She was surprised to hear Wade Baylor's voice.

'Wade, is something wrong?' she asked anxiously.

'Not really wrong. I contacted Zane Felder's lawyer, John Dawson, in Portland. He gave me quite a bit of information. He said the grandfather left Zane a piece of land with a house on it just outside of the Portland city limits. The house is old and in bad shape, but the condition of the bequest was that if Zane accepted the land, he couldn't sell the land or tear down the house for at least five years.'

'Isn't that a strange thing to put in a will?'

'From what I understand, Zane's grandfather was strange. So is his grandfather's lawyer, a guy named Enoch Snyder. What a curmudgeon! Anyway, Zane accepted the bequest with the five-year condition. That was over four years ago.'

'Is there something special about the house?'

'No. I think it had been in Zane's family forever. Dawson told me that Zane's grandfather didn't like him. He thought Zane was a weirdo, but he didn't have any other close relatives. He thought Zane would turn down the bequest rather than pay taxes on an old wreck, but Zane didn't. I called Libby. She didn't know anything about it. Zane seemed to keep it a mystery, which in light of the circumstances – Roxanne being held captive in Portland and Zane being Brody's best friend – seem suspicious to me. I want to see the house. I also want Roxanne to see the house. Maybe she can tell if she ever spent any time there.'

'You want her to go to a place where she might have been held captive?'

'Yes. I know it's a lot to ask, but I need to know. I thought we could go tomorrow.'

'We?'

'You, Roxanne, and me. I also asked Libby to join us since it's Zane's house. Or rather hers – he left his entire estate to her except for forty of his fifty-one percent of Blackbird. That goes to Brody. Anyway, will you ask Roxanne? And emphasize how important this is. She might be more receptive to you than to me.'

Vanessa hesitated and took a deep breath. If Roxanne had been held prisoner in the house, going into it might be traumatic for her. However, if Brody had been the one who kidnapped her, and Zane was his best friend who'd inherited a house no one ever entered, the possible implications were clear. Vanessa remembered Roxanne telling her about the men who'd abused her. Not one man – *men*. Could one of them have been Zane? Could there have been even more who came to that house? They had to know.

'I'll ask her, Wade. You know she'll be reluctant, but I think she'll realize how vital this is and go along with it.'

'Thanks, Vanessa. Tell her how sorry I am to have to ask this of her.'

Vanessa looked at her sister huddled in the SUV. 'Are you all right?'

'Yes.' Roxanne wore jeans, a pink sweater and a jacket. Her hair was full and long, shining golden in the winter sun, and she'd put on lipstick, blush, and mascara, but she still looked slightly ill and scared. 'I wish we didn't have to do this.'

'It won't take long and Wade thinks it's important that we see this house of Zane's.'

'I told you I was kept in different places.'

'But you said you were in the last place the longest. And you walked out of it without a blindfold. You might remember it.'

'Yeah. Maybe.' Roxanne stared out the side window for a minute, then asked, 'Why do you think Grace is so cold to me? She acts like she doesn't want me near her.'

'Grace isn't in good shape physically or mentally. She's not the Grace you knew.'

'Yes, but she's nice to everyone except me. Why?'

Vanessa looked at Wade driving in the patrol car ahead of them and tightened her hands on the steering wheel. 'When you disappeared, Roxy, the family fell apart. No one blamed you—'

'I think Dad must have.'

'To be honest, Dad was so shocked he said things he didn't mean, like maybe you brought it on yourself. He didn't mean it. Anyway, Mommy was already drinking fairly heavily, Dad drank a lot after his father died but he'd gotten sober, then when you vanished he started drinking again, and we were all devastated. Every day we hoped there would be news of you and every day we were disappointed. Grace held it together with her usual strength, but I think we only saw an act. Inside she was torn apart like the rest of us. Then Mom got completely out of control and was confined to her room with a nurse. Dad was a mess, too, and he fell down the stairs and broke his neck. Grace really loved Dad. After his death, I saw her begin to go downhill. She couldn't handle Mom anymore, even though we had nursing help. She had to have Ellen legally declared incompetent and sent her to a permanent care facility. It was for Mom's own safety. Then Grace developed Alzheimer's. This year, I would have had to make other arrangements for the running of the company. I hadn't told her, but she knew.' Vanessa sighed. 'In my opinion, because Grace isn't thinking clearly, in some way, she holds you responsible for the downfall of her family.'

'Oh, God.'

'I said it's because she isn't rational. Five years ago, she wouldn't have reacted this way to your homecoming, but she's not the strong woman she was five years ago. Please try to be patient with her, Roxy. And don't take it personally. Nothing that happened to our family is your fault. Nothing.'

'Maybe I did ask for what happened to me.'

'Then every fifteen-year-old girl with a good figure who wears a bikini is asking for it. Does that sound reasonable?'

'Well, no.'

'Then stop feeling guilty.'

'I can't but I'll stop talking about it. How much farther is it to Portland?'

'Around fifty miles. Why, do you need the restroom? When you were little, we couldn't drive farther than thirty miles without you needing the bathroom.'

Roxanne laughed. 'I got bored in the car. I wanted to stop.'

'We all knew that, but Dad would stop, anyway. It was the one thing you did that got on Mom's nerves.'

'Mommy was incredibly lenient with me. Too lenient.'

'You looked like her. You still do. And you acted like her. I was more introverted like Dad. And you were her baby. I think she'd been told that after me, she couldn't have more children. Then years later, there you were! Her miracle child!'

'Were you jealous?'

'Not at first. As I got older and Mom favored you so much, I admit I resented you a little. I resented her a lot.'

'I'm sorry.'

'Once again, it wasn't your fault. Anyway, do you need the restroom? I can call Wade and ask if we can pull over at a fast-food place.'

'No, I don't need the restroom. I'm just getting nervous. I really don't want to go to this house.'

Vanessa looked at her and smiled encouragingly. 'I'm sure we'll go in, find nothing, and be out in fifteen minutes. Don't worry, Roxy.'

An hour later, Wade pulled his patrol car into the driveway of a ramshackle two-story house that looked as if it dated from 1920. The roof was steep and covered with green asphalt shingles that were beginning to shed onto the patch of weeds that served as a lawn. The porch sagged and two of the steps were missing. An upstairs window bore a long, wiggly crack. A rutted gravel driveway ran beside the length of the house. Vanessa and Roxanne looked at the house, then at each other and started laughing.

'Oh, lord, the police think *that* could have been a prison?' Roxanne asked. 'It looks like it's going to fall down any minute!'

Wade got out of his car and motioned to them. As they were

emerging from the SUV, a blue compact car whipped to the curb. In a moment, a flustered-looking Libby Hughes rushed toward them. 'What's this all about?' she demanded. 'I don't understand. Why are you interested in Zane's house?'

'Zane lived here?' Wade asked in surprise.

'Oh, of course he didn't! Look at it. His ogre of a grandfather left it to him. I just found out about it.'

'Have you been here before?'

'Once. Last summer we got out and walked around the house to see the beautiful view from the back yard. You'd never believe it and you can't even see it from the street. The view, that is. This lot is almost two acres. That's why there aren't any houses crowding this one. Zane asked me if I'd like to live in a *nice* house on this lot. I said yes. I had no idea he already owned it.' She looked earnestly at Vanessa. 'Zane's grandfather was a mean, crazy old coot and he didn't like Zane so he must have saddled him with this place as a joke. And now it's mine, I'm told. Zane left me almost everything. Can you believe that?'

'Yes. He loved you very much, Libby.'

'And he was the love of my life. I'll never marry anyone else.' She looked down at her engagement ring, then back at Vanessa. 'Why are you here?'

'Yesterday I told you we were coming here,' Wade said.

'But you didn't say *why*. Are you trying to make trouble for Zane?'

'I think it's a little late for that, Libby.'

Her big eyes filled with tears and Vanessa put her arm around Libby. 'I think Wade is trying to be very thorough because Zane was a murder victim. He's certainly not trying to cause trouble. He said something that came out wrong. Don't be upset. Do you want to go inside the house with us?'

Wade shot her a quick, annoyed glance, but Vanessa didn't care about anything except soothing Libby's feelings.

'OK, although I don't know what you're looking for.'

'Neither do we,' Wade said. 'Let's hope there's nothing to find.'

Zane's grandfather's lawyer Snyder had left the front-door key in a rusty mailbox that was near to falling off the house. He opened the creaky screen door with torn mesh and inserted the key into the door-handle lock. He had trouble turning it. 'This hasn't been used for a while,' he said. Finally he wrenched it to the side, there was a groaning sound as the bolt slid back, and he shoved open the door.

Wade led the way into a shadowy living room. Thin blinds over the windows let in enough light to show the years of dust and cobwebs covering a scuffed hardwood floor and old furniture that probably dated from the Forties. In corners wallpaper had come loose and hung in dirty desolation.

'Oh my gosh,' Libby breathed. 'This is gross!'

'I'll say,' Vanessa agreed. 'I wonder how long it's been since anyone lived here.'

Wade looked at Roxanne. 'You said when you got free, you ran upstairs and out the front door. Does any of this seem familiar to you?'

Roxanne glanced around and shook her head. 'I was so frightened and I felt weak and sick. All I remember is seeing a door and opening it. I'm sorry.'

'Don't be sorry. You were right to get out as soon as possible.'

'You were in here?' Libby asked, looking bewildered.

'I don't know. Maybe. We're trying to see if I remember anything.'

'Well, no one's been in this room,' Libby said. 'It looks like it hasn't been touched for decades.'

Wade nodded. 'Let's go upstairs.'

'No! Wait!'

Everyone looked at Roxanne.

'When I escaped, I ran *upstairs*, not down,' she reiterated.

'So you want to check out the basement?' Wade asked.

Roxanne nodded, albeit hesitantly.

'OK, but I don't want to spend a minute more in here than necessary.'

They walked to the back of the house. The electricity was turned off in the property, and in the kitchen Wade pulled out his flashlight and shone it on a back door opening to the outside and another door leading down the basement stairs. 'Everyone follow me and watch their step.'

Before they reached the bottom of the flimsy stairs, odors floated up to Vanessa. Patchouli and sandalwood. Cedar was the strongest. There were others, fainter, but those three she knew immediately. Incense, she thought. Someone had burned incense in this basement. Walking into the basement, Wade's flashlight flicked over walls painted black and black-painted wood covering the small windows. The light then caught the shine of brass. Wade focused the light and before them stood a thick brass stick about four feet high with a fat, black candle wedged in the top. Beyond it stood three more.

'Whoa,' he said. 'What are these?'

'Floor candle holders,' Vanessa said. 'They use them on the set of *Kingdom of Corinna*.'

Beyond the candle holders was a long, carved chest. On top stood a boom box with labeled tapes beside it. Without touching them, Vanessa surveyed the tapes: 'Indra' by Thievery Corporation, 'Tubular Bells' by Mike Oldfield. Beside the boom box sat three incense burners, and several pieces of leather. Wade slipped on latex gloves and lifted one, inspecting it closely. 'Is this a mask?' he finally asked in disbelief.

'It's a sado-masochistic mask,' Vanessa said. 'So's the other one. Pick up that piece of leather beside it. That's a sado-masochistic halter. There's also a ball-gag. The other thing is a cat-o'-nine-tails whip.'

Wade stared at Vanessa. 'How do you know all of this?'

'I live in Hollywood.'

He looked at her in disapproval.

'Oh, Wade, I read a lot!' Vanessa managed to laugh despite the circumstances.

'Geez. Give me good old Everly Cliffs any day,' he muttered. Then he flashed the light in the other direction. Everyone went silent at the sight of a bed covered in black velveteen. A canopy loomed over the bed, the velveteen covering it and dipping into fringed edges. The bed stood against a wall where chains were attached to wall hooks. At the end of the chains were metal cuffs.

'What the hell . . .' Wade breathed.

'I don't understand,' Libby gasped. 'A bed? A black bed and *chains*?'

'It's an S & M chamber,' Roxanne said tonelessly, her face colorless. 'I used to lie naked on that bed, blindfolded, my wrists in the cuffs, the collar around my neck, my feet tied with rope, the incense burning – especially the cedar – music playing – blasting – feeling the whip hitting me – not hard enough to cause cuts, only welts – and then . . . and then a man with a hood would . . . would get on top of me and . . .'

She turned, bent, and vomited onto the floor.

SEVENTEEN

Wade called the county police, and while Roxanne sat on the front seat of the SUV, taking deep breaths and trying not to be sick again, Libby paced around wringing her hands, tears streaming down her face. 'I don't understand,' she told Roxanne for the tenth time. 'I don't understand. The lawyer says this house belongs to Zane but that *stuff* in the basement can't be Zane's. It *can't!*'

'We don't know what's happening yet. We have to wait for the county police.'

'What are they going to do? Take that disgusting trash out of the house? Did you see those chains? That *whip?*'

'Oh, please,' Roxanne moaned. 'Don't talk about it.'

Libby immediately kneeled at Roxanne's feet. 'Oh, honey, I'm sorry. But you know Zane didn't have *anything* to do with what happened to you in that basement—'

Roxanne heaved again, Libby toppled backward, and Vanessa grabbed her sister's hair and held it away from her face. 'It's OK,' Roxanne mumbled in a few seconds. 'It's just dry heaves. Can't we leave?'

'No. I'm sorry,' Vanessa soothed. 'We have to wait but not for long. The police are here.'

First one patrol car pulled up and in two minutes another. The uniformed officers gathered in a huddle and spoke with Wade, a couple of them occasionally glancing over at Roxanne. In a minute, Wade came back to the women. 'I'm going downstairs with them but you have to stay. I'm sorry, Roxanne.'

She stood shakily and nodded.

'What about me?' Libby almost wailed, still kneeling.

'They might have a couple of questions for you, Miss Hughes. It would be better if you wait, too.'

'Oh Lord, help my soul. As if my poor Zane getting murdered wasn't bad enough, now he's suspected of doing sick, perverted things.' She put her head in her hands. 'I can't stay! I can't *stand* it!'

Wade cast Vanessa a despairing glance then walked back to the other officers. Vanessa knelt across from Libby. 'Honey, I know none of this seems fair but the police need you—'

'OK!' she snapped. 'If that's what everyone wants, I'll stay!'

'Thank you so much, Libby. That will be a real help.' Vanessa stood and looked at Roxanne. 'How are you doing?'

'All right, considering. I didn't remember that place until I saw it. Maybe I didn't let myself remember it.'

'I'm sorry that you had to see it.' Vanessa scanned the neighborhood. 'There aren't many houses around here. It looks like it used to be a nice place to live but fell out of style. There isn't one even semi-new house here.'

'It's quiet. Very few neighbors.'

'Do you remember any of this from when you escaped the house?'

'Not a thing. It was dark and I was in a panic, waiting for someone to grab me and drag me back to that house. It seemed I ran for a long time, though, before the woman picked me up. Then we drove for a while. I got out of the car. Thank God, I ended up near the bus station.'

'Yes, thank God.' Vanessa paced in a circle. 'They're taking pictures and gathering evidence, but it feels like they've been in there forever.'

Finally they emerged from the house and Wade walked to Vanessa's car. 'I think they got everything they need. They've already gone over Zane's apartment with a fine-tooth comb. Now I'd like to see Brody's place.'

'Brody's? Why?' Vanessa asked.

'He might have left something that would tell us where he is.'

'He's in Everly Cliffs. You know that.'

Wade stared at her but said nothing.

'You think you might find a connection to this house?' Vanessa slowly realized.

'Among other things.'

'Are you up to it, Roxy?' she asked.

'Do I have a choice? What about Libby?'

'I'm going to ask her to come, too. She went there often with Zane.'

'It was the headquarters for Blackbird although it's closed now. What about their employees?'

'We'll talk to them, too, but you don't have to be involved.'
Wade gave them one of his rare smiles. 'C'mon, girls. One more
hour and we'll be on our way home.'

'One hour, Wade Baylor,' Vanessa said. 'Then Roxy and I are
going home, with or without you.'

Twenty minutes later they arrived at a three-story concrete-block
building painted dark gray. The small front lawn was empty of
shrubbery or trees and at the large front window hung beige vertical
blinds. It didn't look like a business and certainly not like a home.

When everyone got out of their cars, Vanessa said to Libby,
'This is so plain.'

'It belongs to Brody and that's how he wanted it. He didn't
have many friends. He always acted like he didn't deserve them,'
Libby replied.

'But Max Newman was a friend.'

'Real casual. He lived a few blocks away. I was here a couple
of nights with Zane when Max came by. He was nice. Brody
seemed to really like one of his employees, Dan Simmons. Both
Zane and Brody think he's brilliant. He's only about twenty-five,
but they even thought about making him a partner. Zane talked
to him after Brody disappeared. He didn't know anything, either,
but that's not surprising considering that Brody didn't let *anyone*
get close.'

Not at all like he used to be, Vanessa thought sadly. He was
outgoing, athletic, popular with girls, and a sort of golden boy.
Then he got sick.

The police opened the front door and they walked into a room
filled with desks, worktables, monitors, and a wall-mounted television. There were five cubicles and a large, round table near a
wall with a whiteboard covered with notes and equations.

'This was the main work room,' Libby said. 'It always looked
like a big mess to me but Zane and Brody made sense of it all.
And the other employees, too. Everybody was really smart.'

They took an elevator to the second floor where there were
racks with cables and equipment. 'This was like a storage room,'
Libby told them. 'Don't ask me what any of this stuff is, though.
All I see are cords and metal boxes. Zane used to say I'm not
computer literate and he liked that because he talked about

computers all day. Brody lived on the third floor. Let's take the elevator.'

The elevator door opened and they walked out into a large, open space with eggshell-colored Berber carpeting, a long, heavily padded tan couch, three matching swivel chairs, beautiful golden oak tables, and ivory walls covered with framed prints of impressionistic art.

'Wow,' Vanessa said. 'This wasn't what I was expecting.'

Libby nodded. 'I was surprised the first time I saw it, too. It's so pretty and almost, well, delicate. Later Brody told me he thought it was calm, restful. I understood, then, considering his mental problem. The only time he ever talked to me about his schizophrenia, he said it made him feel completely out of control and paranoid, like the world was a big jumble. That's why when he was well, he wanted everything to be still and peaceful and serene. I remember that word in particular. *Serene.*'

Vanessa nodded. 'I understand. This room is certainly serene. And lovely.' She looked closely at some of the framed prints. One was the dreamlike *Waterlilies* by Monet. Close by hung *Cliffs and Sailboats at Pourville* by Renoir and *Montmartre* by Van Gogh.

'Zane and I used to come and watch TV with him.' She motioned to the large fifty-five-inch television. 'And we listened to music. Brody's favorite group was The Eagles.'

'Did he ever have a date on these evenings?' Vanessa asked.

'A couple of times there was a girl named Emily. She was very pretty but not very friendly to me. She asked a lot of personal questions and she drank a *lot*. Brody doesn't drink alcohol, you know.'

'When was that?'

'Months ago. Zane told me not to ask about her. I think she found out Brody had a mental health condition and she acted fairly awful about it.'

So a recent break-up hadn't sent Brody spiraling, Vanessa thought. Maybe there had been a girlfriend later that Libby hadn't met.

Roxanne stood close to the elevator doors, her arms folded across her chest. 'Do you recognize this place?' Vanessa asked.

She shook her head. 'I've never been here before. At least I don't think I have. Maybe if I was drugged . . .' She looked at her feet. 'I don't remember everything that happened when I'd been given something.'

Along one wall of the living space was a spotless kitchen, and an island with stools. At the back of the space was a king-sized bed, a dresser and nightstand, and another large flat-screen television. On a wall near the bed hung a framed print of *My Fair Lady* by Edmund Blair. Vanessa looked at the image of a lovely girl descending steps in a long white dress as she held a bouquet of pink flowers. She wore a coronet of pink flowers and her blonde hair hung below her waist.

This was the only space not in pristine condition. The bed was unmade and covered with pictures. A policeman wearing latex gloves picked up pictures of Alexander the Great, Alexandria, medieval castles – Bodium, Dover, Warkworth, Windsor – and women – Eleanor of Aquitaine with blonde hair and blue eyes, several of the Lady of Shalott with a gold ribbon around her forehead, Guinevere and Lancelot – alongside anonymous knights standing in armor, going into battle, riding in jousting tournaments, kneeling at the feet of ladies. There must have been at least fifty pictures scattered on the bed and on the floor beside it.

Vanessa looked at the pictures. 'They're all about ancient life except for these two photos of a tennis tournament. They were taken over ten years ago. There's Christian standing beside him and in this one . . . you and me, Roxy.'

Roxanne glanced at the photo. 'I remember that tournament.'

'Libby, how long ago were you last here?' Vanessa asked.

'Right after Brody vanished. It looked like this. Zane and I didn't move anything. But Zane said he'd been in here about eight days before then and it had looked like always – everything in place, the way Brody liked it.'

Vanessa wandered beyond the bedroom area to the bathroom. She spotted two blue-and-white capsules lying on the vinyl beside the white vanity. Libby walked in and Vanessa held out the capsules. 'Zane and I already searched this bathroom to see if Brody took his prescription meds with him when he disappeared,' Libby said. 'They aren't in the medicine cabinet. I guess he spilled those and didn't see them.'

'Maybe.' Vanessa wrapped the capsules in a tissue and tucked them in a zipper compartment of her tote bag.

Before they left the bathroom, Libby said vehemently, 'Vanessa, I don't care if that hideous room was found in Zane's house. He had *nothing* to do with it. He was a good man – the best I've ever known – and he wouldn't have had anything to do with . . . with *hurting* anyone that way. Do you believe me?'

Vanessa wasn't certain what she believed at this point, but she nodded to Libby.

'No, *say* it. Say that you *know* it.'

Forgive me for lying because I don't know *it,* Vanessa thought. 'I know it.'

Libby smiled slightly then turned and headed toward Roxanne. 'Are you OK, sweetie? You look awful pale.'

Vanessa mentally slapped herself for touring Brody's living quarters instead of looking after her sister who'd lost most of the color in her face and held her trembling hands tightly together. 'Wade, do you need for Roxanne and me to stay any longer?' she called.

'No. I'll call you later. You can go, too, Libby. Thank you for coming with us.'

On the way home, Roxanne barely spoke. Vanessa saw a fast-food restaurant. 'I'm hungry. Do you mind going in?'

'No. I could use something to eat, too.'

Inside Vanessa ordered a hamburger and Coke and Roxanne a large chocolate milkshake. 'Nothing to eat?' Vanessa asked.

Roxanne nodded her head no. 'Only a milkshake.'

When they sat down, Vanessa smiled at Roxy. 'You always loved chocolate milkshakes.'

'I still do. They cure all ills.'

'Are you sure? Today has been terrible for you.'

Roxanne sucked so hard on her straw that her cheeks sunk in. Then she swallowed hard. 'I feel . . . depleted. Not horrified, not sick anymore, just empty. Does that make sense?'

'I have no idea how I'd feel in your position.' Vanessa knew this was not the time to ask questions about what else had gone on in that room, or the drugs Roxy had been given, and especially not about the abortion. 'This evening you can have something solid to eat and maybe we can persuade Christian to prescribe a sleeping pill.'

Roxanne's eyes widened. 'Oh my God! Christian! When he finds out about that room . . .'

'You're right.' Vanessa put down her half-eaten hamburger. 'There's no way we can keep him from knowing.'

'Wade will tell him everything.'

'Yes, of course he will. He should. Zane and Brody were best friends as well as business partners.'

'And probably more.' Roxanne's big blue eyes were full of meaning.

'Fellow perverts?'

'That's one way of putting it.' She looked at her milkshake. 'I'm finished.'

'I think I am, too. Let's get home and try to forget today.'

Vanessa had picked up a few CDs she'd left at Everly House and in the car, she chose *Supernatural* by Santana. 'I know this is dated, but you used to love "Smooth". When you were five and six, you danced to it for the family.'

'Always the show-off.' Roxanne grinned. 'But I'd love to hear the CD again.'

A few minutes later Vanessa looked over to see her sister's eyes closed and her right hand tapping in time to 'Love of My Life'. Roxanne had always loved music and been particularly sensitive to it. She wrote it and she could have been an excellent guitarist. But she was only twenty-three. There was still time.

They entered Everly Cliffs and Roxanne said wearily, 'I'm so glad to be home.'

'Me, too. This wasn't one of the most pleasurable trips I've taken.'

Vanessa stopped the SUV in front of Everly House. As they neared the porch, she could hear Queenie barking inside. 'Someone's missed us!' She laughed.

Then to her surprise, Derek Sherwin opened the front door. His smile was half-hearted. 'You're back.'

'And aren't you supposed to be at your restaurant or your office?' Vanessa asked.

'Yes, but Audrey called to see if I could knock off work early and come to look after the kids.'

Vanessa stopped on the top step, dread filling her. 'What's wrong?'

'Grace had a heart attack.'

EIGHTEEN

Vanessa, Roxanne, and Pete drove through the twilight from the hospital to Everly House. Audrey had waited until Vanessa and Roxy came home so she could explain what had happened while they were gone that afternoon.

'Grace only nibbled at lunch. She said she wasn't hungry and within fifteen minutes she said she felt nauseated and dizzy. Then she broke into a sweat. Queenie came running and stood beside Grace's bed, whining. You know some dogs can sense when a person is going to have a heart attack. It has to do with adrenaline and enzyme levels. When she said her chest felt tight, I gave her an aspirin and called the paramedics. They arrived in record time, but Grace was having pain in her back and jaw by then.'

'Not in her left arm?' Roxanne had asked.

'It's more common for men to have pain in the left arm than women,' Audrey had said. 'The symptoms differ a bit between males and females.' She'd lowered her voice. 'Anyway, after I called the ambulance, I called Pete to come and stay with the children but when he got there, he was so worried I didn't think it was fair to ask him to look after two distressed kids, so I called Derek.'

Vanessa had looked in her rearview mirror to see Pete looking like he was a million miles away. Vanessa had always thought his feelings for Grace went beyond simple respect for an employer.

'Will she live, Audrey?' Roxanne asked.

'I called the hospital right before you got home. They aren't supposed to give out information to non-family members, but Christian was there. He said she's in stable condition, but they don't know how much damage her heart suffered. Her cardiologist is Citra Amir. She's *very* good. We're lucky to have her. She's not taking any chances – she's helicoptering Grace to Portland tomorrow for more sophisticated testing.'

'I keep thinking about how Christian said it's hard to get a good night's sleep in a hospital because they're so noisy,' Audrey commented. 'I hope Grace sleeps well before her trip.'

*   *   *

An hour later Vanessa, Roxanne, Audrey, Pete, Sammy, Cara, and Derek sat at the dining-room table eating leftovers from the night before. No one seemed to have much appetite and Vanessa found herself constantly asking in an overly bright voice, 'More green beans?' 'More carrots?' 'More turkey?' She wished she'd put on some music so the only sound wasn't cutlery clinking against china. The silence was unnerving.

Suddenly Sammy dropped his fork and asked in a loud, quavering voice, 'Do you think I gave Grace a heart attack by reading "The Tell-Tale Heart"?'

'Oh, no you didn't!' Cara cried, her face distressed.

'You're just a kid like me. You don't know.'

'Well, I'm not a kid and I can tell you for sure you didn't cause it,' Derek told him.

'But you're not a doctor!'

Audrey stepped in. 'I'm a nurse. I know a *lot* about illness and I'm absolutely certain hearing a story she'd read a hundred times didn't scare Grace into a heart attack. She loved the way you read aloud.'

Sammy's lower lip trembled. 'Are you sure?'

'Cross my heart.'

'OK then. I believe you.' He looked around the table. 'But I sure wish she was still here.'

Derek smiled at him. 'So do we all, son.'

'I'm afraid you missed dinner,' Vanessa said to Christian when he arrived at the door after dark. 'There wasn't much left from last night, not even cherry pie. I know it's your favorite.'

'And I only came here for cherry pie.' Christian smiled as he pulled Vanessa into his arms and traced her cheek with a gentle finger. 'How're you doing, sweetheart?'

'I'm scared. And upset. It's been a godawful day. I'll tell you all about it later.'

Christian greeted everyone, including Pete who obviously didn't want to go to his cottage and be alone. 'I checked on Grace right before I left the hospital,' Christian said. 'She was sleeping like a baby. Everything seems fine.'

'Thank God!' Pete exclaimed as everyone looked at him.

Audrey offered Christian coffee or something stronger. He asked for coffee and Vanessa knew he thought he might get a call to come back to the hospital. Everyone talked for a few minutes before Cara said, 'Oh my gosh! It's almost time for Aunt Vanessa's show! Can we all watch it together?'

'Sounds good to me,' Audrey said. 'Derek?'

'Sammy and I never miss it.'

Pete turned on the big flat-screen television, fiddled with the remote control until he finally found the right channel, and everyone settled in, the children smiling, Audrey seated in a chair near Derek, Christian and Vanessa side-by-side on the couch. Roxanne sat by herself in a rocker farthest away from the TV.

The rousing music Vanessa knew so well came blaring on. 'Oh, Pete, turn it down!' she said.

'Don't turn it down!' Cara looked earnestly at Vanessa. 'We have to get the full effect. You can't totally get into the show unless you totally get the full effect.'

'Oh. I didn't know.'

'Are you totally getting the full effect?' Christian muttered a moment later, laughing under his breath.

Vanessa nodded. 'I totally am.'

Halfway through the show, King Dominick had been stricken ill just as an uprising of local nobles was forming. Everyone agreed that the nobles would see Dominick's sickness as a sign of weakness and take the opportunity to muster all their armies and strike at the capital. It was the king's chief advisor, Cadmus, who suggested that Queen Na'dya meet the nobles just outside the gates of the capital city with the king's army behind her and talk them down.

The cameras panned over the gathered nobles. Even though each had brought only part of his army, the number of gathered troops was beyond impressive. Then the gates of the city opened. Queen Na'dya rode through on a magnificent black horse. She wore a red-and-gold brocade gown that spread gracefully over the horse's sides. The dress was low cut and on her chest shone a huge gold and ruby pendant that matched her gold crown studded with large, glittering rubies. Her black hair was parted in the middle and unbound, falling over her shoulders and down to her waist, wavy and gleaming in the bright sun. She rode straight and proud, her face classically beautiful, proud, and unmarked by the least hint of fear. Behind her came the king's army – knight after knight after knight until hundreds stood in formation behind her. Then she delivered a speech, telling the nobles that the king was not ill. He was discussing foreign affairs with his most trusted advisors – foreign affairs that if not settled immediately, would threaten the whole kingdom of Corinna and therefore the lands and fortunes of the nobles. She proclaimed that she did not doubt the nobles' devotion to the kingdom that had given them such munificence and that the king was determined would remain theirs. Her speech was valiant, stirring, and eloquent with just a hint of what might happen to those who were disloyal to the king. At the end, the nobles and their armies cheered, and she smiled benevolently.

Audrey, Derek, Pete, and Christian clapped. The children cheered, 'Yeah, Queen Na'dya!' Only Roxanne sat silent, her face expressionless.

'Didn't you like the scene, Aunt Roxanne?' Cara asked.

She suddenly smiled. 'I sure did! I was so caught up in it, I forgot I was watching my sister!' Roxanne looked at Vanessa. 'You were wonderful.'

After the show ended, Audrey announced, 'Bedtime!'

The children groused for a couple of minutes although they knew their cause was hopeless. They stood and yawned and Cara began giving goodnight kisses to Vanessa and Roxanne.

'Audrey, shall I take Sammy home since I'm here?' Derek asked.

'Not unless you particularly want to. You'd both have to get up earlier in the morning so you could bring him back.'

'That's right, Dad,' Sammy said seriously. 'You need your rest.'

'It's very considerate of you to think of me,' Derek answered, straight-faced. He took Audrey's hand and looked into her eyes. 'Thank you for being so good to us.'

'It's my pleasure,' she said and quickly looked away as if no one at Everly House was aware of the growing feelings between her and Derek.

As Audrey walked Derek to his car, Vanessa leaned close to Christian. 'I don't suppose I could talk you into spending the night.'

His straight brown eyebrows rose above his hazel eyes. 'Here? Don't you think anyone else would mind?'

'Audrey wouldn't. Cara and Sammy certainly wouldn't. Not even Grace would care if she were here. She was very modern in her thinking.'

'Then I'd be delighted to stay, but I didn't bring my pajamas.'

Vanessa winked at him. 'You won't need them.'

'This room is beautiful.' Christian's gaze circled around Grace's bedroom. 'It's worthy of Queen Na'dya.'

'I *am* Queen Na'dya, in case you've forgotten. And tonight you're King Dominick.'

'Oh, but I'm ill!'

'You've just had a miraculous recovery thanks to some herbs I picked in the castle garden.'

'Are you sure they weren't poisonous?'

Vanessa frowned. 'Golly, I don't *think* so. How are you feeling?'

'Wonderful.'

'Then I must have picked the right ones.'

He tapped on the wall. 'Is the tower on the other side?'

'Yes. But there's no entrance from the house.'

Christian smiled. 'When Brody and I were young, we never believed that. We were certain there was a secret entrance.'

'You never told me that when we dated.'

'You were still a teenager. I didn't think it was fair to make you give up family secrets in the name of love.' He paused. 'Are you sure it's all right for me to stay tonight? Maybe Audrey won't like it with Cara here.'

'Oh, she won't mind. Please, Chris.' Vanessa's eyes filled with tears. 'After this awful day and what's happened to Grace, I need you so much.'

Christian hugged her. 'Don't cry. Of course I'll stay.'

Vanessa turned the television on low then pulled back the covers on the bed and piled thick down pillows against the headboard. 'Lie down beside me. We can talk and no one will hear us.'

'No one like who?'

'Sammy, although he seemed out for the count when I checked on him. Roxanne might still be awake.'

Christian took off his shoes, pulled off his wool sweater to reveal a white T-shirt, and slid under the covers. Vanessa scooted next to him and he smiled at her. 'Your scene on the horse was especially great.'

'That dress was *so* hot. I was wearing about ten pounds of hair extensions – at least it felt like it. And that crown! I swear it was heavy enough to have been real gold. We had to keep doing takes from different angles and the horse – Diablo – was getting restless. It took all day. When it was over, I was so dehydrated I had to be given water intravenously. But it was a good scene. I felt a little bit proud of it tonight.'

'You should have felt tremendously proud. It felt almost unreal to be in the same room with the woman who was sitting on the horse delivering that speech.' He leaned down and kissed her lightly on the lips, murmuring, 'If your parents had seen it, they would have changed their minds about your acting.'

'Oh, I don't think so. They were intractable about certain things, which seems weird because neither of them was especially strong.'

'Not your father?'

'No. It's the reason he fell apart when *his* father died. Grace helped him as much as she could but Mom couldn't stand her and the constant friction made Dad worse. He started drinking. That's why Grace went to France. She has relatives there, but you know that.'

'And things got better after she left.'

'The business did because Simon Drake came on the scene. But Dad couldn't stand up to him. Simon was taking over. Finally, Grace got so worried about the situation she came back and insisted Dad assert himself more with Simon. I know Dad was trying. And then Roxanne was taken.'

'Do you think there could have been any connection?'

'You mean did Simon have Roxy kidnapped so Dad would be too demoralized to fight him?' Christian nodded. 'Well, I hadn't thought of it and Simon is devious, but it seems kind of far-fetched. A lot of things could have gone wrong.'

'Yes, like what would he do with her after she'd been kidnapped. Still . . .' He sighed. 'Tell me what happened with Roxanne today. Tell me everything.'

'May I get into my pajamas first?'

Christian looked at her quizzically.

'Suddenly my clothes feel too tight and itchy. It's nerves . . .' she said.

Christian said nothing and looked at the television while she quickly changed into a fresh pair of flannel pajamas and joined him in bed. 'Now put your arm around me again.' He did. She took a deep breath. 'Here goes.'

Vanessa told him about the house that had been left to Zane by his grandfather but Zane never used. 'It was an old wreck. It should have been torn down years ago. The first floor was a dusty, creaking mess. I thought it was one of the worst places I'd ever seen. Then we went to the basement . . .'

When she described the hideous basement room, Christian's body stiffened. 'It was a sado-masochistic chamber. Libby was appalled and declaring over and over that Zane couldn't have known anything about it when Roxanne began talking in this strange, robotic voice about things that had been done to her in the room and then she vomited. I thought she might pass out, but we got her outside in the fresh air as fast as possible.'

Christian was silent for a full minute. Then he said, 'Roxanne vomited when she remembered the room?'

'Yes. She remembered everything, right down to the smell of the incense. I smelled sandalwood and cedar. Roxy said the cedar was always the strongest.'

'Cedar?'

'Yes. Why?'

'Brody used to be allergic to cedar oil.' Christian took a deep breath. 'Go on.'

'Well, we went to Brody's building next. I know you already went there looking for him, but the police wanted to see it. Christian, his living quarters are beautiful.'

'I know.'

'I mean, the simplicity, all of those framed prints of impressionist paintings. Libby told me that one time he said he wanted his home to be *serene*. She remembered the exact word. I simply could not reconcile it with the image of Zane with his neck slashed with Brody—' Christian gasped. 'Oh God, I'm sorry, Chris. I didn't mean to say that!'

'But you thought it.'

'Well . . . yes. I don't know much about schizophrenia, but to think that the person who wanted to live in that calm, beautiful room could also murder his best friend so horribly . . .' She closed her eyes. 'I wish I could take back everything I just said, but I can't.'

'Tell me more about Brody's place.'

'Well, it was a shock to see the immaculate living room and kitchen and then see the bedroom. You must have seen all the pictures of medieval scenes scattered everywhere. In the bathroom, I found two blue-and-white capsules lying on the floor.'

Christian's interest quickened. 'Do you have them?'

'Yes. I stuck them in my bag.' She got out of bed, picked up her tote bag she'd left on the floor, and fished out the capsules. 'Here they are. I wrapped them in a tissue.'

Christian took the tissue, opened it and looked at the capsules. Then he rewrapped them and tucked them in the pocket of his jeans. 'I know what they are. Still, I'd like to have them tested.'

'Why?'

'Just to be certain.'

'OK.' Vanessa sat on the side of the bed. 'Did anything I told you mean anything special? Anything about that room—'

'Maybe, but I want to find out more about it – more than what you just saw. I need to know about that house.'

'Then we'll find out, Christian. We're in this together, even if we can't clear Zane.'

'If we clear Zane, we'll clear Brody,' he said. 'I know it.'

He pulled her toward him and kissed her. 'I need you, Vanessa, not just because of this mess but because my life doesn't have much meaning without you. That's what I've learned over the last eight years. That nothing seems like it has any real color, any excitement, if you're not in it. Do you feel the same way about me? Because if you don't, please tell me now before we go any farther—'

'I do feel the same way,' Vanessa said passionately, 'and we can go as far as possible as long as we do it together.'

NINETEEN

At six thirty the next morning, Vanessa and Christian lay twined together in bed. Vanessa's cellphone rang. The sound barely registered, and she shook her head, as if she could shoo away the incessant tone. It rang again. This time she groaned and pulled slightly away from Christian. On the third ring, she fumbled on her night table until she found it and mumbled, ''Lo?'

'Miss Everly? Miss Vanessa Everly?'

'Yeah. I mean yes. This is Vanessa.'

'This is Dr Citra Amir. I'm sorry to tell you that your grandmother passed away in the night.'

'What? No!' Vanessa sat up in bed. 'Her prognosis was good. She was resting comfortably. What happened?'

'We won't know until we do an autopsy, but apparently your grandmother had a serious cardiac event in the night. Her heart probably just stopped, and she didn't feel a thing.'

'What is it?' Christian asked.

'Grace is dead. She's *dead*!'

Christian took the phone. 'Citra? This is Christian Montgomery. Can you tell me what happened?' He was silent for a minute. 'All right. Vanessa and I will be at the hospital within half an hour.'

After he got off the phone, Vanessa looked at him imploringly. 'Please tell me it's not true.'

'I'm afraid it is. Grace had a cardiac arrest in the night. There were no guarantees, Nessa, even though Grace got through the initial incident. Dr Amir was right in assuming there would be another one. That's why Citra was sending her to Portland for more sophisticated testing.'

Vanessa put her head in her hands, but no tears came. She simply could not believe Grace was dead – beautiful, smart, strong, charming Grace whom Vanessa had idolized her whole life. Christian hugged her tightly, rocking her and making soothing noises, but Vanessa gently shook herself free.

'I'm all right. For now at least. And I have things to do. I have to get to the hospital.'

'I'm going with you. You're not in this alone, Nessa.'

They dressed quickly and Vanessa went to Roxanne's room, knocking softly. After the second knock, a drowsy Roxanne opened the door. 'What is it?' she asked in a slurred voice. 'Is something wrong?'

'Roxy, I just got a call from the hospital. Grace died in the night.'

'Died? *Died*?' Roxanne looked like she was collapsing in on herself. 'But I just got home! She can't be dead. She just *can't*!'

Vanessa hugged her but Roxanne didn't return the hug. She trembled, her shoulders slumped. 'Go back to bed, honey. Maybe you can sleep.'

'Sleep? After *this*?'

'Well, just rest then. I'll take care of everything.'

'I should help. I know I should but I don't know what to do.'

'Don't worry about it for now. I won't make any arrangements without discussing them with you.'

'*Arrangements?*' Roxanne asked, appalled.

'Well, there will be a funeral and—'

Roxanne looked as if she was going to burst into tears.

'We'll talk about it later.' Vanessa reached out to her sister, rubbing her arm. 'Go back to bed.'

Roxanne nodded and closed her door without meeting Vanessa's eyes. She turned around and Christian stood behind her. 'Roxanne's not up to handling this,' he said.

'I know,' Vanessa said. 'I'll handle everything I can myself, but I need to tell Audrey.'

Vanessa went downstairs and knocked lightly on Audrey's door. She was already awake and quickly opened the bedroom door. 'Grace died in the night.'

Audrey's blue eyes widened. 'Really? Oh *no.*' Audrey pulled Vanessa into her arms. 'Oh, honey, I'm *so* sorry.'

'Me too. I still can't believe it.'

'What can I do?'

'Nothing except look after the kids. Christian and I are going to the hospital. We'll identify her and sign papers or whatever and then there are funeral arrangements. Roxanne won't be much help. She seems completely devastated.'

'That's understandable.' Audrey stepped back and looked at her earnestly. 'You can count on me. I'll help you with anything you need.'

'I know.' Finally tears began to run down Vanessa's face. 'I can always count on you, Audrey, and that means the world to me.'

As they drove away from the hospital, Vanessa said, 'I feel like I'm dreaming and I can't wake up.'

'Unfortunately, honey, you're not dreaming. I wish you were,' Christian responded.

'She's really dead. Gone. I can't imagine a world without Grace.'

Christian took her hand as he drove. 'I know you can't. Even during the years when she was in France, you communicated with her constantly. She was really more of a mother to you than your own mother was.'

'Yes, she was. She loved me. Ellen didn't.'

'I didn't mean Ellen didn't love you.'

'But she didn't. I was too much like Grace. It's all right, Christian. I came to terms with my relationship with Ellen years ago. And it didn't hurt me. If I'm really honest, I don't think I cared any more for her than she did for me. I suppose that makes me a terrible person.'

'Not at all. I was lucky – I had great relationships with both of my parents and my brother. But just because you're related to someone, doesn't mean you have to love them. That probably sounds cold, but it's how I feel.'

'I suppose I do too, if I'm honest.' She looked at Christian and smiled. 'We have a lot in common, Dr Montgomery.'

He smiled back warmly. 'We always have, Vanessa. Always.'

Audrey ended up going to the funeral home with Vanessa to make arrangements for Grace. Christian had work and Roxanne said she wouldn't be any help. 'I feel like I stopped maturing when I was fifteen,' she told Vanessa. 'I'm sorry to be so useless.'

'You're not useless. I'm going to ask Pete to come to the house and the two of you can look after the children. That's a lot more challenging than making funeral arrangements.'

Secretly Vanessa was relieved that Audrey was going with her instead of Roxanne. Audrey was always calm in an emergency and she'd known Grace better than Roxy did. At the funeral home, she gave Vanessa support and made a few suggestions without trying to take control.

On the way home, they'd avoided the subject of Grace. Audrey had asked some questions about what they'd found in Zane's home but kept her reaction mild, saying, 'Remember that was Zane's house, not Brody's.'

'But they were partners. Before, they were friends when Brody probably stole Roxanne.'

'I thought maybe you didn't believe that anymore, Vanessa. You don't seem to hold anything against Christian now.'

'Eight years ago I believed he was backing his father's lie about Brody being at home when Roxy was taken. Now, even if Gerald was lying, I don't think Christian knew it. And I'm not sure Gerald was lying. Maybe Brody really was at home.'

Audrey was quiet for a moment before she asked, 'Then who took Roxanne?'

* * *

When Vanessa and Audrey got home, the children were playing in the yard with Queenie. Pete stood in the living room, looking worried. 'Miss Roxanne tried being sociable with the kids, but she was upset and they knew it. They're the ones who suggested going outside. I said it was OK as long as they stayed where I could see them. Then Miss Roxanne went back up to her room.'

'So the kids didn't wear you out, Pete?'

He grinned. 'They're full of energy but they are two polite children. You've done an excellent job raising Cara, Miss Audrey, and Mr Sherwin's doin' great with Sammy.' His grin disappeared. 'I just hope that ex-wife of his doesn't get hold of Sammy.'

'She won't,' Audrey said firmly. 'She walked away three years ago to live with a man old enough to be her father. He hasn't married her, and she's made no attempt until now to even see Sammy, much less get custody of him.'

'I know I just got up four hours ago but I feel worn out,' Vanessa said. 'If everything's under control here, I think I'll go lie down for a while.'

'You need to rest. Can I bring you anything?' Audrey asked.

Vanessa smiled sadly. 'Just some peace of mind.'

An hour later, Vanessa lay sleepless in Grace's bed, thinking. She thought of Brody's beautiful loft. She thought of Zane Felder seated at the grand piano with his throat slashed. Most of all she thought of the sado-masochistic room in Zane's tumbling-down house with upper floors that looked as if they hadn't been touched by a human hand for decades. Whose sick minds had planned that room? Whose sick minds had compelled them to keep her sister a prisoner there? Had it been only Zane and Brody? Roxy said there had been several men. Who else was involved?

Suddenly Vanessa had an idea. She didn't wait to decide if it was a good idea – she acted strictly on impulse. She jumped out of bed, got her purse off the dresser, and rummaged through it until she found a business card. Then she picked up her cellphone and dialed the number scribbled on the back of the card.

After the third ring, a loud female voice boomed, 'Hello?'

'Is this Fay Jennings?'

'Well, yes,' the woman said carefully. 'Who is this?'

'It's Vanessa Everly.'

'Vanessa! Vanessa Everly! Oh my God, that's what my caller ID said but I thought it must be a joke. I *never* expected to see you again in person much less *hear* from you after our day on the plane together. Are you really calling *me*?'

'Yes, I *really* am.'

'Oh, I'm sorry. I sound like a fool rattling on and on. I'm so surprised! How are you, dear?'

'I'm fine.' She sighed. 'Well, I'm really not fine. That's why I'm calling. Do you mind?'

'Do I mind if Vanessa Everly calls *me* when she has a problem? Well, I'm simply flattered out of my mind! Oh, that sounded awful. What I meant was that I'm pleased you think you can call me, that maybe I can help you, if you're having a problem. Oh, I'm making a mess of this.'

'No, you're not. Really, Fay. And before we get into my life, how are things with you and Harold?'

'Oh, great! I told you how I love Christmas and it's almost here. I've nearly worn him out stringing lights and dragging in a tree and putting up wreaths. We don't have children but some couples around town are nice enough to come and celebrate with us and I always want the house to look extra special. But that's enough about me. Tell me what's wrong, dear.'

'It's a long story.'

'I have nothing but time. Tell me everything.'

Vanessa began with the kidnapping of Roxanne. 'I don't know if you read anything about it at the time . . .'

'I remembered some of it but when I got home – and I hope this doesn't offend you – I read everything I could find about you on the internet. I also saw that your sister had come home after all of those years. That must have seemed like a miracle.'

'Yes. She'd been held captive for eight years during which she was physically abused, drugged, and used for . . . well, sex.'

Fay gasped.

'I know it's horrible,' Vanessa nearly whispered. 'She spent time in the hospital and then she came home to us, fragile and emotionally scarred but at least fairly physically healthy after she got over a bout of bronchitis and she had plenty of fluids and food.'

'Oh, how wonderful!'

'Yes, it was, but our joy was short-lived. So many things happened immediately afterward.' Vanessa told Fay about Brody Montgomery going missing, the murder of Zane Felder, the attack on Max Newman, Grace's death, and last of all, going to the house owned by Zane and the basement room. By the time she finished, she was in tears.

After a minute, Fay said softly, 'Honey, I am *so* sorry. Last night Harold and I watched *Kingdom of Corinna* and you looked so beautiful and invincible on that horse speaking to all of those soldiers. We both commented on it. And to know that this is what's *really* going on in your life is shocking. You poor, dear girl. I wish I could think of something to say to make it all better.'

'I didn't call for that. No one can make it all better. No one can restore Zane Felder's life. But I hate to see his reputation ruined on top of everything else if he's innocent. He has a fiancé, Libby, who's the sweetest girl you could ever meet. She's shattered by his death and she was with us when we saw that awful room in the house he owns.'

'I'm sure she was. Did she really not know him at all?'

'That's just it. I think she did know him and she swears he couldn't have anything to do with the basement room in the house.'

'But it's his house, isn't it?'

'Yes, but, well . . . it was left to him by a grandfather who detested him and the whole matter of the will was handled by a lawyer named Enoch Snyder who seems to hate Zane, too. Something about it doesn't seem right. This is a huge favor to ask, but I know Harold is a lawyer and I wonder if he could look into the matter. Zane left all of his possessions to Libby along with some shares of the software company. It's her house now and I'm sure she wouldn't mind Harold seeing if everything is . . . well, proper.'

'Oh, honey . . . I'm sure—' Her voice broke off, and she nearly yelled, 'Harold! You're home early!'

Vanessa heard his muffled voice down the line say, 'I thought I'd catch you with your boyfriend.'

'Not today! Vanessa Everly is on the phone. Can you believe it? The poor dear is having some terrible troubles. She wonders if we can help. Well, really you.' Fay came back on the phone. 'Vanessa, honey, do you want to speak to Harold? Tell him *everything*.'

'I don't want to bother him if he just came home for lunch—'

'He's his own boss. He doesn't have a "lunch hour". And you wouldn't be bothering him, believe me. He's here, reaching for the phone right now.'

'Well, OK—'

Before Vanessa could finish a sentence, Harold Jennings was booming, 'Vanessa Everly? Is it really you?'

'Yes, I'm afraid so. How are you, Harold?'

'I'm ten times better than I was five minutes ago. Fay and I were just watching you on TV last night. You were terrific!'

'I'm glad you thought so . . . I'm not so terrific now.'

His voice immediately softened and became sympathetic. 'What's wrong? How can we help?'

'I told Fay a long story. Do you want to hear it all, or only the favor I'd like?'

'I want to hear all of it, if you want to tell me. You sound upset. Take your time, Vanessa.'

She went through the whole story again. Occasionally Harold asked a question, but his voice was calm and professional. 'What I'd really like for you to check on is the house that belonged to Zane. The whole thing doesn't make sense to me.'

'Nor to me. A house that should have been destroyed years ago for health reasons is left standing, untouched, except for a sado-masochistic chamber in the basement? That's one for the books.'

'I know. But our sheriff and I were there with my sister. She threw up when she saw it. She's not confused. That's the house where she was kept. I want to make certain that Zane Felder was the person who created that room, who let it be part of a house that belonged to him.'

'I understand. Now you said that Zane's lawyer is John Dawson. I know him. He's a fine lawyer. I also know Enoch Snyder, who I think should have been ridden out of town on a rail. He's a nasty one. I'll get in touch with both of them, but before I start, I need to talk to Libby since she's the official owner of the house now.'

'Yes, of course.' Vanessa gave him Libby's full name and phone numbers. 'I don't think she'll mind that I'm meddling in all of this. It's for the protection of Zane's reputation. She's a very sweet girl, Harold.'

'I'll do everything I can to help.'

'And send the bill to me.'

Harold laughed. 'You don't worry about a bill, Vanessa Everly. It's a privilege to do a favor for Queen Na'dya.'

TWENTY

'Does this dress look all right?' Roxanne asked. She wore a simple long-sleeved navy-blue sheath they'd selected yesterday for Grace's funeral. 'I haven't worn a dress for over eight years.'

'It looks perfect,' Vanessa said, adjusting a long-sleeved short gray jacket over her own sleeveless gray dress. Grace had hated black.

The last three days had been miserable. They'd tried to make everything normal for the kids, but losing Grace the day before Christmas made it impossible for them to be happy. They'd tried to put on a good show for the adults, but it hadn't worked. Two days later, Vanessa had seen Cara standing beside Grace's hospital bed crying. 'I really loved her like my own grandmother,' she sniffled. 'Sammy did, too. He's been crying, but he tries to hide it because he thinks it isn't manly.'

Vanessa had done her best to comfort Cara but she knew Audrey was better at that than she was. Derek had come over and taken the children to the Everly Cliffs Café before the bed and other hospital equipment had been removed from the library and Vanessa and Roxanne had put everything back the way it had been before Grace broke her hip. Tears had dripped down Roxy's face while they worked. When she'd caught Vanessa looking at her, she'd said, 'I'm sorry to be such a baby when you're so strong. But I just got home and she wasn't glad to see me and I was so hurt. I thought in time maybe things would change, but now there's no chance of that. And here I am feeling sorry for *myself*, as usual.'

'I understand,' Vanessa had said. 'I told you she was very different from the Grace you remembered, but I don't think you had a chance to really process the change. She did love you, though. You were her granddaughter. And she had a good life. She was eighty-six, Roxy. I hope I live that long.'

'Yeah, me too.' Roxanne wiped tears off her face with the back of her hand like a little girl. 'Well, let's get everything done before the children come home. I want things to seem normal for them.'

To their dismay, the kids had seemed upset to see the library returned to its original state. 'Where's Grace's stuff?' Cara wailed.

'It belonged to the hospital,' Vanessa said. 'They needed it, so they took it back.'

'You could've bought it.'

'Sam, that's not polite,' Derek reprimanded gently.

'Well, they could have.'

Vanessa smiled. 'Sammy, Grace designed this library when she got married. She loved it the way it was before she got sick, but we had to put in the hospital bed and the other equipment. This is the way she would have wanted it.'

'Oh. I didn't know. I didn't mean to be rude. It's . . . pretty.'

'You weren't rude and Grace would be happy to know you think the room is pretty. Now tell me – what did you have at the café?'

Shedding coats and hats, the children talked about the apple strudel, cherry-cheese Danish pastries and strawberry-and-cream-stuffed pastries they had sampled. 'I added some new items to the menu,' Derek said. 'They seem to be a hit.'

'The apple strudel isn't new and I could eat my weight in it,' Vanessa had laughed.

Now the mood in the house was somber. Vanessa hadn't heard the children laughing all day and it was two o'clock. She'd told Audrey and Derek that the kids didn't have to attend the funeral, but they both said the children wanted to go. 'They want to say goodbye,' Derek said. 'They both really loved Grace.'

Both Christian and Derek were escorting Vanessa and Audrey. Pete would go with them and he arrived first wearing an ancient dark-brown suit. 'It's the only suit I own,' he told Vanessa. 'I bought it thirty years ago for my sister's wedding. I hope it's all right.'

'It's very smart. Would you like some coffee?'

'I sure would.' He followed her into the kitchen, stumping along on his crutches. 'I can get rid of these dang things tomorrow. Did Wade Baylor ever find out who was hiding in the tower that night?'

'No, he didn't,' Vanessa said, thinking about Christian saying he and Brody used to think there was an entrance from the tower into the house. Did Brody still believe it? 'Milk? Sugar?'

'Now, Miss Vanessa, you know I take it strong and black!' Pete grinned.

'Yes, I do. My mind is wandering today.'

As Pete sat sipping his coffee, the doorbell rang again. Christian and Derek both stood on the porch. 'We arrived at the same time,' Christian said.

'Come in. Would you like some coffee? Pete's in the kitchen having a cup.'

'Sure,' Derek said. 'We don't have to leave for about twenty minutes.'

While they were in the kitchen, Roxanne walked in looking very pale but pretty. 'Coffee, Roxy?

'Oh, I don't think so. I'm nervous enough without caffeine.'

Right after her came Audrey and the kids. Sammy wore a suit, Cara a golden-brown dress that went beautifully with her coloring, and Audrey a lovely dark green suit with her auburn hair pulled back in a long ponytail at her neck. 'Do you want coffee, Audrey?' Vanessa asked.

'No, thank you. I drank too much this morning.' She looked around. 'Everyone looks so nice!'

'My suit is brand new!' Sammy volunteered.

'It's very handsome,' Audrey said.

'Oh yes. *Very.*' Cara added, looking at him admiringly. Then she asked, 'Will people be coming back here after the funeral?'

'Yes. It's tradition,' Vanessa said. 'They spend about an hour eating and drinking.'

'That seems weird.'

Derek frowned. '*Sam!*'

'It seems weird to me, too,' Vanessa told Sammy. 'It always has. I don't know why people think they have to stuff themselves with food after a funeral.'

Sammy and Cara giggled. Even Derek smiled.

The doorbell rang. 'I wonder who that could be,' Vanessa said. 'We're all here.'

Roxanne started out of the kitchen. 'I'll get it.' In a couple of minutes, she came back holding a small package wrapped in brown paper. 'The mailman wanted to give this to someone because he was afraid it would get lost if he left it on the porch.' She frowned. 'It's addressed to me.'

Cara looked excited. 'Open it! Open it!'

'I can't imagine what it could be . . .' Roxanne tore off the paper and took the lid off a small white box. Inside was a card. She read aloud, '"Wear this to your grandmother's funeral. It will look beautiful."' She emptied the box on the counter and there lay a gold, diamond and sapphire ring. 'My birthstone ring,' she said just above a whisper. 'I was wearing this the night I was kidnapped.'

They arrived late to the funeral. After seeing the jewelry, Roxanne had come close to fainting and had trouble getting her breath. Audrey had suggested staying home with her, but Roxanne had insisted that if she could simply have a tranquilizer, she could go to the funeral. As Roxanne got more agitated, Christian asked Audrey if she had any tranquilizers in her medical kit. She did, and when she produced the bottle Roxanne grabbed it, shook out three pills, and swallowed them dry.

'*Roxy!*' Vanessa cried. 'That's dangerous!'

'I have a high tolerance. I'll be all right by the time we get to the cemetery.'

But Vanessa wasn't all right. The arrival of the ring had shaken her to the core. Someone out there had held onto Roxanne's birthstone ring for over eight years and decided to return it on what they knew was the day of her grandmother's funeral. The thought was frightening and she was unable to concentrate on the first few minutes of the minister's graveside service. She knew Roxanne's tranquilizers must have taken effect. Roxy seemed slightly dazed, her face white and blank, her eyes blinking slowly. Vanessa held her hand and instead of thinking about who might be watching them from a distance, reveling in the fear the return of the ring had caused, tried to focus on the multitude of flowers in every color and the blanket of Grace's favorite yellow roses lying on top of the mahogany coffin.

Finally, she was able to shift her gaze and tried to notice the people in attendance without staring at them. First she saw Simon and Jane Drake along with Wade Baylor. Jane stood closer to her father than to Wade and frequently touched the arm of his coat like a little girl seeking reassurance. A bruised Max Newman stood stiffly as if he were still in pain from the injuries to his jaw and rib.

Vanessa's eyes drifted over the faces of some of Grace's close friends, mostly women who had looked up to her as a social queen, which Grace had not understood at all. She'd never considered herself smarter or stronger or higher class than any of her friends, many of whom dated from childhood. There was Verna Hodgkins wearing a net veil; beside her was Esther Edmonds in maroon lipstick; next to Esther was—

Nia Sherwin. Nia Sherwin in a white cashmere coat far too hot for the day with her hair in an elaborate up-do and her make-up perfect. Vanessa glanced over at Derek, who'd also seen her and was pulling Sammy a bit closer to him. She shifted her gaze to Simon Drake who was watching Nia. *Snake*, Vanessa thought. You invited her.

Audrey nudged her and murmured, 'Bow your head.' Vanessa realized the service was over and the minister was saying the Lord's Prayer. Afterward, an endless stream of people passed by, shaking hands, offering condolences, assuming tragic faces. At least Nia didn't have the nerve to approach them, Vanessa thought. That would have been too much.

Her relief was short-lived, though. Back at Everly House, she, Audrey and some of Grace's friends were setting out food for the mourners when Nia passed them holding a cookie and headed like a heat-seeking missile for Sammy. Vanessa broke away from the serving table and followed her. She arrived in time to hear the woman say, 'Sammy, darling, it's Mommy! I came here just to see you. Give me a hug and kiss!'

Sammy's blue eyes were huge and he took a step away from her. She pursued him, grabbed his jacket sleeve and pulled him into a hug. At this point Vanessa cast a desperate look around the room and caught sight of Derek. She made her way to him, explained the situation, but by the time they got back, Audrey was facing Nia. 'You were not invited to this funeral.'

Nia raised a perfect eyebrow. 'It was in the newspaper. Does one need a personal invitation to a funeral these days, particularly one so heavily publicized?'

'It was not heavily publicized. You didn't even know Grace Everly. You came here to see Sammy.'

'And what's wrong with that? He *is* my son, Alice.'

'It's Audrey, and your husband, who has full custody of Sammy, doesn't want you to see him.'

'She's right,' Derek said in a strong voice. The general murmur was dying down as people began to stare. 'I don't want you to see Sam and you know he doesn't want to see you.'

'He's only twelve. He doesn't know what he wants.'

'I do too know what I want!'

Nia smiled grimly. 'Hush, Sammy, Mommy and Daddy are talking.'

'You're not my mother. Not really. Not anymore. You went away with that man and you forgot all about me for *years*.' Sammy was red-faced with fury. 'Now you want me again. Why?'

'That's what I'd like to know,' Derek said. 'But this isn't the place to hash out our problems. I want you to leave, Nia. If you leave right now, we'll talk later. I mean it.'

They locked gazes for almost a full minute as the room became completely silent. Then Nia huffed, stalked to the front door and slammed it behind her. Derek leaned down to comfort Sammy, who stood as stiff and controlled as a soldier at attention.

Guests immediately began talking as if that would obliterate the ugly scene. Audrey and Vanessa moved away from Derek and Sammy. 'Oh, that *woman*!' Audrey almost hissed.

'She shouldn't be anyone's mother,' Vanessa murmured. 'I hope Derek can send her back to her lover soon.'

'I've wondered about that relationship. At first it seemed that Nia was abandoning Sammy because her big-time movie producer didn't want him. What's changed?'

'I'd be the last to know,' Audrey muttered.

'Maybe Derek will find out tomorrow.'

'He might not tell me.'

Vanessa smiled. 'I wish you could see the way he looks at you, Audrey. He's in love with you even if he hasn't said it. I'm sure he'll tell you everything Nia says.'

TWENTY-ONE

Vanessa was bone-tired after the funeral. Audrey and Roxanne were hovering around the kitchen, putting away leftovers and wiping counters. Audrey fixed Vanessa a rum and Coke. 'You need this,' she said. 'I know how much you loved Grace.

Perhaps it will help you sleep. You'll have a busy day tomorrow. A funeral doesn't put to rights the affairs of the dead.'

When she awakened the next morning, she had a vague memory of Queenie walking around her bed the night before, nudging her, whining. Now the dog lay peacefully in her bed, Dom tucked under her chin. *Maybe I was dreaming*, Vanessa thought as she stretched and looked at the dull light seeping in through a slit in the drapes.

'Oh, not another dreary day,' she said aloud. Queenie raised her head. 'I'd hoped we'd have sunshine and blue skies.' The dog made a small sound in her throat. 'You always understand me, don't you?'

Vanessa swung her legs over the side of the bed and Queenie came to her side for an ear rub. Vanessa got up, put on her robe, and headed downstairs for coffee. The kitchen was quieter than normal. The children were eating cereal but not chattering as usual. Audrey wasn't humming as she prepared toast for herself. Vanessa felt like her voice came out too loud and happy when she said, 'Good morning, everyone!'

All three looked at her.

'Good morning, Aunt Vanessa,' Cara said softly. 'How are you?'

'I miss Grace, but she wouldn't want us to be sad. I think we should all remember that she'd be disappointed if we moped around and cried. She thought everyone should enjoy every single day of life.'

'You're absolutely right,' Audrey said. 'I've known Grace since I was a child' – she looked at the kids – 'when I was even younger than you. And I *know* that's how Grace felt. So Cara, Sammy, cheer up. It's what Grace would have wanted.'

Sammy and Cara looked at each other and smiled. 'OK,' Cara said. 'No more tears. Sammy and I will be brave and do what Grace would want us to do.'

Vanessa fixed toast with butter and blueberry preserves and drank two cups of coffee. 'Gee, I feel better!' She looked at Queenie who was licking her bowl clean. 'How about you?' The dog barked and the kids laughed. 'Come upstairs and help me get dressed, Queenie. I need your opinion on what I'll wear today.'

As she passed Roxanne's door, Vanessa opened it and peeked inside. Once again Roxy lay on her right side with her legs drawn up and her head tucked under. Vanessa smiled and decided not to pull up the blanket. She didn't want to wake her.

'Oh, what to wear,' Vanessa said to Queenie as she sorted through the scant wardrobe she brought with her to Everly Cliffs. She chose a pair of jeans, a blouse to wear under a wool V-necked sweater, socks and boots. She brushed her hair and pulled it back in a ponytail. Then she grabbed a jacket and crept downstairs, Queenie on a leash behind her. She felt like taking a walk, but she didn't want the children to accompany her. This morning she wanted to be alone with her thoughts.

The sky was low and the color of flint without a streak of pale yellow or even blue. A light mist still hung over the hill overlooking the beach, which looked bleak and lonely. She closed her eyes, feeling tears pressing, but she couldn't let herself cry after giving the kids a rousing speech about not being sad. Instead she let Queenie lead her through the ragged grass and low undergrowth, trying to keep Grace's face from her mind as she concentrated on Queenie's unusual force as she pulled forward. At last Queenie stopped abruptly and began growling.

'What's wrong?' Vanessa asked. The dog started barking furiously. 'Queenie! Stop!'

Queenie lunged ahead. Vanessa stumbled after her and without even realizing what had happened, she tripped over something and fell. The dog turned to Vanessa but continued a storm of barking. Trying to catch her breath, Vanessa looked back at the obstacle over which she'd fallen.

For a moment she simply stared. Then, with an overwhelming horror, she saw the body of Nia Sherwin lying on her back, her hands folded on her abdomen and holding two white roses, her blonde hair spread gracefully around her beautiful face and a gold ribbon tied across her forehead.

Vanessa didn't scream. She simply clambered to her feet and looked while Queenie barked. 'Quiet. The children will hear you. Quiet, girl!'

Queenie knew basic commands and fell silent, although she stood rigidly by Vanessa's side, as if ready to defend her. But Vanessa wasn't paying attention to Queenie. Her gaze was fastened on the slit across Nia's slender throat and the pool of blood that had spread downward and stained her white crew-necked wool sweater. She wore no coat or shoes. Only black slacks and black stockings on her feet.

Almost without thought, Vanessa called the house. When Audrey answered, Vanessa asked, 'Are the children near you?'

'They're in the other room watching television. What is it?'

'I've just found Nia Sherwin's body.' She heard Audrey's sharp intake of breath. 'I have to call Wade and he'll come with other cops and crime-scene people. Can you take the kids somewhere? Now?'

Audrey cleared her throat. 'Yes. I'll think of something.' Her voice sounded high and strained. 'Are you sure about Nia?'

'Yes.'

'Oh my God.' She drew a breath. 'I'll have the kids out of here in ten minutes.'

When Vanessa saw Audrey's car going down the hill away from the house, she called Wade Baylor. 'Wade, this is Vanessa Everly,' she said formally. 'You should come to Everly House. Nia Sherwin has been murdered.'

'*Murdered?*' Wade almost shouted. 'You mean she's dead?'

'I mean she's been murdered. She's north of the house. Queenie and I will be waiting.'

In what seemed record time, Wade arrived, his expression grim. He looked at the body expressionlessly, walking in a wide girth around it. 'Did you touch the body?' he asked Vanessa.

'No . . . but, oh God, I tripped over her.'

'Is she in the same position as before you tripped?'

'Yes, I think so. She was so stiff that she didn't . . . well, roll.'

'Did the dog nose around her?'

'No. She kept about two feet away, barking.'

'That's good.'

Vanessa remained quiet for a moment. 'Wade, do you have any idea when she might have been killed?'

'She's in rigor mortis, but I'm not sure for how long. We need the experts. I'll call the crime-scene team.'

'What about her slashed neck?'

'I'm not sure. It isn't like Zane Felder's.'

'What? You think the same person who killed Zane Felder killed Nia Sherwin?'

'I don't know, Vanessa. We're going to need a lot of expert examination.'

'But what about Sammy? I know he didn't like Nia but she's his mother!'

Wade looked at her with his sad eyes. 'I know. I'm sorry. Poor little guy. But Nia wasn't exactly beloved by people in this town and especially by her husband.'

'Derek! Are you accusing Derek of doing this?'

'I'm saying he has a motive, Vanessa. Even you have to admit he does. And they had a bad argument at the funeral reception just yesterday. There are a lot of witnesses.'

'Vanessa!' She looked up to see Roxy running toward them. She'd been so worried about the children she'd forgotten about her sister. 'What's wrong?'

Before Vanessa could answer, Roxanne came to a halt beside her, looking at the body of Nia. 'Oh Lord! When did this happen?'

'We don't know. Sometime last night.'

'Her neck is slit!'

'Don't get too close, Roxanne,' Wade said. 'We don't want to disturb evidence.'

Roxanne's long robe blew around her legs in the breeze that lifted her hair. 'He did this, Nessa! Brody did this! Her hair is loose. It's long and the color of mine.' She gazed at Nia. 'Look at the gold ribbon across her forehead. And the roses in her hands.' Roxanne's face was ashen and grave. 'She looks like the women in the prints in Brody's apartment. The Lady of Shalott, some of the others.' She raised blue, terror-filled eyes to Wade. 'Brody mistook Nia for *me*!'

The children came skipping into the house. Cara stopped in front of Vanessa, who was sat on the living-room couch. 'Mommy wanted us to go downtown and look for after-Christmas sales but half the stores were closed! We didn't buy anything!'

'I guess she thought the sales would start sooner than they did.' She smiled at Cara. 'I'd like to talk to Sammy alone for a few minutes. Is that all right with you?'

Cara immediately sensed trouble. 'He didn't do anything wrong, did he?'

'Not at all. I just need a few minutes, Cara.'

As Cara left the room, Sammy stood solemnly in front of Vanessa. 'Something's wrong, isn't it? I could tell by the way Audrey was acting.'

'Yes, Sammy, it is. This is going to be hard to hear . . . Your mother is dead.'

The boy stared at her. 'She's dead?'

Vanessa nodded.

'Did she have a heart attack like Grace?' the boy asked.

'No.' Vanessa swallowed hard. 'Someone killed her. I'm so sorry.'

Sammy looked away for a few seconds. 'Do you know who killed her?'

'No. The police are investigating.'

'Oh.' He went completely still. 'They'll blame Dad.'

'Maybe not.'

'Yes, they will, even though he didn't do it. He was really mad at her, but he'd *never* kill anyone! Not Dad!' His eyes filled with tears. 'Can I go to my room now?'

'Of course, Sammy.'

'And please don't let Cara come in. I don't want her to see me crying again.'

TWENTY-TWO

B y eleven thirty that night, Vanessa was still tossing and turning. The day had been awful and she knew she'd think about every moment of it later, but now all she felt was bereft. From the time she was a toddler, she'd loved Grace more than anyone. Then when she was a teenager and Grace lived in France, they'd communicated almost daily. And after Roxanne had been taken and Vanessa had come to Everly Cliffs as little as possible, she'd still called, emailed and texted Grace constantly. The woman had known Vanessa's almost every thought and feeling.

Now Nia Sherwin had been murdered. She'd intensely disliked Nia but she hadn't wished her dead. And how did Sammy feel? He wouldn't talk and he'd been shut away in his room almost all day. Not only was his mother dead, his father was a suspect. Vanessa knew the police had questioned Derek for hours. Audrey was distraught, Derek had hired a lawyer, and Cara was inconsolable because Sammy had pulled away from her. Roxanne was even more frightened than she had been before Grace's death. All the disasters flashed through Vanessa's mind until she felt as if she'd scream.

Knowing she'd never get to sleep, she got out of bed and put on socks, jeans, a sweater, sneakers, and a jacket, then tiptoed to the kitchen where she made cinnamon tea that she put in a thermos. She found the key to the tower in the antique writing desk and let herself out the front door. Only a few of the porch lights were on and Vanessa was glad they weren't all glowing into the night. She didn't want to be seen. In two minutes she had let herself into the tower, leaned against the closed door, and breathed deeply before climbing the spiral of stairs. At the top, she closed her eyes. She could almost see Grace sitting on the love seat, sipping cinnamon tea and eating cookies they'd brought from the house like they used to do. Then they would look through the telescope at the ocean and finally talk about everything and nothing.

'I miss you,' Vanessa said aloud. 'This was *our* place. We're the only ones who loved it. I know if any of you remains on this Earth, it's in here.'

She poured some tea and sat on the love seat for a while, sipping the tea that brought back so many memories of her confiding things to Grace she would never have told her mother. Grace, in turn, had offered advice and giggled and reminisced, never acting as if she was anything except a friend.

When Vanessa finished her second cup of tea, she stood up and circled the room, looking at framed pictures of ships: USS *West Virginia*; HMS *Victory*; USS *Constitution*; HMS *Bounty;* Captain Cook's HMS *Endeavor*. Then she examined the model ships her grandfather Leonard had built and put in the tower: a three-masted ship; a Spanish galleon; HMS *Leopard*; the *Santa Maria*. Grace said Frederick had shown no interest in the ship models, but Leonard had continued to build them for 'my boy'. 'For his boy,' Grace had laughed. 'His boy couldn't have cared less.'

Vanessa lighted two candles then wandered over to the telescope and sat down, focusing it on the beach. The moon was almost full, bathing the beach in silvery light. Everything looked calm and somewhat lonely at this time of night. The view was making her feel even worse, but then she caught a glimpse of movement to the north. She adjusted the telescope slightly and refocused. She could make out two figures, one much taller than the other. Then she saw a man in dark clothes and a woman in a white top. Her hands were clamped around his arms and she appeared to be fighting, her long blonde hair flying back and forth as he shook her.

Long blonde hair? Could it be Roxy?

Vanessa narrowed her eye, trying to keep the focus as tight as possible. The woman struggled from side to side, then she fell. The man's hands closed around her upper arms and pulled her up. She turned as if to run away and that's when Vanessa saw her face. It *was* Roxanne. And the man was Brody.

Roxanne spun around to face him and wrenched one arm free. She began pounding his chest but he caught her hand. She threw back her head and screamed.

Oh my God, Vanessa thought wildly. *What can I do? What should I do?*

She could almost hear Wade Baylor's voice: *Call 911.*

She grabbed her phone, dialed, and gave a garbled account of what was happening and her location. 'Please send police and an emergency team.' She tucked the phone in her pocket, picked up a flashlight standing on a table and began running down the spiral staircase. Around and around – an endless run, it seemed. Then she came to the door, burst out, and headed across the lawn. She didn't try to find the path in the darkness – she dashed through the trees and brush on the hill leading down to the beach. She slid on damp weeds and slipped on loose dirt but somehow stayed on her feet. By the time she got to the beach, she could hardly get her breath. Gasping, she looked around and saw Roxanne and Brody, still struggling as they moved toward the wreck of the *Seraphim May*.

Vanessa ran toward the shipwreck, her shoes sinking deeper into the wet sand as she approached. Roxanne and Brody had disappeared but Roxy screamed again and Brody yelled, 'Stop! I don't want to hurt you!' They were in the wrecked ship.

Vanessa turned on the flashlight. She shone it on an opening in the hull, stepped inside and began walking carefully on what was left of the soggy sand-covered floor of the ship. She wanted to call out to Roxy but she was afraid her presence would spook Brody. Although during the day sunlight seeped into the ship through cracks and a few gaping holes, at night its darkness was musty and slightly foul, and seemed to swallow the beam of the flashlight. Suddenly Vanessa panicked, feeling as if the rotting hull was moving, closing in on her. She stopped, shut her eyes and forced herself to take a deep breath, even though the air was sulfuric. She choked and tried to muffle her coughs. Then she

opened her eyes, took ten more steps forward and shined a beam
of light, which landed on Brody who was facing her and holding
Roxanne whose back was turned toward Vanessa.

'Brody? Brody, it's Vanessa,' she said gently. 'Please let go of
Roxanne.'

Brody looked up at Vanessa. 'Why are *you* here? No one is
supposed to be here.'

'I came to get Roxanne. She needs to stay with me.'

He shook his head. 'She must *go*. She *must*—'

'I won't! For the love of God, let me loose, Brody,' Roxanne
shrieked. 'Give me to her!'

'No! The voices say you must come with me.'

'Brody, I think the voices are wrong. Roxanne should stay here
with me, her sister.'

'Brody, *please*,' Roxanne begged desperately. 'Let me go to
Vanessa.'

'But you can't stay in this place. You know you can't – I'm only
doing what's best, what you said you need!'

'No, Brody, *you* said I needed to be taken away. I don't! *Please*
let me go to Vanessa!'

'I can't let her have you. I *can't*!' He pulled Roxanne hard
against him. Vanessa watched in horror as they wrestled fero-
ciously for a moment, and then Brody cried out. 'My sword! My
sword . . .' He looked at Vanessa, his gaze surprised. Then he
sank to his knees as Roxanne stood above him holding a knife
with a long blade in her blood-covered right hand.

TWENTY-THREE

Still looking surprised, Brody fell sideways. At first Vanessa
registered nothing except Brody's fallen body and her sister
backing away from him, holding the knife. Vanessa rushed
to Brody, moved his jacket aside and ran her hands over his chest.
She found the wound and pressed her hands against it.

'What are you doing?' Roxanne cried. 'He tried to kill me!'
Vanessa couldn't answer her. '*Nessa!*'

Blood spurted between Vanessa's fingers. She pressed harder

on the gushing hole in Brody's chest. Now his eyes were closed, he made no sound, he didn't move, and he was barely breathing but she held firm. Her hands were slick with blood and her arms were trembling from the pressure she was applying.

'Ma'am, move aside, please,' she heard a man's voice say.

Vanessa looked up at the three men who had appeared, doubtfully took in their uniforms and one holding a medical kit, and finally removed her hands. 'He's been stabbed in the chest. There's so much blood . . .'

'Yes, ma'am. You've done well. We'll take over now.'

Vanessa stood up, still staring at Brody. Then Roxanne grabbed her arm. 'Nessa, he was trying to kidnap me,' she sobbed. 'If I didn't go with him he was going to kill me!'

Reality hit Vanessa like a blast of icy water. She pulled Roxanne to her and held her sister with all the strength she had left. 'Oh, Roxy, my God!'

Another man said to them, 'You both need to leave the ship and wait on the beach.'

Vanessa looked at him blankly then at her sister. 'Why were you outdoors? Where did you meet him? Where did you get that knife?'

'I sort of woke up and then found myself outside. Maybe I was sleepwalking. He came out of nowhere and grabbed me. *He* had the knife! He said the voices were telling him to take me away in a ship and if I wouldn't come with him, he'd have to kill me! He was crazed, Nessa!' Roxanne began sobbing against Vanessa's shoulders, her whole body shuddering.

'You both need to get outside right now,' the man said sternly.

Roxanne began hyperventilating. 'I can't breathe. I can't—'

'Follow me,' the man said.

'OK. It's OK,' Vanessa said, pulling Roxanne along, back through the rotting hull and the smothering darkness. She could hear Roxy dragging air into her lungs, gasping, wheezing. Finally they staggered out of the ship and onto the beach. Roxy's arms began flailing. Vanessa clutched at her. 'Stop! You're all right!'

'I can't . . . breathe,' Roxy rasped out.

'If she can talk, she can breathe,' the officer said in a calm voice. He stepped into the *Seraphim May* and called, 'Can someone look at this woman?'

'Is she badly hurt?' the response came from within the wreck.

'I don't think so.'

'Then hang on a minute, please.'

Vanessa nodded at him then returned to Roxanne and stroked her face and arms. 'Try to calm down.'

Roxanne gave her an agonized look. 'C-can't.'

'I know it's hard but try.' Suddenly Roxanne made a gagging noise and began gulping air. 'You're safe, Roxanne. The police are here. Take slow, measured breaths.'

A paramedic appeared and, using a flashlight, gave Roxanne a quick examination. 'I don't see anything except some minor cuts, but you'll need to go to the emergency room,' he said. 'We've got to get the man there quickly. Do you want to ride in the ambulance with him?'

'He's *alive*?' Roxanne's breath returned with a rush.

'Yes, ma'am, he's alive.'

'No! I can't ride with him!'

'Are you sure? We can get you to the hospital quicker.'

'*No!*' She looked imploringly at Vanessa. 'Please, Nessa. You take me.'

'All right.' The other technicians were carrying Brody out of the wreck. Roxanne turned her head away from him. 'I'll take you, Roxy. You don't have to look at him again.'

Roxy clung to Vanessa as they climbed the hill and walked to the SUV. As soon as they were inside, Vanessa pulled her cellphone from her pocket and called Christian, telling him only that Brody was badly injured and on his way to the hospital. He started asking questions but Vanessa clicked off the phone. She didn't want to say more in front of Roxanne. As soon as she put away her phone, Roxy asked, 'Why did you try to save him?'

'What?'

'He tried to kill me, Vanessa.'

'He's sick—'

'He's Christian's brother.'

'It wasn't because of Christian—'

Vanessa didn't finish. She started the car, trying to shut Roxy's words out of her head. She understood. Roxanne must have seen her act as the ultimate betrayal. Instead, it had been simply blind instinct. 'Can you breathe now?' she finally asked.

'Yes.'

'Roxy—'

'I don't want to talk.'

She stopped trying to think of the right thing to say and concentrated on driving. Although Roxanne remained rigid and quiet, Vanessa felt as if a storm was roiling beside her. She knew Roxy was confused, angry and deeply hurt.

When they arrived at the hospital, Roxanne was whisked away for an examination. Vanessa sat miserable and blood-covered until a nurse suggested she wash. Vanessa stood almost blindly in the restroom splashing water on her face and arms, scrubbing at her hands that wouldn't come completely clean. *I'm Lady Macbeth*, she thought almost hysterically. She even had blood in her hair. By the time she emerged, wet and dripping, Christian was waiting for her.

'Are you all right?' he asked anxiously.

'I'm not physically hurt. Emotionally?' Her eyes filled with tears. 'Oh, Chris, it was awful!'

He took her in his arms. 'Tell me what happened.'

Suddenly Wade appeared beside them. 'First she needs to tell *me* what happened.'

They went to the small emergency-room waiting room and Vanessa recounted everything, including seeing Brody and Roxanne on the beach, following them into the *Seraphim May*, and seeing Roxy stab Brody. 'And then you tried to save him?' Wade said.

'I don't know what I was doing. He'd collapsed, gushing blood, and I stopped thinking and just acted. I tried to stop the blood—' She began to tremble.

'Yesterday you gave me a ring someone had sent Roxanne – a ring she'd been wearing when she was kidnapped,' Wade stated. 'You said she was terrified. Then last night someone murdered Nia Sherwin on your property. With all this, what was Roxanne doing outside at night?'

'I was on the front lawn where there are lights. Brody just appeared.' They looked up as Roxanne entered the waiting room in a wheelchair pushed by a nurse. 'I'd taken a sleeping pill – the kind you're always hearing about making people do loopy, irrational things. Christian prescribed them. If I hadn't taken them, I would have had more sense than to go outside.' She glared at Christian.

Christian looked back unflinchingly. 'I told you to take one pill.'

'I took two. I didn't do anything wrong by going outside, only foolish because my judgment was impaired.'

'OK, enough about the sleeping pills.' Wade sounded annoyed. 'Then what happened, Roxanne?'

'I was standing on the lawn looking at the Christmas lights in town down below and someone grabbed me. Someone tall and strong. Someone who called me "Your Highness Roxanne".'

'That's all he said? Your Highness Roxanne?'

'No. There were other things. "I've found you", "I'm taking you away". I started struggling and he put his hand over my mouth and carried me. He was babbling about how I had to go with him. When I kept struggling, he said he'd kill me if I didn't stop.'

'He actually threatened to kill you?'

'Yes. He had a knife with a long blade. He said he'd stab me. I was terrified.' Roxanne's stony composure broke. 'He was going to *kill* me! Doesn't anyone care?'

'We all care,' Vanessa cried. Roxanne turned her head away.

'So he dragged you down to the beach and headed for the shipwreck,' Wade said.

'Yes. He kept saying we were going away on a ship. We went inside. Vanessa must have followed us. We were fighting and I got the knife away from him and stabbed him. He fell. I'd protected myself and the man who was going to kill me was lying there dying. And then Vanessa had to step in and save the day!' Roxanne's voice broke. 'My own sister.'

Brody Montgomery was still in surgery when Roxanne said she *had* to go home, she *had* to go to bed, she couldn't take any more.

Christian had taken Vanessa aside. 'I know Brody is going to die,' he'd said with a strange calm that Vanessa knew masked unimaginable grief. 'But I can't leave my little brother. I've let him down enough. I won't desert him now.'

'You didn't let him down.'

Christian smiled weakly. 'I did. I know it. I accept it. Anyway, I can't take you and Roxanne home. I have to stay here with him.'

'I drove Roxy here. I can drive her home. Then I'll come back.'

'No. It's my job to keep vigil over Brody. It's yours to help Roxanne.'

When Vanessa and Roxanne got home, they found Audrey

waiting. Roxanne went straight upstairs with barely a word. Vanessa sat down with Audrey and told her everything that had happened.

'My God, Nessa!' Audrey exclaimed. 'I'm so glad the children slept through it, but Roxanne must be traumatized.'

'She is. And she feels betrayed by me because I tried to help Brody. I didn't even think, Audrey. I simply acted.'

'And if you'd had time to think, would you have stood doing nothing while you watched him bleed to death?'

'I don't know.'

'I do. You wouldn't have, even if it wasn't Brody.' Audrey reached out and rubbed Vanessa's arm. 'You're not a killer, Nessa.'

'I wouldn't have been a killer, Audrey! I would have let nature take its course.' Audrey shrugged. 'But he's not in his right mind. Brody doesn't know what he's doing.'

'You know that and it's your answer, Nessa. You wouldn't have been fighting for your life like Roxanne. You were saving someone who couldn't save himself.'

Afterward, Vanessa went upstairs to the bathroom adjoining her room. She turned on the water as hot as she could bear and stood under the shower spray, lathering and rinsing, lathering and rinsing until her skin had started to turn red. She emerged from the shower, swept her long, dripping hair under a towel, dried off, and slathered sweet-smelling lotion onto the skin that fifteen minutes ago had smelled of perspiration and blood. She towel-dried her hair then walked down the hall to her sister's room where she heard Roxanne in a storm of tears. Vanessa thought about knocking on the door, then decided against bothering her. Roxanne simply needed to vent her feelings, cry out her hurt, fear and frustration, and hopefully tomorrow she would feel better.

At 4:45 a.m. Vanessa's cellphone rang. When she answered blearily, not that she was actually sleeping, Christian said, 'Brody's out of surgery.'

'He made it?'

'Barely. I won't fire a lot of medical jargon at you but the knife blade slipped between two ribs and nicked both his lung and his heart. Dr Amir did the surgery.'

'So he's going to live?'

'We don't know yet. If he makes it through the next twenty-four hours, he has a good chance. But he wouldn't have a chance in hell if not for you. He had a massive hemothorax. He would have exsanguinated in that shipwreck.'

'Then I'm . . . glad.'

'You sound like you're not sure.'

'Roxy is so hurt, Christian. Brody might have killed her but she struck first and then I saved him. That's hard for her to accept.'

Christian was silent for a moment. Finally he said, 'I can see how it would be if she blames him for everything that's happened to her the last eight years. But I can't blame him, Vanessa. I just can't.' He sighed. 'I'm exhausted. I'm going home to get some sleep.'

'Yes, please do. You need it. And Chris . . . I'm relieved that Brody is alive.'

TWENTY-FOUR

Vanessa woke up at eight thirty. Her first impulse was to call Christian to check on Brody, but she hoped he was still asleep. If Brody had died in the last four hours, she would know about it soon enough.

In the meantime, she was hungry and desperately wanted coffee. She put on her robe and went downstairs, noting along the way that Roxy's door was still closed. When she reached the kitchen, the kids were eating eggs and toast while Queenie lay at their feet, waiting for scraps. She couldn't help noticing Sammy's serious expression.

Cara looked up at Vanessa and gave her a smile. 'You got in late last night. Did you have a date?'

'It wasn't exactly a date but I did stay up *very* late.' She went to Audrey, who was staring into the open refrigerator. 'Anything exciting in there?'

'More eggs for your breakfast.'

'No eggs. And you're not my cook.' Vanessa gently moved Audrey away from the refrigerator and closed the door. 'Toast for me and I'll fix it.'

'You only want toast?'

'I didn't say how many pieces.'

Cara giggled.

Vanessa leaned in and murmured in Audrey's ear, 'Brody made it through surgery. It's still touch and go.'

Audrey nodded.

'Has Roxy been down?' Vanessa asked.

Audrey shook her head. 'Do you want me to go up and check on her?'

'No. She might be asleep. Or still angry and hurt. Let's leave her alone for a while.'

Vanessa ate her toast and drank two mugs of coffee with the children. When the kids took Queenie outside and began brushing her, she went back to her bedroom, still tired from the horrible events of last night. She tossed herself down on the bed with her arms flung out from her sides, her eyes closed, images of Brody Montgomery clutching Roxanne in the hull of the rotting *Seraphim May* flashing behind her lids. She'd always felt uneasy when near that shipwreck. Maybe that uneasiness had been a premonition.

Finally she left her room and knocked on Roxanne's door. She didn't think Roxy was going to answer but at last she heard a faint, 'Come in.' Inside, Roxanne had pulled the drapes against the morning sun and lay in semi-darkness, propped up on pillows and staring at a blank wall.

'Are you all right?' Vanessa asked.

'I hurt all over but I know it's just muscle strain.'

'I meant emotionally.'

'I don't know how I feel emotionally, Vanessa. Probably as blank as that wall in front of me.' She paused. 'Is he alive?'

'Yes. Barely. He might not make it.'

'Good. I hope he dies.' Roxy looked at Vanessa. 'You think I'm horrible.'

'No. I truly don't. I understand, Roxy. I know why you wish he'd died. I only wish you understood why I tried to save him.'

'I don't have the energy to try to understand.' She finally looked at Vanessa, her complexion pasty, her eyes bloodshot and flat, absent of life. 'I'm worn out, Nessa. Depleted. Empty like I don't even have a soul.'

'Don't say that.'

'Why not? It's true.' She turned away again. 'Please go away. I don't want you to see me like this. Maybe I'll feel better later.'

'I hope so,' Vanessa said as she closed Roxy's door, but she was afraid her sister had reached her limit.

Vanessa was in the kitchen talking with Audrey when her cell-phone rang.

'Hello, Vanessa, it's Harold Jennings,' a mild, male voice said. 'I hope I'm not bothering you.'

'Oh, Harold, of course not. Were you able to find out anything?'

'Quite a lot. Do you have time to talk?'

'Certainly. Just a moment.' She held the phone to her side and looked at Audrey. 'I have to take this in my room.'

In Grace's bedroom with the door closed, Vanessa sat down in a chair near the window and braced herself. 'OK, Harold, tell me everything.'

'I didn't contact Zane's grandfather's lawyer. None of this really concerns him now, anyway, but I talked to Zane's lawyer, John Dawson. I know him by reputation. He's young and very sharp. Even though Zane is dead, John is still bound by attorney-client privilege. However, Zane left a waiver saying that all third parties with which he dealt are not bound by privilege.'

'All third parties? Like who?'

'Agents and business associates for example. Zane Felder left most of his estate to Libby Ann Hughes. I tried to tell her what all of that included, but she's too upset to hear any more. I think she's a very fragile girl.'

'She is. But she's smarter then she seems and I believe she has a toughness she hasn't recognized. She adored Zane and hasn't recovered from his murder. Give her a month. In the meantime, is there anything you can tell me?'

'Yes. I know this shamble of a house Mr Felder left Zane has been the main source of interest. It sits on almost two acres of land and it should have been torn down years ago – it's a public health menace – but in his will, Mr Felder said Zane could only accept it and the land if the house stood for five years.' Vanessa knew all this but kept listening. 'In four months, the five years will have ended. What I gather Miss Hughes didn't know is that Zane intended to tear down the house and build a new one for them as a couple. He'd already filed demolition papers with the county and the permit had been granted. Zane had also been in contact with an architect – a very good one. The architect told me he's been drawing up plans but Zane didn't want to give the go-ahead on any of them until Miss Hughes had approved them. It was to be a surprise. A wedding gift.'

'Oh, she would have been thrilled.' Vanessa swallowed. 'Has anyone told you about that room in the basement?'

'The sado-masochistic room.'

'Yes.'

'I've heard about it. I had my investigator check it out. I know there are no close neighbors, but no one ever saw anyone around that house. Of course it's out of the city limits, the street it's on isn't heavily traveled with no street lights nearby. It's possible that people could have come and gone at night and never been seen.'

'Did your investigator go inside?'

'Yes. The property belongs to Miss Hughes and she gave her permission when I told her that *you* had asked me to check into this matter. She wants to protect Mr Felder's reputation at all costs, but she trusts you. Anyway, my investigator said it was exactly as you described and he took some photos. Shall I send them to you?'

'That won't be necessary. I don't need them. I've seen it for myself.' Vanessa sighed. 'What a mess.'

'I admit that room has me puzzled, especially because Mr Felder seemed very diligent about keeping all of his business in order – surveys, demolition permits, building permits. He had to know that room would be discovered soon considering all the plans he was making for the house.'

'He didn't expect to die though.'

'It still seems like he was taking a real risk.' Harold paused. 'Do you think Miss Hughes will want to go ahead with the plans for a new house?'

'I don't know if she has the money for it unless Zane left her enough after inheritance tax and funeral costs and God knows what else.'

'Well, I don't know the monetary worth of her inheritance, but if she chooses to sell the lot the house is on, she won't have any trouble getting rid of it. It's a good size, outside the city limits but near schools, and it has a beautiful view, if I've been told correctly. What a shame. It could have been a wonderful place for Libby and Zane to live.'

TWENTY-FIVE

Vanessa showered, dressed, and called Christian to ask about Brody. 'He's doing as well as can be expected,' he said. 'Actually, he's doing a little better than expected, but I don't want to get my hopes up. How's Roxanne?'

'Physically, all right. Emotionally? She'll barely speak to me or anyone else. She's holed up in her room.'

'How long do you expect this mood to last?'

'I have no idea, Chris. She's hurt, she's disappointed, she feels let down by me. She's been through *so* much. I don't want to push her. Anyway, I'd like to talk to you about something. Do you have some free time this afternoon or should I wait until this evening?'

'I'll be free around two o'clock. Come to my office.'

'Fine. And Christian?'

'Yes?'

'I love you.'

Vanessa knocked on Christian's office door at 2:05 p.m.

He called, 'Come in' and she found him sitting behind his desk. She'd expected him to be smiling. Instead, he looked grim, almost ferocious.

'My God, what's happened? Did Brody die?' Vanessa cried.

'No. He's all right. Please close the door.'

Vanessa shut the office door and sat down across from Christian's large desk. 'What is it? What's wrong?'

'Remember giving me the capsules you found in Brody's apartment?'

'Of course.'

'I told you I wanted to have them tested.' Christian leaned forward and lowered his voice. 'He takes more than one medicine but the capsules you gave me were Ziprasidone – one of the medications used for the treatment of his schizophrenia. However, inside the capsule was a small amount of Ziprasidone and a large amount of crack.'

'Crack?' Vanessa repeated blankly. '*Crack cocaine*?'

Christian nodded gravely.

'But how—' Vanessa spluttered.

'The crack was broken into extremely tiny chips. If Brody had wanted to use crack, he wouldn't have gone to all that trouble. Do you know the effects of crack?'

'Not all of them.'

'Irritability, depression, anxiety, paranoia, *aggression*. The effects come on more slowly if the crack is taken orally, but in the long run, the result is the same.

'Are you sure he took the capsules?'

'His blood tests are positive for crack.'

Vanessa sat frozen as the shock set in. 'So someone has been poisoning Brody.' Christian stared at her. 'And it started in Portland. That's why he took off and left everything. That's why the delusions came back.'

'Yes. I told you that when I'd seen Brody during his episodes in the past, he'd never been violent. But now he is. He isn't a violent person, Nessa, even off his meds. But he's violent now because he stayed *on* his meds – or what he thought were his meds. He's violent because of the crack.'

'Violent enough to murder Zane? Violent enough to kill Nia and try to kill Roxanne?'

Christian propped his elbows on his desk and buried his head in his hands. 'Dear God, I don't know.'

Vanessa was barely aware of driving home. Her thoughts were a jumble. Brody had not simply stopped taking his medication – he had been deliberately poisoned. Who would do such a thing? Zane because he wanted to take over Blackbird? Zane, Brody's best friend who had been distraught when Brody disappeared? Libby? That was inconceivable.

When she was in his office, Vanessa had told Christian everything she'd learned about Zane's house with the bizarre room, the S & M room where Roxanne had been held prisoner for months, but it seemed almost anticlimactic in light of the news about Brody's medication. The house now belonged to Libby, and Vanessa had no doubt that she would move ahead with the demolition and pray that the room in the basement stayed a secret.

When Vanessa got home, she saw a large arrangement of pink spray roses, carnations, lilies, and alstroemeria in a pink porcelain vase standing on the antique console table in the front hall. She heard Audrey in the kitchen.

'Did we get flowers?' she asked.

Audrey looked up from cookie dough she was putting on a sheet. '*We* didn't get flowers. Roxanne did. They're from Simon Drake. He brought them personally. The two of them talked for less than five minutes and then went outside. Simon said Roxanne needed fresh air.'

'And she *went* with him?'

'Without so much as one protest. Maybe she's still traumatized from her run-in with Brody last night. How is he, Vanessa?'

'Still holding on. Christian said things are looking better for him.' She wanted to tell Audrey about the crack in Brody's medication, but she didn't want the children to overhear. 'What kind of cookies are you making?'

Audrey smiled. 'Peanut butter. Sammy loves peanut butter, as you know. I'm also going to take the kids out to lunch tomorrow.'

'They'll enjoy that. They need to get out of the house.'

Before she went upstairs, she walked into the living room and looked out of the big picture window. Simon and Roxanne stood near Simon's black Mercedes. Simon tilted back his head and laughed. Roxanne stared at him. Then he reached out and touched her arm. Vanessa expected her to pull away but she didn't. Simon slid his hand down her arm, lightly ran his fingers over her bare hand, then clasped it. Roxanne stood perfectly still, looking at him. He leaned toward her as though he were going to kiss her but stopped, smiled, then got in his car and drove away, Roxanne watching him until he reached the bottom of the hill.

When she came inside, Vanessa asked, 'Are you and Simon friends now?'

Roxanne jumped. 'I didn't see you. Were you lurking around, spying on us?'

'You were directly in front of the house. I happened to see you from the living-room window. But you didn't answer my question.'

'He heard about what happened with Brody last night and he brought me flowers,' Roxanne said chillingly. 'Is there a law against *someone* caring about how I feel?'

'Everyone cares about how you feel. But be careful around Simon Drake, Roxy.'

Roxanne gave her a long, hard look. 'I always am, Vanessa.'

*   *   *

Vanessa had thought about Brody's poisoned pills all evening. It had been difficult for her to endure dinner, although Audrey, Sammy, and Cara were in such high spirits they didn't seem to notice. But Roxanne did. Every time Vanessa looked up from her plate, Roxy was staring at her. Finally, she smiled. The smile was small and stiff, but it was a start. Vanessa had smiled back and winked, trying to indicate a sisterly comradery she knew didn't exist right now. Maybe in a few days Roxanne would forgive her for trying to save Brody's life. But Vanessa knew Roxy would never forget it.

Later that night, Vanessa lay in bed sipping a glass of white wine and trying to watch *The Tonight Show*. She couldn't concentrate on the guest promoting his latest movie while the host interrupted with questions intended to get a laugh, but the wine tasted delicious. It had been Grace's favorite sauterne and she could taste the notes of peaches and honey. She could also feel the high alcohol content. She drained the glass, set it on the nightstand, turned off the television, and finally fell asleep.

Her dreams were wild and fragmented. Eventually the fragments slowed and then halted on one scene: the S & M room in Zane's house. 'Indra' played loudly in the background. She was overwhelmed by the scent of cedar. Her dream gaze glanced at the black walls and the covered windows. It lingered on the bed with its black velveteen spread and the matching canopy with fringe hanging down like cobwebs. Her eyes moved to the hooks in the wall, the chains, the steel bands meant to bind wrists. She saw the leather masks neatly stacked on a black table, the fetish whip, the ball-gag, the tall brass candlesticks holding black candles, the incense burners still smelling of sandalwood and patchouli.

The room spread before her in all of its black horror – bizarre, freaky, perfect.

Perfect! Just like the sets on *Kingdom of Corinna*!

Vanessa's eyes snapped open and she sat up. No one had ever been tortured in that room, no one had ever been held prisoner in that room.

It was a set meant for an audience.

TWENTY-SIX

Vanessa didn't wake until nine thirty the next morning. She had a headache but her mind was as clear as her memory – the memory of the dream about the S & M room. She knew the dream had unearthed a thought that had been in her subconscious since they'd first entered that supposed horror chamber. It had taken a while, but she was certain she'd realized the truth.

She picked up her cellphone and called Christian. He didn't answer. She called the hospital's main number and was told that Dr Montgomery was unavailable. *I should have known*, Vanessa thought. He had rounds, he'd be watching over Brody. Besides, there was plenty of time to tell him later.

When she went downstairs, Vanessa noticed that Roxanne's bedroom door was closed. Audrey, Cara, and Sammy were in the kitchen, all seeming happy even if Sammy was slightly subdued. 'Have you seen Roxy yet?' Vanessa asked.

'I heard her in the kitchen in the middle of the night,' Cara said. 'I think she couldn't sleep, so maybe she's making up for it this morning.'

'Was she getting something to drink?'

'I don't know. I was too sleepy to listen really hard.'

'Oh, well, we all have nights when we can't sleep,' Vanessa said lightly, although for some reason she couldn't put a finger on, she felt uneasy. 'How's everyone this morning?'

'Fine,' Audrey said. 'Derek is taking us for a long lunch today. He's picking us up at eleven.'

Derek had not been arrested for Nia's murder due to lack of evidence but the threat still lingered. Vanessa wondered if the lunch was a final celebration before he *was* arrested, or if he was simply ignoring the inevitable.

'Eleven? Isn't that a little early for lunch?'

'He wants to do a few other things. He says they're a surprise. Cara isn't going.'

'Why?' Vanessa asked, looking at Cara.

'Oh, I decided I'd rather stay here and help you take down the Christmas tree, Aunt Vanessa.'

'I'm not actually taking it down—' Vanessa said.

'You're taking off the ornaments. And you're taking down some of the tinsel and other decorations around the house. I heard you saying so yesterday. I'd really like to help.'

'More than going with Derek and Sammy and your mom?'

'They'll have a good time without me,' Cara said dismissively. 'It's my turn to work.'

Vanessa looked at Audrey, who shrugged. Cara didn't sound angry or hurt or jealous, only as if she didn't care about an outing with two adults and Sammy. Maybe her crush was wearing off, Vanessa thought.

'Now you're sure you don't want to come with us?' Audrey asked an hour later, with Derek and Sammy stood behind her.

Cara shook her head. 'Not today. Everybody have a *really* good time but I'm going to stay here and help Vanessa. She needs me.'

'All right, but you'll be missing a lot of fun,' Derek told her.

'That's fine.' The girl began shepherding the three of them toward the front door. 'You'll never even know I'm not there. Bye, bye! See ya later!'

As soon as they were gone, Cara whispered to Vanessa, 'I think a policeman will be tailing them. After all, nobody's found Sammy's mom's killer. They're probably afraid Derek will run away.'

'How do you know that?'

'Television.'

'Is that why you didn't want to go with them?'

Cara grinned. 'No. Policemen don't scare me.'

Vanessa and Cara both tied back their long black hair with matching red ribbons and started to work. They carried in all the ornament and tinsel boxes from the garage where they'd been stored for over a week while their contents were on display.

'Where's Queenie?' Cara asked.

'Pete's taking her for a long walk.'

'He really likes her and I know she'll enjoy her walk, but she'd also be a big help taking down the tree.'

'A big help? Really? Like when we were decorating the tree and she kept running off with the satin-covered Styrofoam ornaments? She thought they were fancy tennis balls.'

Cara bent over laughing. 'Grace thought that was *so* funny! Remember how much she laughed?'

'Sure I do. I don't think she ever had as much fun putting up a Christmas tree.'

Cara picked up the embroidered green felt tree skirt and folded it carefully before placing it in a tissue paper-lined box. 'This sure is pretty,' she said. 'It's a shame you can't see it when all the gifts are piled on top.'

'My mother made it a long time ago for Roxy. She worked on it for a month, sewing on the white figures of reindeers and elves and Santas then embroidering our names on it in script. She could write script.' Vanessa pointed to a name written in script. 'It's very hard to do.'

'I'd like to learn.' Cara looked at *Roxanne* swirling beside a figure of Santa Claus. 'I think my name would look nice in script. So would Sammy's, although his dad would want it to say Samuel. Sammy was named for Derek's father Samuel Allan Sherwin.'

'That's a nice name,' Vanessa said casually, removing a few more ornaments. 'Cara, why didn't you want to go with everyone else today?'

'Well, when Sammy and I are together, we talk all the time. We just can't help ourselves. I thought it would be nice for Sammy to talk more to Mom than he does when I'm around. They could get to know each other better and that's important because . . .' Vanessa raised her eyebrows. 'Because I think by spring Derek is going to ask Mommy to marry him.'

'Do you want Derek to marry your mother?'

'Oh yes! So does Sammy. And I'm sure Derek wants to marry Mommy. I wanted to . . . well . . . help things along.'

Cara looked at Vanessa almost as if she expected a rebuke. Instead, Vanessa threw back her head and laughed. 'Cara Willis, you are one smart girl! In fact, you're beyond smart – you're a strategist. You remind me of Grace.'

'I remind you of Grace? Really?' Cara beamed. 'Gosh, that's the best compliment I have ever had!'

They worked steadily for another ten minutes when suddenly the front door flew open and Roxanne rushed in, looking unkempt and slightly wild-eyed. She slammed the door behind her. 'Where have you been?' Vanessa asked in surprise.

'I took a walk. A long walk. In the woods.'

'Did you see Pete and Queenie?' Cara asked.

Roxanne looked at her in annoyance. 'No. Why would I? What are you doing?'

'Taking down the tree ornaments. Do you want to help?'

'Help? Why the hell would I want to help?' Cara had frozen, ornament in hand. 'I want a shower. *Now*. And don't let anyone else in. Do you hear me, Nessa? *No one!*'

As Roxanne hurried upstairs, Vanessa and Cara looked at each other, bewildered. 'Maybe we should ignore her,' Vanessa said.

But in a moment, a car screeched to a halt in front of the house. Vanessa jumped up and glanced out of the window to see Jane Drake clambering from her small, blue car. She was dressed in nurses' scrubs and clutching something as she ran up the porch steps and banged on the front door. When it didn't open, she screamed, 'Vanessa, I know you're in there! Open the door or I'll knock out this fancy stained glass!'

'Oh, gosh!' Cara cried. 'She sounds really mad but Roxanne said not to let anyone inside!'

'I don't care what she said,' Vanessa muttered as she went to the front door and opened it. 'Jane, what's wrong?'

Jane pushed past her into the entrance hall. 'What's wrong? What's *wrong*? My father is dead!'

'Oh! I'm sorry. How—'

'He was killed. Roxanne *murdered* him!'

Jane marched farther into the house and caught sight of Cara cowering by the Christmas tree. 'Where is she? Where's Roxanne?' Jane demanded of the girl.

Cara stayed mute.

'I know she's here. Where *is* Roxanne?' Suddenly Jane raised her hand. She held a gun and pointed it at Cara. 'Where is Roxanne?'

'Have you lost your mind, Jane?' Vanessa yelled. 'Put down that gun.'

'Yes, I've lost my mind. Your sister *murdered* my father – the man who meant more to me than anyone in the world – and I've lost my mind. I will *kill* her!'

Vanessa took two steps closer to Jane who swung the gun away from Cara and aimed it at Vanessa.

'If you think my sister murdered your father, you should call Wade.' Vanessa's voice wavered.

'Call Wade? Wade with all of his rules and regulations and

passion for the letter of the law? This isn't a matter for him. He's too weak. This is a matter for *me*.'

Abruptly Roxanne appeared in the entrance hall. To Vanessa's horror, she also held a gun. 'Are you going to shoot me, Jane? Because I guarantee I'm a better, faster shot than you are. I've had years of practice. I know what I'm doing.'

Jane fired in Roxanne's direction and missed by two feet. Cara screamed but Roxanne didn't even flinch.

Roxanne laughed. 'See what I mean? You were always a screw-up and you still are. No wonder your father didn't love you.'

'You *bitch*! I suppose you think he loved you,' Jane snarled.

'He didn't love anyone, Jane. He didn't have the capacity to love.'

Another car pulled up out front. Vanessa glanced out quickly enough to see a white car and Max Newman getting out of the front before returning to the horrific scene playing out in front of her. Jane kept her gun aimed at Roxanne but kept glancing at Max, who was unloading a large brown paper-wrapped rectangular package from the back of his car. He carried it carefully up the porch stairs and stepped inside through the open front door. 'Hello! Anybody home! I brought a painting of—'

Stepping into the hallway he saw Vanessa standing tense and white, while Roxanne and Jane aimed guns at each other. 'Good God!' he exclaimed.

'What are you doing here?' Roxanne demanded.

Max swallowed and answered in a shaky voice, 'I brought the second lighthouse painting that Grace commissioned.'

'And it had to be brought *now*?'

'Well, it's done and I wasn't doing anything else and . . . and . . .'

'"And, and, and",' Roxanne mocked.

Max looked at Jane. 'That's not your car out front.'

'I kept calling Daddy but he didn't answer. It was after eleven. I had to check on him. My car wouldn't start so I borrowed another nurse's – oh, what does it matter? I found Daddy *dead*.'

'Oh,' Max said weakly. 'He just dropped dead? I'm sorr—'

'Roxanne murdered him.'

'Murdered him?' Max's voice cracked. 'That's impossible.'

'Oh, is it, Max?'

'Janey, you're upset—'

'Shut *up*, Max. Roxanne killed him. I saw her sneaking out the back door of his house. When I got to him, his body was still warm. He had a needle sticking out of his arm.'

'A needle?' Vanessa asked. 'I know he had diabetes. You said at the party at Nia's that he wasn't always careful with his doses. Did he give himself too much insulin?'

'No, he did not,' Jane spat. 'His kit was on the dresser but very little insulin was missing. I checked that insulin kit yesterday.'

'I'm very sorry about your father, Jane,' Max said in a ridiculously prim voice. 'I think I'll leave the painting and go.'

Roxanne pointed her gun at him. 'You are not going anywhere.'

Cara had lowered herself into a crouch at the far side of the tree, her face white and terrified. 'Please let Cara leave,' Vanessa said quietly. 'None of this has anything to do with her.'

Roxanne glanced at Cara. 'No. She can't leave. I think she'll enjoy this.'

'This?' Vanessa repeated. 'What's *this*?'

'The truth. At last.'

TWENTY-SEVEN

'The truth?' Vanessa stared unflinchingly at her sister. 'You were not held prisoner in the S & M room at Zane's house.'

Rozanne tilted her head slightly and smiled. 'And when did you figure out that, Vanessa?'

'Last night. In a dream.'

Roxanne started laughing. 'In a *dream*? Now I've heard it all.'

'No, you haven't. I know more, but I want to hear everything from you, Roxy, from your kidnapping until now.'

Vanessa felt that her sister's face had changed, the lines harder, the eyes colder. She didn't look twenty-three anymore. She looked thirty-five and full of hate.

'Simon Drake first groped me when I was thirteen. He raped me two days after I turned fourteen.'

'He did not, you filthy liar!' Jane exploded.

'You know he did, Jane. You always have.'

Vanessa was stunned. She'd known Simon was too free with

his hands, but rape? Of an adolescent? 'Even if it happened, why didn't you tell Mom and Dad?'

'I did. Mommy said she was certain it wasn't as bad as I thought. It probably wasn't *rape*. I shouldn't start trouble with Dad's business partner. She actually started shaking all over she was so scared of my rocking the boat with Simon. She was such a *weakling*! And Dad? He slapped my face and called me a liar. He told me to never tell Grace or you. He said if I did, he'd send me to an institution. An *institution*, Vanessa. I was so young, I believed him and the very word made me think of dank cells and barred windows. So I never said a word again, even though Simon raped me at least once a month.'

'Why didn't you tell me when you got a little older?' Vanessa cried.

'You? You who thought Dad was wonderful. And if things blew up between Dad and Simon, you might not have been able to afford your nice apartment in Los Angeles and your fancy drama school. You wouldn't have listened to me. Everyone was looking out for themselves.'

'That is not true. And why, when I asked you when you came back if Simon had ever abused you, did you say *no*?'

'I wanted him to feel safe. I always intended to kill him – *always* – but he couldn't know I was a danger to him. He would have avoided me, maybe left town. It's why I was nice to him yesterday when he brought me flowers. But I always planned to make him pay for what he did to me.'

Color rushed to Jane's face. 'You're crazy. My father did *not* rape you!'

Roxanne's eyes narrowed. 'I'm not the only girl your sainted father abused. Nia for one.'

'Nia Sherwin?'

'She was Nia Jones then. That was three years before me. But there were others. You know that because you *always* watched him and hung on his every word. You couldn't stand it that he thought you were homely and boring. You wanted your father's attention – any kind of attention – but he wasn't interested in you. "Plain Jane" is what he called you.' Roxanne smirked. 'Did you know that? I think you did. He had a type – blonde, blue-eyed, large-breasted with classic features like Nia and me. That's why you got breast implants and long, blonde hair extensions, and a nose job, and contacts that make your eyes darker blue. You've spent a fortune trying to look like Nia and me. Anyone can see it. But Simon still didn't want you.'

Jane looked crushed. She swayed and for a moment, Vanessa hoped she would faint. But she didn't. She stood thin and wooden, her mouth pressed into a nearly invisible line.

'Who kidnapped you?' Vanessa asked.

Roxanne smiled slowly. 'Max.'

His face froze. He opened his mouth to speak but nothing came out. Only his eyes seemed alive, burning at Roxanne.

'Max?' Vanessa asked, stunned. 'Why would Max kidnap you?'

'It wasn't a real kidnapping, you idiot,' Roxanne said witheringly. 'It was part of a scheme to get me out of Everly Cliffs.'

'A scheme? It wasn't real?'

'No. But it had everyone fooled.' Roxanne smirked. 'Pretty smart thinking for a fifteen-year-old girl, don't you agree?'

'Max took you off the beach that night? I thought you barely knew Max.'

'I knew Max very well, even if he was five years older than I was. Max was in love with me.'

'In love!' Vanessa turned to Max, who had set down the painting. 'Is that true?'

Max threw back his shoulders, adopting a steely posture. 'Roxanne wasn't like a regular fifteen-year-old. She seemed older. She was beautiful. And mature. She was crazy about me. But the whole kidnap scheme happened because she was so desperately in need of help. No one would believe her about Simon and she was afraid to run away.'

'You mean running away wasn't dramatic enough for her.' Vanessa looked at Roxy. 'I was the would-be actress, but you were the real actress. And you craved attention. Even when were little.' Vanessa turned to Max. 'Why did you go along with this scheme? Didn't you know how much trouble you could cause for yourself?'

'I loved Roxanne. I was going to school at the Academy of Art in San Francisco. I had a small apartment. I told Roxanne she could just run away and come live with me. She wanted to, but she didn't want her parents thinking she'd run off with me and hunting her down.'

'Why would they have thought she'd run off with *you*?'

Max looked surprised. 'She told me she'd said too much about me. Her whole family knew we were in love and hooking up.'

Vanessa's voice turned to acid. 'Oh, *she* told you. Sorry, Max, but she never mentioned you. No one ever gave you a second thought as someone she had even a crush on let alone as her boyfriend.'

'Well, of course you're lying,' Max said contemptuously. 'Anyway, she came up with the idea of the kidnapping. Brody had gone nuts and everyone knew about him rambling all over town looking for his *lady*. She said he'd get the blame.'

'She hoped a sick man would be blamed for kidnapping her,' Vanessa said with disgust.

'What difference did it make? Brody wouldn't have been held responsible for his actions.'

'He wouldn't have gone to prison. But his reputation—'

'What reputation?' Roxy demanded. 'He didn't have any reputation left except as a nut.'

Vanessa felt like slapping her sister, an impulse that was only held in check because Roxanne held a gun. 'So you ran off with Max. And then what?'

'And then she got restless,' Max said. 'During the second year, she left me. She said she wanted to be free. You see, she was so young when we got together—'

'I'd found another man,' Roxy interrupted. 'A real man, not a boy tied to his mother's apron strings while he dreamed of becoming a famous artist.'

'And how long did *that* affair last?' Vanessa asked.

'A while.' Roxanne sighed. 'And then there was another man and another. At first I had a lot of fun. But the fourth man – well, he wasn't fun. Or kind. Or normal. He got me hooked on heroin. Then I got pregnant. I got rid of the kid and I left him. Then I got clean. I'd had enough of being on my own.'

'That must have been when you came back here,' Jane blurted.

'She came home?' Vanessa asked in shock.

Jane nodded. 'She came to this house. I was taking care of your mother. Roxanne didn't even know I was here. I heard her yelling at her father in his bedroom. She followed him onto the landing. He was standing at the top of the stairs. By then she was screaming at him about my father. She described horrible things my father had done to her. Your dad called her

a "dirty little whore". She rushed at him and *pushed* him. He
didn't have time to brace himself. He tumbled over and over
and hit his head on the floor below. She just stood there staring
at him. Finally she went down and looked in his eyes and took
his pulse. And then she left the house without calling for help
or anything.'

Vanessa was too astonished to say a word. So that's how her
father had died. He'd been drinking, yes, but he didn't have a very
high blood alcohol level according to the medical examiner. There
were whisperings of suicide. No one had ever considered the
possibility of murder.

'I didn't come here to kill him,' Roxy said. 'I was tired. I wanted
to come home. I told him I'd escaped from the man who'd taken
me on the beach, but Dad had been drinking and he was belligerent
and said even if I *had* been taken, I'd chosen to stay away and
put everyone through hell. Then I told him about Simon but he
yelled at me to not start that *crap* again.' She shook her head. 'He
never believed me, even when I was a child.'

'You told lies when you were a child,' Vanessa said coldly.
'Not harmless lies to cover up things you'd done wrong. Lies to
get kids you didn't like in trouble. We all hoped you'd outgrown
the lying by the time you were around twelve, but you hadn't.
Maybe he would have believed you about Simon but you were
the girl who cried *wolf* too many times. You were still lying to
him when you came back – he must have known by your tone.
He was right – you *did* choose to stay away from home and put
everyone through hell.'

'That's not the point, Nessa. He wasn't glad to see me. Like
always. And then he started shouting, and he called me names and
I . . . reacted. Then I knew Grace would be home any minute. I
had to get out and I couldn't come back anytime soon. It would
have looked too suspicious.' She looked at Jane. 'I knew Mommy
was shut in her bedroom and Grace was out. I had no idea someone
else was in the house.'

Vanessa looked at Jane. 'So you've known for over three years
that Roxanne was alive?'

'Yes.'

'And you said nothing.'

'I . . . I was afraid of her.'

Vanessa's eyes narrowed. 'You might have been afraid of her

for yourself, but that's not all that kept you silent. It was your father, wasn't it? You wanted to keep him safe. If Roxanne was around, she might start talking about what he'd done to her.'

'Well, yes. Even though I knew she must be lying, more girls would have come forward. More and more . . . they would have ruined Daddy and Mom and . . . me.'

'Daddy and *you*,' Roxanne sneered. 'That's who you cared about. You didn't give a damn about your mother any more than I did mine. Besides, why would more women have come forward if I was lying?'

'For money, attention, just plain meanness!'

'Or because they were telling the truth. Oh yes, there would have been quite a scandal.' Roxanne smirked.

'I wanted you to go away and never come back again. I went to church and prayed for that,' Jane said fervently, then sagged. 'But you did come back. You're evil and evil always returns.'

'Evil did return.' Vanessa looked at her sister. 'Why now?'

'I've stayed in touch with Max all these years. Sometimes I went to him when things got bad for me like when a boyfriend beat me up and broke my wrist. That took months to heal but Max let me stay with him for weeks.'

'And you paid him back by leaving again,' Vanessa said.

'He was planning on coming back here anyway. We stayed in touch. I was getting really tired of trying to make it on my own, finding men with money who liked me. Then less than three months ago, Max told me Grace probably had only months to live. I wanted her to include me in her will.'

A chill washed over Vanessa. 'You came home because you wanted Grace's fortune? No wonder you were so affectionate with her. It was all another of your acts. How utterly cold and calculating and immoral.'

Roxanne's gaze didn't waver.

'But she died too soon to change her will,' Vanessa said.

'You want me to feel guilty? She wasn't even glad to see me. You saw how she was around me. The woman never liked me.'

'She never trusted you, Roxanne. I've known that since you were young. I made excuses for you then, but she always saw through you. She said little things throughout the years that let me know she had doubts about the kidnapping being what it

seemed. She still doubted you when you came home. I didn't like
that she was being cold to you, but now I understand. She knew
you better than I did.'

'She favored you. She always did. Most people do.'

'Obviously not Max.'

'He's still my best friend.' Roxanne looked at him with abrupt
fondness. 'The only person I've ever really loved.'

Max's voice was flat. 'I wish I could believe that, but it's not
true.'

'You've remained her flunky, haven't you?' Vanessa asked.

'I've never been able to really care about another woman.'

'You made those cruel, anonymous phone calls to me.'

Max nodded. 'I started talking to Grace about the lighthouse
paintings right before she broke her hip. She was out of the room
– her cellphone was lying on the table right in front of me and I
couldn't help snooping. I found your number. I wondered about
how many people would pay to have *that*. But I didn't sell it. I
waited and used it for something else.'

'Something that Roxanne thought up. She knew I liked the song
"Praying for Time". She masterminded this whole thing.'

'She started preparing a couple of months ago, losing weight,
hurting herself with scratches and bruises. Exposing herself to
illness like flu and bronchitis and strep throat. I brought her to
Everly Cliffs and dropped her off. I did it all for her but it was
because I *had* to,' Max said despairingly. 'She forced me.' He
looked at Roxanne. 'It wasn't just love. You've always held that
kidnapping over my head. You were only fifteen when it happened.
Underage. I was twenty. If you told anyone, I would have gone
to prison. You never let me forget that.'

'Don't lie, Max. You stayed loyal to me only because you love
me,' Roxanne said confidently.

Max looked at her with tired misery. 'I've stayed loyal to you
out of fear for my own life. You threatened to confess, to see that
I went to prison. But you're capable of much worse, Roxanne,
and I cherish my life. I don't want to die young.'

'Max, you were always so melodramatic.'

'I don't think so, Roxy. Not after all these years at seeing how
you operate. You have no mercy.'

Jane's hand was beginning to tremble slightly. The gun wasn't
aimed directly at Roxanne. Vanessa knew she had to divert Roxy

until she could think of something to save Cara and hopefully herself. She didn't give a damn about the other three in the room. Roxanne had always thought she was incredibly clever, she thought. Maybe now was the time to appeal to her ego.

'This time you decided not to just return. You claimed you'd been a prisoner and said you'd gotten free,' she said to Roxanne. 'How does Brody figure into all of this?'

'Most people thought Brody took me when I was fifteen. Luckily, Max lived close to Brody in Portland. They'd been friends when they were young. He'd known Zane back then, too. Max had managed to befriend them again. Barely. I knew neither one of them would consider Max *a friend*.'

Max visibly winced.

Roxanne seemed to relish in Max's discomfort. 'But I wanted there to be evidence that Brody – and Zane – had been holding me prisoner and Max was in a perfect position to help me.'

'Why?' Vanessa asked.

'It was more convincing. Daddy didn't believe me the first time I tried to come home. So, this time I had to put on an act.'

'I mean why did you want to involve Zane?'

Roxanne looked at Max and smiled. 'That was really Max's idea. He said Brody and Zane were so close that it would be hard for people to believe Zane didn't know *something* was going on with Brody. And . . . I had another plan for Brody.'

'You mean you wanted it to seem as if he'd gone off his meds,' Vanessa said.

Her sister nodded.

'Only worse. Max, you used to visit Brody sometimes. Libby told me,' Vanessa continued. 'You poisoned his medicine with crack. How could you do such a hideous thing?'

'I told you. Roxanne threatened me and said if I didn't—'

'It was more than that.' Vanessa's voice lashed. 'You hated Brody. Why?'

'I . . . I didn't *hate* him. Back when we were teenagers, everyone acted like he was some kind of god. He was so tall and good looking like his brother. Everyone admired the Montgomerys. My father had taken off years ago, and I was left with a mother who was kind of the town joke with her gossiping and her grande dame airs. And then came the tennis. Brody didn't play better than I did but he always won.'

Vanessa looked at him in disbelief. 'You hated him because he won the tennis tournaments?'

'He didn't deserve to win! I played as well as he did! It was the linesmen and the umpires. They were all against me!' Max went quiet for a moment, seething. 'Then there were our careers. I put my heart and soul into my art. I always wanted to be a great artist, to have my paintings shown in galleries in New York and Paris and Venice. But I was told I wasn't good enough. One teacher told me my work was "barely tolerable". Then along comes Brody and even though he's crazy as a loon, he develops Blackbird. He was going to make millions. And I was just poor old Max.'

'You mean that Brody *and* Zack developed Blackbird. Brody *and* Zack were going to make millions.'

'Yeah. Zack Felder. I knew him when he was a teenager and summered in Everly Cliffs with his parents. What a waste of space – short, pudgy, frizzy red hair, his constant prattling about computers. Nobody could stand him except Brody.'

'But you hung out with them. I remember that.'

Max shrugged. 'I didn't have anything else to do.'

'Because you had no other friends.'

'That's not true!'

'And what happened when you found out you were living only a couple of blocks from Brody in Portland?'

'What do you mean, what happened?'

'You insinuated yourself into his life again. You pretended to be his friend. And Zane's.'

'I was friendly to them. We were adults – over all the kid rivalry and jealousy.'

'Oh, I don't think you were over it at all. And although Brody chose to ignore it, Zane didn't. Zane didn't trust you. Ever.' Vanessa paused. 'Is that why you killed him?'

'I didn't want to. She made me. I was only her instrument.'

Roxanne rolled her eyes. 'You are the most spineless, pathetic wimp I've ever met. I knew it when I was fifteen and you haven't changed a bit.'

'Why?' Vanessa asked Max. 'Why did you murder Zane?'

Max glared at Roxanne for a moment, then said, 'He was suspicious of me. He tried to get Brody to get rid of me as a friend. And when Brody went missing at the same time as Roxanne turned up – well, he really went into overdrive. Couldn't you see the way he was looking at me when he saw us at the Christmas party, Vanessa?'

'He was looking at you the same way he looked at me.'

'No. No, it was different. He was coming after me – I knew it. So I sent him a text sounding like it was from Brody and telling him to meet me at the Diamond Rose. And then I got rid of him for good.'

'And used his house as evidence against him. Whose idea was that room in the basement?'

'Mine,' Roxanne said casually. 'Except Max screwed it up. Everything looked too nice, too well arranged, not like a place where someone had lived for a week much less held a prisoner for months.'

'But you were so overcome you threw up,' Vanessa said.

'Ipecac, dear sister. Vomiting was so much more effective than a maidenly swoon and I can't make my face pale at will.' She smiled. 'It certainly convinced everyone that the room actually horrified me. You all believed I'd been a captive in that place.'

'For a while. Then I realized it looked perfect. And this morning I remembered you saying you'd "slipped" out the front door as quietly as you could. Wade Baylor is strong and the front door of that house is so warped even he had trouble opening it. And I thought of how insistent you were that we go *downstairs* when we'd started up the stairs to the second floor. You rushed it, Roxy.'

'Well, aren't you the brilliant sleuth, Nessa?' Roxanne's voice was scornful. 'Or rather, didn't you become one *after* your renewed love for Christian turn you into Brody's champion.'

'I wasn't his champion, Roxanne, especially after he beat up Max on the beach.' She looked at Max. 'It *was* Brody who beat you, wasn't it? That wasn't a trick, too?'

'It was Brody all right. I wasn't even thinking about him or I wouldn't have been on the beach. But as soon as I saw him, I knew I was in trouble. He wasn't on his medication. Hell, he was on *crack*. I tried to keep him calm, but I couldn't. He was going on about me not being a good knight. He thought I was trying to trick him. And he cut loose on me.'

'Did you know where he was hiding?'

'There are three shacks at the edge of town. They're condemned. I think Derek Sherwin bought them to tear down. Back when

Brody and Zane and I hung out as kids, there was an old guy staying in one. He called himself Captain Morgan. He always invited us in, taught us poker, gave us beer – sometimes harder stuff. He told us stories about his life on the sea and all the women he'd had. I had a feeling Brody might go back there – he loved the old guy.'

'But those shacks were searched,' Jane said. 'Wade told me they searched them three times.'

'Brody seemed to have a sixth sense about when the cops were coming. He hid somewhere else until they left. Then he came back. I kept a close eye on him, per her ladyship's instruction,' Max said scathingly, glancing at Roxanne. 'If I hadn't, I wouldn't have seen that carving knife he left on a table when he went out for a few minutes. I don't know where he got it, but I didn't want to have another encounter with him when he was holding that thing. The blade must have been ten inches long. So I slipped into the shack and took it. Then I ran for my life. I didn't want to be anywhere near when he noticed it was missing.'

'So, which of you killed Nia Sherwin?'

'It was a joint effort,' Roxanne said. 'Jane had finally told Simon she'd seen me kill Daddy. I think she was trying to warn him away from me. But Simon thought he was invincible, even when Nia Sherwin started pressuring him into helping her get Sammy. He wanted her to stop bothering him so he told her about what really happened to Dad. She told me he'd sent her to me to help her because I was in the house with Sammy! And it would be easy for me to get Sammy out of here.'

'Daddy wasn't well!' Jane cried. 'He wasn't thinking clearly or he would never have told her to ask for your help.'

'She didn't *ask*. Nia said if I didn't help her get Sammy out of this house, she'd tell everyone that I hadn't really been kidnapped, and that I'd killed my father. We should have been comrades after what happened to both of us at Simon's hands. Instead she tried to *use* me! She threatened to blackmail me, the bitch!'

'I let her think she'd scared me,' Roxy continued. 'I told her to come here around midnight and I'd have Sammy outside waiting. I sneaked out of the house to where I told her I'd meet her. While I was talking to her, Max crept up behind her and slit her throat. Then we arranged the gold ribbon and the white roses to make it look like Brody's work.'

Vanessa flinched. 'So Max slit her throat. But not with the knife he'd stolen from Brody. Not the knife Brody had when he grabbed you on the lawn.'

'On the lawn?' Max's laugh was dry and scratchy. 'How about on the beach, where Brody was supposed to meet her.'

'That's enough, Max,' Roxanne snapped.

'Oh, is it? I don't take orders from you anymore. We're way past that.' Max turned his attention to Vanessa. 'Roxanne decided Brody had been around long enough. She was afraid he'd be caught and his poisoned medication detected. She thought it was best that he die when everyone was convinced of his guilt. So she had me leave a note on his porch telling him to meet "Lady Roxanne" on the beach. She told me that after Grace's funeral, you'd be sure to retire to your tower. With any luck, you'd be looking through your telescope. She had the whole scene planned. From your viewpoint, it would look like Brody was abducting her and when she fought him, he tried to stab her. But really, he was only trying to get her in the shipwreck because he was trying to rescue her. He didn't threaten to kill her. *She* had the knife. She stabbed Brody and he would have bled to death if it hadn't been for you, Vanessa. You ruined her plan, and she despises you for it.

'Nothing is going right for her and I knew she was about to spin out of control when she told me she was going to kill Simon Drake,' Max went on. 'She wanted to know if I still had any of my mother's insulin. I did, and I gave her the insulin and Mother's kit. I thought she was going to wait until tonight to do it but I didn't intend to hang around here waiting to see what happened or what she'd do next. I only came by to get my pay for the painting and then leave Everly Cliffs as soon as possible.'

Jane glared at Roxanne. 'So you broke into my father's house and murdered him!'

'I didn't have to break in, Jane. He came here yesterday with flowers and reminiscences about the *hot* sex we used to have. I let him think he was seducing me, the old fool. We made plans for me to spend the night with him. He made my skin crawl, but it was worth it to know I was ridding the world of him. I went after midnight. We had sex. As much as he could handle, which wasn't impressive.'

Jane's face crumpled.

Roxanne continued. 'I stayed awake until morning when he was still asleep and used Max's mother's insulin to give him a fatal dose. Then I had to wrestle him into his chair, find his own insulin kit and needle, and inject some of *his* insulin into him. That's why I waited until morning. I wanted his body to still be warm so it would look like he'd accidentally given himself a morning overdose. It took longer than I thought it would and you – Plain Jane – had to come barging in to check on Daddy. Unfortunately, I didn't get out of the house quick enough.'

'He was my *father!*' Jane screamed.

'He was a sexual deviant, a blight on the Earth. I got rid of him.' Jane started to sob.

Vanessa looked venomously at Roxanne. 'My God,' she breathed. 'Roxy, my little sister, orchestrated everything.'

'Yes, I did.' Roxanne sounded proud. 'You always thought you were the imaginative one. You weren't. *I'm* the smart one, *I'm* the imaginative one, *I'm* the shining star in this family.'

'Don't smirk, Roxy. You're insane.'

Roxanne's face was so full of fury Vanessa knew Roxy had considered the possibility and it terrified her. 'I'm *not. Brody* is insane!' Roxy spat.

'He isn't. He's just a guy who's sick and whose life you've almost ruined—'

The front door opened. 'We're back!' Queenie bounded in with Pete right behind her holding her leash. 'We had a great walk!'

Jane shrieked and fired a shot that hit the wall beside Vanessa's head. Queenie jerked her leash from Pete's hand and charged Jane, knocking her to the floor. Vanessa heard Jane's head crack against the leg of the hall table. Without thinking, Vanessa darted forward and took the gun out of her limp hand.

'What's going on here?' Pete asked in a high, tight voice. 'Is she dead?'

'I don't know. Stand still, Pete. Roxanne has a gun.'

'*Roxanne?*' Pete looked at her in shocked bewilderment. 'Why does everyone have a gun?'

'Only two of us have guns,' Roxanne said. 'And only one of us has the courage to use one.'

Pete's face tightened. 'Grace told me you were dangerous once, Roxanne. I didn't believe her, but she was right. This time you're not going to hurt *anyone.*'

His body tensed and took two steps toward Roxanne before she shot. Cara screamed as Pete staggered backward. 'Pete!' Vanessa screamed as he hit the floor.

In a flash, Roxanne ran into the living room and jerked Cara to her feet, holding the child in front of her like a shield. 'Don't get any ideas about shooting me, Vanessa. You're not a good enough shot to be sure you'll hit me instead of her.'

A shudder coursed through Vanessa. Cara looked terrified and Roxanne looked determined. She would have no conscience where the child was concerned, Vanessa thought. She didn't care if Cara was injured or even killed. Roxy's only concern was herself.

Roxanne began pushing Cara toward the entrance hall. The girl's ribbon fell from her hair and she was trying not to cry but tears streamed down her face as Roxanne held her tightly with her left arm while pointing the gun at Vanessa and Max with her right hand. 'Cara and I are going to leave now,' she said in a creepily casual voice. 'As long as I get away from this place, she'll be fine.'

No she won't, Vanessa thought. *You'll kill her to prevent her from saying where you were headed.*

As if making her final bow, Roxanne said with a flourish, 'It's been a most interesting afternoon.'

They were almost to the front door when Max made a nervous move. Roxanne lowered her gun and shot him in the leg. His high-pitched squeal echoed around the entrance hall.

'You're not going anywhere – certainly not with me,' Roxanne snapped, visibly annoyed. 'You've always been such a dope, Max Newman. I don't know how you've lived this long.'

Roxanne pulled Cara onto the porch, glanced at the cars, then headed for Max's. She opened the driver's side door, shoved Cara in, and got behind the steering wheel. When the car started, Vanessa knew Max had left his keys in the car. Roxanne must have known he always did. She spun the car around and headed down the hill.

'Oh God, she's taken off in Max's car!' Vanessa cried. 'It's white but I don't know the make—'

'It's a Chevrolet Trax,' Pete said.

'You're alive!' Vanessa cried, running to him.

'She just grazed my shoulder. The shock knocked me down.'

'Stay down. You're bleeding heavily.' She pulled his cellphone from his jeans pocket and handed it to him. 'Call Wade Baylor. Tell him I've gone after Roxy and my iPhone has tracing software. I'll leave the phone on, I think he can trace me.' She picked up her iPhone from the hall table, Cara's red ribbon and called for Queenie. 'I'm going after them.'

TWENTY-EIGHT

Queenie, dragging her leash, jumped onto the second row of seats in Vanessa's SUV. Vanessa got in front, laid the gun and ribbon on the seat beside her, started the car and wheeled it around. She drove down the hill, not as fast as Roxanne, but above her normal speed. This was a big car and she wasn't completely accustomed to driving it. She had to be careful, she reminded herself. She couldn't let panic overwhelm her and make a mistake because she might be Cara's only hope of survival.

The morning had been lovely with pale blues and yellows, but now the sky had turned to dove gray and lilac. This would have made a beautiful twilight, but it was only two fifteen in the afternoon. A storm was coming.

'Do we need a storm *now?*' Vanessa asked. Queenie, standing on the seat with her head beside Vanessa's, chuffed loudly. 'That's what I said. Not now, God, *please.*'

Vanessa turned right at the end of the drive and started down Preston Street, heading for the highway to Portland. She couldn't see Roxanne's car but she thought her sister would go to a city she knew well enough to easily find a hiding place.

And then what? Roxanne wouldn't drag Cara around with her, making her more obvious, slowing her down. And Cara meant nothing to Roxy. That sweet, innocent little girl meant absolutely nothing to Roxanne.

Vanessa tried to concentrate only on the road ahead of her and not consider that she might be headed in the wrong direction. She knew Pete would have called Wade by now. Thank God Pete knew the make of the car. Also, by now the emergency services would probably be at the house tending to Pete's shoulder. She was glad Roxanne had shot Max in the leg. He couldn't flee. And what

about Jane? Was she alive? If so, how could she possibly explain
to Wade that she'd known for years Roxanne was alive? And would
she care if he forgave her? The love of her life – her pervert of a
father – was dead. Vanessa had a feeling nothing would ever really
matter to Jane again.

Vanessa called Pete and told him she was on her way to Portland.
He said that the emergency services and the police had already
reached the house. Jane was alive but had concussion. He and
Max were ready to be taken to the hospital. 'Did you talk to
Wade?' she asked.

'Yes. I said Roxanne was armed and had taken Cara with her
in Max's car. I gave him the make of the car and told him to track
your phone. When he heard you'd gone after Roxanne, he swore
a couple of times.'

'Wade knows me too well to not think I'd try to chase her down.
Has Audrey called?'

'No.'

'If she does, please don't tell her what's happening. Let's give
her another hour or two of peace.'

'I understand, but I won't lie to her.'

'Don't lie. Just stall. I have to get off the phone now.'

'Good luck, Vanessa.'

Normally Queenie would have lain on the seat but she seemed
to sense Vanessa's tension and stood, looking out the windshield.
When they turned on to the highway, Vanessa sped up and the dog
sat down, still peering ahead. After ten minutes of driving, Vanessa
began looking in the rearview mirror, hoping she wouldn't be
pulled aside by the highway patrol for speeding. She wished she'd
grabbed a jacket on the way out the door and turned the car heat
on low. Almost instantly, the sky opened up and rain drenched the
highway and the car. She flipped on the windshield wipers but
vision was still difficult.

Her shoulders were stiff and her hands clenched on the steering
wheel. She'd taken a deep breath, trying to relax, when she saw
a car overturned on the other side of the road. Vanessa slowed and
peered at the wreck. Clearly the car had spun out of control in the
rain, shot across the wet pavement, and rolled over, coming to a
halt beside a bank. A white car.

Her heart slammed against her ribs as she saw a car door open
and Roxanne climb out, clutching Cara's hand. The child was

crying but Roxanne kept jerking at her until she'd gotten her out of the wrecked car. Vanessa slowed and the sisters' gazes met for a full, challenging minute before Roxanne held up her right hand with the gun while she pulled Cara behind her and dashed for the woods bordering the road.

No other cars were around. Vanessa pulled off the side of the road, picked up the gun and Cara's red ribbon from the seat beside her. She held the ribbon under Queenie's nose. Collies weren't tracking dogs, but Vanessa had to try. 'Find Cara!' The dog snuffled the ribbon. 'Follow Cara!' She got out of the car, opened the second door and grabbed Queenie's leash before the dog leaped from the car.

The dog shot across the highway. If a car had been coming, they would have been hit, but luck was on their side. Roxanne and Cara had already vanished into the woods as Vanessa and Queenie began climbing the hillside. The ground was already soggy and rain dropped heavily from tree leaves. Vanessa wished she had a jacket. The temperature seemed to have dropped at least ten degrees since the rain began and her hands were chilled. She couldn't see very far in front of her – she depended on Queenie to lead her through vines and over dead, molding leaves.

The deeper into the woods they went, the tighter Vanessa's chest grew and even her throat seemed to be closing. *It's only panic*, she told herself. *You're not having a heart attack, you're not suffering anaphylactic shock. You can breathe fine if you don't give in to fear. There's not a monster ahead of you. It's only Roxy.*

But Roxy was a monster. Roxy was the mosgrum Vanessa had feared for so long. The realization made her vision darken. She wanted to sob, she wanted to scream her despair to the heavens, she wanted to magically turn her sister into a good-hearted gentle girl like Cara. But Roxy wasn't good-hearted and gentle. She never had been.

A western meadowlark let out a shrill song above them. Vanessa almost screamed and Queenie barked as the bird soared away in the rain. Then Queenie jerked forward, dragging Vanessa behind her. Vanessa's clothes were soaked, feeling like they weighed several pounds, and she thought of the elaborate brocade gowns she wore on *Kingdom of Corinna*. The difference was that she often had them on in the heat. Now the clothes were lighter but also colder, her jeans clinging to her legs, her sweater drenched, her shoes feeling leaden with water and mud.

Her own hair ribbon had fallen out and now her long hair hung in heavy tendrils around her face. She tried pushing the hair behind her ears, but it wouldn't stay. Even her long eyelashes were wet, pulling down her eyelids. She kept wiping a hand across her face, trying to focus. Her thighs were beginning to burn and a sharp pain kept stabbing her side. She needed to work out more, she thought as she tried to keep her mouth shut although she wanted to pant.

Queenie stopped and looked from side to side. *Oh no*, Vanessa thought. *Please don't tell me she's losing the scent.* Then Vanessa heard a thin, heartrending wail come from ahead of them. Cara. If running through the woods was hard on Vanessa, it had to be grueling for a child being dragged. Roxy's voice floated back to them. 'Shut up! Get up you little—'

'I *can't*. I want my mommy!'

Queenie took off so fast that Vanessa almost fell. Drawing on every ounce of strength she had left, Vanessa ran, ignoring the cold, ignoring her shortness of breath, ignoring the pain in her legs. She wasn't certain how much farther she could go at this speed when she heard another cry.

Queenie lunged even farther forward, jerking Vanessa behind her, then stopped, went rigid and began growling. Vanessa shambled to a halt and looked at her sister, sitting on the wet ground, her face wrenched in pain as she rubbed her ankle. She looked up at Vanessa with pure hatred in her blue eyes.

'Cara, are you hurt?' Vanessa asked gently.

'Not really,' she sniffled. 'I'm s-s-scared.'

'She's "s-s-scared",' Roxane mimicked. 'Shut that dog up!'

Vanessa stroked Queenie. 'Hush, girl. It's all right. You found her.'

The dog quietened but maintained her stance, her gaze fastened on Cara. 'Is that better?' Vanessa asked Roxanne.

'Slightly.' She tried to move her ankle and winced. 'I'm surprised that the glamorous TV star gave chase through the woods.'

'Give Cara to me, Roxanne.'

'I don't think so.' She still held the gun in her right hand and pointed it at Cara. 'Cara will stay with me.'

'Why?'

'She's the only thing keeping me alive until I'm able to walk. Unless you suddenly develop enough courage to shoot me with that gun.'

'Do you really think I'm going to let you go, Roxy?'

'Do I really think you're going to shoot me?' Roxanne laughed.

Cara was trembling violently but Roxanne had a firm grip on her arm.

'I won't let you hurt that child, Roxy,' Vanessa almost growled.

'I'm not hurting her. She's scared and uncomfortable, but she's not hurt. Turn around and go back to your car and she'll be just fine.'

'I don't believe you,' Vanessa said tonelessly. 'You'll only keep her alive as long as you need her.'

Cara began to cry. 'Now look what you've done. *You*, Nessa, not me. Go back to your car.'

'Not without Cara.'

'What is so damned special about Cara? She's not *your* daughter.'

'She doesn't have to be my daughter for me to love her.'

Roxanne began laughing loudly. 'Oh, what a lovely sentiment! Did they come up with that for you on your show? Because I know better. I know you've never loved anyone except yourself. It's people like you who rule the world – narcissists – who look out only for themselves and always come out on top!'

'That is the most ludicrous thing I've ever heard you say! Do you think I didn't love *you*?'

'No. You didn't. I was just a nuisance. Mommy didn't love me – she loved her alcohol and her pills. Dad certainly didn't love me. And Grace? Grace hated me from the time I was in the crib because I reminded her of Mommy!'

Suddenly she jerked Cara and glared at her. 'And it will be the same for you. You don't even have a father! He ran off as soon as your mother told him she was pregnant with you. And all these years have gone by and you *still* don't have a father. No one wants you, Cara! No one ever will!'

Cara began sobbing.

'Roxanne!' Vanessa cried. 'How can you say such things?'

'Because they're true!' She looked back at Vanessa, her eyes blazing. In fact, her entire expression had changed. Her features seemed to have twisted and hardened until she didn't look at all like the beautiful Roxanne Vanessa once knew.

She's finally lost it, Vanessa thought. *She's actually gone completely insane.*

Roxanne pointed the gun at Cara's head. 'I'm finally going to do something good in my life. I'll put this little girl out of her misery.'

'Roxy, no!' She raised her own gun. *'Don't hurt that child!'*

'Why not? There's nothing ahead for her except loneliness and heartbreak and rejection. She'll end up old and bitter.'

For an instant, Vanessa thought she saw movement behind Roxanne. She must have imagined it, she thought, and kept talking. 'You don't know what's in Cara's future, Roxy. Give her a chance to grow up!'

'Why? Grow up to be like me, sitting in the rain with my sister pointing a gun at me?'

Now Vanessa definitely saw a flash of Wade Baylor's face. He was moving so slowly and stealthily that Roxanne was totally unaware of him. But Queenie wasn't. She glanced up at him. Terrified that Roxy had noticed, Vanessa shouted, 'Roxy, I swear to God if you don't take that gun away from Cara's head, I'll shoot you!'

'No, you won't. You don't have it in you, Vanessa. You're the sister everyone looks up to, but you don't have strength or courage or just plain guts.' She cocked her gun and Cara moaned. 'I'll show you who does.'

A shot rang out in the woods. Birds shrilled, Vanessa cried out and closed her eyes, while Queenie barked furiously. Another shot followed. The woodland sounds died down but Vanessa couldn't open her eyes until she heard Cara cry out and then felt the child fling her arms around her. Vanessa looked down at the rain-drenched little girl holding her tightly. 'Oh, Aunt Vanessa, I knew you and Queenie would save me!'

Vanessa glanced at her sister lying on her right side, her knees drawn up, her head lying on the wet, moldy floor of the woods. Wade Baylor was stooping over her, taking her pulse. He looked up and shook his head.

Vanessa remembered letting out a long sigh before the world went dark and she sank to the ground, still holding a sobbing Cara.

EPILOGUE

One week later

A fire burned in the beautiful fireplace and Vanessa ran her foot up Christian's bare leg under the comforter. 'Even though the house is empty, it feels cozy up here in Grace's bedroom,' she murmured.

'Who are we missing? Audrey, Cara, Sammy, your sister, and Grace. Well, we're not *entirely* alone.' He glanced over the side of the bed. 'Queenie is keeping watch over us.'

'Queenie is asleep.'

'A sound sleep for a noble dog.'

'I had no idea if she'd track Cara or not. For all I knew, she would have run wild in the woods. But she understood her mission and carried it out masterfully.'

Christian stroked her cheek. 'Are you lonely here during the day?' he asked.

'I haven't had time to be lonely. Audrey helped me organize Roxy's funeral, small though it was, and considering that Roxy was going to kill Cara, I think she deserves the Medal of Honor. But that's the kind of friend Audrey is. She and Cara moved back in with her mother yesterday but I have a feeling Audrey will be looking for a house with Derek before long. Derek found someone to look after Sammy now that school's started again. Cara told me Sammy likes the new woman fairly well, even though she's old. I believe she's around fifty.'

'Decrepit.'

'Yes, isn't it? At least he's taking his mother's death well. But she hadn't really been a mother to him for years. Pete's in his cottage. Everyone is back where they started. Even Roxanne. For eight years I thought she was dead. Now she is.' Her voice had thickened.

Christian pulled her close to him. 'I'm sorry, my darling.'

'I'm sorry she was so terrible. I'm sorry that only death could stop her before she did even more damage. Poor Zane. Poor Brody.'

'Brody's doing fine. He'll have to go to a clinic when he's physically well enough, and they'll get his medication straightened out.'

'Is he going through crack withdrawal?'

'A mild one but he didn't have a lot over a long course of time. Still, the thought of it is horrifying. How could anyone be fiendish enough to do that to him?'

'Max Newman on orders from my sister.'

'Well, Max will be going to prison soon and he won't be able to do any more harm for a while. As for Brody, he's not feeling sorry for himself. You can't really have a long, coherent conversation with him yet, but I've learned a few things. First of all, the Roxanne he was always trying to rescue was not Roxanne Everly. It was Alexander the Great's wife. She and their son were murdered several years after Alexander's death.'

Vanessa's eyes widened as Brody continued. 'Brody even wrote a story about saving her when he was about thirteen. It's called *The Rescue of Roxanne*. He got it the night he came in our house before I got home. When I came in the house, I felt as if someone had been there, but nothing seemed to be missing. He'd only taken some of his books and that carving knife Roxanne used on him. I didn't check the silverware that night.'

'Why did he want the knife?'

'For protection after he thought he was being threatened on the beach by Max. He couldn't go in a store and buy one. So he took one from our house. Instead, Roxanne turned the tables on him.'

Vanessa shut her eyes, thinking of that night in the shipwreck.

'He was the man in your lighthouse the first night you were home,' Christian said. 'He says he thought it was the turret of a castle and he was trying to hide.'

'I knew it wasn't kids playing a prank.'

'Also, he knows Zane's dead. His heart's broken over it, but he's still making plans. He says Zane would want Blackbird to "fly".' Christian smiled. 'A guy named Dan Simmons worked with them and is brilliant. When he's well, Brody's going to keep the company going with him as a partner.'

'Oh, great!' She paused. 'Jane won't fare as well. Now that Wade has learned she obstructed justice by witnessing Roxanne murder our father and not saying a word, I can't see him staying with her, no matter what the law does to her.'

Christian slowly ran his hand down Vanessa's side. 'And what do you plan to do with this grand house Grace left to you?'

'I've given it a lot of thought. I can't live here, Christian. It was never a happy home for me. Mom and Dad didn't get along, I adored Grace and she left, then Roxanne . . . disappeared. Afterward it became like a tomb. Now I know that she killed our father here. And this was her home, too. I can't be happy in a home I shared with her.'

'I understand. You'd always be thinking about her.'

'When I met Fay Jennings on the plane to Portland, she told me she and her husband wanted to retire to Everly Cliffs in a year. One day it simply hit me what a wonderful bed-and-breakfast this place would make. There are five bedrooms upstairs and a big one downstairs. This house has a beautiful view and the unique miniature lighthouse. I called Fay and told her what I was thinking and she agreed that it would be a great idea. I asked if she and Howard would like to move here and manage the place for me. She had to discuss it with him but the next day they came up here, toured the place, and Howard said he was thrilled with the prospect of managing Everly House. So I'll still own it, but Fay and Howard will manage it. And they'll keep Pete on to do the handiwork so he won't lose his home.'

'I think that's one of the best ideas I've ever heard. Really, Vanessa. It's great.' He sighed. 'Now there's only me.'

'You?' Vanessa ran her finger along his jawline. 'And what are you feeling?'

'I'm feeling that I don't even like Everly Cliffs anymore. Too much has happened here. Brody's condition, all the rumors about him, Zane's death. And Brody won't be living here. When he's well, he'll go back to Portland and his business.'

'So what would you like to do?'

'Go somewhere new.'

'Really? You've lived here most of your life.'

'So have you but you want to go. I *need* to go. Got any ideas?'

'Well, I've been giving that possibility some thought. I know I'll still be on *Kingdom* for two more years, and I hope for even more years – I'll never have such a great acting job again. I'll be traveling a lot for seven months, but when I'm not, I've grown very fond of Los Angeles. And unless I'm mistaken, they have quite a few hospitals in the area.'

Christian laughed. 'To say the least.'

'Hospitals that need doctors. I'm sure you could scrape up *some* kind of employment.'

'Really? What else, sweet pea?'

'Sweet pea? I'm not certain I want to go on if you're going to call me *sweet pea.*'

'What? You don't like it? It suits you perfectly.'

Vanessa tapped his arm. 'It does not. I like *darling*, or *my treasure*, or *precious.*'

'How about *darling*?'

'Fine. If you're certain you want to give up Everly Cliffs Hospital, you could move into my humble apartment in West Hollywood with me while you look for another position. When you find one, we could get a nice house near it, something convenient for you.'

'And we'll cohabitate in this nice place for a while, *darling*?'

'Cohabitate doesn't sound too romantic.'

'No, it doesn't sound romantic at all. Let's think of something better.'

'All right.' Vanessa looked deeply into his hazel eyes. 'We could get married.'

'Married? Are you proposing to me, Miss Everly?'

'Yes, I am.'

'I thought the man proposed.'

'This is the twenty-first century, Christian.'

He smiled, his eyes glistening. 'Then here's to the twenty-first century, darling. I accept with all my heart.'